BEYOND THE VEIL

NICKY SHEARSBY

SRL PUBLISHING

Also by Nicky Shearsby

To the Bitter End
Green Monsters
Black Widow

SRL Publishing Ltd
London
www.srlpublishing.co.uk

First published worldwide by SRL Publishing in 2023

ISBN: 978-1915073-15-0

1 3 5 7 9 10 8 6 4 2

A CIP catalogue record for this book is available from the British Library

SRL Publishing is a Climate Positive publisher offsetting more carbon emissions than it emits.

One

The Others

I can loiter in the darkness for hours, undeterred, unencumbered, just watching, nothing more—waiting for an opportunity to change a supposed *innocent* life forever. It is a gratifying, albeit disconcerting, emotion despite a painful truth my feelings are of little concern to *The Others*. They do not appreciate I find it difficult to express emotions when left alone, when the silence of the night is all I have for company I probably do not deserve. *Innocent*. The very word amuses me, implicating some blameless act these people believe they have played no part in creating. I can assure you there is nothing *blameless* about any of this. I glance around. Most of the lights in nearby buildings have long been turned out, heedless dwellers already in their beds. It is a shame they are unaware of the malingerer in the shadows beyond, a deep slumber able to locate them with ease.

I take a breath. The cool air is refreshing against my algid skin, a light breeze brushing over me—nothing more than an old friend it is pleased to see. I appreciate, of course, my lingering position may look sinister to those who do not know me, know of my need, my very presence left to the wild uncertainty of a failing world that has, too often, failed *me*. Yet, this is the time of day I enjoy the most, when I leave the supposed safety of my home, venturing into the night towards potential acquirement most will never have the capacity of mind to understand—personal appeasement something I *need*. I am, in fact, misunderstood, although such a concept has been savagely misinterpreted, leaving me mostly forgotten in a world that will never really know who I am.

No matter. I am here now, a willing participant, able to achieve my goals with ease, this night more than capable of providing me with the gratification I desperately desire. I am standing in a prolific part of Eastcliff, beyond normality, beyond the veil of accepted society, hidden from view behind several dustbins—rats the only creatures willing to share this foul space with me. I do not mind. These innocents have far more in common with me than those deranged *animals* already intoxicated and violent within the heated walls of downtrodden buildings around me—humanity wholly capable of shunning what they cannot possibly understand.

Yet only those in search of self-gratification venture to this degenerate location—men with urgent needs, females in need of critical financial gain. It is precisely why I am here now. Not for sexual enjoyment, you understand, but to satisfy a personal urge I have been unable to sedate for a long time. It is an impulse few sane people will *ever* understand. I take a breath, several females pacing the quiet roads behind me, their overbearing perfumes blending with their overrated mannerisms, their heels clicking impatiently: this moment perfect for the picking. I need to choose—choose and dissect, if you *excuse* the expression. Yet which one? The tall, slim framed wretch with boots that disappear to her thighs; the older, more accomplished one of her trade; or the petite, nervous young thing who appears out of her prevailing depth?

I smile, wetting my lips, the decision made as I step from my hiding place into the cool, fresh air, my body confident in its pending mission. My shoes beat the pavement in time with my heart, my body in sync with the tune of the night. I smile, she smiles, simple pleasantries exchanged. She asks what I want. I ask what she offers. All the time my heart is pounding, threatening to expose my desires with exorbitant force. We leave that location together, my hand on the small of her back, her scent overpowering—this victim unappreciative of my *true* intentions. No one questions my motive, those around us in search, it seems, of the very same thing.

I do not talk much during our short journey, grateful this young girl does not expect conversation. She expects to be fucked, swiftly, her limited time with me paid for in full by the appearance of several carefully counted banknotes placed into clammy palms that have seen much action already this evening. Polite conversation is not required, not expected. Our time together is purely transactional. The simple truth is that I cannot speak because if I do, I will not hold back, poisoned words allowed to spill from my tongue like acid, capable of burning through the most solid of objects. Only my pending goal keeps me motioning forward, the anticipation of what is coming, most appealing.

I park out of the way, far beyond the town's edge and potential watchful eyes, along a narrow lane towards a desolate location I know and love well. I have grown rather fond of the isolation this ruined building provides, the solace I can therefore claim with ease. The female does not question my choice as she climbs from my car into the darkness, awaiting payment for services she believes will be swift. *She has no idea.* She turns, opens her mouth to speak, yet I am already a step ahead (forgive the expression), my hand covering her mouth. The stench of stale tobacco procures what her perfume fails to disguise, her hair in need of a wash—foul sweat still lingering on her body from the last male who grunted himself into her in the fumbling dark.

She struggles, but I am quicker, bringing my free hand to the back of her neck, a simple incision rendering her immobile. My blade is fast, slicing deep, severing her spinal cord, the oncoming paralysis entirely unexpected. With eyes set wide, she falls against my awaiting arms as I lower her to the ground below. I smile, more a grimace, my sinister appearance unanticipated. I cannot help it. She cannot move, cannot speak, tears already spilling from terrified eyes that cannot see the reasons behind her forthcoming demise. I know what she wants to say, of course. *Why me?* Yet, my excitement ensures I cannot answer. Instead, I remain smiling, focused now on removing her clothing, her arms and legs compliant as I unbutton garments, sliding underwear freely from her body. I remove her shoes, jewellery, a plastic hair clip that breaks beneath my grip, placing them inside polythene bags that I seal and discard in the boot of my awaiting car.

I do not wish to partake in sexual activity. My needs are far greater, this moment more important than mere acts of carnal pleasure. Besides, I do not find the female form attractive, especially wretches of *this* calibre. Her naked body is no more inviting to me than a freshly slaughtered pig. She has no choice but to lie still, of course, her spinal cord damaged, my hand still pressed over her trembling mouth to prevent unwitting, unwanted outbursts.

She gags and convulses, an unexpected moment occurring when the creature vomits into my palm. I do not wish for her to choke to death, her full attention required whilst I perform my duties. I need her to witness this act, appreciate the beautiful art I only dare practice in the dark. I pull my hand away, disgusted, disgruntled by remnants of her last meal that spill from her lips, her continued choking infuriating. I reach forward, slap her across the face, my hand now in need of clean water, a towel to wipe away this unrequited bodily fluid. She has wet herself, too. I know this by the stench of urine, the dampness between her legs threatening to soil my own. I have never understood the workings of the human body, functionality often lost to the concept of terror.

I take a sawn down broom handle from my car. It is nothing special, the thing adequate enough for the job as I drive it firmly inside her. The sound she makes is somewhat amusing. She has sex for money, every night, the filthy whore no better than a street dog. So *why* is she not moaning with assumed pleasure now? I ram it hard, force it deep, only prepared to stop when blood pours along my wrist, spitting from her terrified mouth in unison. That is deep enough, I think. The victim gags blood and vomit across her cheeks, her body succumbing to my heinous act, the disgusting creature almost passed out. Her anus will be next. Had she been male, this would be more appealing, yet she is neither appealing nor inviting as I drive my wooden length inside her once more. Another involuntary yelp, this time accompanied by a strangled groan, more blood trickling from her trembling lips. She has bitten her tongue, too, almost clean off. *Oh, dear.* What a shame.

I take a moment, composing myself, ready to bring my scalpel to her belly. The sound of flesh peeling open as I slide the sharp blade along her skin is alluring, my heart quickening, my head light. She cries out again, knowing she is done for, yet her irksome outburst is distracting, forcing me to hit her across the temple with the very handle coated now with sticky blood. The strike is hard enough to knock her unconscious. *Damn it.* No matter. Instead, I take a breath, losing myself in the act of opening her up, exposing her insides as I pull out organs, slicing them free from their unwanted positions, carefully cutting each breast from her now ravaged body that I place inside previously prepared sterilised jars. She will be dead soon enough. Blood loss is entirely normal. I check for tattoos, those things an identifiable marker, wiping my blade carefully across my sleeve before cutting thickened pieces of skin from her body and placing them inside more jars for later assessment.

Cutting into flesh is far easier than removing limbs; hence I always leave such an exhausting act until last. Once I am certain she is dead, several organs now placed mockingly across her bloody corpse, I move on to the action of removing her teeth and hands. Both can identify her, and whores should *never* be identified. They are not worthy of such privilege. I slam my blood-soaked handle forcefully into her jawbone, breaking every tooth from her head with relative ease. These, too, I save, remove from the scene, removing her features in the process. It is almost poetic.

Hands are attached via tendons and bone, a saw blade required for this act. Unfortunately, my instrument is not as sharp as I would like, and I am forced to hack and chop rather than carefully slice. The deed is done, my night complete. I simply need to leave this place, go home, wash myself head to toe in bleach, burn any offending item that might link back to this moment—a moment that will live forever in my mind, if nowhere else.

I stand in the darkness afterwards, the corpse at my feet. I have done the world a great service by removing this whore from their midst. Women like this should never be allowed freedom of movement, either by day or by night. I sigh. As much as I love this location, it is irritating that dog walkers often frequent these parts, a simple, early morning stroll holding the potential to see me caught in the very act I enjoy more than anything else in the world. A distant bark, a rumbling voice carried against the breeze. I have no time left to complete my mission, required to retrieve my trophies and drive into the night, the body left to its unnatural, unfortunate fate.

I close my eyes. The Others are close now, whispering into the looming darkness, the surrounding trees eagerly calling my name. They often whisper in the shadows when no one else can hear. They talk to me, tell me their deepest secrets, my history bound in shared suffering from which I can never escape. It is regretful. Still, I am what I am, no chance of changing such a terrible truth about the man forever hidden in the blackened gloom of a damaged world. We are, after all, bound together by circumstance and time. Everything we do, everything we have ever been now forms a unique bond few people will understand. It is a shame, I know. It doesn't matter.

Two

Newton

How perplexing is it that a simple walk to my car had me wishing I'd stayed in bed? It wasn't even eight o'clock in the morning, and yet I'd already lost my glasses, my car key, prepared to also lose the breakfast I'd hurriedly forced myself to consume—the unsuspecting curb side falling victim to the remnants of a piece of toast. The fact I'd forgotten to do the weekly food shop, *again*, confirmed my distracted mindset with gusto—my much-required morning coffee jar currently sitting empty on the kitchen countertop, mocking me from a distance, laughing at my inability to think straight. My day of pre-planned mayhem now threatened to dislodge my sanity before I'd made it five feet outside my front door.

I despise being late, although it's something I seem incapable of avoiding these days. Rushed mornings oddly now form my daily existence, leaving me vaguely perturbed as to how I might, by some feigned miracle, change anything about *any of it*. The more demands my day makes of me, the less I find myself capable of achieving everything I tell myself I *must* do—those little things we all deem a requirement, important, necessary to our survival. Such as *buying coffee*.

I should, of course, be used to these intense morning dashes. My average day is not contained to increasingly overbearing university lectures that, to be honest, before I took the job, I was not expecting to become so demanding. The back seat of my car was perpetually crammed with disorganised, mismatched paperwork I really should sort out, read and assess, hand back to my poor unwitting students. I'm sure some of those essays have been lurking back there for several weeks, gathering dust, requiring urgent marking, long overdue—my students' grades in need of desperate attention. However, instead of acting the professional college professor they should have come to expect, my poorly determined mindset and shallow conjecture have conspired against me to bombard my brain with complete nonsense. It doesn't matter. Coffee usually fixes that problem. That's if I ever manage to get some.

I took a breath. Where on earth was my car key? I patted myself down, a haphazard array of A4 folders balancing precariously underneath one arm as I checked every pocket I possessed in haste. Nothing. Retracing my steps probably wouldn't help. I couldn't even recall leaving my flat. I scanned the pavement, jabbing a wayward foot between overgrown weeds that threatened in the early morning sunlight to ambush my declining basement flat steps, ruin my already ageing shoes and destroy this unfathomable morning once and for all. Honestly, it must have taken a few minutes before I realised the damned thing was dangling from my gritted teeth. *Okay.* Take a breath, Newton. *Breathe.*

I mused over the relentless demands on my time, from students with too many opinions and too few priorities, to the Eastcliff CID, who assumed I was always available when they needed me, requiring assistance—none of them aware of my degrading state of mind. I scoffed loudly as an unsuspecting morning jogger ran past, the poor chap momentarily assuming I'd scoffed at *him*. I nodded a half-hearted, demented apology his way, still balancing several student folders in my failing spaghetti grip, trying not to drop them, attempting to get my damned car key into the slot whilst avoiding vomiting into the road. *Perfect timing, Newton.*

Despite my lateness, I couldn't help but watch the lycra-clad runner with trainers that looked far more comfortable than they probably were, disappear from view—my existence, unhinged state of mind and overall general failings of no concern to him. Is it my imagination, or are we *all* savage slaves to our morning routine? Focused only on where we *believe* we need to be at any given moment, we permanently equate our daily existence to life's relentless demands, that deluded jogger included.

I thankfully managed to unlock my car without further trouble, dropping the heavy folders onto the passenger seat, no time to check that everything was in order before embarking on my first lecture of the day. I was already late, my students prepared to filter out of the building, bored of waiting for their elusive professor, unexpected freedom pending. I needed a moment to catch my wayward thoughts, take a breath, grab that coffee. Was such a concept so impossible? The way my day was going, probably. I casually glanced in the rear-view mirror and spotted my glasses perched carelessly on top of my head. *Right.* So, it was going to be one of those days, was it? *Perfect.*

I rolled my eyes, glancing towards an expanse of blue beyond the windscreen, an exasperated shake of my head coming from nowhere. I was glad it wasn't raining. Considering I didn't own a brolly, things could have been far worse. I slammed my car door shut too fast, catching my fingers, sharp air struggling to locate my overworked lungs — hovering between debatable sanity, a car door I now wanted to kick, and my elusive cup of coffee. If it was the weekend, a heavy duvet could be pulled over my throbbing head, allowing me to forget my name for a few hours. As it was, my ears were ringing loudly, too much on my mind, too many ideas, many impossible thoughts left to roam free. My mobile rang. I almost didn't acknowledge it.

'Newton Flanigan,' I stated with half-hearted disinterest into my ageing mobile phone, glad I hadn't lost that too, not convinced I hadn't already lost my mind. I was rubbing my temple awkwardly between my less than soothing fingertips.

'Newt. It's DCI Mannering. Have you got a moment?'

'Paul, hi. Sure. Is everything okay? Seriously, what's with the formality?' I wanted to laugh, make light of how he'd introduced himself to me as if we were strangers, nothing but passing acquaintances, his job finally getting the better of him.

Paul Mannering only *ever* referred to himself as "Detective Chief Inspector" when he was knee-deep in formality; such rank distinction usually only aimed towards suspects, victims, strangers. We were friends. Or at least, I assumed. He did not need to concern himself with titles on my behalf. I was now slightly irritated, to be honest. He knew about my week's packed diary, the relentless lectures we both wished I could swerve, too many chattering students needing undivided attention I wasn't confident I could provide. Why he sounded so pointed, so distracted, I couldn't tell.

'Sorry. It's been one of those mornings,' he muttered, busy elsewhere, distinct clattering and page rustling telling me he was multitasking, as always. I smiled. Oh, yes. I could relate to *that*.

'Is everything okay?' Something in his politeness unnerved me. I was usually pleased to receive his calls, grateful for the distraction. Today, I wasn't confident I'd make it to lunch.

'Yeah,' he mumbled, whispering something into the ear of a nearby police officer I didn't catch. 'I was wondering if you had time for a quick chat? I have an unusual case that could do with a second opinion.' He sounded stressed. I know how he felt.

'Unusual, how?' My interest was mildly piqued now, at least. Despite my preoccupied and unwarranted rationalisations, I was keen to know more. I was glad of the interruption that might momentarily remove me from thoughts of my pending day, thankful to have been given an additional moment before my teenager filled morning commenced.

'Some random guy came in, confessing to a murder.' Paul sounded distant, as if his relentless multitasking was becoming a cause for concern, the poor sod too busy undertaking several things at once, speaking continually to other people in the room—my call simply another thing he needed to tick off a long list of encroaching priorities. At one point, it sounded as if he had dropped his mobile, the incoming muttered 'shit' not lost on me as he grappled to locate it from the floor. I refrained from laughing, instead pressed parched lips between my teeth in protest of my inappropriate response. Stress, it seems, affects both our daily lives. I was oddly relieved by such a concept. I no longer felt so alone in *my* daily struggles.

I shook my head, shaking off distracting thoughts I didn't need. 'And?'

As happy as I was for the temporary distraction, this wasn't exactly breaking news. I'm sure the police saw confessions of crimes every day of the week, many (slightly) unstable citizens confessing to the odd murder or two, most of them wishing for nothing more than a night in a warm jail cell. Such a location would be more hospitable than the street corners they were usually forced to endure, a hot cup of tea something those poor sods would be in much need of—not unlike me and my morning coffee.

To any police department, this type of incident was nothing new, although I imagined it would become exhausting after a while. I resisted the urge to confirm this aloud, my own irritation prickling now. To be honest, I didn't fare well without a morning cup of coffee or two in my system, so I could forgive myself for this unanticipated emotional response.

'He knew the whereabouts of a body.' At least Paul had refamiliarised himself with his mobile again.

'Okay.' I was still listening, still pressing throbbing fingertips against my temple in a vague attempt to sedate coffee withdrawal symptoms, my mobile balanced under my chin, trying not to lose a recently consumed slice of dry toast to the confinement of this rapidly overheating car. 'So?' I wished he would get to the point.

'*So*, we found the body. Exactly how this guy described it, precisely where he said it would be.'

Great stuff. I could sleep soundly now, knowing the police were doing a fantastic job. I swallowed my unkind thoughts, developing a nasty headache I didn't need.

'Sorry, Paul, but what does this have to do with me?' I was now precisely eighteen minutes late for the start of my first lecture, a conference hall filled with students awaiting my arrival, and still, not a single drop of coffee had passed my lips. I didn't mean to sound so irritated. It was hardly the detective's fault. My friendship with DCI Paul Mannering and overall involvement with the police meant they often called me when details of crimes made little sense to them, when they needed a professional opinion, a clinical theory, a fresh set of eyes. To be honest, I enjoyed working with Paul far more than a room of hormonal teenagers. Not that I would ever openly admit such a thing, of course. I needed the pay packet.

Paul sighed, some punch line he hadn't yet shared with me still dangling from his lips, awaiting my frank acknowledgement. 'Because we honestly don't know how he could have known this.'

'Why?'

There was a pause that, for a moment, threatened to tip me over the edge entirely. Paul sighed. 'Because the guy who confessed to the murder is only twenty-six years old.'

I raised my eyebrows, allowing the glasses I'd earlier forgotten about to slip from my forehead onto the bridge of my nose with a thud. 'So?' *Talk about dragging out the drama!* I don't believe being *twenty-six* prevents anyone from committing murder.

'Because, Newt, the body we found is at least *two hundred* years old.' Paul emphasised the numbers, ensuring I'd heard correctly, appreciated the significance.

'I beg your pardon?' Surely he meant twenty years?

'Yes, you heard me. Two *hundred* years old.'

Okay, he now had my full attention. I could see how such an incident might require a professional opinion, further investigation, more thought. The potential mental health issues of fellow humans were never far from my attention, it seemed. Oh, the irony.

'Fine,' I sighed, the intruding sounds of relieved teenagers already filling my head. 'I'll be there in twenty minutes.'

Three

Newton

I begrudgingly made my way across town to the police station, my morning lectures abandoned. I'd potentially left a trail of gleefully satisfied teenagers in my wake, at least making a *few* people happy today. *Well done, me.* It was unfortunate I visualised the university Dean just as clearly, his face flushing wildly, eyes bulging—*not* so happy. He was probably already on a mission to ensure I never returned to teach another day, many hapless students left now to roam the campus grounds unchecked, run amok, ruin *his* day. He might even classify me a fallacy, a fake, my recent hard work and loyal service over the last few months seemingly all for nothing. Still, I couldn't overthink it.

By the time I'd found a parking space, I was hot, flustered, a headache I couldn't dislodge creating irritation I didn't need, my throat feeling as if it had been slashed. If I didn't get that coffee soon, I might not be responsible for my actions. At least I was in the right place to be locked up for a few hours, should I become hysterical, claim temporary caffeine-infused insanity, throw a tantrum.

'Newton, thank you for coming in so quickly.' Paul greeted me before I'd even closed the station door. He looked as flustered as I did, uncertain what he was dealing with, still wondering what to make of the situation he had unwittingly found himself in.

'Any chance of a coffee?' I couldn't help asking. I was dying here.

Paul nodded, laughed knowingly, holding a hand towards an open door in front of us. 'Obviously,' he laughed again, leading the way. He knew me well. 'How're the lectures going?'

I narrowed my eyes in defensive response, nothing for me to say about that.

'Oh, sorry. Did I interrupt?'

I nodded, raising my eyebrows. 'I hope this is more important, or they could never ask me to return.' I might have sounded casual, but I was deadly serious. I'd spent months prepping for these lectures, my recently acquired job as Professor of Psychology at Springfalls University, something I was pleased to secure. It meant more money, better career prospects, less stress due to fewer travel requirements, the university campus literally on my doorstep. Or at least, that was the plan. I'm not convinced I'd nailed the *less stress* part of the equation very well. Paul needed to know my day entailed more than assisting the police with criminal profiling, advice often requested at the most inopportune moments. Like *now*, for instance.

'I hope *you* think so,' my friend replied as we stood next to a keenly awaited coffee machine. The inviting aroma almost witnessed me clamp my open mouth over the coffee spout in eager anticipation. I took a breath. Maybe I needed rehab? Paul handed me a paper cup filled with strong, black coffee, he knew how I preferred it, two sugars to remove the edge, soften the incoming bitter taste of this cheap brand, wake me up, shake me vigorously out of the self-absorbed slump I couldn't recall slipping into. I needed this energy boost more than he could appreciate, my mind unwilling to cooperate with anything I instructed it to do.

'Okay, what was *so* important it couldn't wait until tomorrow?' I wanted to confirm that two-hundred-year-old bodies weren't exactly going anywhere, yet such a proclamation would have been inappropriate, even for me.

Paul stared at me blankly, unsure what to make of his apparent discovery requiring my immediate attention. 'It's probably best I show you.' He led me to a corner of the incident room where several photographs and sheets of A4 paper were laid out in preparation for my arrival, a discarded desk now littered with information I was yet to become familiarised with. Judging by the little space it took up, the police deemed this case of little importance, its priority a mere formality.

'Do we know much about our would-be killer?' I asked casually, taking a seat whilst sipping my much-needed coffee. I was concerned I was becoming neurotic, addicted to a substance I couldn't live without. 'He obviously wasn't responsible for the death of the body you found,' I continued, attempting to sound rational. 'Unless he's *really* bloody old?' I resisted an urge to laugh.

Paul thankfully ignored my sarcasm, taking a seat opposite me as he leaned back, thinking. I liked Paul Mannering. He was a fair officer, a decent guy, able to remain calm in turbulent situations whilst eagerly dissecting evidence that ultimately helped catch the culprits, close case files, get results. It was why we worked well together — usually. We enjoyed the process of gathering evidence, understanding events yet to be disclosed, ensuring that, between us, we got the bad guy. Well, *mostly*. He wasn't much older than me, our dry sense of humour, quick wit and calm approach to criminal investigation similar.

'We *obviously* know our man can't have committed the murder,' he replied flatly, discarding my attempts to make light of a situation I wasn't yet familiar with. 'But we don't understand how he knows so much about it.' Paul tapped his fingers on the table, readying himself to show me what they currently had.

'What do you mean?' I was now staring at several photographs of the apparent victim, nothing more than bones slowly dissolving to dust, the poor sod still draped in what was left of his clothing — rags, most of the fibres already claimed back by the ground in which he'd lay.

'The body, everything we found. This guy knew it all. Right down to the tiniest of detail.' Paul pointed to a photograph of skeletal hands with seemingly no fingers. Or at least, I *think* that's what it was. 'He described these in perfect detail. The way he claimed to have hacked off the guy's thumb in a temper, taking part of his hand with it.' He stabbed an index finger over several mud-coated bones that, to me, didn't resemble anything remotely recognisable. I resisted the urge to turn the photograph around, just in case I was looking at it wrong. I did not dare tilt my head. I didn't want to look stupid.

'Could he have read about an old murder, somehow?' I was still enjoying my coffee, not yet fully absorbed in my surroundings, still not fully awake. I still had bits of toast in my teeth.

'I doubt it. We pulled every record of unsolved cold cases we could find, dating as far back as we were able to go, but nothing came up. There was nothing in the newspapers, yet the press of two hundred years ago was hardly documented as it is today. Shit, Newt, we didn't even know the body was down there. How *he* knew, we can't yet say.'

I sighed, my coffee cup now empty. 'Could it have been a local story or some long-dead relative, perhaps? Someone somewhere might have bragged about a murder, the information passed from generation to generation.'

'That's what we want you to help find out.'

I shook my head. 'I'm confused how you got the results of the bone age so fast?' Those types of forensics usually take weeks.

'What do you mean?'

I glanced around. 'Well, I take it you've been holding this guy since yesterday?' I assumed, at least, that was the reason for the urgency now, the need for my pressing attention. The police only ever had a measly twenty-four hours to work with—charge him or release him.

Paul laughed. 'Christ, no. It took over three weeks for the bloody lab to send us the information.'

'Jesus, Paul.' I almost regurgitated my coffee. 'So, how on *earth* do you still have this guy?' Was that even legal? I glanced around, keeping my voice low.

Paul shook his head, offering me a knowing smirk. 'Of course we don't still have him.' He refrained from adding "you idiot". I was grateful. I shuffled in my seat. 'We had to take his initial confession seriously. He even took us to the burial site and showed us the body's exact location. I had no reason to suspect it had been there that long. Bones are bones at the end of the day. They all look the same to me.' Paul shrugged. What did *he* know of such things? 'I assumed it had been there no more than five, ten years, max. I arrested him as soon as we found the evidence but had to let him go when forensics noticed how long it appeared the body might have been down there.'

'Okay.' That was a relief to hear. No law's broken there. 'So, remind me, *why* do you need me again?'

'The guy keeps showing up. Every goddamned day. It's annoying.' That explained Paul's stressed look, at least, the lines on his face seemingly deeper than they were the last time we'd met. 'He turns up every day, always with the same confession, usually first thing in the morning, looking as if he hasn't slept. He *refuses* to go home. He's been practically camped outside the station for weeks.' Paul motioned a free hand towards an open window as if half-expecting some desperate, demonic face to be pressed against it. 'That's why I called you. We appreciate this guy couldn't have killed that male, but I was hoping you could find out what he knows. He's not making much sense, to be honest.'

'What do you mean?'

Paul glanced my way, an uncertain look on his face. 'You'll find out when you meet him.'

My attention was caught, Paul's vague words having the desired effect of waking me up. Either that or the coffee had kicked in. 'But surely this is just basic police work?' They didn't need me to confirm the guy was claiming murder for *attention*. I wanted to laugh, roll my eyes behind the protection of an empty paper cup I'd been absentmindedly chewing the rim of for the last few minutes. Paul wasn't laughing. I turned my attention to the printouts in front of me, tracing a finger across several extensively written notes. I needed to at least *act* professional. 'He told you about detailed injuries to the body, broken bones inflicted *before* death, things he did to the victim?'

'Yep.' Paul handed me a sheet of paper. It was a statement they had taken three weeks previously. 'He confessed to the killing of six people in total but claimed he could currently only remember the whereabouts of our friend here, *conveniently*.' It was Paul's turn now to roll his eyes, jabbing an exasperated finger against the tabletop. 'But, he knew every single injury on the body.' Paul slid several photographs towards me. 'A broken wrist. A broken neck. He claimed the guy put up a hell of a fight, stated his apparent reputation on every detail he was able to provide, even describing the clothing the guy was wearing.' I was staring at an image of a belt buckle in the shape of a crow's head, something that looked like a piece of leather still attached to it. Or, at least, I think that's what it was. It was covered in mud, rusted and ravaged by time, a written statement the only clear description we had.

Paul continued. 'Someone *must* have told him what had happened to the victim. We just can't get much sense out of him.' Paul resisted the urge to laugh. It was as if he was finding the entire thing irritating.

'Where exactly was the body found?' My detective mode had kicked in. Hallelujah for caffeine.

'The old factory ruins on Adderson Street. He was buried beneath a tonne of concrete flooring. It was deep, too. We probably would have given up digging if our chap hadn't continued his annoying rampage. No one was ever going to find that body again without prior knowledge the bones were there.'

'The old miller's place?' The old factory had burned down decades earlier, yet nobody had bothered to demolish it. It was typical of modern society to leave unwanted things to rot, paperwork and planning permission often too extensive, legal complexities overriding common decency.

Paul nodded, clicking his tongue against his teeth. He often did this when he was stressed or couldn't figure out something that should have been obvious, straightforward.

I sighed, knowing my job was simply to evaluate this guy, assess his mental state, find out who *told* him about the body beneath that factory floor. 'Could he have any connections to the cotton mill around that time?' We were talking about the early eighteen hundred's, when life was very different to how it is today. I was impressed I remembered. *Thank you, Mr Ellington, for your primary school history lessons.*

'We looked into that. Pulled every record we have for anyone who went missing in the area between 1800 and 1830. Nothing. Nada. Not a damned thing.'

'Okay. And do we know who our victim is yet?'

Paul shook his head, giving me one of his "are you serious?" looks. 'What do *you* think? All we know is that whoever killed him pulled every tooth out of his head. Even with today's technology to back us up, it would be near impossible to identify him.'

I scanned the table for evidence of Paul's shocking declaration, picking up two images of what looked like a toothless skull taken from different angles, bludgeoned holes where a jaw once sat, nothing much left now that would confirm the shape of a head at all.

'Forensics claim it's possible the killer cut off his victim's fingers *before* disposing of the body.' Paul shook his head. 'Either that or the poor sod's fingers went missing by themselves.' He laughed. It was hardly appropriate. I resisted an urge to sigh.

'So, where does *your* man fit in?' My empty cup was annoying me now, my brain needing a second fix, more caffeine to keep me functioning. Paul reached out, took my cup and got to his feet. He knew me well.

'He claims his name is Adam Mires. Comes from the local

village of Shelby.'

'Shelby? Wasn't that place turned into a market town back in the sixties?' It wasn't even seen by the locals as a stand-alone town now, more an extended subsidiary of Eastcliff, the entire country merging via overpopulation, relentless consumer demands.

Paul nodded. 'You're starting to understand what I've had to put up with for the last three weeks. There's something off about him, to be honest. Very nervous looking, not the type you'd think capable of killing anyone.' He paused. 'He's a little odd, in my opinion. Slightly theatrical. A bit weird.'

'Why?'

'As I said, you'll find out when you meet him.'

'So, why not the type capable of *murder*?' I rolled my eyes. People don't wear signs around their necks to confirm such a status. "Look at me, I'm a killer." It was unfortunate I appeared more confused than I felt.

'The guy seems to suffer from manic depression. Very edgy and anxious.'

'It's called Bipolar, and you do realise that anxious people often make the *best* killers.' I sighed, needing my friend to understand not everyone is like him, apparently perfect, yet Paul's blank features gave nothing away of his actual thoughts on *that* subject. Maybe he didn't care. 'Have you been able to pull up any previous on this Adam Mires?' I continued, no point in correcting my friend's wrong assumptions.

'Nope.'

'Why not?'

'Firstly, the *only* Adam Mires from Shelby we managed to locate is twenty-six years old. The guy currently sitting in that interview room has to be in his late thirties, at least.' Paul was pointing over my head now, towards a closed door and an unknown man I was oddly growing curious by.

I looked puzzled. 'And secondly?'

'Adam Mires is dead.'

Four

David

There is a relatively little known, somewhat uncomfortable, fact about me that I often find myself in situations where I can become momentarily unfamiliar with my surroundings. It is akin to how a dream feels when waking from a deep slumber, often unable to retrace steps taken before emerging in a different location entirely. Not unlike sleepwalking, I should imagine. Today, for instance, I have found myself sitting inside a relatively small police station interview room, providing them with a statement that, to be honest, I am uncertain what I am *meant* to be declaring. Sadly, this isn't the first time I have found myself unwittingly without prior knowledge of my alleged actions. It is the way I am, the way I function. I should be used to it by now, of course. This is nothing new.

I have been given a cup of tea, which was a mildly

pleasant, albeit brief, occurrence. However, the tea could have been brewed a little longer in my opinion, the cup provided slightly warmer, my mind left to now ponder the mysterious reasons behind today's unjust treatment along with bland tea. They have not even offered me a biscuit. They *have* left me alone however, deliberately, in order to watch my movements from behind a thin piece of glass they assume I am unaware exists. Allegedly they are collating important information they claim I have already provided, yet I cannot recall doing such a thing. *How odd.* I wish these people would hurry things along so I may go home. My birds need me. They must be hungry by now. I certainly am. I cannot recall eating breakfast.

I am relieved when the interview room door opens, and a gentleman wearing a dark grey tank top steps into the room. I know instantly, instinctively, we will form a strong connection. His face is contorted into confusion as if the poor chap recently experienced a conversation he has since been unable to unravel. I know *precisely* how he feels. I enjoy watching his face as he spreads photographs and files out in front of me. It has an unexpected upside of calming my mood, although he is not aware of this fact or that the items in his possession are becoming contaminated with aftershave and traces of hand cream dispensed too generously, most likely in a hurry.

On the other hand, I do like the way his brow furrows into two neat lines that meet frantically between his eyes, leaving an indentation that does very little for his appearance other than to make me smile. I want to tut, offer him my advice on how to better care for his skin, smooth away unnecessary furrows with my fingertips, but I glance away, suppressing a smile I do not feel he will appreciate. This poor chap obviously has far more to deal with than my unfettered observations of his daily hygiene habits or rising stress levels.

His hands are not ageing well, which is a shame because I sense this gentleman could look appealing if he took a little extra time over his appearance. However, his skin has the look of a fellow who has neglected himself long enough. He's in his thirties, no doubt, although he might soon pass for forty if he isn't careful. Deep creases are already forming at the knuckles, the beginnings of sunspots he probably hasn't noticed. He has a slight tremble in one hand as if stress is beginning to take a toll he is equally not yet aware of. The poor fellow needs to be more careful, look after himself better, relax. He smells of strong, cheap coffee. That might explain the jitters.

'Adam? Adam Mires?' He glances my way, holding a prematurely creased hand towards my own. *Adam.* Oh my goodness, why am I *not* surprised? I resist an urge to sigh loudly into this confined space. At least, that explains *this* unfortunate moment. I lift my hand (he assumes I am about to shake his), but instead, I brush a stray hair from my cheek that is threatening to bristle my eye socket, scratch my pupil, cause unrequired irritation. That will *never* do. I require a clear view of this chap. I oddly wish to get to know him better.

'I'm afraid not, my dear fellow,' I reply, somewhat begrudgingly, inwardly berating Adam for arriving so promptly and then retreating to leave me, as usual, to clear away *his* mess.

'Oh?' The poor vexed chap is standing in front of me now,

palms clammy with overwork and stress, hair already dulled from a cheap shampoo he isn't aware is not helping its condition in the slightest. He glances at several files in front of him that he has seemingly not yet looked at, towards notes he now assumes has been given in error. He looks around, towards the door, back to me. Then he sighs. I do wish I could help in his moment of need. As it is, I can only sit and watch. 'I'm sorry, but they told me your name is—'

'I'm terribly sorry that your time seems to have been wasted.' I cannot help but offer the poor fellow a sigh of my own now, unwilling to explain things further to this unassuming wretch standing awkwardly before me. 'But you may call me *David*, if you wish.' I nod my head, remembering my manners. After all, polite etiquette is required when meeting new people. I must retain composure.

'David?' Again, with the confused, bemused, half-berating stare. I immediately confirm that he is not a police officer. The police do not care for matters of polite discussion, merely facts, statements, records they wish to file away quickly. Tick those little boxes that seem to keep them all so very busy.

'David Mallory,' I confirm, bowing my head, our introduction complete, irritated that this guy has not yet introduced himself to *me*. He begins writing something on a piece of scrap paper he has pulled from his pocket. He sits down, still flustered, still unsure *why* he has been called here today. He is reading something, confusion apparent, yet seemingly unwilling to concern himself with facts neither of us can change. When he finally looks my way, I am almost taken aback by the brilliance of his striking blue eyes. My pupils have dilated. I cannot help it.

'Okay then. Well, good morning, David. My name is Doctor Flanigan.' *Doctor?* Well, well. That *is* a much better introduction, if I do conclude, although a doctor in what, exactly? I take my time absorbing his presence, hoping he cannot see my increased interest. He is certainly not qualified in anything medical. His hands are far too shaky to practice any potential surgery, and I equally conclude he is also no police doctor, judging by his current mannerisms and failing presence of mind. At least the poor sod seems to have composed himself now, thankfully. We might resume a relatively normal conversation. The good doctor attempts a smile, thinks better of it, turning his mouth slightly at the corners before turning his attention to notes we both know he has not yet had time to read. *No.* He is certainly no medical doctor. A psychologist? Yes, indeed. How *typical* of the Eastcliff Police to introduce such a person to *me*.

I nod. 'Doctor Flanigan,' I repeat calmly, the chirps of my beautiful birds forming in my head, my mannerisms, although outwardly relaxed, requiring much-needed fresh air, an escape from this room, an escape from this man. From *Doctor* Flanigan.

He smiles, allowing me to see teeth that are straight, white enough to be considered hygienically acceptable. Relatively few fillings, I am glad to note. I glance towards the table in front of us, my heart beating a little faster than intended. It is hardly appropriate.

'May I ask you a question, David?' the good doctor has now placed those generously moisturised hands on the table in front of me, folding his fingers together casually. He reminds me of a teacher I once knew.

'If you must,' I reply with a curt tone. He is beginning to bore me now. It is a shame.

'Why did you tell the police your name is Adam Mires?' He is pointed in his assumptions that I have lied and therefore must be lying now. The poor man is unable to fathom such wayward motives from a seemingly rational individual.

I tip my head backwards, focusing my attention on the ageing, peeling polystyrene ceiling tiles overhead that I am perturbed to discover, require a clean. 'I do not control what Adam does, my dear.' It is true. Adam is his own man. His actions, therefore, have nothing whatsoever to do with me. I am, however, beginning to form a better picture of his recent actions. Today's police interview is something I know only *he* could have instigated. How infuriating.

'I still don't know who this *Adam* person is?' The good doctor is relentless in his quest. I would usually be intrigued by his interest. Not today.

'Why do you need to know?' He is irritating me now, and unfortunately, I am in no mood for irritation. The day is waning.

'Is Adam a relative of yours?' This fellow is trying, I'll give him that much.

I laugh, unable to prevent my throat from forming an automatic response to his unexpected probing. 'Something like that.' I have no immediate intention of expressing more about myself or Adam today. Come to think of it, this moment is hardly deserving of such a personal introduction at all. I hardly know the man. It would be entirely inappropriate.

'Well, I can't speak candidly with you unless I know *why* you are now claiming to be someone else. Who exactly is Adam Mires to *you?*' He taps a chewed pencil against a file in front of him. I want to remove it from his hand and lay it on the table. Remember your manners, my dear fellow.

I swallow, shrugging aching shoulders now in need of a hot bath. I breathe in the intoxicating scent of this man, private thoughts left to linger inside a mind that I do not currently wish to acknowledge.

'The police are under the impression that your name is Adam,' he continues, oblivious to my private musing. 'So, why are you now claiming to be called David?'

'My name *is* David Mallory. I have already told you as much.' I glance skyward, pressing my lips together in protest of words I cannot speak. Whatever Adam has or has *not* done has nothing to do with me.

'Okay.' The good doctor is sitting back in his chair, chewing his bottom lip. I sense this is an unconscious decision. I'm confident the poor man does not realise that his lips are already looking sore in places, in need of lip balm. I have some in my pocket, yet I refrain from offering it. I do not wish to offend. 'Then why did you come here under the false name of Adam Mires?'

'I did no such thing.' I cannot help offering him a sharp look, my irritation prickly. It is unfortunate. When my anger becomes aroused, terrible things happen. He has, in fact, aroused me in more ways than one today. It is a shame he is unaware of such a truth.

'You know it's a crime to lie to the police, don't you, David?'

I glare at this man. How dare he assume to know my thoughts? *'Why* do you care so much about Adam?'

'I don't even know Adam. But *you* obviously do.' He refrains from adding "I can see it in your eyes." It's probably just as well. Nothing good exists there.

'What exactly did Adam confess to this time?' I sigh, wishing to understand what he has expressed so I can set these people straight on the matter. Go *home.*

The good doctor glances towards his extensive notes, including several photographs of skeletal remains that sit casually on the table in front of us. 'If you don't know what Adam gets up to, how do you know he confessed to *anything?'*

I take a slow breath, holding it for several seconds, willing this impossible moment to end. He is definitely a psychologist. 'Adam is *always* confessing to something.' Usually the same thing, over and over. The fellow is rather tedious.

'Apparently, you have been coming here for the past three weeks, confessing to murder.'

'Not me.' I shake my head. He needs to understand this truth.

'Do you have a twin?'

I tut. *Of course, not.* His joke is not appreciated. 'May I go home now, please?' I stifle a yawn. I do not wish to continue this conversation further.

'Avoidance of the question will not help you, although I see it often in my line of work.' The good doctor is continuing his quest for knowledge, as if my opinion is of no current relevance at all.

'Oh?' *See what often?* He hasn't yet confirmed his *actual* line of work. I no longer care. 'I would like to go home, if you don't mind,' I state again, as calmly as I can, knowing these people have nothing that will in result in a charge being brought against me. I know Adam. *Nothing* he could have said to these people will see me arrested today, charged with any potential offence.

'I'm afraid that won't be possible at the moment.'

'Am I being arrested?'

'Not just yet.'

I smile. I can see they have nothing on me, nothing on Adam. 'So why can't I leave?'

'Because, David, for the last three weeks, you have been walking into this station as Adam Mires, confessing to no less than six murders. And now, you claim, your name is David Mallory. I'm sure you can see my confusion.'

The poor chap does indeed look confused. On the other hand, it makes him look appealing, oddly attractive. Oh, dear. Here we go again. I will deal with *Adam* later.

Five

David

I have no idea how long the good doctor has been staring at me, but we must have sat together in silence for a few minutes, neither of us willing to reinstate our earlier conversation for reasons unbeknown to us both. I watch him absently chew his bottom lip as he glances around the room, attempting to entertain himself with the folder in his possession, no doubt because he is now unsure how to address *me*. Eventually, thankfully, it is he who breaks the unbearable silence.

'Tell me, David. Why would you assume the identity of a dead man? You must know Adam Mires is *dead*? Are you lying to me now about who you are?'

'I *never* tell lies,' I spit, rising to my feet in defence. How *dare* this man presume to know anything about me? It is unfortunate the poor doctor already believes me a liar, due in part to Adam's relentless quest for penance no one is ever going to provide. I am not expecting the interview room door to burst open so violently, yet two uniformed police officers march into our once perceived tranquil location as if readying themselves for a fight. I hold my hands aloft as the good doctor also rises to his feet, seemingly coming to my defence. My outburst is most regrettable and one I immediately retract.

'It's okay, chaps. David and I are just getting to know each other.' The good doctor turns to me. 'Aren't we, David?' At least the man is no longer determined to irritate me beyond belief. His well-placed comment might even hold the potential to calm me a little, cast much-needed clarity onto my unravelling mindset. The officers offer me a look of vague complacency before leaving the room, leaving us to our "not so private" conversation. 'Did I hit a nerve?' the good doctor asks, resuming his seated position. He is writing something on his notepaper.

'I apologise,' I reply, swiftly. 'I do not usually display such wanton outbursts, especially in front of someone I do not know.' I nod, flattening the lining of my jacket neatly across my lap as I retake my seat, smoothing my hairline at the front. I wish to relocate my manners. Discomposure is something I refrain from displaying in public. 'But I will have you know, Doctor Flanigan, I never lie. *Never.*' It is true. I avoid a response entirely if I need to divert the truth of a situation. The good doctor does not need to know this, of course. Not yet.

'That's okay,' he responds, unshaken by my previous outburst. 'But, if you are not lying now, am I correct in assuming you have a medical condition we need to know about?' I cannot help but sigh. We both know precisely to what he is referring. This man has either done his homework on me, is a *very* astute man, or seemingly understands little about how to address strangers. Anyone else might take offence. I sit upright, stiffly, offering a well-formed smile of my own.

'What exactly do you know of such matters?' I ask, mildly amused.

The good doctor grins, those perfectly aligned teeth drawing more attention from my private thoughts than is potentially safe for him to provoke. It is unavoidable, slightly uncomfortable.

'Forgive me,' he mutters apologetically. 'I forget my manners.' He laughs, reaching his hand towards mine that I take now, begrudgingly. It is soft, warm, far too tempting. I resist the urge to bring my hand to my nose, ingesting the faint scent of moisturiser that now lingers on my fingertips. That would look somewhat out of place, I'm sure. *Rather odd.* 'I am a clinical psychologist,' he continues, his wayward effect on me of little concern to him. 'I work with the police when they need to make assessments that require a specialist insight into the mind of someone who may require a little extra *assistance.*' I glare at him, noting how he has emphasised the word "assistance", although he does not seem to notice. Either that, or he is very good at ignoring people's emotions. I assume it might be the latter.

'I work closely with those displaying mental health issues.' Again, the good doctor smiles, although he does not indulge me with those beautiful teeth this time. What a shame. This new smile is oddly conceited, matter-of-fact, cold, as if he has just remembered his place, his position. 'Would this correctly describe you, David?' He is waiting for my response, doing his job, hoping to provoke a reaction. Yet, I am in no mood for such a private introduction to my mental health issues today.

I allow an unfiltered sigh. He will, of course, require a response at some point, a full, uncensored evaluation. 'I do not enjoy the term *mental health issues*,' I confirm. 'Adam likes to pretend we do not exist. It is annoying. However, he is as much a part of *me* as the rest of them.'

'The rest of *them?*'

The good doctor's eyes momentarily light up, as if my words have brightened his day. Oh, dear. I have said too much? 'You seem a smart enough man,' I offer, attempting to keep this otherwise overbearing conversation light, discrimination free. 'I'm sure the police did not ask you to simply uncover what you assume is my hidden mental health issues.' My *hidden* problems.

The good doctor flicks a dry tongue over his coffee deprived teeth, seemingly unsure how to respond. 'Well, actually, they *did* ask me to assess your state of mind. But you're right. They didn't *only* ask me to talk about your mental health.' He sits upright in his chair, suddenly needing to bring our conversation back on track. 'I was asked to speak with you because they know that Adam Mires died in 1818. Therefore, the police are curious as to why you are confessing to murders occurring over two hundred years ago.' It was a simple enough question, I suppose, asked out of required obligation.

'What exactly do you have on Adam Mires?' I ask. I am fully aware I have disconnected myself from Adam for the time being. I do not need him in my head. For now, I wish to understand what the imbecile has implied.

The good doctor shakes his head, a blank shrug of his shoulders I cannot read. 'That's just it, David. We don't yet understand the connection between a dead man, a dead body, and your constant appearance here, every day for the last three weeks.'

'Three *entire* weeks?' Why do I sound rattled by such a concept? So depleted? Oh, Adam, what *are* you doing to me? I lean back in my chair. This is exhausting.

The good doctor nods, sliding several photographs across the table so I can finally gain a clear view of the skeletal remains that have been resting upside down since his arrival. The body is still in its recently uncovered grave. I almost do not want to look. *How disgusting.*

'Do you have any idea who this man is?' He points towards a selection of A4 printed pages as if he honestly expects me to know.

I want to laugh. I am confident the man is unaware he has provided such a ludicrous statement. 'Sorry, please forgive me. I must have misplaced my "corpse identity kit" today,' I chuckle slightly. I cannot help it. How in God's name does he anticipate I might, in any way, know of the identity of bones? I glance between each photograph, none of which hold an ounce of recognition for me. 'I am not sure about this one?' I jab a finger across the face of some toothless shape that might have passed for a skull at some point. 'It isn't a face I have seen recently. He appears to be missing some teeth. Maybe, if you could locate his dentures for me, I might have a better chance of offering a more formal identity. Was the poor man not wearing his name tag?' I cannot help the low chuckle that leaves my throat. The good doctor does not smile or indicate he appreciates my little joke. No matter. I raise an index finger to my lips, forcing back yet more unwanted nonchalance. 'Forgive me. Just a little joke for you. To lighten the mood.'

'Indeed.' The good doctor does not look amused as he grabs the photographs from the tabletop, sliding them back into the folder. Have I hurt his feelings? *Oh, dear.* 'Well, maybe you can explain who Adam Mires is? And why you have continually shown up over the last three weeks, claiming to have murdered six individuals.' The poor man honestly sounds perplexed with me now. *Six? My goodness, Adam, you have been a busy fellow.*

I shrug. 'As I have already expressed, I make no claim over what Adam does or does *not* do.'

'But Adam Mires is long dead. So why are you assuming his identity?' I can tell the good doctor is baffled by the concept. I would be, too, under any other circumstance.

'My name is David Mallory.' I am bored now.

'Yes, you told me.' The good doctor is tapping his pencil again. 'We are not getting very far, are we, David?'

I shake my head. Finally, we agree on something.

'You mentioned something about "others" earlier.'

'Did I?'

'You did, yes. Care to elaborate?'

'Not really, no.' I lean back in my chair, exhausted now, needing sustenance neither this man nor this room can provide. I need the friendly chatter of my beloved birds, fresh air in my lungs—a moment to relax. 'How long do you intend on keeping me here?' I already know the answer. They have nothing on me. Nothing on Adam. His confession equally means nothing if he isn't available to speak to these people, confirm such offences. They already know the man is *dead*. Case closed. This has nothing whatsoever to do with me.

The good doctor rises from the table, picking up his folder as he turns towards the door. 'Will you excuse me for a moment?' he states, his question requiring no reply. He taps the door of the interview room; it opens, allowing him to leave, leaving me to the profound solace of this space and momentary peace of my unfettered mind. *Thank God in Heaven for small mercies.* I hope he will not return. My early assumptions of the man may have been rudely unrewarded.

Six

Newton

By the time I left the interview room, I needed yet more coffee and a quiet moment of reflection. This guy was clever. He knew the system, understood the law—precisely the type of person I was glad I didn't encounter daily. He was displaying classic symptoms of Dissociative Identity Disorder (DID), yet he could be playing me, playing the game, capable of causing trouble for the sheer hell of it.

'Newt?' Paul was walking along the corridor, the air refreshingly cool after being cooped up inside that room, a worried look on his face that matched my own. 'What the hell was *that*?' He'd been listening in on the interview, out of view, out of earshot, quietly allowing me to do my job.

I shook my head. My only intention was to head directly to the awaiting coffee machine, towards sustenance continually eluding me this morning. 'Well, it was *not* a guy called Adam Mires,' I confirmed, glancing over my shoulder. I have no idea why. It was an automatic response. Something about him unnerved me. 'Are you sure you've got the right person in there?'

Paul gave me one of his looks. I smiled. No need for him to answer *that* question. 'Who the hell is David Mallory?'

I shrugged. 'I was hoping you'd tell me? He seems to know Adam, though, or at least some version of the Adam Mires he was pretending to be when he arrived this morning.' Unless the guy has a *twin?* I resisted the urge to express my thoughts. From his accent, his mannerisms, it was obvious David saw himself as a person of prestigious distinction, a man of higher social ranking than the rest of us mere mortals.

'He's taking the piss now. Acting all posh and know-it-all. Maybe I should charge him for wasting police time? That might take him down a notch or two.' Paul ran fingers through his rapidly receding hairline. It did nothing for his appearance whatsoever. 'What the hell is his game?' He was leaning against a radiator, tapping irritated fingers across the ageing metal. 'We'll have to send him on his way. We can't hold the guy for knowing about some old murder case and pretending to be someone else.' I could tell he was seriously considering charging him with wasting his valuable time, though, if he could get away with it.

'I think there might be more to it.' I was already pouring coffee, its inviting aroma filling my nostrils.

'Like what?'

'I'm not exactly sure what we are dealing with. It might be DID.'

'DI what?'

'DID. Dissociative identity disorder. It used to be known as a multiple personality, or split personality.'

'Schizophrenia?'

I shook my head. 'No. Schizophrenia doesn't morph into *actual* personalities, simply giving the sufferer consistent voices inside their head they feel they must act upon. Often with plenty of paranoid thinking, hence the common term, *paranoid* schizophrenia.'

'What's the difference?'

'Quite a bit.' I glanced at my friend. The fact he was unfamiliar with such differences was annoyingly common. Many people couldn't separate them either.

'Yeah, whatever.' Paul waved a dismissive hand in the air, discarding my words, disinterested in the concept and what I had to say about it, happy to leave the psychology stuff to me. 'So, in your *professional* opinion, would you say he's a nut case?' He sighed, equally uninterested in any potential response I might have to offer. 'Just some guy in need of attention.' He scoffed, knowing how many people like David he'd witnessed in his career. Deluded, demented, too many drugs resulting in too few functioning brain cells.

'As I say, I haven't reached any conclusion yet. It's too early to say much of anything.'

'Keep questioning him. I'll do a search on this David Mallory. See what comes up.' Paul tapped the wall and radiator simultaneously as if trying to recreate some annoying song lodged in his head. 'Deal with him, Newt. He's driving me insane.' He headed along the corridor, still tapping, whistling now, out of tune, not caring who overheard. 'That guy isn't even old enough to remember potential stories passed down by his ancestors. Unless he knows the secret to eternal youth.' He laughed at his apparent joke, leaving me to my coffee in peace.

~

I stood staring at several police posters on the wall above the coffee machine, attempting and failing to make sense of David's actions. Why did he initially pretend to be someone else, only to then change his story midway through a police interview? It was a serious confession, told under caution, the guy already guiding the police to the location of a body. *He* was the one claiming murder, demanding attention, and no matter how ludicrous the entire thing was, David had no one to blame for this unwanted attention now, but himself. I glanced at his statement, needing to understand what initially took place. I couldn't go back inside that interview room until I understood a little more about him—ready to offer advice I wasn't confident he'd want to hear.

The initial report was a handwritten page, nothing more, yet the accompanying paperwork was vast—typical police bureaucracy. The name, Adam Mires, was written at the top of the sheet, as was his age, and the date and time of his confession. He was twenty-six. *Yeah, sure.* The guy claiming to be David Mallory must be in his late thirties. Either that or he's had a hard life. I leant against a desk, perched uncomfortably, coffee cup in one hand, the folder on my knee brimming with loose sheets of paper I struggled to hold onto.

'Need some extra leg room?' a uniformed police officer asked with a laugh as she passed by.

I shook my head. 'No, thank you, I'm good.' I didn't glance her way, instead continued reading, my eyes straining to focus without my glasses. I should have checked these notes first *before* speaking with this guy. Nothing made sense.

I, Adam Mires, aged six and twenty years as of this very day, hereby willingly confess that between October 1817 and March 1818, I did thereby murther six people, the full identities of which I will gladly divulge in due course.

I confirm that, during the early hours of October 28th, 1817, I disposed of the first body beneath the recently dug foundations of the yet-to-be-build cotton mill along Old Adderson Lane, on the outskirts of Eastcliff.

I removed the teeth of my victim, breaking his jaw, wrist, and neck, each finger severed so that, should the poor fellow be found, he would not fall victim to his own identity and subsequently conclude my fate. I know the location of his body and am willing to disclose his final resting place in return for my immediate incarceration.

Two further bodies reside still in shallow graves, forgotten now, most regretfully, I know. Ensure my capture, and I shall reveal the location of their final resting place henceforth. At this time, I am unable to recall where precisely, but these things do tend to come back to me with time.

I read the statement twice, lingering over words potentially unfamiliar to myself and anyone else on the force. *Murther?*

Was that a typo or a strange way of spelling? Equally, Old Adderson Lane was actually Adderson *Street*. Was that also an error, or was David making this shit up as he went along, unable to recall facts in any relatable order? It added to my assumption that if David was pretending to be a dead man, claiming to have murdered six people in the early eighteen hundreds, some of his inventions would be inconclusive. Yet, why didn't he provide the apparent victim's names in this statement, too? It would have made for better reading. He sounded sorry for his crimes, referring to the corpse as a poor fellow. A second sheet described the victims clothing, none of it collaborated apart from a crow head belt buckle and a pair of cowhide boots barely surviving the test of time.

I'd seen this before, many times—unstable patients confessing to murder on a daily basis. Most were locked up, drugged up, not able to recall their names from one moment to the next. Yet, why would David assume a dead man's identity? He claimed to have killed six people, yet he speaks only of three bodies. Who were the other three? And where were they? I drank my coffee quickly, needing another, not wishing to return to the interview room with my mind anywhere but in the right place. David was playing us for a fool.

'Newton?' Paul strolled along the corridor, a sheet of paper in one hand, anxious uncertainty in the other. He was still absentmindedly tapping that annoying tune against his leg as he handed me the page. 'Okay, so we found David Mallory. Thirty-eight years old. He's been living in a mental institute for the last seven years. Got out just over a month ago.' He stared at me, handing over an unflattering photograph of David, obviously taken during his recent incarceration. 'Want to know why he was institutionalised?'

'Let me guess? Dissociative identity disorder?' I scoffed, knowing I was right.

Paul shook his head, something in his expression telling me he was about to relish this moment for a very long time. 'Nope. Paranoid schizophrenia.'

~

'Okay, David, you're free to go,' Paul stated blankly as we stepped into the interview room. David was tilted backwards on his chair, face pointed towards the ceiling as if he was searching for something, obviously finding this entire morning tiresome. I know how he felt.

He sat upright, a relieved sigh escaping his lungs as he allowed the legs of his chair to fall to the floor. 'Finally.' He rose to his feet, smoothed the palm of his hand across the front of his hairline, and straightened his jacket. I'd never met anyone so calm, so collected in thought or posture. 'Good day to you, Doctor Flanigan.' David tilted his head in my direction. 'It was nice to meet you, my dear fellow.' Although polite, I didn't appreciate his darkened, perplexing tone. The way he looked at me. There was something behind his eyes, something in his mannerisms. Something he wasn't yet expressing. I smothered a sigh, holding my breath too long, this room closing in on me too fast. As frustrating as this situation had become, there was nothing more I could have done, nothing more to be said on the matter.

The man now referring to himself as David Mallory had done nothing wrong, and as Adam Mires was refusing to co-operate, the guy was free to go. His previous confession and intention to divulge the names and whereabouts of a further two victims seemed a fruitless task. The police had nothing to link David Mallory, or Adam Mires, to the body found in Adderson Street. Other than a seemingly impressive guess, the guy had done nothing to warrant an arrest. The police had already concluded he must have heard about some unrecovered body during his incarceration, tipping the police off to an ancient murder they would *never* be able to tie him to. Was this entire thing some bet he'd made with a fellow patient? A way to tie busy police officers in knots? Frustrate everyone involved? Was this a game to him?

I hoped the poor man was receiving help for his mental health issues, yet my gut told me the diagnosis of schizophrenia was probably incorrect. My brain swam with thoughts I didn't need as I headed out into the car park to collect my thoughts, my car, my sanity. I should have been glad for the fresh air, a moment of peace, but instead, my mind twisted violently with the events of an unexpected morning, my body now exhausted from too much exertion, chatter that made sense to no one, too little coffee in my system for my brain to function with ease.

My distracted thoughts ensured I didn't notice David standing some feet away, hovering with uncertainty, perplexed, somewhat troubled. I was busy fiddling with a mobile phone that mostly refused to co-operate, my car key momentarily disappearing into the lining of my cluttered jacket pocket. I had no clue where I'd left my reading glasses. I assumed they were still in the car, *somewhere*. It had been one of those days already, the entire morning's lectures abandoned, the university staff notified, mortified. I assumed my students would be pleased by the sudden change to their timetable, disinterested in my disappearance anyway. I was grateful the university understood that police work would always need to come first. When called to action, Newton Flanigan *must* go. However, a morning with three-dozen bored students would have been preferable to the company of that man. David Mallory. He was an enigma, a problematic individual with darker thoughts swilling in his mind than he was willing to express.

It was unfortunate (for me) that, by the time I glanced up, David was heading across the car park, too late to escape his unwanted attention or pretend I hadn't noticed him. I dipped my head, assessing the location of a key that mocked my unexpected panic with its continued absence. I willed my mobile to ring, anything that might provide a moment of distraction to free myself from further communication with this impossible man. I've met many unpleasant people in my life, yet David Mallory seemed to affect my mindset in a way no one ever had. Despite his probable condition, he unnerved me. I had no idea why. It was hardly his fault.

'Hello David,' I had no choice but to address him, no chance to hide, run away, the man now standing a mere six-foot from my car. *Damn it.* I needed to remain calm, show him that his presence did not bother me. I blinked, swallowed, still fumbling inside my pocket for that damned car key, finding only fluff, and sweet wrappers. David seemed distracted, as if he was uncertain who I was. A look of panic shot across his muddled eyes, the man I'd spent the last hour of my life with now displaying a completely different set of mannerisms entirely. I found my key and grabbed it firmly, an unexpected tremble forming in my hand as I jammed it into the lock, the doors unlocking with a click. Why was I so anxious around this guy? I was used to these types of people, had dealt with them often enough. He was biting his bottom lip, a trait I knew well. I'd done it myself for years. Still do, ever since we lost my older brother, Isaac. It isn't something I talk about often, his death not a memory I need in my head.

'Do you know me, sir?' David asked, closing the six-foot gap between us, pressing sweaty palms flat against the roof of my car. What was he talking about? Of course, I knew him. We had literally spent the last hour together. He was speaking now in a detached tone, the man failing to retain any previous composure. He dithered in front of me, dancing from foot to foot, no longer confident in his mannerisms. Did he need the toilet? I opened my car door in response to his approach, needing to retain some distance as he slid trembling hands along the car roof towards me, needing support he feared might not be so forthcoming. We were inches from each other, my open door the only thing separating us, my hand on the handle, his breath shallow, nervous.

'David? Are you okay?' I was shocked to notice tears in his eyes.

The man swallowed, appearing as if he wanted help he

wasn't confident how to ask for. 'I beg of you, sir. You *must* help me,' he muttered, lunging forward, grasping my shoulders with both hands.

Seven

Adam

I am genuinely perturbed that, still, after three *unimaginable* weeks of continued discussion and much pleading on my part, none of these dubious fellows have the capacity of mind to take me seriously. I have no honest knowledge of how many times I will be forced to show my face at this slovenly place before they omit their lunacy, lock me away. It is, after all, only what I deserve. I could head back inside the building, of course, demand immediate action, although those oddly dressed constables already hold a detailed account of my crime. There is nothing more I can tell them. The fact I have been thwarted from my proposed mission many times since, has now found me standing, once again, in this stoic location with numerous, may I add, indecently dressed, overly painted womenfolk who seem to hold more sway over me than should be considered acceptable.

How can so many females hold the rank of *law enforcer?* I have never seen anything of the like. Indeed, the way they are dressed mocks the very virtues of womanhood, seemingly happy to vex me with their continued ignorance, dressed almost as men. Do they possess no common decency amongst them? My confessions have been openly ignored, my words holding no meaning for any of these people. Surely they must *understand* my words? Are we not, after all, conversing in the same language? I take a breath knowing that, for now, I must keep a level head. My disdained nature is making things worse.

An odd-looking man is staring at my back when I turn around, dressed head to toe in vulgar clothing that consistently reminds me I am out of place here, out of my prevailing depth. There is, however, something about him that makes me want to run to him, wrap perplexed arms around his shoulders in urgent desperation, abate increasingly ludicrous emotions slowly swamping my mind. No. That will never do. Such an act of wanton abandonment would be utter madness. He may take a sudden aversion to my presence, leaving me in no doubt about his potential indifference.

I wonder if I am able to ask kindly for his aid, my mind requiring anything that may help it ease a little. Yet such a request may appear dubious. I smile, contemplating impolitely if I can simply walk over to him without appearing out of place. I shake my head. Of course, I cannot. The fellow would probably thwart my efforts. Still, it would be worth asking the question, nevertheless. Despite his attire, he indeed appears a fine figure of a man. I cannot help but stand and stare at him for a lingering moment, unable to prevent myself from gnawing the rough skin from my bottom lip with incumbent intent. Why I do this, I have no idea. It is a habit long acquired since childhood.

'Hello, David,' the gentleman calls out in my direction, seemingly holding prior knowledge of who David is. Yes, indeed, I might have known that *he* would have had something to do with my undesired removal from this location. My persistent candour in providing them with the confirmed location of a corpse would, of course, not be enough if David has had anything to do with it. I need now to acquire the information passed to this man, if any at all, to understand how much of my dear friend David Mallory he has been unfortunately forced to deal with.

'Do you know me, sir?' I call out, my bumbling frame scurrying perplexingly across the grounds of this disgusting hovel towards a man I have never before met. It is most troubling I would indeed have, at one time, given my life to go to bed with such a male. He is a handsome chap if ever I saw one, though not in a conventional sense of the word. He might, assumingly, not look twice at me, and understandably so. My increasingly uncouth, quelled appearance has become unbefitting of the man I once remember well. I am, however, not a total buffoon. On the contrary, I know how to act upon a first meeting. I simply do not feel altogether confident in this time or place. I glance around me. It is an unforgiving time, it seems.

My balance falters a little as I reach what I assume is his

vehicle, grabbing the roof with both hands. What an imbecile must I appear? Might he now believe me a heathen, a caper who loiters like a dog amongst these indignant dwellings, no better use of my time to be had? I cannot help but feel slightly contrived by the idea of becoming unavoidably bilious over this beautiful creature. I almost choke back the truth of my emotions. I require aid I feel may not be so forthcoming. Anyone with a molecule of brain cell capacity might have the license of mind to see such a thing. However, I probably look to this man now as if I am nothing more than a drunkard, already swayed by the thought of his beauty.

'David? Are you okay?' he asks. My goodness, this man is *truly* magnificent.

I swallow, requiring attention I do not know how to obtain. 'I beg of you, sir. You *must* help me,' I mutter, unconvinced this swain even understands my meaning. I have found myself surrounded by naked heathens, each using a dialect unfamiliar to my own. I do not intend to cause a commotion, of course, but I lunge forward, grabbing his shoulders with both hands. A gesture of my pending appeal for support I am uncertain how else to request. This man *knows* me. Or, at the very least, he knows *David*. It is a starting point, although somewhat unfortunate for me that I do not understand who *he* is.

He has a taut body I wish had the capacity of mind to...

I shake my head in disgust, dislodging uncomfortable, inappropriate thoughts from my mind, knowing I am acting impertinently, vulgar in my thinking, this moment oddly perplexing to my senses.

'Forgive me, sir,' I whisper, removing my now trembling hands from his shoulders. His scent is intoxicating, inviting. It is a shame he appears as vexed as those constables I have left behind, every one of them acting as if I have attempted some incumbent malice they wish to remove themselves from. I am fumbling awkwardly, my words emerging no better than the bark of a dog.

'Do you need to sit down?' he asks, a kindness I am not expecting. I stare into his eyes, deep blue, a hint of green that almost takes my breath. If this were a different time, I may very well believe myself to be in love.

'How is it, sir, that you know of me?' I need to calm myself, the need to keep this fellow on my good side, strong enough to maintain my wavering composure. The very last thing I need is for him to retreat into the shadows and be lost to me once more. I glance around, motioning forward, only for the poor unsuspecting victim to retreat backwards, attempting to climb into his vehicle. 'No, please, a thousand apologies again, my good fellow,' I state, holding my approaching arms aloft, needing to calm this situation, compose myself. I do not have a good history with men. It is unfortunate.

'Have you forgotten our interview already?' This delectable gentleman is giving nothing away of his emotions, aside from the fact his scent has increased, his natural body odour forcing the clarity of my senses in more ways than I would like to admit.

'You have spoken with David?' I hope he has conversed with *only* him and not The Others.

He offers me a smile, a quiver lingering at the corner of his luscious mouth. 'Adam?'

I gasp, grateful he knows my name, thankful, if nothing else, that I am not of unsound mind. 'Oh, yes, sir,' I breathe, intoxicated by his mannerisms, relief evident in my declaration. 'I thank you heartily.' I cannot say why I am openly expressing gratitude, merely relieved to hear my name spoken aloud with willing acceptance.

He nods, discarding what I can only describe as a carrier of some description, along with a folded document onto the rear seat of his vehicle. I jest that my freedom of movement has been prohibited for too long, nothing of my surroundings familiar now.

'How can I help?' he asks calmly. He does not possess a wedding band. Does this fellow, like me, prefer the company of men? The thought almost brings an unfettered smile to my lips.

I take a much-needed breath. 'I have failed in my mission for them to take me seriously, sir. Therefore, I am feigned to know how much is understood as to why I am still a free man.' I must admit I am rather distressed by the concept. 'But seeing as you freely called me David, and without assistance, I hope you will help those constables see just cause to incarcerate me.'

'Take you seriously about the body they found?'

Ah yes. The body, indeed. 'Why yes, sir.' I nod my head, grateful he understands my urgency, knows of my crime.

The gentleman sighs, closing his metal-framed door and stepping towards me. He appears far less concerned by my appearance than he did a moment ago. I am grateful. 'How did you know where the body was, Adam?'

'Because I placed it there,' I state clearly, solemnly, bowing my head in acknowledgement. Yet such an act is hardly worthy of this cool-hearted gesture, I know. My past deeds are not acceptable, my shame unforgivable.

The gentleman shakes his head, dismissing my words. 'You couldn't have done. That body has been in the ground for over two hundred years. I'm sorry, but you don't look that old to me.' Is he attempting to make light of my situation?

'Sir, I will have you know I will be seven and twenty years on the next year of my birth.'

'Exactly.'

'Exactly, what?' Indeed, what does he mean by *that*?

'Adam, I'm afraid you would need to be well over two hundred years old, I'm sorry, but you don't exactly look it.' He is staring at me now as if he believes me ill-minded, ill-informed.

I step backwards, dejected, peevish and resentful of words he cannot appreciate have not been expressed in good taste. I could quarrel with him, of course, throw myself onto the mercy of his good nature, but that would neither help him nor I in this unfortunate moment. I sigh, unable to comprehend the reasons behind this distinct lack of appreciation. *I have confessed.* What more am I now required to do?

Eight

Adam

I have no forethought of mind to see beyond the concept that this day might, by some miracle, be my last as a free man. Yet, I feel this fellow is mocking me, laughing at my words, able to form malice where, only a moment earlier, there was none. Why is he unwilling to take my confession as truth? I have forcefully expressed the whereabouts of that unfortunate body, taken several men in law enforcement to the precise location. Why am I, therefore, currently still free to roam as I wish?

'Do not rail me, sir,' I whisper sharply, ready to remove myself from this vexing situation if the moment should call for it. I am perturbed by his throwaway utterings as if my emotions matter little in this instance at all. He has taken my need, turning it into malicious lies that do not sit well with me.

'Sorry. Christ, I would never willingly do that.' He holds out a hand as if to calm me. How durst he laugh at me whilst claiming withdrawal of his noxious words, presuming now to care for my welfare? And, to take the Lord's name in vane like that. How *disgraceful.*

'I did murther those six people. You need to understand.' I hope my statement will sicken him, force him to take me in hand, drag me by the collar into the building beyond, towards several awaiting constables, my fate certain. I wish only to display brevity now. Nothing more will suffice.

'Murther?'

'Yes, sir.' Why does he mock me? And why is he offering such a strained stare?

'Meaning?'

'Meaning, sir, that I took the lives of my fellow compatriots who had caused me no direct harm.' I close my eyes, unwilling to linger over the concept a moment longer. I am not pleasured by this truth. I hang my head low.

'You mean *murder?*'

'Is that not one and the same thing?' I chastise. How has the English language changed so much since I was a young man in my prime?

He nods, finally appearing in agreement with my utterings. 'Apparently so.' How can he appear so calm whilst equally confused in his *own* mannerisms?

'Please, I beg of you. Why will they not imprison me?' I am beginning to panic now, my body trembling beneath this hazy midday heat. I do not wish to withdraw my continued questioning. 'I implore you. I do not deserve to be anywhere other than inside a jail cell.' Potentially hanging from a rope, already a rotting corpse on display for the entire town to view.

'Why do you feel that way?' The fellow looks puzzled, if not curious, perplexed by my utterings, perturbed in appearance and failing to appreciate my urgent desire.

'Because of The Others, sir.' I glance around, praying they haven't overheard. It is somewhat incumbent that they appear to be constantly listening, hiding amid the shadows of my darkened mind, waiting to remove me from a cruel world I have never understood.

'What others, Adam? Do you mean, David?'

'David, yes, and-' I pause, unable to bring myself to utter their names aloud for fear of what that might provoke. 'David will not tell of such matters. But if you aid me now, I promise heartily I shall give you precisely what you require.' I lunge forward, needing him to hear my words, to understand that I *need* his urgent attention. Once locked away, I will willingly testify to everything I know.

Seeing me head towards him with intent, he flinches, catching his footing in a grate beneath him, twisting a heel. He cries out, forcing me to catch him before he falls to the ground below us. I cannot help wrapping my arms around his body. I do not wish to hurt him, although I cannot speak for The Others, of course. They do not readily display emotion in such matters of the heart. He is pulling away, troubled, momentarily anxious.

'A thousand apologies, sir,' I am babbling again, I know. I cannot help it. I mean him no distress or to digress from my mission.

'It's okay, Adam,' he says, reclaiming composure, getting to his feet.

I disagree. Nothing of this matter is okay in the slightest. I cannot have those constables believing I could hurt this fellow by any means. I glance over my shoulder, a momentary idea forming in my wayward thoughts. Such an act *would*, of course, have the willing procurement of seeing me inside the very jail cell I have been imagining. At the very least, it would bide the little time I sorely need. I often find it unfortunate to consider the idea that David or one of The Others can appear at any given moment, fully able to prevail over me, chastising my worth as if I am nothing more than a noxious substance unbefitting of anyone's attention.

Of course, I do not wish for The Others to arrive. I do not believe this poor gentleman would understand who and what those men are. I drop my weight to the ground, my shame too much, curling into a ball in front of him as if I am nothing but a child about to be punished by his master. I have made myself look awkward—a foolhardy man with no capacity to hold a conversation.

'Advise them to lock me away. *Please*, I implore you with everything that is good and holy. I know they will listen if you tell them I affronted you, hurt you, procured a moment of malice.' Tears are falling now. It is ridiculous. *I am ridiculous.* He continues to stare at me as I curl further into a ball at his feet. The Others will reprimand me, I know, but I cannot help what I am—nothing more than a weak, foolhardy heathen, overtaken by impossible euphoria that I do not understand where else to place. Such lunacy I am displaying. It is all madness. *Madness*, I tell you.

'Adam?' The gentleman's voice is calmer now. It is as if he understands my fears are unnecessary, unrequired. He is kneeling at my side, his hand pressed against my arm. I glance at his face, my own paling by comparison. 'Why don't we sit down and talk about this.' He offers calm words matched by a lingering smile, his previous fears leaving his foreboding eyes before I am able to ascertain further probing.

I nod, reaching my hands for his, hoping he will aid me in my thwarted mission. They feel warm against my palms as he pulls me to my feet. I appreciate strong men, always have. Yet, I wish now only to keep him safe. Safe from The Others. Safe from everything I do not wish him to know about me.

'They do not yet know I am intent on exposing them all,' I whisper into his inviting ear as he leads me to the safety of his vehicle.

'Expose what, Adam?' I love his voice. It is soft yet focused, able to maintain the very composure that has seemingly escaped me. His accent is quite something. Strong, inviting. I find it alluring.

'That they are all killers too.'

He stops for a moment and regards me. I wonder if I have the power to shock him, change how he sees me. 'Oh?' Something in his voice wavers, as if he has taken a sudden aversion to my words. He wonders what I may divulge next. I can see it in his eyes.

I lick my lips, salty tears coating the thin skin around my mouth, my cheeks wet with fettered embarrassment. 'They are all dangerous men. I wish only to be free of their wrath.' I do not add "once and for all". It would be inappropriate.

'How many of them are there?' This fine fellow is nothing if not consistent. 'And *how* can I possibly free you?'

'Four. There are four of us, sir.' I have no honest notion of how I will ever be free of them. It is near impossible, of course. I cannot tell him this truth. He would never understand.

He stares at me. 'Four?'

I nod. 'Yes. It is unfortunate, I know. They are not like me,' I am disheartened to convey. I hang my head, overtaken by shame I have nowhere to place.

'Oh? And what are *you* like?' I enjoy his probing tone, his questioning abilities. I want to offer him a smile, but I refrain.

'I will never again hurt a living soul.' I had, in fact, vowed such a truth long ago.

'But you already confessed to the killing of six men.'

His words cut me, nothing more than a sharp blade to my belly. 'My victims were not *all* men, sir,' I state coldly, distressingly. I cannot help the melancholy memories that flood my thoughts, sounds of that poor woman's terrified screaming I wish I had the power to revoke. I can *never* put it right. 'It is the very reason I wish to confess all. To tell them what I did and why I did it. I have felt so much hatred for so long, yet I do not know what is to be done.' I am crying again. Foolhardy Adam. *Stupid damned fool!* I close my eyes. I cannot be confident this fine gentleman believes my words.

'Have you been taking your medication? I assume you must be on some.' The fellow is asking questions as if confirming a list of requirements he assumes important, although I have no idea to what he is referring. I must have expressed a withdrawn glare because he sighs, shaking his magnificent head. 'Adam?'

'No sir, I take no medicine for my troubles.'

He looks at me as if an idea has formed in his mind. 'Why don't I drive you home?' he offers, his kindness emerging from nowhere. I step back, uncertain how to proceed. I do not know how I should feel about such a suggestion. My thoughts about him are not entirely innocent.

I shake my head. 'No, sir. I cannot go home this day. *He* might be there.' Have I spoken such words aloud? But, of course, I am only expressing a half-lie. I do not wish to be alone with this fine fellow for long. It is most unfortunate.

'Who?'

'Jacob.'

'Who's Jacob?'

I glance towards a face that knows nothing of my predicament, nothing of who I am, entirely innocent in his query. 'He is the worst of us, sir,' I find myself replying, my voice no longer rational.

'And you don't like him?'

'None of us enjoy the company of Jacob, sir. You would not wish to be in his company either if you knew him as I do.'

'How often do you see him?' he is bringing forth relentless questions, disinterested in my responses.

'We try to keep him away. David is good at that.'

'You mentioned there are four of you?'

I nod. 'Indeed, yes. David, Jacob, Simon and, of course, myself.'

'Simon?'

'Yes. However, poor Simon is a little strange of mind.' I cannot tell him more than that. I cannot wish to see such discontent in his eyes whenever he looks at me, knowing I am to blame for the way of things.

The gentleman looks as if he wants to laugh now, yet his tone is able to retain a calming influence I have already grown fond of. I assume he believes us *all* a little strange, in our own way. Perhaps he is correct in his wild assumptions.

'Please, allow me to take you home, Adam,' he repeats. 'You look shaken. The police are *not* going to arrest you for a crime committed a long time before you were born.'

What on earth is this good fellow talking about? I shake my head, confused. 'I murthered that man. I can prove it.' I killed them *all*.

'But that murder was committed in the 1800s.'

I narrow my eyes. I know this fact, of course. I have lived with the memory of such an occurrence for so long. Why is he offering me such a dubious look? 'Yes, of course.' I stare at him, wishing only to dissect his thinking. It is impolite. I cannot help it. 'Do you believe me to be a simpleton, sir?' I do not wish him to think of me like *that*. Such a concept would be burdensome to my increasingly damaged emotions.

'No, of course not,' he smiles. I admire his teeth—pristine, wonderful. 'But you claim to be only twenty-six years old?' Again, he regards me as if I have lied.

'Why, certainly.' *Only twenty-six?* I wish I had the capacity of mind to smile. As it is, I am finding this entire morning somewhat troublesome. My age was once considered advanced. I should have been married by this stage of my life, settled, fathered children, able to provide for them with relative ease. It is unfortunate that such a concept was never something I could have undertaken. No matter what was expected of me. I refrain from expressing my distaste of ever taking a wife.

'Then, you couldn't have committed *any* murder.'

I shake my head. Why would he display such vulgar indifference? 'I am afraid it is you who are mistaken.'

I cannot grasp the look on his face, yet it appears as if he is no longer able to see me as I once hoped. His thoughts now seem to have trailed towards something else entirely. We are both muddled, it seems.

'Get in the car, Adam.' His demand is unexpected yet oddly inviting to my senses. I do as instructed without further ado.

'Forgive me, sir, but I am not yet acquainted with *your* name?' I glance around, not knowing what else to do. I have never found myself in a situation such as this.

'It's Newton,' he states calmly, whilst closing the passenger door. The interior of this odd-looking vehicle is disgusting. It smells of dust, sickly air and heated leather I am not accustomed with.

I smile. 'Newton? As in, *Isaac Newton?* The natural philosopher, mathematician, and physicist?' I refrain from offering a gleeful outburst that would look misplaced in this moment, seeing him throw me, once again, into the road beyond. 'No. I think not, sir. I think not, indeed.'

Nine

Newton

I have to admit, I was shaken by Adam's unexpected appearance, the confessions he'd made now wholly unanticipated. Yet it was his eluding presence that baffled me, his persona, the way he carried himself, his *odd* choice of words. Despite being diagnosed with paranoid schizophrenia, I couldn't help assuming it was an incorrect prognosis, although why his doctors had it so wrong, I was yet to appreciate. DID is very real, of course, but those inflicted with this rare identity disorder usually, unconsciously, *create* each of the personalities inside their minds. Although every variation might indeed manifest as either sex, varying sexualities, differing ages and personas, they do not claim names of the *dead*. Adam's behaviour was strange, new, something now niggling me I couldn't place.

The concept that Adam claimed to have lived during a

completely different time period was unusual for DID. Dissociative identity disorder involves a distinct lack of connection with any sense of identity, their memory and consciousness often incomplete. Sufferers will subsequently create varying personalities in order to handle aspects of themselves and their lives they might otherwise find difficult, including potential trauma they may have been unable to deal with in the past. The whole thing results in manifestations that, without which, they would probably struggle to cope with daily life. Paul had already confirmed that Adam Mires was a dead man; the guy in front of me now speaking almost in tongues. I would probably need a dictionary to understand much of what he said.

I was, however, impressed by how David was able to shift mannerisms effortlessly, readily able to recall historical information and phrases on cue. I could only assume his personalities were purposefully created from long-dead people to shock. But why would he do that? Why would he claim the past of a man capable of committing murder, only to then want to repent for that very same crime? I needed to uncover more about Adam and The Others living inside one man.

Despite his earlier, demanding need for attention, Adam remained relatively quiet on the drive to his house, his nervous, anxious tone replaced with a calmer, more subdued character. I initially equated his change in behaviour to a change of environment. My car was capable of putting anyone to sleep with its incessant rattles and knocking I've been trying to ignore for a while. He was pressed back against my headrest, his eyes closed, occasionally rubbing his neck with both hands—awake yet unwilling to chat, offering the odd sigh I equally attempted to ignore. I tried not to take it personally.

I shouldn't have offered to drive him home at all, I know, yet leaving him in such a state outside the station would have resulted in a less favourable outcome than the one I'd probably triggered now. Adam did not appear as sinister as David, more desperate than anything else, *poor sod*, and for that, I was grateful. Yet, it remained in my mind that, at any moment, one of his unwitting characters might make an unexpected appearance. The confines of my small car would be too much for such an introduction.

I usually find no issues sparking conversation with strangers, keeping chat light, carefree, especially around those who need careful mental health consideration. Yet, I was rendered uncharacteristically speechless once we were together in my car alone, our proximity slightly uncomfortable, our elbows accidentally brushing every time I changed gear. There was something about this guy I couldn't put my finger on. David had displayed a curt, uptight, obnoxious manner, whereas Adam appeared laid back, albeit unsettled. Even his eyes appeared softer, brighter, a different colour entirely. It made my skin go cold, and the tiny hairs on the back of my hands stand to attention. So, instead of launching into general chitchat as I usually would, I simply asked for his address, to which he responded coldly, a flat tone I'm sure wasn't there a moment earlier.

By the time we arrived outside the property, our silence

was becoming overwhelming, the midday heat overbearing, despite many pointed questions aimed his way to help ease the tension that had oddly formed from nowhere. I spent too long casually commenting on the weather to quash the otherwise unbearable hush lingering between us. It was a strained conversation that teetered on deplorable small talk, and I hated every second of it. Eventually, I gave up, concentrating my efforts on driving, the traffic unrelenting.

Adam's house was a whitewashed building of three storeys, peeling paintwork, exposed crumbling bricks, an overgrown front garden needing attention. I concluded swiftly that Adam, David, or any combination of the men living inside this guy's head had seriously failed to take care of this place. You'd assume between the four of them, they'd be able to keep the weeding to an acceptable level. The fact David had been living in an institute for the last seven years gave him the perfect excuse, I guess, for this lapse in kerbside appeal, but this building had been left far longer than a few forgotten years. I wasn't about to express my thoughts, of course. It would be rather rude.

Adam climbed out of my car without offering any thanks, closing the door in silence as he stepped light-footedly towards the building, his awkward, bumbling way of walking replaced now with a lighter variation that disturbed me. David had walked stiffly, as if he dared not bend his body for fear of snapping something. Adam was on a different planet altogether. Now, the guy walking towards a dilapidated front door appeared to be neither of those two men at all, almost feminine in composure as he floated towards the door. I swallowed, glancing around this unfamiliar neighbourhood. What was I even doing here?

I got out, closed my car door, popping the key inside my trouser pocket so I wouldn't lose it again if I needed it in a hurry. Why such a wayward thought jumped into my mind, I have no idea, but I coughed, freeing my throat from the choking ideas that threatened now to spill into my increasingly muddled mind.

'Adam?' I called towards the open front door, stepping forward, hating my feet for automatically pointing me in the wrong direction. I should have climbed back into my car and driven off. Adam was home. Safe. That is all I had promised him. Instead, I allowed my feet to climb several weed-ridden steps towards his front door, my brain (almost as if watching some crazed horror film) loudly yelling at me to not go inside the "scary house". It was dark in there. Everyone knows you never enter a dark, spooky building—especially not alone. My brain was screaming profanities. *Don't go in there, you idiot!*

The property was mid-1920s, complete with a wooden veranda built over a damaged porch. It was probably once adorned with white paintwork, maybe cream, inset with dark olive-green edges popular of the period. Yet that same paintwork now looked rotted to near dust, barely any colour left on its worn surface that might pass for paint at all. Stained glass panels reflected deep red and blue onto the parquet hallway flooring beyond, laden now with dust and leaves blown in from the outside world, forgotten, left to rot where they sat. Discarded mail sat abandoned where it had fallen from the letterbox, some of it yellowed with age. It looked as if no one had been here for decades. Footprints led along the hallway towards the back of the house, the soles of Adam's shoes gathering the very dust that had lay untouched for years.

'Adam?' I called again, the darkness of this old building becoming more apparent the further I stepped inside. Should I call David's name instead? Simon? *Jacob?* Although the sun was bright, this place had the look of a condemned building, large cracks in the ceiling that crept down the walls like giant fingers reaching out, threatening to destroy it all. There was a strange smell, not unlike old rotten meat, as if someone had forgotten a beloved pet, left to decompose. Against my better judgement, I motioned into the hallway, several decaying floorboards groaning beneath my incoming weight. An open door at the far end allowed a trickle of light to showcase dust motes that flooded the space around me, an offset staircase leading to a darkened landing above. I dared not look upwards.

'Adam? Will you be okay if I leave now?' I didn't want to leave without saying goodbye, it would appear rude, yet I equally couldn't get my legs to propel me any further into the house. My brain was happy about that concept, at least.

Footsteps, light, quick. A shape appeared in the kitchen doorway and stood staring at me, a free hand held aloft. 'My dear man, please do not stand in the hallway with the front door wide open. Anyone could walk in off the street. You're letting the wind blow all sorts in.' He waved a casual hand towards the open front door before he spun on his heels, heading back into the kitchen with a disinterested flick of his head. Okay. *Not Adam.*

A distinct clanging of pots and pans reverberated around me, much muttering and sighing happening in the next room. I swallowed, not about to close that front door for anyone, no matter how polite the request had been. I wished I'd stayed outside, listened to my brain. Instead, I turned around, creaking the door closed enough so it appeared as if I had latched it. I hadn't. I then forced my feet to walk the length of the hallway towards the kitchen, my mind mocking the fact that if I'd driven away, I wouldn't be in this situation now at all.

The kitchen was lighter than the hallway, thank goodness, although only just, and I had to stop myself gasping when I walked through the door to the sight of Adam, David, or some alternate manifestation, standing at an old-fashioned sink. He had his back to me, frantically tapping the side of a tap in a vague attempt to locate water, a large copper kettle balanced in his outstretched hand. The kitchen looked as if it hadn't been updated since the house was built. There was a solid oak table in the middle, a cast-iron range beneath a chimney breast in one corner, a free-standing sink unit that Adam was struggling with. He turned when he saw me, offering a smile I wasn't confident I liked the look of.

'Oh, you wouldn't mind giving me a hand, would you, my dear? This old thing has troubled this house for many a year.' He grinned as if this was an average day for him, tilting his head to assess me better. I didn't want to, but I walked over to the sink to hold the kettle whilst he busied himself with the task of getting water to come out of the tap. The unit was in a filthy state, so rusted in places I could see straight through to the brick tiled flooring below.

'You actually *live* here?' I didn't mean to sound so shocked, so pointed. I was surprised that *anyone* could live in such a place. It looked like a museum. A bleak, untouched one—no visitors, no life.

'This was my mother's house.' He laughed, offering me a sideways look. 'Although it was in far better condition when she last saw this place, I can assure you.'

His tone had changed, so had his manner of speaking, the way he held himself. I concluded I was no longer communicating with either Adam or David. 'Your mother?' Was I talking to Simon or Jacob now?

He laughed, more a giggle, raising a hand to his mouth as he pressed a thumb across his smiling lips. 'The Others dislike me coming here. They do not care much for the old place, sadly.' He glanced around, taking in his surroundings, seemingly happy to be home. I was glad I couldn't understand the thoughts swimming inside his darkened eyes. Nothing good lived there. He took the ageing kettle from my hands, filling it as best he could before turning off the tap, the action causing much protesting from several old pipes. The kettle was leaking. I dared not tell him. He took it over to the old stove and stood it on a black iron grate, muttering to himself, my presence of no concern. 'Matches, matches, I can never find any matches when I need them.' He searched several shelves, pulling out decayed boxes that allowed dust to fly into the air above us.

'You were telling me about your mother?' I asked,

attempting to keep my tone casual, needing to create a conversation. He stopped, turning to stare at me. I swallowed. 'Forgive me,' I found myself muttering. 'We haven't yet been properly introduced. My name is Newton. Newton Flanigan.' I attempted a smile that never made it to my lips.

'Simon Frederick at your service, my dear,' he replied, raising disinterested eyes to the ceiling before returning to his previous, frantic pursuit for matches to light a stove which now housed a puddle of stagnant water from the leaking kettle. He stood with his back to me, delighted when he finally found what he was searching for, an orange flame flickering to life in front of him. 'Although I am intrigued to learn precisely *what* you have heard about my mother?' His tone had darkened, as if I had accidentally hit a nerve by mentioning her.

'Oh, I know nothing of your mother, I can assure you. You mentioned this was her house.'

He turned, smile wide, eyes resuming their previous brightness. 'Oh, yes, this was my childhood home. It was full of life back then, of course.' He giggled again, not unlike that of a young girl. 'Now, where are those blasted teacups?'

'It's okay, I don't want any tea,' I replied, hoping he would forget the idea for a moment. I feared he might accidentally burn the entire house down, the two of us inside, mocking the fact I'd agreed to such a ludicrous invitation in the first place. The old stove didn't look as if it had been lit in years, a distinct smell of burning already filling the room, filling me with dread. 'You mentioned that The Others don't like it here. Do they live elsewhere?' I wondered when Simon Frederick had climbed into my car instead of Adam Mires. It had been a stressful morning, but how had I missed *that?*

Simon turned to face me, tapping a hand freely against his hip. He appeared very feminine, openly expressing gentile emotions with ease. 'I suppose they do. I, however, prefer it *here*, whenever I am allowed the freedom of choice.' He sighed, running a hand across a dusty kitchen table. It had remnants of what looked like a loaf of bread sitting on a forgotten chopping board. Although it was grey now, turning black, furred over with a vast colony of bacteria that made me gag. I did not imagine for a moment that Simon would be willing to give me David's address.

'How often do you come here?' I already knew the answer to that question: *Hardly ever.*

Simon sighed. 'Not as often as I would like. I have special memories here, you see, my dear. Special trinkets and mementoes I cannot share with The Others, especially Adam.'

'Oh?' I tried to remain casual, yet I knew Adam had wanted to expose them all. Killers, he called them. I swallowed, almost choking as something in the air tried to disappear down my throat.

'Adam doesn't appreciate our art. He believes we should atone for our sins. He isn't like the rest of us, you see.' Yes, I'd confirmed as much.

I thought about David, wondering what his apparent crimes had been. He'd wilfully protested an innocence I now oddly wondered about. 'Your art?' I probably shouldn't have asked.

Simon laughed, tapping his toes together and standing

straight, not unlike a ballet dancer about to perform a pirouette. I flinched, the protesting groans of this ageing building sending shockwaves through my body. Simon didn't notice. 'Darling, art is subjective, don't you agree? Although I'd prefer it if you didn't ask about such personal matters. We hardly know each other.' He chuckled, still searching for teacups.

I made my excuses, needing to leave, grateful that Simon seemed more occupied by his childhood home than by me, happy to allow me the escape I needed. Decades of dust had gathered in my nostrils, and by the time I stepped onto the front porch, I was ready to either sneeze or cough up a lung. I was grateful I'd managed to subdue the urge until fresh air filled my chest; the distinct impression forming that Simon wouldn't have cared much for my unanticipated bodily fluids aimed towards his mother's possessions.

'Do call again, won't you, my dear. I rarely get to converse with many men these days.' He was standing inside the entrance porch, his slim frame confident, almost arrogant. I nodded, grateful I was walking back to my car, the soles of my shoes sticking to the pavement as I strode from the house as fast as I could. Luckily Simon didn't notice. Instead, he waved once before closing the front door, leaving me to ponder alone. He'd mentioned nothing of Adam or his earlier confession. Indeed, nothing was discussed how I had come to find myself inside the house of his probable *dead* mother. I shuddered, wondering when she died, *how* she died. I did not assume I wanted the answer.

I climbed into my car and kicked off my shoes, glad for the

freedom my socked feet provided, coated also in dust now, annoyingly. I couldn't imagine how Simon Frederick could happily muse around that place with no trouble at all, overlooking the state of the property entirely. I thought of my own, less than presentable basement flat, still with last night's take-away curry box sitting on my cluttered dining table, several coffee mugs on my rug. I probably did the same, to be honest. Did I even own a vacuum cleaner? No. Unfortunately, I do not believe I did.

Ten

Simon

It would be insincere of me to claim I am rarely startled by the appearance of people I have never before met, because I am. It is genuinely distasteful. However, I should be used to such occurrences by now, not always in control of my actions. Jacob and David do not entertain, so I hardly need to bother about those two. They are, like me, loners preferring their own company. Adam, however, is an entirely different matter. Oh, how I *loathe* that man. If I possessed the psychical capability to do such a thing, I would have already taken his life by now, adding his pathetic corpse to my splendid collection. As it is, to do such a drastic thing would end my own life. It is unfortunate. We are connected, after all, bound to one another by time, life, and impossible circumstance.

I am relieved once that frightful man has left my house. He told me his name, but I cannot recall what it was. My mother would have scolded him for dragging his cheap, crudely manufactured shoes around her beautiful parquet flooring, the man no better than a Neanderthal, a brutish thug surely capable of breaking something if left alone too long. He is an imbecile, nothing more. I did not like the way he continually scanned my mother's possessions, as if he was disgusted by the sight of them. Yes, granted, things have no longer remained in their once pristine state, yet I can do little about that. This house seems to drift further into dilapidation with each of my increasingly rare visits. How this is continually able to happen, I have no idea.

I glance around, attempting to survey what that horrid man was staring at. Everything appears to me as it always has. There may be a little dust here and there, perhaps, yet the pantry remains stacked with an abundance of tinned goods and essential baking accessories, pie dishes that reach the ceiling, a distinct aroma only made possible from a brimming, healthy food storage. Remnants of butter, apple, and blackberry pie, flour containers probably still containing the very flour my mother once used to produce an array of delicious baked products for our friends and neighbours. Her teapot still adorns the kitchen table. Two cups are set, one for each of us. The old range, a prized selling point of the house and the reason my father purchased this property for my mother in the first place takes centre stage beneath the chimney breast, complete, may I add, with bread oven—a rarity for its day. I fold my arms across my chest. Yes, indeed. Mother would be proud I have taken good care of the place for her.

I enjoy the tea I earlier offered that infuriating man, still uncertain why he turned me down in such a way, chastising myself for forgetting his name. It was rude of him to refuse my polite offerings. Yet, that may be the reason I have chosen to disregard his identity now. Mother would have been most aggrieved. I close my eyes, in need of respite from today's events, a little time to muse over my private thoughts and ponder new ideas that often drift around my mind unchecked. I hasten to conclude I now enjoy the simple pleasures life has to offer, sitting with a nice cup of tea, the sound of birdsong beyond my mother's kitchen window appealing to my ravaged senses. I enjoy it when this place is quiet, when no other soul has the potential to disturb my thoughts. I finally understand why Mother was always so keen for solace, a little quiet time in which to reflect upon the day. It took me a while, I know, to see things as she once did. I did not always appreciate her when she was alive. It is upsetting.

Swilling remnants of tea from the pot under my grumbling kitchen tap, I set it aside to dry, perplexed as to how the old sink has formed a hole in one corner, rust threatening to devour it. I will need to deal with that problem swiftly, of course. Mother would be mortified should any of the neighbours call unexpectedly. I wonder why I've never noticed before.

I set about tidying my mother's house the best I can, wiping windows, shaking rugs into the overgrown garden, and removing old net curtains from even older frames. I wonder how long it has been since anyone has taken a cloth to the surfaces, the entire place stale and stayed. I am on a mission, my mind no more able to think about my mother's decaying house than the state of her decaying corpse, her bright soul sadly long departed, lost to me forever.

I am, however, shocked at how well the apples are growing. It is a welcome distraction. Thick, ripe balls of juice hang from branches in giant clusters, the likes of which I haven't seen for some time, even in the most prestigious of Eastcliff's organic grocery stores. Mother always said the fruit grew better here because of the ripe sea air and her dorsal tones cutting through the open windows. Indeed, who am I to argue with that? My mother's tone certainly had a way of clearing the cobwebs from us all.

I ascend the creaking staircase, away from the grandfather clock in the hallway that has stopped ticking, along the landing into my mother's bedroom. I am uncertain if I should enter as I hover by the door. Nothing has changed in here since I was a small boy. It still has the same handcrafted counterpane over the bottom of her bed that I used to pick the threaded cotton with my fingertips until all was left were tiny, pinpricked holes in the pattern. Mother never knew, of course, or if she did, she never mentioned anything to me. A giant stuffed rabbit with velveteen ears still sits on my grandmother's old rocking chair. It was old, even when I was a child, and it often terrified me in the looming darkness, especially in the middle of the night when the house fell silent. I no longer have any troubling thoughts about greyed, fibre-filled objects, considering what looms below me in the basement.

I glance around. A three-fold mirror still rests on my mother's dressing table, those ageing Victorian perfume bottles she used to collect now smelling more of dust than the fragrance they once housed. When I sit on the bed it creaks angrily beneath my weight. I was never allowed to do that when I was small, and it still feels odd, even now. Mother always wanted the sheets to remain smooth, crisp, perfect to any potential onlooker. It's a wonder she even slept in it. It is a shame they now look frayed, damp in places, rotting away with time and neglect. Mother would be most incensed.

I lie back, unable to prevent myself drifting into a deep slumber, dreaming of my cherished men I wish I could converse with now, lavish gifts I lovingly gave them, declarations of devotion that reside these days only in my deepest thoughts. Even that infuriating man, with his tank top attire, overbearing scent and cheap shoes, manages to pop into a dream. *How annoying.* I do not even recall falling asleep. Still, I awaken sometime later to the feel of a spider crawling across my cheek, a stiffened neck, not even the sound of birdsong beyond the window to diffuse the increasing noise in my head.

Despite everything, I enjoy my time here. It allows me to feel close to my family once more, my mother and beautiful men still speaking freely from these darkened, decaying walls. Whenever I find myself elsewhere, be it in David's residence, walking the streets of Eastcliff, or strutting around like a madman inside Adam's unforgiving mind, I always try to find my way back home, to where I am once again complete, safe, surrounded by the love I once knew and cherished well.

I amble into the kitchen, my bare feet the only sound to break the silence I do not expect to overwhelm me so much. Although my mother is long dead, items we bought together are still dotted around the place, including things I no longer enjoy. Although she died slowly, painfully, she still managed to leave behind our old life for me to deal with and process alone. I trip over a rug that has seen better days, feeling a staggering urge to take a knife to it and shred it into oblivion. However, I refrain from my frenzied knife attack and instead make myself a cup of earl grey.

It has been one of those unfortunate weeks where everything seems wrong. This house is the same, of course. Eastcliff is still on the same part of England's east coast that it has always been, and I am the same, inside. Yet, something now feels painfully different. My tea tastes bland. I have nothing to consume besides a forgotten fruit loaf that has turned a strange shade of grey, eggs that are *seven* years out of date, a bottle of unopened milk in the pantry no longer resembling milk at all. It has solidified, looking more now like yoghurt. Or cheese. Surely it has not been so long since I was last here?

I sigh, sitting in silence, not even turning on my mother's old radio in case the unwanted noise distracts me from the solitude in which I now prefer to live. *Is this my life?* Consisting of little more than a house readily crumbling around me, inedible food, lying awake at night with memories in my head I no longer wish to recall.

The years have passed slowly, yet time is moving relentlessly forward without me. I notice this far more when I am forced into the world beyond these walls. Everything appears differently now from my recollection of those earlier, precious years with my mother. At weekends I rarely leave the house at all, my social life having previously been tied to mutual friends Mother and I once shared. Now those people are gone, existing only in fading photo frames still resting on dust-laden surfaces in her front parlour. It matters little to me, I know, yet it helps cement the truth of my new way of living. I am alone, isolated, lost in a world I fail to understand. When I summon the energy to leave the house, it is to always stand in a town that no longer feels familiar, waiting for unknown men to pass me by, as if somehow, one day, I know *he* will be there. I need a sign, just one, that all this is real and not simply a ridiculous story that lives inside my head.

Eleven

Newton

I was barely a mile from Old Trent Road and Simon Frederick's overbearing property when my mobile rang, thankfully returning me to the real world and much-needed rational thinking. I was flustered, perturbed by the personality shift one man could make with ease. I grappled along the dashboard to retrieve my phone, disgruntled by the mess that met my outreaching hands; a half-empty crisp packet spilling its contents alongside a toffee that had glued itself firmly to my sun-beat windscreen. *Seriously?*

'Flanigan,' I stated plainly, distractingly trying to wipe traces of melted sugar and crumbs from my hand. Why did I have such an obsession with sticky sweets?

'Newt, it's Paul. You free?'

I thought of David Mallory, my mind twisting words left unsaid into something rather ugly. 'I am now. Why?'

'I could use your help.' He paused, his request enough to make me sit up and take notice. I resisted the urge to lick toffee from my fingers. 'A body has been found.'

For a split second, I wanted to laugh, although it wasn't funny, I know. 'Did Adam Mires confess to yet more *murthers?*' I chided, smothering my inappropriate outburst against the sweat infused sleeve of my shirt, repeating the unusual word Adam had used, his voice lingering in my head long after we parted company. All I could see were forgotten bones, a decaying loaf of bread, dust I couldn't dislodge from my shoes or my sinuses.

Paul sighed, no doubt trying to cover his increasing irritation. '*No*. This has nothing to do with David. But I would like your opinion if you don't mind.' There was something in Paul's tone that told me to keep my jokes to myself, for now — that it wasn't appropriate.

'Okay. Where are you?'

'You'll never guess.'

'The old factory ruins on Adderson Street?'

'Bingo.'

~

Without running the risk of overthinking everything that had happened today, I concluded the location of this recently discovered body was because the place was underwhelmingly underused — overgrown with everything from nature to fly-tipped junk. It was the perfect environment for anyone to dispose of a body no matter what century it was discarded. I arrived on scene to the sight of several police vehicles already dotting the area, passers-by and dog walkers gathered in clusters, chatting amongst themselves, taking pictures and videos, wanting to know what was going on—every one of them attempting to extract any gossip to post to their social media accounts.

A flash of blue flickered across the tree line, outlining several dilapidated, crumbling walls, a once beautiful building nothing now but a long-forgotten ruin. Even the low rumble of engines and distant chatter failed to showcase anything inviting about this old place. I accidentally parked in a puddle, my right shoe and hem of my trousers confirming the error with annoyance as I climbed out of my car in haste. *Bloody hell.* I was still shaking yesterday's rain from my now soaked foot when Paul walked up the sodden path to greet me. Dressed in wellington boots and wax jacket, my friend looked every bit the local farmer instead of the important Detective Chief Inspector he actually was.

'Thanks for coming,' he stated casually, noticing my damp lower leg. He sounded as if I was joining him for a relaxed coffee, a beer, his tone kept purposefully casual, too calm for the magnitude of this moment. I understood why Paul was clad in wellies now, at least. He could have warned me.

'No problem,' I muttered, wondering if someone had a towel I could borrow, a fresh pair of socks. Instead, my damp foot was forced to squelch mockingly beneath me as we trekked downhill towards the ruined remains of the town's once-prized tinned soup factory, the much earlier cotton mill no longer standing the test of time. There was nothing left now but forgotten walls, many no longer standing at all, a gap where the main door would have once stood, plenty of overgrowing weeds claiming back this vast space with force. Someone held up a length of printed blue and white tape wrapped around several nearby trees, allowing us to enter a segregated zone, a pre-laid plastic sheet ensuring we were careful to leave no lasting trace of our presence behind. I was handed paper slippers that would at least hide my damp foot; at least the rainwater had washed the dust off.

A white tent had been erected some feet away, no doubt hiding the unfortunate body that lay beyond. A few people stood around, taking photographs, creating possible scenarios in their minds, periodically being yelled at by uniformed police—told to stay back, go home.

'I warn you, it isn't a pretty sight,' Paul stated flatly as we neared the tent, nodding towards a colleague who handed him a pair of surgical gloves he subsequently gave to me. I glanced his way, assuming nothing of what I was about to see held any potential to shock me. *I'd seen it all.* Up until now, I'd been given no information about this discovery. A body. That's all Paul had confirmed. I assumed this was my friend's way of containing the situation at hand, allowing me the fresh perspective of an initial inspection. Shapeless forms in paper suits floated in and out of the tent, carrying toolkits and cameras, their faces blank, whispering amongst themselves so no one else would hear. I pulled on my gloves and paper slippers, waiting.

I failed to appreciate the reality of the unfortunate body that lay a couple of metres in front of us as Paul lifted a breeze-induced flap, allowing me to step inside the tented area ahead of him. A young woman was on the ground, covered in dirt and blood, naked, on her back, legs spread, as if someone had recently finished having fun with her before leaving her to her fate. I have no idea what I was expecting to see. *A body*, of course, probably female, a child even. I was prepared for that. I'd seen such things before, no matter how uncomfortable it always was. *But this?* As much as I'd grown accustomed to seeing dead bodies in varying states, varying locations, the sight of this poor girl came as a shock. I tried not to cover my mouth with my hand, failed, clamping my gloved palm against my jaw in automatic response.

'I told you,' Paul muttered, standing behind me now, arms folded across his chest, waiting for my thoughts.

I glanced over my shoulder, allowing a sigh I couldn't help, a deep breath escaping my chest without warning. I could taste sick. *What the hell?* The poor girl was missing a few *vital* body parts. No hands, just brutish stumps on the end of each arm, no teeth and (I motioned closer), more importantly, no *breasts*. I carefully stepped around her damaged body, mindful not to disturb the gruesome scene that lay in front of us. She'd been cut from the middle of her rib cage to her pubic area, her internal organs now lying cold across her mutilated chest.

'Jesus Christ, Paul.' I couldn't help blurting out the words, glaring at my friend for his lack of ability to warn me of several important things today, my damp foot now the least of my concerns.

'My words precisely,' Paul agreed, missing the point.

'Who on Earth would do something like that?' I asked, more to myself than the man at my side. As much as I wanted to, I couldn't tear my eyes away from her internal organs; her heart, liver, intestines, something I couldn't identify lying discarded at my feet.

'You tell me, you're the psychologist.' Paul refrained from laughing, instead turning his fickle comment into a deep sigh of his own, his eyes diverting as he spoke.

I knelt closer to the body. The woman's eyes were set wide open, as if the last moments of her life were recorded somewhere in the deepest areas of her brain, still fully able to recall her killer with ease. I felt slightly embarrassed for her, to be honest, wanting to remove my shirt and cover her modesty. Or, at least, what was left of it. The stench of congealed blood was overwhelming, the heat of the day too much. Even flies were unsure how to react. The rustle of a paper suit interrupted my thoughts as the attending forensic pathologist, Bernard Taylor, stepped into the tent, nodding a swift hello to Paul and myself, dancing around us in the confined space with a muted apology.

'Okay, so what do we know?' Paul asked, his tone blank.

'She was probably killed around ten to fifteen hours ago, I'd say. No longer than that. Might have been at some point in the early hours of this morning or late last night.' Bernard lifted one of the woman's handless arms with the end of a pen, revealing heavy bruising around her ribs and inner torso. I often wondered how the man could do his job without vomiting. 'She was kicked a few times at some point by the looks of it.'

That was the *least* of the poor girl's worries.

'Cause of death?'

Bernard looked at Paul for a moment as if he was being stupid, although thankfully, nobody confirmed how ludicrous his question sounded. It was obvious what had killed her. Horrific, brutal trauma.

'It's difficult to say at this stage if her organs were removed pre- or post-death, but judging by the sheer blood loss, I presume she would have been alive whilst she was being cut open. I'll know more when I do the post-mortem.' He turned the girl's head to one side, revealing a deep incision on the back of her neck. 'She may have been fully awake while she was being cut open, completely paralysed and unable to fight back.'

Did I hear that correctly? I had to look away, the thought of this poor girl's potential terror too much for my muddled mind to deal with.

'And it appears she may have been raped. Brutally. Though *what* he used, I'm yet to confirm.' He hovered an index finger over her vaginal area, heavily peppered with blood, torn in places. There were bruises around the tops of both legs and buttocks, although there was too much dried blood to appreciate the significance of her suffering. It was challenging to decipher what I was looking at. I dared not get too close. I wasn't sure I wanted to know.

'What is *that*?' I asked, pointing to a fleshy lump of blood that lay across her rib cage.

Bernard looked at me blankly. 'That, my friend, is her womb.'

I swallowed. *Shit.*

'Have we found her clothing yet?' Paul stepped in, trying, as was I, not to lose his breakfast.

Bernard shook his head. 'Not a thing. Nothing at all to say who she was. No bag, purse, or mobile phone. It looks as if she might have had tattoos, although judging by these wounds, they were removed by a sharp instrument.' He pointed to a bloodied square patch of missing skin on her forearm, a large section on her shoulder blade, another on her upper leg, as if someone had carefully cut away huge chunks of flesh for fun. I hadn't noticed, too busy trying not to stare too long at what was left of the rest of her.

'Knife wounds?' I found myself asking in automatic response.

'More like a scalpel if I had to hazard a guess. The cuts are clean. Even sharp knives leave noticeable marks, score lines. Knife blades are usually too thick to cut with any precision. These wounds are perfect.' He pointed to an almost flawless incision made across her torso and her missing breast area. 'If I didn't know any better, I'd say a surgeon did this.' I wondered what kind of a person would attack someone so violently, so savagely, then carefully remove body parts, carving tattoos from their victims skin with precision? *A surgeon?* It didn't bear thinking about.

'What about the hands?' Paul chipped in, writing the findings in his notebook for later assessment. Someone was still taking photographs.

'That's the odd part. Her hands were hacked off, seemingly in a temper. The teeth were punched out, too.

Either with a fist or a blunt object. Whoever killed this poor girl seriously didn't like her or didn't want her to be identified.'

'So not carefully removed, like the organs and skin were?' I asked.

Bernard shook his head. 'No. Not at all. Done in anger, I'd say.'

'And the—'

'Breasts? Again, carefully removed. It was almost as if the killer wanted—'

'A trophy,' I concluded, noting there was no sign of either breast at the scene. I swallowed, not entirely needing *that* image in my head.

'Indeed.'

It wasn't a pleasant thought. The idea of someone now possessing whatever tattooed skin this female once had, along with her female anatomy. Maybe he would keep them in a freezer until he could preserve them better. The idea made me feel ill. Bernard left us alone to conclude our findings before the body could be taken to the lab for further investigation, a full post mortem pending.

'Thoughts?' Paul asked once we were alone. No time for niceties today.

I stared at her bludgeoned features. Did she put up a fight? Did this woman know her killer? I shook my head. I couldn't exactly tell, but she didn't look that old.

'Beating someone to death, hacking off their hands and punching out their teeth shows a severe lack of respect, anger even. Someone who has a lot of pent-up frustration,' I muttered. *Anyone* could see that. 'But it doesn't tie in with the care taken in slicing off her breasts, cutting out her organs, removing tattoos.' The very thought formed a lump in my throat, causing me to wince at the idea.

'No,' Paul said, thankfully removing my unwanted thoughts. 'It doesn't.'

We stood staring at the unfortunate body at our feet, neither of us willing to acknowledge this woman wasn't much older than his eldest daughter, currently at sixth-form college, hopefully safe, drinking hot chocolate with friends, oblivious to this poor girl's plight. The idea that someone would deliberately go out of their way to hurt a fellow human in such a way made me feel sick to the stomach. After all, who would want the idea placed in their head that anyone, male or female, could find themselves like *this*?

I still had David on my mind, the way he was, Adam Mires supposed victims, missing fingers, teeth, old bones, rotting bread. 'Bit of a coincidence, don't you think?' I couldn't help expressing my thoughts aloud. I needed a second opinion.

'What is?' Paul was already halfway out of the tent.

'That this poor girl ended up in a similar way to the victim your guys dug up the other week?'

Paul glanced over his shoulder, shaking his head, furrowing his brow. 'Hardly.'

I turned to face my friend, still hovering by an open flap. 'No?'

'You can't seriously assume the remains of some two-hundred-year-old corpse is in any way linked to *this* poor sod?' He glanced towards the blood-let corpse one last time before stepping out into the afternoon sunlight, grateful for the fresh air.

'Not directly, no,' I agreed, stepping outside now too, also thankful for a fresh breeze that took my breath, happy to leave the police to zip the poor girl into a body bag, take her away. 'It's just I can't get David out of my head.' I honestly couldn't. It was uncomfortable.

'David Mallory is a nutcase who needs to go back to that institute if you ask me,' Paul scolded. *Say it like it is, why don't you?* 'Why they let him out is anyone's guess. But to suggest he had anything to do with that,' Paul pointed towards the tent, 'is ludicrous, even for you, Newt.'

'I'm not suggesting he *was* involved, but I—'

'You're not paid to link my cases, just to evaluate the living, assess the dead, get me results where possible. Do *that*, and we might both sleep a little better. Other than that, please leave the police work to me.' Paul removed his paper shoes and gloves, screwing them into a ball before tossing them into a plastic bag Bernard had left out for us on the sodden ground. When had I ever done anything else? Maybe David had got under my skin, but there was more to this than either of us knew. I couldn't shake the feeling that there was a link, a connection. I just didn't know what it was yet.

Twelve

David

Few people have the power to influence my mood. It is the way I like it, the way I have always preferred it. It provides me with my own power to subsequently influence how I am viewed by a world I often find myself somewhat out of touch with. It is, therefore, most unfortunate that since returning from the police station, I oddly now feel uncomfortable in my surroundings. I do not know why. My private space is as it has always been—my beautiful birds willing to provide me with an undemanding, undeniable company I know I can never live without.

I adore my birds, each one able to appease my cluttered mind on cue. Such simple creatures do not confuse my thinking, their varying dorsal tones fully capable of lowering my heightened agitation whenever the need arises. They have a quiet manner about them I wish I had the power to extract, absorb when required, share with the world. Humans do not display such a calming influence. Indeed, this is potentially the very reason my thinking feels different today, ensuring I have acted offhandedly, oddly spontaneous. It is the good doctor's fault, I know, and the rude interruption to my daily routine by the unwanted appearance of Simon. I agitatedly shake bird feed into containers lining a spacious aviary, glad of their chatter as they greet me with excitement, thankful for Frank, my ageing neighbour who has taken good care of my feathered friends during my absence.

Until today, I have never felt the need to tell anyone about The Others, not even the doctors paid to dissect my ravaged mind. It matters little to them that I was forced into therapy under duress, my treatment dependent upon an apparent mental health condition they never appreciated I had. Now, all I can think about is *Doctor* Newton Flanigan and his probing questions. His aftershave and moisturiser still linger in my nostrils long after we have parted company, those beautiful teeth, the way he speaks—the poor man unaware of the slight twitch in his right eye. A weak muscle, no doubt, easily rectified with rest I feel he does not take often enough. Yet, even my precious birds cannot suppress the anxiety that burns steadily now in my chest, my mind too busy for such unwanted distractions, my berated mind unhinged, devoid of simplicity I wish, just once, I could experience.

I enjoy living in Eastcliff, grateful to my parents for leaving me this house, no rent requirement, no fuss. There is always so much noise here. Even at two o'clock in the morning when most are asleep, Eastcliff is *very* much awake.

A little like me, in a way. It is why I choose to remain in the midst of it all, this town steadily developing into the surrounding suburbs, threatening to reach the very coastline it was named after. As long as I have continued background noise, I can pretend for a while that the voices in my head aren't real. I sleep with the window open in the midst of winter so my mind has something to focus on. Anything to steer my thoughts from what is happening inside my head.

Despite my usual outer calm, most people would never look at me the same if they knew the whole truth of who I really am. When The Others are close, I often grow suspicious of those around me, unable to connect to the outside world, incapable of determining what is real from what is not. It isn't pleasant. I do not wish the good doctor to view me with such indifference. I have not felt this intrigued by the potential of male company for quite some time. I genuinely want to get to know him better.

I head into the house and stare out of my front window, the afternoon commuter traffic already building. Parents late collecting their restless children from school find themselves interwoven with those leaving work early, tension increasing with each passing second. Delivery vans fight for parking spaces, gesturing to anyone who dare cross their path, anger and frustration apparent. Cyclists, pedestrians, buses, non-commuters, all thrust together like cattle, wishing they could be anywhere else but here. I, however, *love* this time of day. It is a time when I can watch strangers from a distance, unaffected by thoughts left to wander unchecked, my mind willing to create ill-favoured excitement from whatever I choose to channel my energies on.

A child is crying outside my window, her face soaked with tears that her mother, already, irritable from the day's stress-induced mania, wipes firmly from reddened cheeks. This woman is either late for something or is having a bad day. It is difficult to say which. I rate myself as reasonably intelligent, yet here I am, not unlike that unfortunate wretch beyond, unwilling to comprehend how I can change *my* life in a way that means I enjoy my actual existence beyond a daily battle with The Others.

If I close my eyes, I can hear them clearly. Simon, Jacob, Adam. It isn't pleasant, hearing their thoughts, recalling painful memories none of them cope well with—subjected daily to relentless noise I wish I had the power to silence. Although I was diagnosed with paranoid schizophrenia some years ago, I rarely tell people about my *real* problems. I certainly cannot disclose what is going on in my head. If I told my ageing father, he would laugh, the man continually seeking stability and rational logic in a world he believes he understands better than most. According to him, I should be settled by now, a wife and several offspring to pass down potential knowledge he assumes I have already acquired, my so-called *normal* life complete. But I do not need a wife, and I most certainly do not consider myself anything other than normal. The very thought infuriates me. The old man is deluded, ignorant. He knows what I am, what I have always been—no partner of the opposite sex capable of changing who I will always be.

I cannot help but feel incensed with the world for how it

has treated me, my father included, ultimately turning me into what I am now. I am thirty-eight years old, and yet this world (with all its memories), including pain I wish I could dispel, has ensured I indeed feel the two-hundred-year-old soul I *know* I have always been. I miss my mum, of course, and her apple pies I readily baulked at as a child before eagerly consuming and enjoying. I could never tell her such a thing, not openly. She would give me more of the same. Now I wished she was able to do so. It's a shame she died far earlier than she should have. No matter. What is done is done.

I stare at a photograph of my parents, the fading holiday so long ago. It is a shame my father never got over Mum's unexpected passing, failing to sustain the pretence of our fragile relationship until he was no longer able to sustain his own existence. He still talks of my mother, on good days. He would often send care packages to the institute that consisted of tiny home-brewed bottles of cider. They were always lovingly wrapped in dark blue tissue paper, slotted neatly inside cardboard boxes with upright supports so the glass wouldn't break during transit. Not that I was ever allowed to consume any. Not on my medication. I assume the staff at Manor Hill enjoyed it immensely, though. I miss those care packages.

I often lay awake at night, worrying about him, wondering what he would do with himself once the fruit my mother lovingly grew in their garden dwindled to nothing—my father left to fester away alone, our family home slowly becoming ravaged by the ocean air along with the steadily declining mental health of my one remaining parent that eventually saw him admitted to a nursing home not long after. In fact, the last time we spoke, he sounded quiet, subdued. I must call him soon. See how he's doing. He knows how busy I am, of course. Most days are far too hectic for me to remember my name, let alone consider a phone call to my father. It's no excuse. I know. It is a shame that some days, my father doesn't remember my name either.

I allow a sigh. The world beyond my window will *never* understand the truth of David Mallory, my parents included. They left me this house, which was good of them, although neither of them understood my problems. They never appreciated how I can live with so much noise in my head. Of course, we cannot always comprehend everything about this world or the people in it, especially those we believe we know well, despite many assuming they do. I find it perplexing how humanity is able to keep their metaphorical eyes closed, their hearts devoid of the limitless possibilities awaiting them— motiveless minds focused only on moving from day to day, nothing occurring that might upset a somewhat deluded balance of a limited self-belief system thrust upon them from birth.

I cannot help but scoff now as people hurry by, existing only from personal experience made possible by what they are taught as children, their reality created from innermost private thoughts they assume no one will ever know. They hope only to reach the end of their short, poisoned lives with bodies and minds as intact as their shallow lives have allowed. As if *this* is all there is. And then, for them, it ends. If lucky, some of those people might even mourn those left behind, recalling the very air they once took for granted. They then spend years trying to get over the apparent loss. Or at least that is what they tell themselves.

I am irritated when I hear a knock on the door, the intrusion enough to force me back into a reality I do not want. A small brown box is sitting on my doorstep, wrapped in a hastily tied dark blue string, the delivery driver already halfway down the steps, eager to complete his daily requirements. He nods. I return the gesture. The parcel is from my father. I'd recognise the handwritten address label anywhere. I haven't spoken to him since leaving Manor Hill over a month ago, despite several messages that have all gone unreturned. He can be a little sulky sometimes. It's annoying. I should probably visit him, but as I say, I have been rather busy of late.

I pick up my package and head into the kitchen, momentarily glad of the distraction, grateful The Others are keeping their relentless conversations to a reasonable din. I untie the string and peel away the brown paper packaging, uncovering a much-anticipated bottle of cider. I laugh, expecting nothing else, a melancholy emotion bubbling in my belly for my father's brief moments of clarity. Included is a hastily written note, the same untidy handwriting spread across its crumpled surface. I smile, visualising how my father would often sit in his makeshift brewery shed for hours until my infuriated mother would be forced to intervene and bring him in from the cold. He would carefully brew cider from the vast quantity of apples and pears growing in the garden that would now never become anything but rotting bird feed falling from overgrown branches, my mum's handcrafted labels and uneaten produce slowing dwindling to nothing.

I pour myself a glass of orange juice and unfold my father's note, which, of course, smells of the apple fragrance mum always placed into her homemade candles, many of which are still dotted around this house. I am surprised the care home allows such an indulgence, his tiny, overheated room brimming with the cider making equipment he insisted he took with him when he moved into the place. Though, I doubt he is allowed to use any of it, judging by the shop-bought label on this bottle.

My father's handwriting seems hurried, scruffy, as if he had trouble keeping his hands still whilst writing it. I wish he would learn to use a mobile phone. It would make both our lives far simpler. I expect the usual words, declarations of love, hoping I am well, simple talk of his daily life, life without Mum. Yet, this hastily scribbled message makes little sense.

My dear David.
I know your secret.
Your mother wishes for you to atone for your sins.
Love always. Dad. xxx

I scan the note, needing to decrypt my father's ridiculous handwriting in order to read the thing properly. *To which secret is he referring? What sins?* The man has never been one for lengthy words or expressing emotion, his open distaste for my repulsive existence remaining unresolved. He is a practical man, probably always will be, but I struggle to understand the concept of this declaration. He is speaking of my mother as if he conversed with her on the subject of their only son this very morning, yet has expressed nothing behold basics I firmly struggle to appreciate.

He cannot be talking about The Others, of course. I have never told a soul about them, not even the parents I will always adore, despite their blatant failure to accept the son they wished was different, or the institute paid to keep my mental health in check. I assume he is having a rare moment of lucidity, his mind remembering that I am a gay man. I cannot presume he knows anything further, and I certainly cannot overthink it for now. I am due to call the care home soon. I will ask him to explain himself when I speak to him next.

Thirteen

Newton

I tried to bury uncomfortable thoughts of David Mallory as deep as I could, pushing our earlier encounter to the back of my mind. I drove back to the police station in a state of shock, too many unspoken words leaving me perplexed, confused. The police had been left behind to tidy the scene, collate evidence—give back that poor girl some goddamned dignity. Visions of missing finger bones blended with missing hands, damaged skulls combined with blood-stained faces, and mutilated body parts swarming my thoughts as I drove, relentlessly unable to dissipate vile ideas about the type of person capable of doing such a thing. It was raining but I barely noticed until the world beyond my windscreen became scarcely visible, Paul's car ahead nothing but dulled lights matching my rapidly dimming mood—the entire world blurring into obscurity.

The drive across town was relatively short, not enough time allowed me to organise my mismatched thoughts into any logical order. Neither did it help that the CID incident room at Eastcliff police station oddly matched the shabby look of my flat, adding to my confusion and giving me a headache. Put together in haste, the entire space appeared unconcerned by aesthetics or visitors. Trailing cables and computer equipment created many trip hazards, as did several discarded boxes of case files far heavier than they looked, already brimming with information too daunting to sift through, unashamedly left to their own devices. Whiteboards were covered in photographs, from mugshots to snapshots, nothing but A4 paper pinned to hurriedly derived street maps, hastily scrawled marker pen handwriting, words highlighted in red, others scrubbed out in frustration. So much clutter littered the space. It took a moment for me to absorb it all. The subdued tones of those police officers working on so many different cases sparked a plethora of suspicion aimed in every direction, many bad moods now wandering freely in the heat.

'Okay, guys, can I have your attention, please?' Paul's voice boomed into the ample space. Everyone stopped, turning their attention to the boss.

'An unidentified female was found this afternoon along Adderson Street by a couple of kids on their way home from school.' He pinned several images to a whiteboard he'd made available for this new case, the body we'd recently endured the misfortune of viewing up close, now available to everyone here. A few people muttered their shock. 'At this stage, we don't know anything about her other than she was probably late teens, early twenties, white, found naked, assumed raped, *obviously* mutilated.' He was busy writing "Adderson Street factory ruins" next to an image of the poor girl. I couldn't help wondering about the kids who'd found her. Surely they would be in shock too, needing urgent therapy.

'Boss?' someone called from across the room.

'Yes, Averly?'

'*Kids* found her?' I was glad I wasn't the only one thinking the same thing.

'Unfortunately, yes. They've been taken home. We will need to question them at some point, but they are both in a bit of a state at the moment, as you can imagine.'

DI Averly raised his hand once more. 'And the victim was raped as well, you say?' Everyone knew what he meant. This was already an extreme murder, an excessive way to cause suffering. To then add *rape* to the equation? The whole thing seemed incomprehensible.

Paul nodded. 'Until we get the pathology report, we won't know for sure, but yes, it looks that way. But let's keep the speculation to ourselves for now, shall we.' A few officers muttered profanities in low whispers, trying and failing to keep their opinions to themselves. 'I need officers on the ground, going door to door, asking the usual questions. Did anyone see or hear anything suspicious late last night? Find out if anyone's daughter, sister, or friend didn't arrive home as planned.' Paul looked stressed as usual; today's discovery another in a long list of victims he dealt with each year.

I stared at the photographs. One showed the poor girl flat

on her back, her recent trauma on full view for the unwitting camera, several more displaying close-ups of mutilated body parts; including one of her face—or what was left of it. For the next hour, the team mulled around me, creating a detailed collection, logging their findings, the large whiteboard slowly filling with facts, questions, theories. Someone had placed her body on its back. Was she penetrated before or after death? Something else *must* have been used other than the killer's penis, judging by the extensive damage. Nobody assumed a woman could have done this. We were looking for a man. Number one on a vast list of possibilities, ticked. I wrote the words "male killer" next to an image of her spread-eagled body with a permanent marker, realising my error too late, not able to rub my speedily written words away no matter how much I scrubbed. Maybe it was a sign? A sign I needed coffee.

I sighed, tapping the pen against my teeth, again an error I could do nothing about. This wasn't just rape, but anger, revenge. But revenge for what? The positioning of the body was interesting. Beating someone to death, knocking out teeth and hacking off hands expressed brutality. Therefore, the subsequent disposal of the body should have been careless, as if throwing it away like a piece of rubbish. Yet, she was seemingly laid carefully on her back, her breasts precisely cut off, her abdomen sliced open, removing her womb and several organs as if someone had taken their time over such intricate detail. Both hands were missing; no teeth left inside the poor girl's head to identify her. Tattoos, usually a significant indicator, were cut away. Neatly. Precisely.

I closed my eyes, visualising her last moments. Did she put up a fight? I assumed she must have. There were significant, painful-looking hack marks and bruising on her arms. Potential defence wounds maybe? Had she held up her arms to stop the incoming blows from something heavy? Did that, therefore, mean her attacker would have been hiding potential wounds, too? Fingernails would have been scraped by now, any trace of the killer carefully collected. But in this instance, there were no hands for anyone to collate evidence from, no fingerprints to confirm. If her DNA wasn't currently on file for any previous conviction, the police would have a Jane Doe on their hands. I couldn't overthink the concept of someone potentially severing her spinal cord, the deep incision Bernard had discovered on her neck hopefully insignificant. The alternative didn't bear thinking about.

Where were her clothing and personal effects? Stripping someone in such a brutal attack is unusual enough. Removing clothing is an act of intimacy, a ritual. It signifies care, consideration. I took off my jacket, folding it, unfolding it, resting it on the back of a spare office chair before picking it up again. I was trying to get a feel for how the killer might have felt. Did the victim remove her own clothing? Did the killer remove his? Was this all just a sick game to him? It was a possibility the poor girl could, in fact, have arranged to meet her killer, to enjoy the company of another man. After all, the Adderson Street ruins would have provided the perfect opportunity for privacy, the location dedicated to a single forgotten building. Yet, why would our man then remove every trace of her clothing from the scene afterwards? Taking clothing, keeping the hands, breast tissue, teeth, and tattooed skin indicates a sinister act. What type of mind would do this?

'Coffee?' someone asked. I was still staring at the photographs, still trying to figure out the deranged mind of this brutal killer.

I turned around to see the welcoming sight of one of Paul's team holding up two empty mugs, a large grin on his face. 'Please,' I smiled, noting the ring of coffee and traces of lipstick around the rims of each cup, hoping he was planning on washing them before handing one back to me. Would it be rude if I vocalised my thoughts? Paul was busy dividing his team into sections, with different jobs allocated to various officers. I wasn't listening. Someone was missing this young woman. A parent, a sibling, a spouse.

'It's bad enough when we have fingerprints and teeth to get an ID from, but this?' Paul came up behind me, scoffing deeply into a steaming mug of tea. 'This is just sick.'

It *was* sick. Somebody had not only removed her dignity but had deliberately removed her identity as well. *But why?* Did it matter to the killer who this person was? Why remove the identity of his victim? Unless he had issues with his *own* identity? Surely the killer would have been far more concerned with covering his own tracks than that of his victims?

'Guv?' DS Alice Baker yelled across the room, taking us both by surprise.

'Yes, Baker?'

'Last month, a young woman was found on the outskirts of Lockhurst Lane, about a mile or so from Digsby.'

'So?'

She shook her head, seemingly troubled by her recent discovery. 'Same type of attack. No identifying marks were left behind. Her body was mutilated beyond recognition.'

'Did they identify her?'

DS Baker tapped her keyboard. 'No. The case was filed as an unknown and closed due to lack of pretty much any evidence at all, and no one came forward to confirm anyone missing.'

'Was she—'

'Raped? Oh yeah, brutally. But not in the traditional sense of the word. Some bastard had used the handle of a sledgehammer. They found large pieces of wood and splinters inside her vagina and anus. It made a right mess of her insides, according to the lab report. She was also found naked, with no teeth, no hands, no clothing.' She paused. 'No breasts either. Her womb, heart, and a section of her intestines were also missing.' Several male officers sucked in air sharply.

'Tattoos?'

'There was a deep square of skin cut from her shoulder. The lab wasn't sure what it was at the time, but it makes sense now to assume a tattoo was removed.' She paused. 'There was also a deep incision, about an inch in diameter, on the back of her neck.'

'Shit.' Paul stepped around a collection of messy, disorganised desks towards DS Baker, the tea in his hand threatening to spill. 'Good work. Print out what you have. Looks like this twisted bastard has developed a taste for mutilating young women.'

Fourteen

Newton

By the time I arrived home, it was early evening, the day passing in a blur—the whole thing too much for me to ever want to remember it again. I showered, spending too long in the bathroom, glad of the warm water cascading over my body, my thoughts draining into the shower tray along with sorrows I didn't expect to develop. Neither did I anticipate how quiet an empty flat could be until I found myself alone in mine, nothing to distract me but the television and a cavern of random thoughts racing through my brain. The truth was, I had no clear idea what to make of this murder case. I'd seen my fair share of dead bodies, my fair share of death, but I'd never witnessed anything so cruel, so *brutal*. Today's unexpected encounter with that poor unknown girl was bad enough, but it now seemed we had two victims. Murdered a mere month apart, both women were beaten to death, mutilated, callously attacked—ultimately discarded like rubbish.

I unenthusiastically tidied my flat as much as my aching mind would allow, picking fragments of a broken mug from the floor I couldn't remember breaking. My flat wasn't anything special, of course, but I was lucky enough to say it was all mine. I had no monthly rent to find, no hefty mortgage, thanks to a brother I'd be forever indebted to. It is odd that, whenever stressed, my thoughts often wander to my brother. Isaac made some excellent investments in his life, made a decent amount of money, and, luckily for me, was just as forthright in sharing what he had. Then he died, unexpectedly, the oncoming bus driver needing several weeks off work to process the fact that none of what had happened was in any way his fault. He was simply walking to work when he slipped off the curb, his mobile phone the reason for such an unplanned moment of distraction. No day has ever been the same since—not for me, his wife, or his poor kids. He left me enough money in his will to pay for my flat outright. The rest, as they say, is history.

My big brother was an incredibly astute man, always ensuring everything was in its place, including me. That was, of course, until it wasn't. His missed footing now the very reason I make the seventy-something mile journey to London every month to visit his grieving widow, Stephanie, and my two rapidly growing nephews, Peter and Timothy, in constant need of appeasement. I try not to recall that fateful day too often if I can help it. It helps no one to dwell. He would, however, be perplexed by the fact I barely find time to tidy the home paid for by his hard work and unrelenting dedication.

As it was, dozens of books and half-written thesis papers now littered every available piece of floor space I owned, despite telling myself I'd get round to putting my much-needed bookshelves together at some point, eventually. It took several twisted ankles and torn book covers before I considered doing anything about my self-created mess, my foot twisting badly the very day I managed to get the flat-packed pieces out of the box. That is, however, how the damned things have remained, still propped against the same pile of books causing the very issues I have been trying to remove.

I sat cross-legged on my lounge rug, a large mug of black coffee in my grip, those unfortunate bodies at my feet. Left naked and brutalised, both girls were now discarded on my lounge floor, nothing more than printed A4 images I could barely bring myself to observe. I closed my eyes, allowing my mind to drift. It needed a moment, anything to distract me from my work, those poor dead girls—my big brother.

I stared at a piece of laminated wood propped against one wall that, under the right circumstances, would have passed for a bookshelf—a screwdriver and patience the only things required to achieve that end. I couldn't say how long I was planning to remain idle on my rug, no strength or enthusiasm to move, several police files and photographs spread out in front of me, mocking me, waiting for attention I wasn't convinced I could provide.

Eventually, I turned my attention to the window, to several birds that danced across low passing clouds, the late summer sun slowly dying—a pang of envy twisting my stomach for a simple existence I wish I had. I was hungry and I needed the toilet, yet I dared not move a muscle for fear of interrupting this moment of quiet solitude I rarely found the time in my racing brain to create. It was unfortunate the whole thing had a side effect of accidentally launching my mind into an unpredicted overdrive, my grumbling belly dissatisfied. I needed something, *anything* to distract myself from what I should have been doing. Yet, with not even the buzz of the refrigerator to break the otherwise stillness of the building, this place felt too quiet now for my anxious disposition to cope with. I couldn't even recall the journey home, too much left unsaid between David and myself that I chastised myself strongly for.

When the doorbell rang, I wasn't expecting the distraction and almost ignored it, the buzzer ringing loudly for several moments before my brain registered the intrusion. I cast a fleeting glance around my lounge, wishing I had the forethought of mind to have at least cleared this morning's breakfast dishes or last night's takeaway curry cartons still scattered over the dining table. It didn't matter. No one ever came to my flat, not even Paul, and so, over time, I guess I had become used to my unfortunate existence. I was certainly not expecting visitors this evening. What I wanted was to ignore everything beyond these walls, this day taking a toll I wasn't expecting. I glanced at the clock. It had just turned eight. *Bloody hell.* If Paul was deliberately keeping his finger on the buzzer to annoy me further than I already was, he could turn around and go away. I was in no mood for a lecture or his theories right now.

Reluctantly I lifted myself upright, my knees creaking with the incoming burden. My visitor was going nowhere, the buzzer ringing incessantly, the presumed solace of my private space broken—my private moment, gone. I yanked open my flat door, irritated, the unexpected image of David Mallory standing on my front porch entirely unanticipated.

'Doctor Flanigan. May I come in? I am terribly sorry to have troubled you so late in the day.' David attempted a smile that he immediately retracted, a quiet unrest lingering between us I couldn't place. It was weirdly uncomfortable.

'How did you get this address?' I muttered. Indeed, how *did* he get my private address?

'Details, my dear doctor.' David shook his head, shaking off my concerns, waving a wandering hand towards me as if to confirm I should not worry myself over such a trivial matter.

'May I come in, *please?*' he queried again, firmer this time when the overbearing entrance to my basement flat threatened to become too much for the both of us, the weeds at his feet overwhelming his recently shined shoes. I was momentarily grateful for the open window behind me, the bustle of a town unaware of my current suffering and unfettered state of mind. I couldn't bring myself to look directly at him, his face already a twisted expression of events he'd readily created in his mind. It told me everything I already knew about the probable state of his brain, the reason he was here now, needing undivided attention I wasn't willing to give. I didn't need clarification of his emotions.

'Sorry. Yes, of course.' I shook my head, stepping to one side, allowing the man I'd shared an earlier strained conversation with to step into my flat, against my better judgement, against the grain of my chastising mind. I closed the front door, turning to see David already standing in my front room, staring blankly out of the window, uncertain hands trembling by his side. *Shit.* I licked my lips, racing into the very room containing information on a murder case not yet made available to *anyone*, including information on David himself I'd written on sheets of discarded kitchen roll; just passing ideas through my wayward thoughts, musing potentials, random possibilities. I gathered the documents, scooping them into a pile with a muted apology before placing them haphazardly on my dining table to join the clutter hell-bent on mocking my inability to clean. What *was* he doing here? And why could I smell bleach?

I glanced his way, but David averted his attention to something unimportant in the room. He appeared subdued, as if he wanted to talk, yet wasn't convinced he could. Eventually, it was me who broke the silence. I couldn't stand listening to David's shallow breathing a moment longer than necessary, secretly scoffing at twisted thoughts I couldn't help having in private.

'So, how exactly may I help you?' I muttered, eventually. I had no idea why the man confused my mind so much, why he unnerved me as he did. How on earth did he get my address?

'Doctor Flanigan, please forgive me. I wish only to apologise for my behaviour earlier. I acted rudely, and—'

'It's fine, really.' It wasn't fine, but I was in no mood to discuss it now. Not with David.

'I can assure you, my good man, the way I acted was anything *but* acceptable. I wish only to apologise and explain my unfortunate position in the hope I may reintroduce your favour.' David pressed his fingertips together, the prayer position it created almost angelic, yet the man was anything but, entirely unsure what to say next. Was he talking about our time together at the station, in my car, or at the house? We hovered in silence for probably no more than a few seconds, yet it was enough to send my brain into reticent turmoil. 'I wish for you to appreciate what it's like, living inside my head,' he continued, requiring an appreciation of emotions I wasn't convinced I wanted to know.

David lowered himself onto my sofa without being invited and stared into space, thankfully unconcerned by the mess surrounding him, an odd smell I'd only just noticed lingering now in the stagnant air. He looked out of place, out of his depth, no doubt already going out of his mind. *I know how he felt.* 'I do not wish for you to view me badly, my dear man. It isn't easy being me, I can assure you.'

'Oh?' By asking the question, sounding mildly interested, I had invited more detail, ensuring he would remain in my flat longer than was comfortable. Should I offer him a cup of tea? Coffee?

'I assume by now, you must already know of my past troubles?' David glanced my way briefly as if embarrassed by the fact he had been living in a mental hospital for the last seven years. He would have known such an event would be common knowledge to the police, to me.

I nodded, unsure how to respond, still wondering whether or not to put the kettle on or continue in the hope he might take the hint, leave my flat, leave me to my previous self-absorbed brooding. I was oddly enjoying the silence. What's more, the police still needed a detailed profile on a killer now dubbed "The Eastcliff Ripper", the university leaving several irate voicemails regarding today's non-existent lectures that would also require my attention at some point.

'You have to help me, please,' he muttered, his desperation coming from nowhere. 'I have done my research on you, Doctor Flanigan. You have quite the reputation in your field.' He smiled, nodding my way.

I sighed. *Damn it, Google!* I wasn't sure what unnerved me the most. The fact that David had looked me up or that my contact details seemed to be out there for full public viewing. I've seen the insides of many prisons and mental health hospitals in my time, yet none of those spaces bothered me like this. I wasn't used to dealing with potentially (excuse the expression), unhinged people in my own home—mutual, communal areas adequate for such unrehearsed conversations.

'It has been brought to my attention that you were in the institute with paranoid schizophrenia.' I didn't wish to provoke a reaction, yet I needed to confirm what I already knew. It was an incorrect diagnosis.

David nodded, hanging his head lower than appeared comfortable. 'I'm afraid it isn't as simple as taking my medication and hoping the voices go away.'

'Oh?' I wished I wouldn't keep inviting further

information. *It wasn't helping.*

'I do not entirely know what is wrong with me.'

'Dissociative identity disorder,' I couldn't help confirming it. To be honest, I was surprised no one else had.

'Sorry?' David looked up, narrowing his eyes.

'DID. It used to be known as a multiple personality disorder. A *split* personality.'

David nodded again, this time offering a smile that seemed to linger longer than I found comfortable. 'You see, Doctor Flanigan. *That* is why I came to you.'

I ignored his flippant comment. 'Has no doctor or specialist considered the diagnosis?' It seemed simple, obvious. I sat down, my attention caught now on the possibility of this blatant misdiagnosis.

'You really do *not* want to know.' David sighed before rising to his feet, pacing my lounge that suddenly looked cramped, stepping around several discarded books and flat-pack furniture still half-torn from cardboard boxes. He was right. I didn't. What I *wanted* was for him to leave. 'What are these?' he queried. Out of everything in this room that might have taken his attention, annoyingly, it was the images of those naked dead girls gathered now in a haphazard pile on my table that he chose to rest his prying eyes on.

'Nothing for you to concern yourself with.' I gave him a look, shot to my feet, bundling the offending items into my hands in a vague attempt to prevent unwanted attention. I had enough problems without a presumed mental patient getting wind of those vile crimes. I didn't know what kind of response such visions might provoke. I was being unkind, I know, the stress of the day too much. David was probably harmless. I could *hope*.

'Maybe, I can help?' He stepped forward, eagerly tilting his head to get a better look of the pale flesh pressed now between my pale fingertips. I slid the images between a vase of dusty plastic sunflowers and several forgotten pizza boxes. *Christ*. When had I become such a slob?

'You can't help,' I confirmed, probably too forcefully. I didn't mean to sound irritated. It was hot in here.

David nodded. For a moment the man looked fragile. I felt sorry for him. 'Then maybe you can help *me?*' He almost whispered, allowing his words to emerge like a small, frightened young boy as he dropped once more onto my sofa.

I glanced at the clock, knowing I was needed elsewhere, my time never my own for long. Paul would have to wait. 'Do you *want* to talk?'

'I really do,' David offered, a smile creeping over his face. He crossed his legs and placed his still trembling hands in his lap, staring at me, waiting for my full attention.

'Okay,' I sighed begrudgingly. 'I'll put the kettle on.'

Fifteen

David

I like the doctor's apartment. It has a lived-in look about it that makes me smile—inwardly, of course. It would be rude of me to sit and *outwardly* grin at his lack of housecleaning, a probable lack of ability in areas of domestic bliss stemming from painfully prolonged bachelorhood. It is warm here. Far warmer than my ageing, drafty house, the constant bustle outside oddly ensuring I feel safer here than I might elsewhere.

'Are you taking your medication?' the good doctor asks, placing a hot mug of tea on the table in front of me. He hastily puts milk and sugar, still in their original packaging, unopened might I add, on to the table next to my mug, needing to slide several items out of the way to create a space. No biscuits? Oh dear, what a shame. I press my lips together so as not to invite a smirk at the thought of my unwanted inner musing. I doubt this man has *any* biscuits at all, least not anything suitable for passing guests. Equally, the fact he assumes I am on medication is somewhat disconcerting to my thinking.

'They confuse me,' I confirm, lifting my tea from the tabletop and taking a sip. I do not require milk or sugar. Both commodities possess the ability to bring forward The Others. I do not need them here today. I do not need that kind of confusion adding further turmoil to this already muddled day.

'Oh? Don't you need them?'

I smirk inappropriately. I cannot help it. 'There are a great many things I do *not* need, Doctor Flanigan.'

'Call me Newton, please.'

'Like the famous mathematician?'

The doctor nods, smiling to himself more than to me. I assume it isn't the first time he's heard the similarity, potential jokes aimed his way, no doubt since childhood. I know precisely how he feels.

'The tea is nice,' I lie. It is a shame that far too many Englishmen do not know how to make an adequate cup of tea. A slice of lemon might help lift the taste, but I doubt he has any to hand. I glance towards several pizza boxes piled next to a vase of dried sunflowers that have seen better days, none of which clearly know the location of the nearest dustbin. I assume he did not buy those. I wonder what kind of woman would have placed them there? Certainly not a wife. This place does not possess a woman's touch—or at least, not anymore. I try not to stare at the discarded plates next to the sofa. Something in the air smells off. I try not to retract in muted disgust.

'Why don't you tell me about Adam?' The question comes from nowhere, throwing me momentarily off-balance. Yet, isn't that why I am here? To discuss The Others?

'He can be a little highly strung, as you have probably noticed.'

'Well, he certainly doesn't act or speak as you do.'

I shrug, no longer wishing to pretend I am enjoying my tea. I place my oversized mug onto the tabletop, wondering when teacups went out of favour. I miss saucers. 'Adam is old school,' I confirm. 'He has a different way of doing things than the rest of us.'

'Oh?'

'You've met him, spoken to him. So you know to what I am referring.'

'The way he speaks?'

'Yes. Amongst other things.' The way he acts can be inappropriate, too. I shuffle in my seat. I do not wish to express my intolerance.

We sit, regarding each other carefully, absorbing each other's presence, the good doctor's slow breath distracting yet oddly inviting. His features are stretched into firm concentration. I like it. Probably more than I should. The way his brow creases in the middle. I can still smell the aftershave he overly used this morning, although it has become muted slightly now, mixed with his increased body odour, despite taking a shower at some point, his hair still damp.

'Can you tell me why one of your alters would know the

whereabouts of a dead body?' he asks, emphasising the word "alters" as if he knows what he is talking about, appreciates my problems. Oh, dear. I should have known he would be more interested in that unfortunate corpse than of my immediate needs.

One of my alters. What a curious choice of words. Anyone might assume I chose to pluck the things from fresh air, a throwaway action I am somehow able to control. 'I cannot control what someone else does,' I confirm with a sigh, loud enough to irritate us both. 'After all, Adam Mires is what he is.' I am talking in riddles. I cannot help it.

The good doctor stares at me as he drinks strong coffee I cannot abide the smell of. I wonder how he can consume the stuff so readily. 'You do realise the manifestation of DID does not usually include inventing surnames for the personalities living inside the heads of those afflicted?' he questions. He has become quite serious. Again, I find it attractive in an unkempt, chaotic sort of way. I like this man very much. However, he is wrong. I have invented *nothing*.

I shrug. 'I really cannot say.' He assumes I have invented those characters for effect, for fun, my way of coping with past traumas he obviously believes I have. He is telling me nothing I do not already know, yet, why would I do such a ridiculous thing? I cannot tell him, of course, that when The Others arrive, I cannot always recall anything of what happens whilst they are in control of my mind. It is the reason I am here now, asking for the much-needed help of the good doctor.

'I'm sure you're fully aware of how such a problem occurs, Doctor Flanigan?' Of course, he knows. He is a psychologist, after all, and a most admired one, at that.

I might have accidentally invited a speech as the good doctor launches into theories he seems excited now to share with me. 'We often think of someone with DID as having different identities. However, some researchers, myself included, believe those identities are nothing more than different parts of *one* identity that cannot function properly together.' The good doctor assumes he is speaking the truth. He has *no* idea. 'Did you experience trauma in your childhood, David?' He is leaning forward, ready for my response.

I press my lips firmly closed. Not as such. No. Yet, I cannot tell him the truth of what happened to me. 'Why would you suggest such a thing?' I am deferring the question, I know.

'DID is usually caused when a person experiences severe trauma over a long period, potentially during childhood. By experiencing such a trauma, you might have found yourself taking on different identities and behaviours in order to protect yourself. As you grew up, these behaviours would have become more fully formed until it now looks as if you have several differing identities inside you. However, it is, in fact, different parts of your *own* identity which are not working well together.' I almost want to applaud. Is the man quoting directly from some textbook? He is certainly living up to his highly regarded reputation.

'You still assume I even have this DID thing?' I brush fluff from the arm of my jacket, casually noticing a photograph sitting on his mantelpiece of a young male with two small boys. It is not the good doctor, although they look very much alike.

He continues excitedly, oblivious to my query and recent discovery. 'Do any of these feel familiar to you? You dissociate regularly and have done so for a long time. You might dissociate in separate, regular episodes. Between these episodes, you may not notice any significant changes. Or you might have something called "dissociation from coercion", whereby someone else forced or persuaded you. For example, if you were brainwashed or imprisoned for a long time. Or your dissociation might be acute, your episodes short-lived but severe. It may be because of one or more stressful events. You, therefore, find yourself in a dissociative trance, with little awareness of things happening around you. You might not even respond to things and people around you because of the trauma—'

'My goodness, Doctor Flanigan, take a breath. Please, my dear Newton.' I stare into his dark eyes, a curl in the corner of my lips ensuring my unexpected smile is near completion. His name lingers intriguingly on my tongue. The good doctor is on his feet now, pacing as he speaks, this wonderful account of my mental health firmly in his forethought. Maybe he devours books for breakfast. He certainly speaks as if he does.

'Do *any* of those things feel familiar to you, David?' he repeats, stopping only for a moment to glance my way. His hair is ruffled, his cheeks glowing. This man enjoys his work. How admirable.

'Who is that?' I ask then, pointing towards the very photograph taking centre stage in the room, needing a moment to catch my breath. 'Is it your partner?' I do hope I am correct in my desired considerations of this fellow. I *would* truly like him to be homosexual. Is that so terrible of me?

The good doctor falters, obviously startled by my interruption. 'That's my brother and his boys.'

The man appears shaken, as if he is not comfortable with my question. 'Oh?'

'I don't want to discuss it.'

Oh, dear. Have I hit a nerve? 'Forgive me. I did not realise that you and he were *estranged*. What is his name?' I am inquisitive, wishing to understand the good doctor a little better. I see no photographs of anyone else. I am still clinging to the absurd possibility that he may, at some point, find *me* as attractive as I find him.

'His name was Isaac—'

'*Was?*' Oh, dear. I really *have* gone too far now.

'He died. Now can we please—'

'Isaac and Newton?' I laugh, unable to prevent my outburst, willing to skip over the uncomfortable topic of his poor brother's death. I hope it wasn't a recent passing. What kind of parents did those poor boys have? Ones with a twisted sense of humour, no doubt.

'Yes, it's an old joke. Ha, ha.' The good doctor has gone bright red. But, of course, it isn't as if he's not heard it all before. Many times. I can see that.

'Forgive me. Where were we?' I stiffen slightly, needing to regain composure. Where are my manners?

'Do any of those things feel familiar to you?' he repeats, quieter now, resuming a seated position on an armchair adjacent to mine.

'All of the above, my dear fellow,' I state calmly, as if my earlier outburst never happened. I do not wish to divulge the details.

The good doctor breathes out, allowing a half-smile, a nod of his head. Well done, Doctor Flanigan. Well done indeed.

'But I am still confused as to why your diagnosis seems to be incorrect?' he queries.

I laugh, almost ejecting saliva that I quell with the back of my hand. Oh, dear. I really am failing in my composure. 'Quite simply because they all firmly believe I made up The Others in order to get attention.' I do not wish to recall my unfortunate time at Manor Hill.

'Why would they do that?'

'Because my dearest Newton, Adam, Simon, and Jacob are *real* people. They lived. They died. Has no one confirmed this for you yet? Tut tut. According to my doctors, a person cannot live with the personalities of people *long dead* inside their head. Or so I have been told.' I am deadly serious. Only a handful of people have ever known this unfortunate truth about my life. It is a shame that none of those same people lived to appreciate the significance. No matter. The good doctor stares at me, thinking, potentially hurting his brain with so much clutter.

'They assume me deluded, for obvious reasons, as I am sure you now share the same conclusion.' I close my eyes, not wishing for him to see me in a lowered light. 'They know I often talk to myself. I cannot help it, yet they presume I suffer only with hallucinations, the voices in my head nothing more than that. *Voices.* They tell me The Others are not real, ironically, and that I have created a disconnection to my reality. Yet they are more real than you could possibly understand. You call them alters, but I can assure you, they have nothing to do with any *altered* mental health problem I may or may not possess. My behaviour in the past has been less than satisfactory, you see, disorganised, often catatonic. A classic classification of schizophrenia do you not agree, Newton?'

'And *have* you displayed catatonia often?'

'Oh yes, many times. However, it is usually Adam who brings out such an unwanted emotion in me. He is always proclaiming guilt for past actions that nobody even cares about anymore. You've witnessed this first hand. The tiresome fellow is always confused, restless, agitated, demanding to be locked away from society.' I take a breath, take a moment. 'Although he certainly got his wish this last seven years.' Why is the doctor avoiding the elephant in the room? My so-called alters, as he calls them, are not *made-up* characters. They are real men with real lives. Real problems. Still.

'And I assume your disorganised thinking is—'

'Associated with a combination of everything I have to deal with. You have heard the language Adam uses, I know. He isn't quite in the present moment, is he? Have you met Simon yet?'

The doctor nods. 'At your house, earlier today?'

'My house?'

'Old Trent Road.'

I shake my head. 'Not mine, my dear fellow. Simon's *mother's* house. It is not a nice place if you ask me. You should steer well clear.'

He gives me an odd look. I cannot read it. 'And Jacob?'

'Oh, you do not want to *ever* meet Jacob.'

'Why not?'

'He, my dear fellow, is the worst of them all.' The worst of *us* all.

'Tell me about him.'

'No.'

'Why?'

'Because he might believe he has been called. Summoned, so to speak. He is not required just yet.'

'Maybe I want to meet him.'

'Believe me, Newton. You do not.'

'David, please—'

'No,' I state firmly, my irritation rising. I am glad when a mobile phone rings, steering us away from our little debate. I am trembling, although I try to disguise it. The good doctor almost loses his composure as he yanks the phone from his pocket. An ageing solid block slides across the floor, still ringing. He grabs it, scrambling from the room, answering his phone in the hallway beyond. I hear muffled words, although nothing I can comprehend clearly. I try not to glance towards those unfortunate photographs of bloodied, naked females now lying next to his uneaten pizza. He does not realise, of course, I can still see them from where I sit.

'I have to go,' he states firmly, stepping back into the

room, his mobile still in his hand.

'The police?'

'Yes.'

'Can I help?' I *can* help. If only he'd ask.

'No. Go home. Get some rest.' The doctor sounds stressed, something in his tone I cannot understand.

'Okay. Well, thank you for your time today.' I want him to know I have appreciated his thoughts on my apparent health, glad to have conversed with him, if only for a short while. I nod, rising to my feet, happy to leave him to it, for now. I rest my eyes, once again, on a partial image of what I assume is a dead body that has been on display since my arrival. I *could* help, but only if the good doctor would be willing to allow me such insight. Yet, what am I to do about such matters? I can hardly explain my involvement, can I?

Sixteen

Newton

My life in Eastcliff has become so engrained with my perceived normality that my sister-in-law, Stephanie, has recently, expressively, begun telling me I have forgotten how to slow down. Live a little, she now often exclaims, usually with more enthusiasm than I'd like. Relax, before I do myself a palpable injury. Isaac would have been very disappointed in me—*apparently*. She has, in fact, expressed this opinion more than I'd comfortably prefer. However, it now sadly appears she may be right. I have seemingly forgotten how to converse with humanity, too, my home a place I've kept private for too long. I glanced towards my now brimming coffee jar, glad I hadn't forgotten to purchase *that* on my way home this evening.

The unexpected arrival of David Mallory has verified Steph's deliberations with volatile force, our conversation currently not going as well as I'd like, my mind elsewhere, my thoughts drifting wildly. I stood in the kitchen making tea for my unplanned guest, hoping I had milk in the fridge, sending a text message to my sister-in-law to confirm she might have a valid point about the current state of my general wellbeing. Steph replied with a simple smiling emoji. She knows me well. *No need to elaborate.* I smiled. It was a heart-warming moment.

By the time I ventured back into my lounge, David was once again staring out of the window, positioned a little too closely to those unfortunate images of mutilated females I wish didn't exist. I couldn't overthink it. They didn't appear to have been moved, thankfully. We sat and talked for a while, the man kind enough to allow an uncensored insight into his mental health I found oddly enlightening. I didn't know if he absorbed much of what I was explaining to him, however, *and* he left his tea to go cold. I found *that* extremely rude.

When my phone rang I was immensely grateful, something about this man's presence made me uncomfortable. I shot upright too fast, jarring my neck, dropping the damned thing onto the floor. It bounced aggressively across the room, out of sight, forcing me to take a breath I felt might not be forthcoming. I needed to calm myself, praying that David hadn't noticed my failing composure. What on earth was happening to me today? Despite a comical and futile panic, I grappled under the sofa for my phone in a frantic attempt to subdue my absurd thinking. By the time I found my phone and pressed the accept call button, I was beyond frustration.

I wasn't comfortable leaving David in my front room alone again, knowing full well the sensitive information currently stuffed beside those pizza boxes would be enough to disturb anyone's mindset. Yet, Paul wouldn't be impressed either if I ignored his call. This wasn't *all* about David Mallory. Luckily, I managed to get the detective off the phone relatively quickly, ensuring David knew how busy I was. I needed to leave. I was a busy man. Of course, I didn't want to bundle the poor sod out of my front door without some kind of apology. It would have appeared thoughtless, rude. Thankfully, he noticed my discomposure and left with no further agitation expressed. From one madman to another, we seemed to understand each other's immediate requirements. It wasn't an enjoyable moment.

Once he was gone, I picked dirty plates from my lounge floor and dining table that had been mocking me for the last hour, forcing my brain to take a well-needed break from its erratic, irrational thinking. The entire day had built to this point, my brain now overthinking everything. Thoughts of that poor man's misdiagnosis sat uncomfortably in my mind as I pulled my flat door closed behind me, checking twice that I'd locked it before heading into the night.

~

The station, as always, was a discordant mixture of abandoned activity created from relentless demands never quite met. Discarded, untouched files were left strewn across tabletops, cluttered desks, the floor. Mugs of varying sizes and designs contained contents in various states of consumption—forming thick skins, milk curdling, smelling off; the entire place in need of a deep clean. It ironically reminded me of my flat. That probably explained why I felt so at home here. Sharing banter, case histories, an irrefutable inability to keep anything clean—each day different, unrelenting, unforgiving. Sounds about right.

'What's so urgent you couldn't tell me over the phone?' I asked Paul as we stood staring at a whiteboard brimming with information; peppered with potential new leads, theories, ideas, although the only urgent thing I needed right then was my bed.

'We did some digging. Turns out we might now have three potential victims. They were all killed in the same way,' he sighed, 'potentially by the same person.' Paul was hunched over, concentrating hard, hands on hips, his protruding belly not accustomed to the volume of take away meals he consumed between the time he left home (telling his wife, Adele, he wouldn't be late) and the time he actually arrived back, exhausted, usually in the small hours. Today would be no different.

'Three?'

'Yeah, a school teacher. Thirty-five years old, found on an industrial estate just over seven years ago. Again, naked, mutilated, no teeth, no...' he paused. I didn't need the confirmation.

'You managed to identify her?'

'Yes. Luckily our murderer must have been disturbed. He

only managed to hack off *one* of her hands.' I cringed. Paul nodded. 'It seems our man has improved his technique over the years.' *Was that a joke?*

I didn't offer a response. The moment didn't call for one.

'Rachel Gates was formally identified due to her fingerprints and a tattoo of a lioness angel across her shoulders,' Paul continued, unconcerned by my musing. 'It appears that, seven years ago, our killer wasn't overly concerned by identifying marks. Either that, or he wasn't as accomplished as he seems to be now. When we cross-referenced missing women between the ages of eighteen and forty, Gates was flagged immediately due to the nature of her injuries. Unfortunately, neither Rachel Gates nor the unknown victim from last month were killed on our patch, so the deaths weren't linked.' Paul sighed, irritated by the continued lack of communication between stations. 'However, her husband was able to identify a photograph of her tattooed shoulder.' Paul looked at me, knowing the poor man wouldn't have been able to identify her by any other means.

'You had her fingerprints on file?'

'Yeah. There was a minor assault a few years ago on some random in a supermarket.' Paul spoke as if her past crime was unnecessary, unrequired, just grateful she was identified at all.

'That was lucky.'

'Not for her, it wasn't.'

Paul was right. She wasn't lucky. She was dead. 'Seven years is a big gap, considering we've had two new deaths in the last month alone.' I was chewing the skin from my bottom lip, thinking.

'That isn't all.' Paul paused.

'What now?'

'Rachel Gates had a brother.'

'And?' Why was this relevant?

'His name is *David Mallory*.'

'Seriously?'

Paul nodded. *Christ.* I had a nagging feeling that David was somehow linked to the victims, but not like *this*. That might explain his incarceration. Fragile minds don't need much tipping over the edge. We glanced at each other, neither of us wishing to confirm our thoughts.

'What on earth was the killer doing for those missing seven years? Killers don't just take a break.' It was true. If anything they become more proficient, more active over time. I couldn't help connecting David to the missing seven years that he, himself, was locked away. It wasn't helpful.

'That's your job to find out for me.' Paul smiled, his toothy grin unnecessary in this moment. I rolled my eyes.

'Cheers for that.'

'You're welcome.' He slapped my arm with a chuckle before leaving me to ponder these new findings alone. A takeaway curry was calling from his office, threatening to go cold in his absence, my stomach reminding me of my own continued disinterest for basic survival.

I stared at the whiteboard. What type of psychopath would gladly remove vital organs and identities of total strangers? That's assuming, of course, those women *were* strangers to our killer. What was the percentage of people who knew their killers again? I shook my head. I doubted this was a contributing factor. More "wrong place, wrong time" than "planned execution". He had killed three women now. Or at least three we *knew* of. I maintained the assumption that our killer was a man. Women usually kill from the perspective of passion. These poor sods had been abused, abandoned, discarded in the most unsavoury of places, in the most disgusting way.

I was staring at yet another dead body recently added to the growing collection. Her photograph was pinned beside the other two, a smiling headshot the only one among them resembling anything close to normality. She, too, had been left on her back, as if the killer was busy enjoying himself, spread eagle as if he wanted to humiliate her, looking to the world as if she had fallen asleep after sex. Yet, *this* poor woman looked as if she had been tossed to one side, forgotten, left in haste, her arms and legs not as carefully positioned as the other two victims, no organs removed despite a deep cut along her abdomen. She was much older, too, the other girls seemingly late teens.

I grabbed a marker, keen to write my thoughts before someone interrupted my random idea. I wrote, "Positioned as if content. Happy?" One question mark. No. Two. *Bloody hell.* To me, it appeared that these victims were made to look comfortable, *happy* to have enjoyed their "session" with their killer. That word again. Happy. Were these women *consenting* adults?

'Paul?'

'Yeah?'

'Where any of our victims sex workers?'

Paul strolled over to me, a plastic container in his hand, chewing loudly. 'To be honest, I have no idea. Tony, try and find out—'

'Yeah, I'm on it,' a muffled voice echoed across the room, momentarily bringing me out of my private thoughts. It seemed I wasn't the only one in demand today, not the only one expected to work late, disregard a life neither of us probably had in the first place. I thought about Tony's partner, Paul's wife. At least I didn't have *that* problem. The police seemed more concerned for the dead and their families than they were for their own, the very motives of a killer in question. Yet, they had a job to do. I understood that more than most.

If these girls were sex workers, and if our killer had been friendly to them, maybe they went with him freely. Maybe they removed their clothing willingly in anticipation of a sexual act. But where on earth did their clothing subsequently go? I wrote "Consenting women?" in hastily scrawled handwriting, trying to empty my thoughts onto the board in front of me, along with the word "gay?" underlining it twice, a nagging sensation that it was somehow important. Our killer either despised females or he had a serious issue with *himself*. I couldn't determine which.

Just as I was beginning to make sense of the crime scenes, my phone rang. I didn't recognise the number. I muttered my name absently into my ageing mobile, too busy organising my brain and this whiteboard into some potential pattern, my mind elsewhere.

'Newton, it's David,' a small voice emerged. I took a breath. Shit. *Not again.*

'David? How did you get my number?' This guy was relentless, slightly irritating. He was panting, as if he'd run from somewhere, or *someone*, his breathing short, his words stunted.

'You have to help me... please.' He genuinely sounded terrified. 'He's trying to get in.'

I visualised an intruder currently attempting to get into his property. 'David, calm down.' DI Tony Averly glanced my way. I didn't acknowledge him. '*Who's* trying to get in?'

Silence for a few seconds, then a quiet, troubled voice. 'Jacob.'

Seventeen

David

I have no one else to call, no one else to ask for the help I am uncertain I even need, yet I automatically call the good doctor. He seems to understand how my mind operates, how my thoughts can often slip into overdrive when left unchecked, my private demons prepared to creep into every aspect of my life without warning. I am clinging to my phone, clinging to sanity, hoping the poor man will come to my aid. It is not a pleasant sight, I know, a grown man cowering in the corner of his kitchen, quivering, no better than a pathetic, petulant child—the thought of being overtaken by a brutal killer something I have never been able to acknowledge. Who can I tell of such things? Who will *believe* me?

'David, calm down,' I hear him say, the telephone cold against my ear. 'Who's trying to get in?'

'Jacob,' I mutter, no hesitation required. I speak quietly

enough so that only the good doctor and myself will hear my strained words.

'Where are you?' His voice is calm. Too calm for the likes of me.

'At home, my good fellow,' I reply, staring frantically towards the ceiling as if searching for absolution, needing the good doctor to appreciate that, at any moment, Jacob *could* appear, grab me, seize control of my mind. I need him to come to my aid, to rescue me from the hell I now call my life.

'Stay there,' I hear, grateful for his trusting words. 'I'm on my way.'

The phone goes dead, leaving me alone with thoughts I do not wish to contemplate. I have no doubt we all exist locked inside private, often twisted thoughts, believing our self-created existence as if we are nothing more than victims of our own cruelly designed fate. Yet I do not assume many will understand my predicament. I am, of course, certain I am not unique but it often feels I am alone in this *world*, a mere curiosity to most, nothing more. Not unlike the good doctor, I should imagine.

I am usually able to maintain ease with the existence of The Others. I have, after all, had many years to become acclimatised to my unusual situation. Yet today, something is oddly threatening to tip my composure towards a darkened place from which I feel I may never return. It has the unfortunate ramification of placing *me* in danger, other people, strangers—even the good doctor. Am I right to ask for his help? Do I have the right? Is it too late to call him back, change my mind, express valid remorse for my unplanned phone call?

It would be unfortunate if Jacob were to *actually* arrive when the good doctor is inside my house. I clamber to my feet, my legs unstable. I can hear the voices. The Others. They are always lingering in the background, never far from mind—too often when I am in bed, attempting to locate sleep that no longer comes readily to me. It is mostly just noise, I know. Mere memories left to linger long after the sunlight begins to trickle through my closed bedroom curtains, long after I have lost all hope of rest.

I close my eyes. All I honestly wish now is to drown their relentless chatter, momentarily calm the irritation that races through my mind every second of each unforgiving day. I amble around my parent's Victorian kitchen, a distant sea breeze cutting through the cracks in the window frames, my parents long gone, guilt over my mother's loss forcing my father's mind to unravel with as much speed as my tiresome demands for appeasement. I cannot dwell. I feel bad enough as it is. I do not have the strength for both myself *and* my father right now. The voices are growing louder. I cannot dwell on *that*, either.

It is strange being here without the laughter and comforting chatter my parent's presence once brought to this space, my time in the institute ensuring I did not appreciate such impending solace until now. I wonder how my father feels, his nights spent alone without his wife for company. Without her apple pies, constant laughter, and bright smile to fill his life, he would have been lost. He probably still is. I glance out of the window towards a once loved garden, the imposing darkness removing any ability to see beyond the glass, my reflection the only sight I witness staring back. It seems odd to think of my mother's fruit trees that now dance in the breeze alone, the fruit no longer consumed. Forgotten. A little like *me*. Still, I cannot ponder distasteful thoughts. It helps no one to mull over events no longer changeable.

I sit in my kitchen staring at a plate of uneaten fish I cannot recall preparing. A solid oak table dominates the space, mismatched chairs with equally mismatched seat cushions set to unravel my mismatched mind. Despite my efforts, the voices have increased over the last few hours—my usual need to keep them to a passable din, now worthless. Of course, I have known something is very wrong with me for some time, yet I am still shocked to admit I have never told a living soul about my problems, even the very parents I once professed an unconditional love for.

It is odd now to admit I often sit alone in my family home wondering why I do not feel especially aggrieved by my mother's passing. I miss her, of course. Daily. Her absence has left a hole that none of us expected to experience, my father especially. Yet, I know it is because I miss having someone to share my continued existence. The concept has left a bitter feeling I am unable to placate. Am I such a compassionless man that I cannot express genuine emotion over losing the woman who birthed me, other than slight unease at being left alone in my family's cherished house? It is difficult to appreciate that, since then, nothing and nobody has been able to appease my increasingly low mood. Only the good doctor has been able to place a smile on my face, yet the poor man does not even know.

I have researched online and off for others like me, the truth behind those malignant voices living inside my head. Paranoid schizophrenia is a term I have learned to live with, of course, but I am neither paranoid nor delusional. I do not intentionally display negativity in my life and have never held any false beliefs. Yet, no one believes my voices are genuine, authentic people who lived and died. I am therefore left to conclude I might be going insane—slowly, painfully. I cannot live this way anymore. It is unpleasant. I press my hands over my ears with a sigh, wanting to scream, knowing I cannot escape. *Why will they not leave me alone?*

I do not notice the knife at first until it is already in my hand. It may be easier if I end this thing now. No one else should be forced to suffer because of me. All I require is a little respite, a calmness I do not know how to demonstrate, The Others hell-bent on manifesting on cue. It is exhausting. Yet will this *ever* end with me? My past is constantly looping around, over and over, the voices in my head wanting freedom I cannot find yet can never prevent. Will I, David Mallory, become another voice in someone else's head, my future self continuing this pattern of madness?

I am almost glad for the knock on my front door, the distraction welcoming, although it is more a frantic banging, the relentless drumming expressing concern for my welfare, my caller demanding attention. I lunge forward, shocked that my legs no longer want to walk in a straight line. I still have the knife in my hand, yet I do not intend to use it. All the same, the good doctor's face is priceless as I pull open my front door, his mouth set in shock at the sight of cold, unyielding metal in my grip.

'David, are you okay?' his voice is warm, like honey. I wish only the forethought of mind to invite him in, show him the *David Mallory* most people fail tragically to understand. The good doctor motions to step forward, then stops, displaying hesitation I am unprepared for. Why is this poor fellow looking at me in such a disgruntled way? He glances towards the knife, pondering my intentions. *Oh, dear.*

I glance downward in automatic response, noticing the blood only when my eyes are, once again, able to focus on the potential reality of this moment. My hand is cut, badly, deeply by all accounts, a trail of blood now snaking mockingly along the hallway behind me, towards a kitchen table still set for dinner.

I do not know what to say, my embarrassment evident to us both. I open my mouth, but no words emerge. 'I'm—' I wish to express I am bleeding, unexpectedly, but I do not understand how I could have cut myself without any sensation of pain.

Noticing my predicament, and, rather expertly might I add, the good doctor steps forward, carefully removing the knife from my grasp and placing it on the cabinet behind us. He then guides me into the kitchen, turning on the tap, allowing warm water to pour into the sink, over my freshly torn skin. Still I feel no pain. I struggle to comprehend my racing thoughts as this incredible individual (that I have oddly grown fond of) washes blood from my fingers and behind my nails, wrapping my hand in a towel, searching cupboards for a first aid box. I have become blinded by raw fury today, rendered incapable of knowing when something is evidently real. Indeed, is *this* moment real? With a jolt, I realise I must be going insane, old memories too vivid, my imagination and dreams left to linger unchecked. It is honestly alarming.

I could easily shout, punch walls, tell the good doctor everything I know about The Others, about Jacob. I could beg for understanding behind my actions, plead, cry even. But I do none of those things. Instead, I stand at my kitchen sink feeling nothing but despondency at the way my life is slowly dissolving to dust. I dare not move, not even when dear Newton places an innocent hand across my shoulder blade to steady me. I can, in fact, no longer *breathe*. How am I meant to respond to my irrefutable, irrational existence? I stare into the good doctor's unseeing eyes. How can I ever tell him the truth?

Old memories continue to flick through my consciousness, yet, over time, I have weirdly been able to accept them as if they are old friends. I can vividly recollect the lives of Adam, Jacob, and Simon, a constant overwhelming feeling of love for the men they once were, the occasional new memory overthrowing my thoughts, set to surprise me some more. It is a feeling I cannot shake and the reason I feel so drawn towards the good doctor.

He has bandaged my arm, although I have lost several precious hours of this day along with several pints of blood, more valuable moments passing unnoticed. He is speaking to me, yet I cannot understand the words leaving his mouth. It is not always appropriate to admit that when The Others invade my mind, I do not remember large chunks of time. It is as if I disappear, allowing strangers to possess my body. Today is one of those days. I like the good doctor. I would like to recall the feel of his hands over my bare skin, even if it is only to dress an open, angry wound.

'David?' he is looking at me now, his searching eyes darting across my face in need of a response.

'Sorry?' I fumble with my sanity, hoping I have done nothing that might infer further potential disgrace on my part.

'I said, are you feeling any better now?'

I want to shake my head. *No.* No, my good fellow, I am most certainly not. I am not a well man. However, I nod, requiring a moment to reclaim my composure, reaching for an empty chair that seems too far from my grasp. A bloodstained armrest has been scrubbed, damp now, deep red fading to a pale, muted brown. The good doctor helps me to sit, handing me a glass of water. I struggle to take it from him, my trembling hands ensuring I look as unbalanced as I feel. I do not wish for Doctor Newton Flanigan to see me like this. It is embarrassing, overwhelming.

'You sounded worried on the phone,' the good doctor is still speaking to me, although, through sips of ice-cold water, I am unable to think straight. I wonder for a moment if he has opened my freezer, yet if he had, we would not be having such a calm conversation now.

'Where is he?' I ask, recalling that I have already spoken about Jacob, only wishing to reclaim composure in my own home. I need the good doctor to maintain the illusion that I *need* him. It is not entirely a lie.

'Who?' The good doctor is either being kind or has become distracted. He has attempted to wipe clean the blood that trailed into the hallway beyond, judging by traces of smudged pale pink still lingering between several cracked tiles. I would have liked to watch him on his hands and knees. No matter.

'Jacob,' I mutter, his name nothing more than acid on my tongue. It feels as if the word is being torn from my throat, ripped out painfully by a blunt instrument. I am hardly acting the composed gentleman I usually aim to display, barely the well-presented man I wish *only* for Newton to see. I glance at the good doctor, already seated at my kitchen table, his hand resting against an empty cup. I have not even offered my newly acquired friend a drink. *How rude.* He will need a cup of coffee, no doubt, something to calm his frayed nerves. 'Forgive me.' I nod my head as calmly as I am able. I am fooling no one, I know. Still, I cannot help such things. 'What must you think of me, my good man?'

Newton shakes his head, offering a sympathetic smile I do not need. 'Why don't you tell me about Jacob?' he asks quietly. A genuine concern in his tone that threatens to expose me where I sit.

'I cannot.' Where would I begin?

'But you called me about him, upset.'

I glance upwards. Upset? *Women* become upset. *Children* become upset. I scoff. I do not intend such nonchalance, not in the good doctor's presence.

'I may have been a little hasty, I know,' I confirm, knowing I needed his undivided attention. He seems to calm me. It is unusual, unnatural, my feelings apparently one-sided. Still, here we are.

The good doctor is staring at my bandaged hand, traces of blood already seeping through the white cloth, mocking my words, ensuring I appear as hideous as I feel. I pull my arm away from his gaze, rising to my feet.

'You didn't tell me that your sister was murdered?'

I am not expecting the question, though Newton cannot help his querying tone. I wonder how long he's known. 'My dear fellow, why would such a painful incident be of any consequence to the *present* moment?' I do not wish to speak of my poor departed sister. I do not wish to be reminded.

'I'm sorry, forgive me. I only found out today and wanted—'

'Wanted to pass on your condolences?'

The good doctor nods, lowering his eyes to the floor.

For a moment I falter, knowing I have invited more into my home than just an innocent acquaintance. 'I have made a mistake in asking you here. Please, forgive *me*.' I am muttering now. I cannot help it. I need him to leave. Leave or suffer the consequences.

Eighteen

Newton

I did not sleep well last night. I was constantly drifting off to visions of dated kitchens, broken clocks, a hallway holding more secrets than I dared imagine—jolting myself awake too often by the sight of David's face and an overwhelming stench of bleach. I spent many of the early hours drinking coffee I couldn't recall the taste of, research the one thing keeping me focused. Seventeen, Old Trent Road, still to this day belonged to a woman called Violet Frederick. It was never sold. Her unexpected disappearance in 1936 had ensured the house remained untouched ever since. I could testify to that truth, the current condition of the building requiring work that would not be happening any time soon.

David's place wasn't in a much better state either, the title deeds of Forty-three, Crescent Avenue in the name of his elderly father until seven years ago when the house was transferred to his son. Thomas Mallory was in a care home now, ravaged by dementia—no longer concerned by home improvements or his wayward boy, David, no doubt glad no equity would be drained to pay for continued care. I stared at my laptop in a darkened kitchen, grateful for no ticking clocks in the background to remind me of time relentlessly passing by. Nobody needs that kind of reminder at four o'clock in the morning.

According to my research, Simon's house was originally purchased in 1926. The owner, a Mr Albert Frederick, passed away three years later, leaving behind his widow and her young son, Simon. He was just thirteen. If Simon Frederick were still alive today, he would be one hundred and ten years old—possible, of course, but not entirely probable. It was confirmation of yet another dead man's identity that David had oddly claimed for himself.

But *why* was this guy pretending to be dead men? It made no sense. I thought about Jacob, knowing I hadn't yet been given any insight into *that* personality. To be honest, I wasn't certain I wanted to. There was something about David's tone that unnerved me. Something off. Something dark. Adam had confessed to murder, several of them, in fact. Would David have created a similar, somewhat twisted personality for Simon Frederick? For Jacob? Were those men killers themselves, and if so, how the hell did David get access to such information? I called Paul, forcing him out of bed, no apology made on my side, simply needing the institute's name that David was committed to and yet another cup of coffee.

~

Manor Hill was neither on a hill nor did it resemble any manor house I'd ever encountered. It was, in fact, a relatively new build, large windows, flat roof, more office block institution than insane asylum—the type you see on modern science park developments, thrown together in haste, profit an overriding factor. I was almost relieved by the sight of it, my nerves shredded by overbearing thoughts of David morphing into Simon in my dreams, Adam screaming in the darkness about bodies long forgotten—the house on Old Trent Road swamping my entire night with ease.

I parked carelessly, unconcerned by allocated parking bays as I poorly positioned my car sideways across several thick white lines. I was distracted, thankful Paul was willing to provide details of David's previous incarceration as I headed towards a looming building I didn't wish to think too long about. He was apparently already camped outside the police station, *again*, having arrived an hour earlier, demanding to be arrested—once more claiming the name of Adam Mires. I sensed they were growing tired of him, anxious now to receive my profile on the man hell-bent on disrupting their day. I was fully aware that Paul did not yet believe my theory of DID— Adam, David, or whoever the guy chose to call himself, beginning to irritate them all.

The reception space inside Manor Hill appeared unwelcome, stark, with little furniture to invite potential comfort. I peered through the large windows, no sign of any chairs in the space beyond to welcome relatives, no pictures or plants to brighten this desolate void. I got a distinct, uncomfortable impression that visitors came here by appointment only, purely of their own volition, *and* only if they were brave enough. The main door was locked, obviously, my continued pressing of a security buzzer mocking my very existence, this day just one in many I wasn't prepared for. I was relieved when a young woman opened the door for me with a smile, not overly concerned by my demands for attention. Her nametag telling me her name was Janet.

'Hi... Janet.' I leant towards her, narrowing my eyes, my reading glasses forever elusive. 'My name is Doctor Newton Flannigan,' I beamed brightly, a casual wave in her direction entirely unnecessary. To be honest, I did the same thing whenever a camera was pointed my way. Janet nodded, noting the flush of my cheeks, the heat of the morning already consuming. I probably should have left my jacket in the car. 'Sorry to bother you so early, but I'm a clinical psychologist and criminal profiler working with Eastcliff police. I'm currently investigating one of your previous patients. Do you mind if I ask a few questions?' I held up my identity badge. I was smiling widely, fluttering my eyelids at the poor girl like a demented idiot. In fact, the only thing I didn't do was get down on my knees and beg.

Janet thankfully ignored my outward façade as she glanced at my badge, her turn now to lean towards me before offering a smile of her own. She opened the door wide, confirmation of my police involvement literally all she needed. 'Of course. Who is it you wish to find more about?' she stepped aside, allowing me entry.

'David Mallory,' I replied, tucking my badge inside my jacket pocket, glad this vast space was cooler than the morning air behind us. Despite its appearance, it could almost pass for welcoming.

Janet took in a short breath, too sharply for my liking, as if the very mention of the man was unexpected so early in the morning. 'David?' she queried, as if his name instilled bad memories. I nodded, wondering if, like me, the man made everyone else around him feel uneasy, too. 'My goodness, that isn't a name I ever expected to hear again.' She smiled, although it wasn't the same as the one I'd witnessed a moment earlier. I hoped she might elaborate. She didn't. Instead, she made me sign a visitors book before handing me a badge on a ribbon that I hung around my neck. She then directed me along a narrow hallway to a closed door that opened to a stuffy room stacked floor to ceiling with books and folders, a tiny statured man hunched over in the midst of it all. I didn't dare assume this space was that poor guy's office, the desk he sat at seemingly a temporary aid.

'Doctor Connor, I'm sorry to bother you, but I have a visitor. He's with the police.' Janet didn't bother confirming my name.

The small man rose to his feet, his legs almost failing to comply. 'How may I help?' he offered, no smile on his lips to brighten the space, no window in this room to lighten the mood—a skylight in the roof, the only natural light available.

Janet motioned me into the room with a nod, leaving me

to get to know my new acquaintance, pausing by the door briefly to ask if I needed a tea or coffee, not wishing to forget her manners. I asked for coffee, of course, although I didn't need a drink, I needed answers.

I smiled, the heat of the room already too much in contrast to the space beyond. I considered leaving the door ajar before changing my mind and closing it with a thud. 'I'm hoping you might be able to help me with a former patient?' I queried, unsure whether to sit down or remain where I was.

'Who?'

'David Mallory.'

The doctor released a grunted sigh, nodding a fattened head my way with a smirk telling me more than he intended. He pulled a thick folder from a dusty shelf and dropped it onto a nearby desk. 'This is David's file,' he offered, pulling out a chair he assumed I would want to sit on at some point. Doctor Connor paused. 'But I warn you. It doesn't make for good reading.'

'How well did you know him?' My curiosity was now well and truly piqued.

'Well enough.' The doctor smiled, yet neither comforting nor convincing.

'I believe he was here for seven years in total. Is that how long you knew him?'

He laughed. 'Thankfully, no. I started working here three years ago. But that was long enough for me to learn all I needed to know about David Mallory.'

'Why was he released? If you believe he wasn't ready?'

'I don't believe I said anything of the sort—'

I smiled. 'You didn't need to. I saw it in your face.' Sometimes I think people forget it is my job to read them, to see what they are thinking, even when they haven't said anything at all.

'David Mallory is a very clever man. He comes across as being extremely calm, together. *Sane.*'

'Oh?'

Doctor Connor didn't respond.

'And you believe he shouldn't have been released?'

'Read his file. See for yourself.' He motioned towards the folder, and I sat down, peeling open David's file. I wanted to understand the man behind those multiple personalities he seemed hell-bent on sharing, whether I wanted him to or not, the likes of which couldn't have been more different from each other if he'd tried. His notes were extensive.

'David Mallory was admitted to Manor Hill after an incident in a supermarket, whereby he attacked a male employee with a kitchen knife.' The doctor was speaking, but I was now firmly absorbed in the sheer volume of incident reports in my hands. Many problems that David had readily created now existed in detailed recordings on paper. Doctor Connor had disappeared behind a bookshelf.

'A knife?'

He reappeared, carrying a second folder handing it directly to me. It was almost as thick as the first. 'Yes, but after spending a night in a police cell, David came clean, confirming his real name instead of the *Simon Frederick* initially arrested.'

I glanced up. I'd experienced such a stark change in David

myself, first hand. 'What happened? At the supermarket?'

'I don't know all the details to be honest with you, but apparently he stabbed an employee unprovoked. He claimed his sister had wrongly defended the guy a few days earlier, and David blamed the employee for turning her against him.'

'His sister?'

'Yeah... what was her name?' Doctor Connor closed his eyes. 'Rachel, I think.'

'Rachel Gates?'

'You know her?'

I shook my head. 'Not personally.' I couldn't tell him the poor woman was dead. At least it explained the incident that saw Gates arrested for the minor supermarket incident. But why would she attack her brother? She must have died not long after. Maybe Rachel's death somehow tipped David over the edge?

Doctor Connor continued. 'A police doctor was called in to assess him, concluding swiftly that David required urgent mental evaluation. He was admitted to the hospital, where he was promptly diagnosed with paranoid schizophrenia, subsequently sectioned and brought to Manor Hill after displaying disruptive behaviour around hospital staff and patients alike.'

'Do you agree with the diagnosis? Of schizophrenia, I mean?' I was curious, keen to know what this established psychologist believed.

'Throughout his stay, David's behaviour deteriorated rapidly, often hearing voices that manifested several times each day. All medication failed, spiralling him into a pattern of continued depression and negative behaviour. He tried three attempts on his life before being admitted to the high-risk section of this hospital.' He motioned forward, pulling a sheet of paper from between several others. 'This is a list of the symptoms he displayed. See for yourself.'

I glanced at the handwritten notes, not entirely convinced by what was written.

- David *sees and hears things that others around him cannot.*
- *He is suspicious, with a general fear of other people's intentions.*
- *He suffers persistent, unusual thoughts or beliefs often manifesting as memories.*
- *Has difficulty thinking with clarity.*
- *Is often withdrawn from staff.*
- *Shows a significant decline in self-care, usually accompanied by manic states and depression.*
- *Experiences volatile hallucinations of other time periods, different places.*

Classic paranoid schizophrenia.

I sat back and stared into the dust-ridden space around me, the sun barely able to penetrate the filthy ceiling window overhead. It reminded me of Old Trent Road. David had clearly displayed many separate personalities, yet schizophrenia did *not* usually bring on sudden and rapid changes to a person's actual character. Someone suffering from PS is still *one* person. Not several. They mostly hear voices telling them to do things uncomfortable for the rest of us to acknowledge. I assumed the staff had initially equated David's condition to his otherwise unfettered delusions, the hallucinations they believed he was having, those unexpected outbursts I'd witnessed myself. Several incident reports outlined detailed attacks on both male and female staff, including several fellow inmates, spanning six of his seven years here—and then nothing at all during his last year in this place.

'What happened during his last year?' I needed to know, my demanding questions emerging relentlessly.

'David was eventually placed on a concoction of drugs that seemed to calm him and help his condition.' Doctor Connor was standing amid his pile of books again, too busy to concern himself with my needs.

'That explains why he was eventually released, but *surely* he would have been answering to different names during his incarceration here.' I needed to find details of his alternate personalities.

The doctor shook his head. 'There should be my full assessment in this file somewhere.' He began sifting through the paperwork, many sighs leaving his mouth, confirming he had more important things to deal with than my boring company. Eventually, he pulled out a file, handing it to me before returning to his desk, far more pressing matters calling.

I scanned the contents, keen to understand what Doctor Connor honestly felt about David Mallory.

David Mallory appears to have active paranoid schizophrenia. Often consumed by delusions or hallucinations, the vast majority of his energy and attention is focused on keeping to, and protecting, his falsely held beliefs.

His symptoms of schizophrenia, including common hallucinations and delusions, occur less often than I would have presumed, yet are possibly more likely to have simply gone unnoticed. After a prodromal phase, the patient entered the "active phase" of schizophrenia, during which he experienced many debilitating thoughts and perceptual distortions. In addition, he often demonstrates impaired motor and cognitive functions, including disorganised speech and catatonic behaviour.

David's paranoia stems from delusions that often manifest as active personalities, rather than voices more commonly known to people with schizophrenia. His many firmly held beliefs continue to persist, however, despite evidence to the contrary, including several hallucinations, behaving abnormally and often not able to recall the identities of staff. These experiences can be persecutory or threatening in nature. David seems to hear voices in his head that he does not recognise as his own thoughts or internal voice. These voices can often become demeaning or hostile, driving him to do things he would not otherwise do, unable to recall his actions at later times, including an incident where he tried to cut his own throat.

I read the information twice. The doctor honestly believed he had given him the correct diagnosis, and, reading his report, I could understand why. Yet, I wasn't convinced. I got to my feet, keen to find Janet, eager to leave this suffocating room and difficult man behind. She knew more than she was telling, probably understanding far more about David than I did. I made my excuses and left the psychologist to his books, not waiting for a response before I swung open the door for some much-needed fresh air.

'Is everything okay?' Janet asked as I walked across the hallway towards her. She was typing something into a computer, not overly concerned by my requirements or the fact that poor Doctor Connor had been left speechless by my sudden unexpected departure. I couldn't even remember if I'd said goodbye.

'Did David ever refer to himself by other names?' I asked, exasperated that I hadn't yet found *any* reference to his alternate personalities, infuriated by his non-compliant psychologist. I still had the report in my hand.

Janet sighed, bringing her hands together and cupping them under her chin, a quiet deliberation I couldn't read. 'We were never supposed to write them down. Doctor Connor assumed it was simply David's manifestations causing him to invent alternative names for himself, nothing more.'

'So he *did* have other names?'

Janet nodded. 'Yes. He would change personalities several times a day. Doctor Connor did not assume such a thing to be important, yet, to me, David's behaviour didn't seem normal for someone with schizophrenia.'

'What do you mean?'

'It was as if, whenever he "became" someone else, he took on a far sinister role. David was always calm, collected, as if nothing in the world could bother him. But The Others. The Others scared us. They certainly scared me.' She shook her head, lowering her voice. 'It was odd that Doctor Connor *never* witnessed any of David's other characters, though. He only saw *David*. I'm certain he orchestrated it that way so the doctor wouldn't notice anything out of the ordinary. He would visit his office once a week, on the dot, taking the medication he was prescribed without incident. Doctor Connor assumed our concerns were nothing more than David's ongoing psychosis battle and that there was nothing to worry about as long as he took his medication and kept himself calm.'

'Can you remember the names of David's other personalities? If you don't mind helping me.' I smiled, hoping to look as needy as I felt.

Janet nodded, taking out a notepad that she scribbled something down on before handing me a sheet of paper. On it was written David's four *alters*. Seeing them in solid ink was nauseating.

David Mallory. This seems to be his normal state.

Simon Frederick. Hates his mother.

Adam Mires. Terrified of everyone. Often confesses to murder.

Jacob Pointer.

I glanced towards Janet. 'What do you know about Jacob?' I asked. The mere fact I had a surname for him gave me the creeps. She had written nothing next to his name that might provide any clue about *that* personality. I couldn't shake the fact that David had lived here for the last seven years, released a only month ago. It may have been a coincidence that his time here matched the dates for our dead girls, but it didn't sit well with me.

'You don't need to know much about Jacob, Doctor

Flanigan,' she replied, her voice raspy as if I'd accidentally provoked some painful incident she was trying to forget.

'Oh? Why not?' I was curious now. Needing more.

'Just pray you never have to deal with him,' she said, nodding her head. She rose swiftly from her desk, stepping around me and out into the bright reception space, more important matters to attend to. It was as if her thoughts had trailed to somewhere dark, and she now needed some air. It was odd, considering that as yet, I hadn't dealt with him at *all*. I could hear David's earlier warning. It made my skin go cold.

~

I was thankfully allowed to make photocopies of David's file, the police happy to confirm my authority on such matters, Doctor Connor happy for me to leave the building. I left Manor Hill with a handful of paper stuffed under my overheating armpit, my mind racing, heart pounding. Janet appeared equally glad to have rid herself of my presence, thoughts of David Mallory something she didn't need inside her head. By the time I arrived at the university, I was once again late for the morning's scheduled lecture.

I was glad my first class of the day was an hourly slot and not the usual three-hour endurance sessions my students had grown uncomfortably accustomed. My mind was elsewhere anyway, set firmly with David and his increasingly curious behaviour. I sat behind an empty desk in front of a large lecture room, coffee in one hand, Janet's note balancing on the keyboard of my laptop. I'd set my students a task I knew would keep them busy for a while, currently researching DID for an assignment I hadn't anticipated providing, the true purpose of my mission solely that I needed a second opinion, my students able to provide several.

There are no limitations to the number of personalities a sufferer of DID can display, created purely from a deep-rooted, often profound need for acceptance they feel other people will not understand in them. And yet David had claimed the names of a dead man, possibly two, Simon Frederick no more a hundred and ten years older than I was.

I searched the census records for Simon Frederick, shocked to discover he too had been missing since 1936, the very same year his mother vanished. No bodies were ever recovered, and they were both declared legally dead by the courts seven years later. He had no other family. No wife or children in which to confirm his unexpected disappearance. He was just twenty-three years old.

I already knew Adam Mires was dead, Paul providing such details with a roll of his eyes and a shake of his head. He hated time wasters and assumed David was one of them. Adam had hung himself inside his prison cell in 1818, convicted for the killing of three people, at the time awaiting execution. He had brutally caved in the head of a young man outside a local Inn in March 1818 after a brawl got out of hand. The other two were a married couple, found dead outside their own home the same evening. Adam provided no valid reason behind those killings that might have seen him evade the hangman's rope. Instead, he died ranting, looking to the outside world as if he had lost his mind.

David Mallory, on the other hand, was very much alive and well, his current living status confirmed on the electoral roll. I stared at Jacob Pointer's name. He was the only one I knew nothing about, a search for him returning no results at all. Maybe David had made him up. After all, sufferers of DID do not have personalities of *dead* people in their repertoire. I could live with that. It made him less terrifying in my mind.

When my mobile rang, I was grateful for the distraction, stepping out of the lecture room into the corridor beyond, my muttered apology earning me several frustrated eye rolls I happily ignored. When did teenagers become so opinionated?

'Newt, that goddamned guy won't go home.' It was Paul.

'Which one?'

'It's not funny. Can you come in? He's refusing to speak with anyone other than you.'

It probably wasn't funny, but I laughed anyway. I glanced over my shoulder, grateful my lecture was about to end. I assumed my students would be grateful too. 'Give me thirty minutes.' I needed to speak with Adam again anyway. He seemed the only one happy to share what he knew. I hoped I could get to the station before one of The Others turned up, David especially. He had a knack of doing that. I dared not think too long about Jacob Pointer. Nobody needed that kind of image in their head.

Nineteen

Adam

I am glad of the traffic and the light breeze that brushes my face, ruffling my hair, providing a welcome moment of solace. I cannot recall the last time I was given such vocal placidity. Morning revellers amble around, men and womenfolk in similar attire, leather cases matching leathered faces, none of which can seemingly breathe in the ensuing commotion. Dog walkers and strangers converse privately inside small, flat objects held firmly in their grasping hands, unable to see where they are walking, strangers unable to see anyone, even each other.

Despite the daily bustle, I try to ignore my surroundings where possible, the lives of strangers meaning little to me now. I am glad for the fresh air and noise, travellers dressed in little more than cotton undergarments, regretting their dubious decision in the fresh morning breeze, a bright sun giving false expectation of a summer still lingering. I wish I had the capacity of mind to tell The Others to silence. Indeed, I wish I held sway over *my* mind, able to scream at this wretched world to make them stop. But I never do. I might never, in fact, be so bold as to bring forth an incumbent and personal chasm that I have been forced to endure for so long. I would despair for those I do not know to look at me with such vile distaste.

My brain pulls naggingly, torn to pieces by fragments of prevailing memories I can no longer make sense of—a jigsaw puzzle if you like, many of the pieces missing. It ensures the picture will never again look complete. I compose myself as I pull open the heavy station door, the concept of gaining transparency over my uncontrolled senses failing to resonate. I need the constables in this building to understand what has happened to bring me here now—how, in fact, I have ended up in this harrowing place at all.

I am forced to sit in silence, told to wait, this space too encumbered for my unravelling mind. I am not alone, yet not able to converse with those around me, their silence more imposing than my own. I have specifically asked to speak with Doctor Flanigan—*only* with Flanigan. No one else will understand. No one in this building seems fully able to appreciate what I require. He appears to understand me, if only a little, the last time we spoke, he ensured my mind was somewhat set at ease. I hope he will appreciate I am conveying the truth, only the truth, and nothing but.

So far, the constables have failed to heed my confession, unwilling to listen to reason. I scoff, uncertain if they will readily listen now. I wish he would hurry, the one who shares a *famous* name. The Others are never far away, never far from mind. I do not have long, I know. Nevertheless, I am perturbed to find myself in this stoic location once more, my ultimate capture uncertain. How often must I confess, only to be wholly ignored, sent on my way? I have provided the location of the first body, and yet still they fail to take my words seriously. Maybe, if I disclose the whereabouts of the other two, they will have little option but to lock me away, remove me from a society I no longer wish to be a part of. Indeed, I *must* be locked away, and soon. I am not safe as a free man. The Others remain a continued nemesis I can abide no more.

I hail from the northern borough of Shelby, although much of what I remember has been lost to my failing recollection. It is unfortunate and, I hasten to add, troublesome for me to acknowledge. Eastcliff, Shelby's neighbouring community, has equally changed dramatically over the years, the two communities destined to converge now as one. I am forced to remain forever indifferent, this abated, once quiet corner of the country unable to slow to the gentler pace it once afforded, the pace I remember, many strangers now housing every available square footage of street. Their relentless chatter is enough to confuse my muddled mind whilst holding the potential to cease the noise in David's. I cannot get him out of mine now as I sit alone in this space, a bandage wrapped tightly around my right hand unable to recall the incident.

I close my eyes briefly, opening them to the sight of a

perplexing young swain standing to the far end of this waiting room, a grimace set upon his burdened face I do not entirely appreciate. It is unnerving, imposing. I admit I usually enjoy the indifference Eastcliff affords me, the community unconcerned by my existence. However, I do not frequent myself with those who live here now, their strange mannerisms telling of a culture not my own, the people residing here far removed from my own time and place. There are too many heathens, delinquents, and potential murderers in Eastcliff. Of course, I do not include myself in this unfortunate consideration, although it is an unforgiving downside of who I am. Still, I try not to dwell on matters I cannot change. It helps no one to license such candour.

The young lad cannot be any older than twenty, maybe younger, thwarted to procure any stubble that might potentially pass for a beard. He is dressed in an overcoat too large for him, trying to prevail a size not his own, failing in his mission, though not for want of trying, I see, attempting to appear older than he is. His hair is ragged, unkempt, unwashed. I take a breath, swallowing the unwanted desire to remove myself from his presence, yet with nowhere else to go, I am forced to remain still. Instead, an uncomfortable delirium now lingers in my thoughts.

I do not wish to ponder this young thing for long, knowing he is amused by my momentary lapse of any befitting surroundings, my longing for a home far away, having an undesirable effect on my thoughts that I have not anticipated. Now, for the first time today, I wish only for an escape, to quell this lunacy, willing to wait for Flanigan beyond these station walls. However, I remain seated, even when a hooded figure looms into view, coming to a halt as the main doors open ahead of him, allowing access—much-needed freedom awaiting *me*. The stranger walks on, unconcerned by my existence, that young male unmoving, his lingering stare something I cannot abide. I glance his way. He nods, a crooked smile most threatening.

Under normal circumstances, such actions would amuse me. I have often found myself surrounded by swaths of modern townsfolk, crammed together and behaving unconcerned by what has happened in their relatively short lives to force them to such crowded conditions each day. I, in fact, usually revel in the bustle. It means I do not need to think about anything else for a while. Now, unfortunately, I am oddly concerned for my wellbeing, the welfare of this poor young thing in my presence something that might equally be in danger if I am left alone with him much longer. He knows nothing of The Others, although what does he know of life? Of death? What do any of us?

The main door opens once more, and I motion to leave, heading towards the exit, hands clasped together, heart in my throat. I shudder, pulling my clothing around my body in a futile attempt to warm a part of me that has suddenly turned icy, despite the increasing warmth of the morning. Distant footsteps are misplaced as they ascend nearby steps, louder than I would like, oddly vexing. I turn around several times to ensure I have not been followed. The Others are never far away, I know. I must look ridiculous. I check the entrance once more, turning around to the sight of that troubled young man being led away by an attending sergeant, his thoughts no longer resting with me.

I am grateful when Flanigan finally walks through the doorway, time slowly ebbing away. He appears flustered, irritated, as if he has not slept, and there is something in his mannerism that vexes me. I hope *I* am not the cause. I stand to greet him, hoping he appreciates the urgency of my visit. I hold out a hand, glad he takes it, his handshake welcoming. I am then ushered into a small room, the only light in this space emanating from a thin buzzing tube overhead. My untethered thoughts are exhausting, this room smaller than I would have hoped, closing in around me, threatening to choke. I am growing weary of fighting to keep David and The Others from taking over, forcing me aside, as always, as if I matter little to them at all. I need to *do* something. I will even turn to drastic measures if I deem it necessary. But I digress. This is *not* why I am here.

'Adam?' Flanigan asks the question as if he isn't confident which version of me he is addressing.

'Indeed, sir,' I reply, a nod of my head denoting politeness. However, inside I am anything but calm.

'How can I help?' he asks, gesturing me to sit. I have been offered tea, something called coffee, and even a glass of water when I refused both. I do not require their pleasantries, merely an aiding hand in matters of much importance.

'I have very limited time, sir,' I reply, my words emerging solemnly yet with a frantic tone I cannot hide. I am fully aware that, at any moment, David, Simon, or even Jacob, *God help us all*, might locate me, removing me from rational thought, expelling me from truths still requiring this good man's attention. 'I wish to know when I am to face my penance,' I state. As yet, I have been given nothing but my marching orders.

Flanigan sighs, crossing a leg across his knee, leaning back. A thin, plastic carrier with handles of the same material rustles loudly at his feet. I wonder if it contains trinkets important only to him. Did I hear the clang of a glass jar?

'I'm all yours,' he states, retaining a calming tone that helps ease mine.

'I need to tell you about the bodies. About the other two men I killed.'

'Adam Mires died in 1818. You *do* know this, don't you, Adam?' He is frustrated. I can tell.

'But, of course. I recall that fateful day well.' The day I *died*. 'I hoped to serve my penance, serve my time. I was due to be hung from my neck the following day.'

Flanigan leans back further. 'So why do *you* believe Adam took his own life?'

It infuriates me how this man is referring to my past as if it belongs to someone else. I shake my head. 'And watch in horror as my poor parents looked on, the hangman readily tying a noose around my throat? No, sir. Such a death was not for me. On the contrary, I wished only to spare them the indignant pain, my lagging tongue, my rolling eyes.' I close them now, remembering with bitter malice the torture of that day.

'Okay, I'm listening. Tell me about the deaths.'

'Which ones?' I do not mean to sound flippant.

Flanigan smiles. 'Why don't you start at the beginning?'

I nod, clearing my throat, needing to unburden myself, share what I know while I am able to do so, hoping the man before me might aid my impossible quest. I am glad he is willing to listen, at least.

'I was—' I pause, 'still am, a homosexual male, sir.' I glance upwards, daring to look into the eyes of the only human I feel might aid me, fearing what I might see in them now. His tone remains unchanged. I am grateful. 'Life was very different back then, you see. Of that, I can assure you.'

Twenty

Adam

Where do I begin? I glance towards Flanigan, glad I have been given the freedom to discuss personal matters with an open heart, grateful for the chance to reveal my past, revel in my *truth*. He remains relatively still, head to one side, nowhere better to be, it seems, but right here with me, this room dimly lit enough to allow my memories to drift unheeded. I close my eyes, the smell of fresh rain on my skin, the taste of my beautiful man lingering—still.

~

It began in the winter of 1817, a simple year of promise and harvest. A year when I believed all good men existed and that incredible things could happen if a person held such strong beliefs within their heart. A sharp, relentless winter wind had cut through the village that year, forceful, unforgiving, bringing with it sombre clouds and rain so penetrating that any further outdoor pursuits would be out of the question. Such weather ensured we were set in pure delirium, James and I, nothing to do but spend the darkened evenings together, not always alone, of course, yet never thwarted from what we both knew would eventually happen, the indifferent views of our once cherished neighbours and compatriots providing license for much frivolity we did not anticipate possible.

I close my eyes, recalling a far better time, long gone, of course — these memories often fleeting, painful. At the time, I did not know what name to give it, but the simple verity of this matter was, and still is, that I was in love. There is nothing more than that to tell, nothing that might otherwise make for better acknowledgement of my unfounded emotions. James and I began as allies, our mutual companionship developing into friendship, then towards something neither had expected. We held firm trust in each other, the world made all the better for his laughter and simple, raw beauty that shone even when the sun did not. We shared a joyous, outrageous passion for art, music, anything, in fact, that might procure to somehow elevate our small world beyond what we already knew existed — the world beyond our simple farming lives of Shelby as unobtainable as the relationship we did not intend to begin.

I must confirm with strong validity that I did not set out to *kill* anyone. Never for a moment had such an atrocious thought passed my incredulous mind. It is a painful truth that I have been unable to share with a living soul before now, my former captures included. I recall how the church constables treated me, how they abused my body for days through lack of food, warmth, clothing. The beatings I took because of what I was, *what I am*—what I will always be. I was a young swain, naïve in my thinking, unworldly in my ways. James appeared so handsome to me, more, in fact, than anyone I'd ever before encountered. More than the fair maidens living in either Shelby or Eastcliff at that time, more than any female ever could hold sway over me.

A ceaseless rain had softened the ground that fateful night. Storm damaged trees and shrubs stood in shrouded dampness, along with a volatile wind that swept leaves and debris into the penetrating night, leaving behind nothing of value that might explain our elevated mood. James and I were giddy on ale and each other, our illicit love affair ready to take its natural next step amid the life we both knew we could never truly have. We had already left the safety of Shelby, you see, venturing south towards Eastcliff, our companionship requiring privacy, a place where fewer people knew of us. We staggered playfully together into the night, intoxicated, neither of us aware of what we were about to begin, or that we were already being watched from the shadows. Dark, condemning eyes lingered on our naked forms, the moonlight dancing above as we danced together in perceived private, exposing our bodies and noxious delirium, unintentionally, I can assure you, to one of the town's most prestigious dwellers.

Once the wind had abated a little, I stepped outside to catch my breath, take in some much-anticipated air, still inebriated, still flush with the warmth of my lover's heady scent on my skin. I left James asleep in a barn used rarely by anyone, satisfied, unencumbered, his skin like porcelain in the fresh evening air as I traced fingertips over his goose-bumped body. For the first time in my life, I was happy. It was the most profound emotion I'd ever experienced, and I revelled in the glory of it.

Robert Peel was Eastcliff's most exemplary, God-fearing lawman, hired by the church to ensure the safety of its much-loved community—righteous, forthright, often unforgiving in both temperament and the actions he carried out in the name of his beloved Christ. I was unaware of his presence at first, unaware of the knowledge and power he had now gained over us, my thoughts only on James, our secret love affair beginning in earnest.

When he cornered me, stepping out from a deepening shadow, I denied the truth, rejected my lover, my potential embarrassment overshadowing any candid emotion I might otherwise have expressed. I was mortified, unaware, as was James, that Peel had already witnessed him uncovering my manhood, taking it in hand, other deeds the poor man was unwilling to acknowledge, the prevailing darkness able to disguise it all. *I take a breath, unable to help a shudder that forms in my body at the memory of such a beautiful act of love—of such a beautiful person my dear beloved James once was.*

I did not know what to do, most of my clothing still on the ground behind me, James' sleeping naked body on full display amid hay bales soon to become our notable downfall. I was fambling wildly, pleading for Peel's silence I knew in my heart would never be forthcoming. I could not blame the drink, I know, my drunkard state not in any way to blame for my willing actions, for James' part in our love-making decision. I wrongly chanced Peel to be in good humour, the evening most pleasant, albeit a cold one, attempting to quell this solitary moment by bringing forth a bottle of rum I hoped he might take with good grace. I was endearing in earnest to acquire his good favour, of course, yet he was having no part of my lunacy. He was peevish, resentful, his mission to thwart our uncouth relationship, bringing our grotesque sins to the full attention of the innocent people of both Shelby and Eastcliff alike.

When Peel turned around, his back to mine, his aim was intentional. To expose our deeds to the community in the way our naked bodies had been exposed to him. I did not mean to fly into an uncontrolled panic, and neither did I intend to pick up the axe, my innocent aim solely to reclaim power I did not possess. However, a dark rage sprang forth, from where, I do not know, but it forced me to strike him across the back of his head. He fell henceforth with a thud, landing on the sodden ground at my feet, no better than a pig brought in for slaughter.

I feared the idea of heading home, my bloodstained fingers and clothing intact, blood on my skin I could never wash away—not even the wild stream beyond my home enough to cleanse my now damned soul. Yet, worse still was the thought of leaving him in the icy mud to be discovered by an innocent passer-by, a virtuous child, a stray dog. Moreover, I was not yet convinced I had intentionally murthered him, his body knocked into a deep slumber by the wrath of my unyielding hand. Indeed, what was I to do? Should he awaken, he would cast me in irons, ensuring my body was hanging from the gallows before that very day was done. Where then would that leave poor James? Hanging by my side, no doubt, much shame brought upon his entire family, upon mine.

The low horizon was already bringing in a new dawn, so I dragged forth the body, glad it was easily moveable in the slippery mire, this moment rendering me liable to strange penance. By the time James had awoken, the deed was done, Robert Peel's body now buried deep beneath the freshly dug foundations of a nearby, newly intended mill that was subject of much talk by everyone I knew. However, he landed badly, breaking his neck, not yet dead, the incoming grunt and sharp snap most unexpected. I am ashamed to confess that, by the time I'd left him to his fate that day, his face was brutally pulverized. I could not allow him freedom of identification, lest his corpse should be discovered.

I broke his wrist with a pitchfork, taking with it a part of his thumb, accidentally, of course, his hand reaching towards the breaking dawn, towards salvation and mercy I was unwilling to provide. There was no turning back for me, the moment of sanity gone, a fleeting idea now passing my mind that I might *profit* from my unanticipated deed. I was unable to remove his jewels, his body fattened over the years by wild pig and wine. Cutting off his fingers would rectify the problem, hence I was then able to remove said trinkets with ease. I mistakenly believed selling those items may enable

James and I the freedom to leave Shelby and begin a new life elsewhere, a place where we could remain unknown, our private world kept so.

I stuffed his bloodied fingers deep inside my pockets, mocking gold glistening in the moonlight. Although, in my haste, I accidentally left a crow headed belt the man often whipped his children with, still attached to his body, a discerning identifiable factor I'd overlooked. Despite my grappling hands for several minutes, I was unable to exhume the body, the mud thickening by the second. There was no time to think, no chance to search any further, nothing more to be done.

When daylight broke, already sickened with guilt, I readily explained to James what had happened, exposing my position, our relationship now compromised. Of course, I did not expect him to take such news well, yet I could not have foreseen his reaction. The poor man was mortified. It was unexpected. I'd concealed our scandal, you see, protecting our fate, my clothing now needing to be burned in my fire grate.

Yet James was never the same after that day—never again comfortable for us to be seen together in public, in either Shelby or Eastcliff, his own embarrassment far outweighing mine. He distanced himself from me for weeks, despite much pleading. Then one evening in early spring, his conscience piqued, threatening to expose what I had done, confirming he could no longer live with himself and the secret I'd vulgarly forced him to keep. We quarrelled, fought each other promptly for the heinous right to keep such a painful truth the secret it needed to remain. For both our sakes.

He waved a knife towards me, frustration and fear building, although his intention was not on anything sinister, I can assure you. The poor man was beside himself. However, it was enough for the situation to take an unexpected twist. He stabbed me in the abdomen, superficially, a flesh wound nothing more. Yet my reaction was misplaced, punching him in retaliation, an automatic response on my behalf I admit. He fell, hitting his head against a water trough, the incident too swift for my mind to revere. *I close my eyes, remembering now. Nothing good came from that night.* I could not allow him to speak out against me, you see, expose our truth and what I had been forced to endure henceforth—my only aim to protect the man I adored.

I did not intend for such an expression of repulsion. Yet, he died on that road all the same, on his back, on his way home, a local tavern mere feet from my own, my arms set around his, his blood-soaked hair seeping wilfully into my skin, his brain too damaged for recovery. I vowed there and then I would never trust another man, never love again the way I loved James Lambert Collier. *I do not wish to continue, but I must. I glance towards Newton Flanigan, observing the lines beneath his eyes. I cannot read him. I cannot see beyond my own pain.*

William Collier was James' brother. He and his wife Elizabeth had been kind to me, and I had nowhere else to go. With a heavy heart and thunderous soul, I headed directly, heartbroken, to their humble home, my intention to express to his brother the truth of what had happened, what I had wrongly done and request their protection. It was an accident, nothing more. Surely they could see? I loved James. I was still covered in my beloved's blood, my own wound angry, still holding the very knife I had taken from his unwilling grasp, knowing he never intended any actual harm to come to *me*.

It was late, the lights all out, the village long retired, a full moon the only lingering companion showing me the way. William was roused by my pitiful calls for help, stepping into the cool night to quell my malice. "How durst I wake his wife at such an ungodly hour?" he chastised. I was crying. I could not help it. When he saw me, saw the blood, he threw into a rage, punching me hard, forcing me to the ground below. He no longer concerned himself with thoughts of waking his sleeping wife, waking the entire village. So, with no further assistance afforded me, I was forced to kill him too.

His wife was screaming. Of course, I had to silence her. Everything happened so swiftly, no time to think, no logic to my actions. I strangled poor Elizabeth on the doorstep of her own home, needing her silence, her husband already dead on the sodden ground behind me, a knife deep in his belly, my beloved James still on the very road I'd left him. *I can still smell the blood, if I try.* The entire moment numbed my body as if I was already going to hell for what I had done, four deaths by then, each one my fault.

Everything spiralled out of control from that moment on. I could no longer live with what I had become, and so I ran, my intention only to hide away, no better than a dog with no place to be, my thoughts drifting to dark places they had no business being.

John Bull was the local blacksmith. He and his son, Henry,

often worked late into the evening, shoeing horses, forging irons for local fireplaces. It was customary to see the glow from their fire pit, a comforting vision I was always heartened by. James and I could often be seen lurking there, always intoxicated, lingering beyond that stoic location, wishing only to get to know each other better, Shelby knowing nothing more of our culpable intentions.

As it was, I was standing now on the precipice of hell, memories I did not want in my head allowed full control of my brain, unaware that father and son had witnessed the commotion outside the Collier residence, set on notifying the church of my sinful deeds. His son was only seventeen, could never now unsee what I'd unwittingly forced the poor boy to witness, their conversation not as private as they had perceived, my conversation with William exposing my truth. I could not allow them to spread such news, my entire existence now in their hands.

I lured them onto my father's farmland under a false proclamation that, if they were to keep quiet about such an unfortunate incident, my father would reward them handsomely, willing to pay heavily for their silence. My father and John Bull were close friends, allies, no reason for him to believe my words were untrue. Yet, lied I had, and willingly so. There was, of course, no such proclamation. The Bull's were a greedy family. John had no reason to assume I was lying to him, trusting my word for what he believed it was.

I wanted to warn him off, that's all, ensure his silence but he was furious. I had little time to think, pushing John into a hole recently dug to extend the only riverbed, passing for little more now than a stream. Henry was young yet felt able to help his father whilst thwarting me. However, the poor boy broke both legs during his own, ill-placed jump into a hole far deeper than he had appreciated. Of course, I tried to reason with both men, but to no avail. I was subsequently forced to hit them both over the head, ensuring their silence, killing them instantly where they stood. I then coldly cut off the fingers of both men, hacking each tooth from their skulls, just as I'd done with Peel, no one now able to learn their true names should they stumble upon this villainous deed. I buried them together in that unforgiving hole and never returned.

~

I am staring at Flanigan now, a man who has allowed my vulgar rant to go unchecked for some time. I know what he is thinking. How was I eventually caught? How did I end up in a jail cell, six dead people and hanging from the same rope set aside for my ultimate end? By the time I have finished speaking, my life has been exposed in all its gruesome finery. I am beyond hot, tethered to my fate, my voice now that of a small boy with nothing left but pain of a life long passed.

Flanigan has not spoken a word, simply happy to allow me to spill soiled words into this room without potential fear of reproach. He stands now, allowing a moment of silence to linger between us.

'I loved James, sir. I need you to understand that truth.' It is a painful one, at that. I do wish this room had a window. I need air I feel may never arrive. 'I could not simply discard his body and carry on as if nothing had happened.' It was unfounded that I had, indeed, disposed of three bodies with no thought of it. William and Elizabeth remained where they dropped to their untimely end, ensuring I became a wanted man in that heinous moment, nothing but a common caper, a killer in their midst. I killed six people for the love of one and I had nowhere left to go. I was nothing but a vile wretch of a man, no future, no absolution, so without further ado I handed myself into the local church whose constables threw me henceforth into a jail cell with the intention of putting me to death. I deserved nothing less.

'Thank you, Adam,' Flanigan offers. He is pacing the room now, stretching his legs. 'So the other two bodies?'

'John and Henry Bull?' The very names instil a twisted animosity onto my thoughts I have never been fully able to atone for.

Flanigan nods.

'Well, sir. Unless someone dug them up, I assume they are both still resting in the very grave I gave them.'

'Do you remember the exact location?'

'Of course.' It is, in fact, a location I will never forget. 'Beyond the outskirts of Shelby, deep within Chestermill woods, you will find a clearing running alongside the narrowest part of the riverbed. A large rock, set deep into the landscape, carved by nature in the shape of a demonic hand, and a large oak tree, marks north of their position. You will find both men beneath the clock tower bridge.' No actual clock tower was ever built in that location, merely a name given to a simple footbridge with a misguided notion that one day, my father would help extend our humble village. I close my eyes again, my father's once prized land still so very vivid to my poisoned memory.

'May I ask you a question, Adam?'

I nod.

'Why did you not offer this information three weeks ago, when you first came in to the station?'

I take a moment, hindsight not something I find easy to convey. 'Memories are fleeting, Doctor Flanigan. I find it most distracting, as I am sure you appreciate, but events come to me sporadically, not always in the correct order. Whenever I feel a pulling clarity of mind, I wish only to unburden myself.' I hope he understands. I do not always.

Flanigan nods and leaves the room, leaving me to painful memories that sickens me still. Memories I do not feel relieved to have finally shared with someone else after all these prevailing years.

Twenty-One

Newton

Paul was hovering in the corridor as I stepped out of the interview room. My head was throbbing, my brain ready to explode with information overload I wasn't convinced Adam had intended, lack of sleep to blame for my encroaching exhaustion. After being shut in that small room for the last hour, I was glad of the cool air now drifting across my flustered cheeks—Paul's rattled composure confirmation I wasn't going out of my mind.

'Well?'

'*Well*, it seems Adam Mires has been a busy boy,' I chided sarcastically while heading towards the coffee machine. I didn't mean to diminish the poor man's troubled mind. It was hardly appropriate, or professional.

'Funny.' Paul rolled his eyes with a scoff, bored of the continued disturbance by so-called dead men, his time better spent working on *actual* police work, dead bodies they might one day find closure for, families they *could* potentially help. 'I may have to charge him with wasting police time if he doesn't take the hint soon.'

'His story was detailed enough, though.' I was still reeling from the depth of information the man provided so readily, hardly needing to take a breath for most of it, the entire morning ensuring I now needed a moment to catch *my* breath.

'So was Stephen King's novels. But I don't see *him* waiting in line to confess the crimes of his fictional characters.' Paul was being facetious, of course, making light of the moment, nothing else to do, no other rational explanation as to the continued appearance of David Mallory and his unrelenting sidekicks.

'I have the location of the other two bodies, if you're interested,' I confirmed, rolling my eyes at my friend's continued irritation.

'Not really,' Paul shook his head. 'I'm sorry, Newt, but I can't send my officers to investigate a potential location of two-hundred-year-old buried corpses. It was bad enough digging up the first one. If we'd known it wasn't linked to a recent death, I wouldn't have bothered.'

'Why not?' I didn't mean to narrow my eyes.

'Because, my friend, two-hundred-year-old bodies don't have desperate family members requiring closure. Think about it. There must be hundreds, if not thousands of unidentified bones scattered worldwide in unmarked graves. I can't go to the chief superintendent asking for funding on that kind of thing. Adam needs an archaeologist, not a copper.'

He was right, but it didn't make it right. 'Yeah, but—'

'Sorry. No. I can't spare the manpower.'

I sighed loudly, muffling any potential sigh Paul might have already given *me*. I oddly felt sorry for Adam, David, whoever the guy might have become by the time I made it back to the interview room. 'Okay, fine.'

'I need to focus on the here and now. On the bodies that *do* need my attention.'

I thought of the recent victims, a shudder forming unexpectedly as a cold finger of dread ran along my spine. 'Did you ever find out if any of the dead girls were sex workers?'

Paul raised an eyebrow. 'The first one definitely wasn't, but the second two, possibly. They had track marks on their arms from possible drug use, and both girls had traces of semen on their bodies. One also had some inside her mouth.' Paul shook his head, rubbing a stressed hand over his forehead, neither of us needing to visualise the poor pathologist whose job it was to discover that.

'The same guy?' *The killer?*

'No. It looks as if they had consensual sex with at least three different men before they met our man, so the conclusion is they probably were sex workers.'

I thought of poor Rachel Gates. 'Do you think the killer targeted Gates by mistake?' How could you mistake a school teacher for a prostitute?

Paul nodded. 'It looks that way.' He sighed. 'That isn't all. I'm afraid we might have another.'

'Another body?'

'A nineteen-year-old female was reported missing this morning by her mum. She didn't come home last night.'

'But that doesn't mean—'

'No. It doesn't. But for now, my priority is finding this young woman, hopefully drunk in a ditch somewhere, fully clothed, intact, fully compos mentis. Simply having forgotten to call home.'

'Is she—'

'Oh yeah. She's a sex worker too.'

~

Woodbine Avenue was nothing special, its name denoting a far better image than its actual location permitted. Dozens of Victorian terraced houses were jammed together like sardines on both sides of a narrow street, hardly any greenery amongst them to invite nature, aside from stray dogs, urban foxes, and plenty of discarded rubbish bags. We knocked on a dilapidated front door to the sound of a snappy, high-pitched dog that irritated me more than I wanted to admit. A woman appeared behind a clear glass panel, her face reddened, eyes swollen, as if she already knew our routine visit was futile.

'Mrs Cormac?' Paul asked, aiming his voice towards a damaged letterbox that probably did nothing to keep out the prevailing wind. He held his identity badge in front of him. 'It's DCI Mannering.'

The door opened to a tiny-framed female in a dressing gown who stood trembling in front of us, the yappy dog in her arms shaking violently. Her hands were unsteady, no doubt a restless night from worry and little sleep, heavy bags already forming beneath her puffy eyes. She nodded a tear-filled head while stepping aside, fully aware the police would be attending her house today. Nobody confirmed it would be *helpful*.

'Daisy, shush,' she muttered to the dog, who, still desperately wanting to know why we were invading her space, was now wriggling frantically within her grasp. The little dog simply needed the freedom to nip unwanted shoes and claim back a much-protected territory. 'Sorry about the dog.' Mrs Cormac ushered the tiny Pomeranian into an even smaller kitchen and closed the door. It was a shame the high-pitched barking did not abate, scratching and confusion erupting from the poor thing as the woman took a disinterested seat by the fireplace.

'I know this is upsetting for you,' Paul said, already perched on the edge of a sagging sofa, glancing my way as if he hated his job sometimes. I assumed this type of conversation never got any easier for him. 'We just need a little more information about Annie, if that's okay.'

Mrs Cormac nodded, pulling a tissue from the inside of her sleeve and wiping her nose forcefully, her bloated face bearing the brunt of her frustration. 'Annie *never* stays out all night, and if she does, she always lets me know.'

I glanced around the dimly lit living room. The curtains were still pulled together, cabinets and bookshelves brimming with photo frames of all shapes and sizes displaying a child's development from toddler to teenager—the young female in every photograph looking happy and content. I mused around allowing Paul to do his job, my presence here purely to evaluate anything of interest the police might accidentally overlook.

'Is this Annie?' I asked, picking up what looked like a relatively recent photograph, knowing, of course, it *must* have been. There were no pictures of anyone else in the room. She was blond, pretty, sitting on a beach somewhere, tanned. No cares in the world.

Mrs Cormac glanced up. 'Yes. That was taken last year, before—' she trailed off, forcing me to look her way.

'Before?' Paul queried. His tone remained calm and neutral, attempting a friendly approach that didn't come naturally. He'd never learned the art of diplomacy when it came to fellow humanity.

'Before all the nasty business began.' Mrs Cormac shook her head as if she didn't want to think about the dark thoughts now twisting her mind to shreds.

'Care to elaborate?' Paul asked, thankfully calmer than I'd ever seen him. I was impressed. Unnerved, obviously, but impressed.

'Before she met that man.' Mrs Cormac shook her head again, gritting her teeth as if she didn't want to say his name aloud. '*Tony McNally.*'

'Who is Tony McNally?'

Mrs Cormac stared into space. 'Some boyfriend. Or so she claimed. But I'm not convinced he took a shine to Annie because he liked her *personality.*' Paul nodded, allowing the woman to continue in her own time, a tactic I'd previously taught him to use in these situations. I was impressed he remembered. 'After just six months, he had her working on the street, hooked on drugs, a totally different girl to the one I raised.'

'When was the last time you saw Annie, Mrs Cormac?' Paul had his notebook ready, standard questions asked.

'Yesterday morning, before she headed out to college.' Paul was writing now, concentrating. 'She goes out every morning. Comes home every afternoon with coursework in her bag. I assume she must go to her lectures.' Annie's mum was clinging to hope.

'What is she studying?'

'Business studies.' Mrs Cormac allowed a smile at the thought of her daughter's education. 'She's a bright girl.' Her impromptu smile slipped, the tissue in her hand disintegrating as she wiped away a stray tear. 'Please, find her for me. I couldn't bear the thought of losing my girl. She's the only thing I have in the world.' I stared at the vast array of smiling faces set inside flat, cold frames, a single-parent family explaining such beloved possessions, the barking dog no part of the equation, it seemed.

I was having a hard time thinking about Annie Cormac as a sex worker. She didn't look the typical type, although that might have been stereotypical on my part, I know. She was in a loving family, studying at college, just an average young girl, by all accounts. I placed the photograph back on the shelf as carefully as I could so not to deter Paul from his current mission or risk upsetting Mrs Cormac further.

'May I take a look around her room?' I asked, needing to know more about Annie and the type of people she would associate with. Mrs Cormac nodded, allowing me to slip quietly from the room, ensuring Paul was free to continue building a picture of her last known movements.

Upstairs, the sound of the dog was thankfully not so disturbing to my senses, my attention turned now to a strong scent of sweet perfume lingering in the heavy air. I fought an urge to open a window, the priority of fresh air not something Mrs Cormac would be overly concerned by. Instead, I followed the scent into Annie's room which looked typical of a young woman; all cushions and candles, discarded clothing, an unmade bed, trinkets, fairy lights not yet turned off, and cut out photographs pinned to a large mirror over a cluttered dressing table.

I stepped over several pairs of discarded, mismatched shoes, wandering around this private space in a vague attempt to find out what made Annie Cormac tick. A folder was open on a chest of drawers showing an assignment half completed, confirmation this young girl was, at some point, still attending her classes. What on earth would make her turn to sex work and drugs? It didn't look as if she needed the money, her room filled with many possessions, happy memories. I couldn't help wondering if many of these items had been purchased by Tony McNally. Whoever *he* was. Did he have something over her? Was it the other way around?

I stepped back onto the landing to the sound of Paul talking softly in the room below, the little dog's bark nothing more now than a strangled whimper, no doubt tired of being ignored. I couldn't imagine what that poor girl's mum must be going through. It's bad enough to receive news that someone you love has been taken from you suddenly. I could *personally* appreciate how that feels. But to not know where your loved one is? The idea made me feel sick.

I descended the staircase to the now-familiar sound of a troubled dog, wondering if the poor thing hadn't barked herself hoarse in pursuit of freedom and much wanted attention. I had as much as I was going to get from Annie Cormac's room. For now.

Twenty-Two

Newton

Visions of Annie Cormac, David Mallory, and brutally mutilated bodies drifted around my mind for the rest of that day. I fully understood why the Eastcliff police could not send officers to the location of remains discarded potentially two centuries ago—two unfortunate souls amongst many undiscovered corpses littering the world, long forgotten. Yet, nothing was preventing *me* from undertaking a private investigation of my own, nothing more to do than settle my increasingly inquisitive mind.

An hour with Adam was enough to shift my perspective on the man. He knew too much. He knew too much detail. The way he spoke—far removed from how we converse today, nothing for me to do but buy into his theatrics. Equally, as much as Paul and his team were ready to discard Adam's confession (or should that be David's?), I was curious. I couldn't get Annie Cormac out of my mind, a nagging, lingering thought remaining with me that somehow, her disappearance and those recent murders were linked. Even if David had nothing to do with Annie's current whereabouts, there were too many abhorrent killers in the world for the poor girl to encounter. That truth alone provided enough momentum for me to take things into my own hands.

It was odd. Today, Adam had displayed the look of a broken man—a man worn down by life and everything in it, unkempt stubble left in a chaotic state, unlike David, his continued pursuit for perfection. His hair, already allowed to grow long, rested against his shoulders dishevelled and dirty. It was the first thing I noticed when greeting him this morning. His eyes seemed different too—darker, duller than David's, if that's possible. I swear David had *blue* eyes. David always presented himself well; his hair, although obviously the same length, was usually combed back away from his face. But not today.

I drove out of town with a nagging feeling I couldn't shake. I'd only dealt with DID a handful of times in my career, yet every one of those people required much attention and plenty of medication. David was different, his version of the condition manifested from personalities of men long dead. *But why?* It was abnormal. Why would he claim characters of mortal men, able to provide vivid recollections of what he *must* have read about in decades-old journals and newspaper clippings, no doubt pouring over old library collections for several months? Years? I was honestly impressed with the man's memory. I wish I knew his secret.

I'd tried and failed to locate anything of significance on the body found beneath the Adderson Street factory ruins; anything potentially documented about a man missing from Eastcliff in October 1817 now long gone. Either that or I wasn't looking hard enough. The body was buried deep, as if whoever put him there did not want him found, the original foundations more than capable of concealing his corpse forever. If the bones had been in a shallow grave, as you'd expect, it would have been found in the 1820s when the original mill was built. As it was, it took a team of police officers, several forensics experts and two diggers before they found the remains. And, only then because Paul was convinced he had a murderer sitting in an interview room, a dead body needing closure for a family it had unwittingly left behind—no time for mistakes or missed discoveries.

I could fully understand his hesitancy now, of course. It was funding the police could ill-afford. Yet Adam had willingly provided the location of two more potential victims, his elaborate story fitting neatly with those old events—the wounds found on the original body including a documented case of Adam Mires, the confirmed and convicted killer of three in 1818. The guy *actually* existed. Because of this truth, I was heading now to a new location on the outskirts of what was once known as Shelby village, around five miles or so from Eastcliff. I loved my ageing Volkswagen Beetle, of course, but it rarely left the security of Eastcliff's smooth, well-maintained roads, my daily commute short, my monthly required trips to London to see Steph and the kids achieved via train.

Chestermill Woods were out of the way, out in open countryside, beyond the trappings of normal life, where the world is able to slow down a little. I usually hated the silence, my mind always full of ideas brimming with potential I had little capacity for. Today, however, I was glad of the peace. The last few days had ground me down, the very reason my brain was now uncooperative, almost ready to reject sanity. I might have blamed David, of course, but that would be unfair. It wasn't his fault his brain didn't function the way it should have. He needed help, not persecution.

It was getting dark by the time my ageing car made it to my chosen destination, a dense tree line creating ghostly shapes against a fading sky that danced and played together in the hush now surrounding me. Only the occasional shriek from a nearby wild animal kept me on full alert as I took a torch and shovel from my boot—just a fox, no doubt, nothing more. Why did those things always sound as if someone was being murdered in the dark? *Oh, the irony.*

A putrid whiff of damp and rotting wood peppered the air, including something that had died not long ago. It threatened in the encroaching darkness to combine random thoughts of murderous beasts along with David's malignant breath—nothing more than a breeze, I know, yet enough to drive me to unwanted distraction. It tugged at my sanity, this very night destined to become too much for my overloaded brain as I trudged along the softened ground. For a brief moment, I feared exposing my position in a flash of irreversible electricity, my body holding enough energy to light up my location like a giant homing beacon. *Come and look at the daft psychologist on his futile mission for nonsensical answers!*

The woodland irradiated around me with flashes of torchlight aimed in all directions, my hands unsteady with demonic shapes thrown against a backdrop that looked as sinister as the magnitude of the situation I'd found myself in. Constant low voices prodded the breeze, some more profound than others sounding as lost as I felt. I tried not to overthink it, telling myself it would be nothing more than sound travelling with the wind. Dog walkers. Poachers. My vivid imagination.

I walked for a while, losing my bearings on several occasions, cursing my lack of navigation skills. The whole place was overgrown, the earth beneath my feet long since changed by nature. The deeper I ventured into those woods the darker it became, turning my surroundings almost pitch black. All I could see now was a faint glow of distant stars as the evening sky attempted to guide me, a single beam from my torch highlighting trees that danced in the breeze like ghosts around a midnight campfire. I stopped, took a moment, considered turning back—a wayward curiosity and Adam's annoying compulsion overtaking any reasonable logic that the bodies would be here at all. *What on earth was I doing here?*

There would be a clearing, Adam said. Next to a dwindling riverbed. *What river?* I'd never heard of *any* river this far inland. I closed my eyes, straining to listen to any potential running water, yet there was nothing to deter my wandering mind other than a gentle rustle of leaves. I shone my torch around, wishing I'd come here during the day (when I could actually see), the fact I couldn't bring myself to go home to an empty flat the very reason I was here now at all.

He'd claimed there would be a large rock in the shape of a hand and an oak tree. Large rock? *Seriously?* I must have stumbled around for twenty minutes or so, nothing but a blanket of trees for company before the inevitable happened. I lost my footing, almost breaking my neck as I tripped over something solid at my feet. *Shit.* I shone my torch towards a large piece of wood, greyed with time, decayed to the point of no return. I should have turned back, of course, cursed my feigned stupidity and unsuitable shoes and gone home—but it was then I remembered Adam had also mentioned something about a bridge.

Motioning my torch frantically along the ground, I spotted more wood, not fallen branches but purposefully sawn timber, long-forgotten now, of course, broken into several pieces by age. When I stepped in something wet, I realised the riverbed Adam had described was nothing more than a carpeted mossy mess, a simple marsh not able to pass off as a stream, overgrown and strangled by a continued lack of maintenance. Left to its own devices, it had become entwined with twisted branches and long thick grasses, wholly capable of holding back any potential water flow, creating a sludgy bank of unpleasant algae I was now standing ankle-deep in. *Brilliant.*

I shone my torch into the air, hoping to find the oak tree that would by now have grown quite large. Yet what did an oak tree look like? I cursed my lack of interest in biology, faded images of leaf shapes and trees in school textbooks blending together in a sea of relentless green. It wasn't until I leant against something hard that I realised I was propped against the very rock Adam had spoken about. That too was now covered in years of plant growth, nature slowly taking it back, shielding it from view. At least I was in the right place.

I must have looked ridiculous scrambling around in the darkness. To be honest, I didn't anticipate finding anything out here—least of all, the long-buried bones of two dead males, father and son forever together in this desolate space. My cursed curiosity had got the better of me. Still, I was here now. I pulled my mobile from my pocket. No signal. *Typical.* It had just turned nine-thirty. I glanced skywards, searching the heavens for sanity I wouldn't find, knowing it would be much lighter out by the car. Late summer still lingered, these dense trees capable of hiding anything—history, murder, Newton *stupid* Flanigan.

I couldn't help the sigh that left my lips, echoing throughout the landscape, extenuating the fact I had probably been hasty in my questionable pursuit. With nothing to lose now and nowhere else to be, I laid my torch on the ground trying to figure out the best place to bury bodies, hiding a horrific crime from this world forever. Unfortunately, there wasn't much left of the environment Adam had vividly described, two hundred years enough time for nature to claim back its victims, hide a dark truth I wasn't convinced I believed.

I cursed myself for absorbing Adam's words as I began chopping large sections from the overgrowth at my feet, the tip of my shovel offering no genuine assistance that might aid my mission. I was grateful for the sodden soil below, slackened with continued penetrating rainwater. I had no genuine idea how the man could have learned of such a murderous location. He must have spent months, years even, researching possible sites of time-aged crimes he could lay strange claim to. Either that or he had made the entire thing up to annoy me. I thought of Paul shaking his head at the concept of me standing amid overgrown thickets of shit with soaked ankles and ruined shoes, a knowing roll of his eyes with his hands on his hips. What the *hell* are you doing, Flanigan?

Yet I couldn't ignore the fact that Adam had been right about the previous body. No one could have known it was buried so deep below a long-forgotten factory floor, destined to lie untouched forever. I stopped, closing my eyes needing a moment. Was I doing the right thing? Adam Mires died in 1818 having hung himself in a local jail cell. *David* was the one who had told me of the bodies. David alone had engaged in conversation and turned up at my home, cut himself in his own. What if the man was playing me for a fool?

I kept digging despite my brain telling me to stop being an idiot and go home. It was becoming a vendetta now anyway. I searched for what felt like hours, pouring with sweat, glad I had the cool, dense air of Chestermill Woods as my unwitting protector. I was almost as obsessed as Adam, my focus set on locating something, *anything*, that might prove I wasn't as deluded as him. I dug three holes each around five feet deep, my clothing and hands so blackened by soil and dirt that I almost blended perfectly into the night. Nothing. Exhausted, I slumped to the ground glad for a moment to rest, a much-needed respite from my rapidly untethering mind, my arms throbbing. When I noticed something poking from the mud amid a thin beam of light, I almost ignored it. Set at an awkward angle, the thing stood out against the night, my torch aimed perfectly towards its unwitting location. I narrowed my eyes, unable to presume it would be anything other than a piece of discarded plastic or a stone.

I clambered forward on exhausted hands and knees, an overwhelming stench of rotting vegetation threatening to make me as sick as I assumed David's mind already was. With fingers numb and muscles aching, I peeled the pale shape from its surroundings, lifting it out with trembling fingertips.

I swallowed. *You have got to be kidding me!*

Stepping back, I collapsed onto the dirt with an unceremonious thud, not caring that I now looked as if I'd messed my trousers. There in front of me lay a bone. It was just a fragment, nothing more, but I could clearly identify a broken tibia, its distinct shape practically unrecognisable against the dimly lit surroundings. *Human.* I swallowed, daring myself to dig further, my bare hands scrabbling around in the mud for further proof that tonight wasn't a total waste of time. Finally, after several frantic moments of feeling nothing but soil and earthworms, my index finger prodded something hard. I pulled at it roughly, firmly, bringing a fully intact rib bone to the surface. *Bloody hell. Adam was right.* With the offending bone still in my grip, I clambered out of the hole back to the presumed safety of the surrounding grasslands, my hand unwilling to acknowledge what it was holding onto.

I had no idea which way my car was located, my bearings all but lost to the darkness around me. I needed to call Paul, tell him of my discovery. He couldn't ignore this. His entire career would be in jeopardy if he did. How would his bosses react to the fact he had ignored confirmation of the whereabouts of human remains located in nearby woodland? Not good. The Eastcliff police would not understand the concept of these bones being hundreds of years old, only that bones had been uncovered in the first place. I glanced skywards hoping for a miracle that would guide me out of these woods in one piece back to my awaiting car, preferably alive, continued fox calls holding the illogical power to have me believe that, if I wasn't careful, I might be killed tonight. I knew Paul would be furious with me, but I needed to know the truth. I couldn't let it lie.

It was already long past midnight by the time I finally made it out of those woods, back into the light of a welcoming full moon and open fields. Distant lights denoted the location of Eastcliff, a place I wished I'd never left the safety of.

'Newt? Where the hell are you?' Paul's groggy voice filled my ears making me momentarily glad of his metaphoric company. He sounded tired. I hope I hadn't woken him. Knowing him, he was probably still working at the station, avoiding his *actual* life.

'Chestermill woods.'

'Why?' I heard a rustle, creaking of aching bones, a spring.

'I found bones. Exactly where Adam said they'd be.' I was

out of breath, probably out of my mind, covered in mud, my car still some distance from where I'd emerged. I had no idea how to direct the police to the correct location. It didn't matter.

'*What?* Shit, Newt, I told you not to probe.'

'I was curious.'

'Christ. So, now I'll have to send a team, won't I?'

'Yep.'

'Jesus, Newton.' I could hear Paul walking around, grabbing clothing. 'Why the hell can you *never* leave things alone?'

I smiled. It wasn't my job to leave things alone. I didn't get paid to develop theories and leave them to it. The police employed me to achieve those much-needed results they might not otherwise find without me. The concept made me feel more important than I probably deserved, but I didn't care.

Twenty-Three

Newton

A lack of sleep, lack of understanding, and a total lack of support had all but rendered my mind obsolete. I arrived home at five o'clock in the morning after locating my car, a lengthy perimeter sweep with far too many expletives leaving my irritated lips. It had taken an age for the police to arrive, promoting far more annoyance from my brain than was comfortable, yet, once on-scene, they'd been swift enough to cordon off the area, dawn steadily breaking over the site, revealing this isolated location in all its true beauty. The foxes had gone to bed. *Thank Christ.*

Several uniformed officers headed into the woods, their mission to confirm my grisly discovery, emerging some time later with shocked looks on their faces and mud on their shoes. Paul arrived not long after them, a scowl welded to his face that told me I should go home and leave them to it, the forthcoming day now requiring a full excavation of the site. I'd done enough, apparently, according to the lingering glare he gave me by my car.

Now, after two hours of lying on my bed staring at the ceiling with nothing but bones and murderous foxes for company, I'd failed to locate any sleep at all. Paul was avoiding me, avoiding answering his phone, avoiding the lecture I knew was heading my way. I had a student lecture this morning too, yet the university had oddly slipped down my list of priorities, my bosses growing tired of my continued absence. I appreciate, of course, that I need to teach in order to subsidise my income, my students nothing but victims of my constant, unapologetic disappearances. Yet, bodies long dead have oddly now become more important to me than those alive, often disgruntled and bored in forgotten lecture rooms.

Again, it would have been easy to cry off work and head to the station, my head on the chopping block anyway. Yet that wouldn't be fair on my students. I toyed with my limited options for a few minutes before reluctantly heading to the university where, instead of apologising to Paul Mannering, I apologised to my students, proceeding to set a detailed assignment on the inner working minds of paranoid schizophrenics and how this mental health condition differs to DID. I received many groans and comments I didn't wish to acknowledge or repeat. It didn't matter. They were here to learn psychology, I was here to teach it to them, and, as long as their final grades emerged unscathed, they had nothing to complain about. I then gave them the morning off, a study period I claimed, the real reason being that I needed sleep. I was glad when Paul sent me a text message confirming they had, once again, taken David in for questioning. I made my apologies, excused my disgruntled students, and drove directly across town to my unwitting accomplice.

Twenty-Four

David

I have found myself, once again, in an overbearing police station interview room, devoid of stimulating conversation, a cup of weak tea I cannot bring myself to consume, many thoughts flicking through my head. I should, by now, be accustomed to this location, the probing, relentless questioning I do not appreciate, perplexed by the *continued* annoyance of it all. I am tapping my fingers against the tabletop, waiting impatiently, hoping someone will have the good grace to explain why I am here and what they want with me *now*. I am a busy man. I have other, more pressing matters to attend to.

I do not even know if I am relieved or frustrated when the door opens and the good doctor walks in. As usual, his hair is dishevelled, stubble littering his chin as if the poor man hasn't slept. I smell shower gel, the cheap sort usually found on supermarket shelving. It would appear that he has washed his hair with it, for quickness no doubt, traces of dirt left to linger behind fingernails he has sadly overlooked. Tut, tut. I wonder what he has been doing to make him appear so flustered and out of place this morning.

'Doctor Flanigan,' I state, my tone flat. I am exhausted. It is unpleasant. 'Do you mind telling me why I am here, yet again? *Please.*' I do not mean to sound so flippant, so irritated. I refrain from rising to my feet to greet him.

'I need to speak to Adam if you don't mind.' The good doctor's tone is chipped, relatively blank, matching a cold look on his face. I cannot read him. Usually, he is easy to read, easy on the eye. But not today. Oh, dear.

'I believe I have already told you. I do not control—'

'Cut the shit, David. We found the bodies.' The good doctor does not usually sound so *pointed.* I have certainly never heard him swear. It does not become him, yet I cannot tell him. It would be rather rude of me. He leans across the table, willing, it seems, to drag Adam from my unwitting body in pursuit of knowledge he assumes me rightfully able to provide.

'Bodies?' For a moment, I falter, wondering what he knows and what, if anything, they might have uncovered. I then realise it will be Adam, yet again confessing to murders none of these people care a damned thing about. 'Oh, my goodness, not again.' I am growing tired of the man now, unable to prevent my exasperated eyeballs from rolling back inside my head.

'How are you getting this information, David?'

I look across the table at the good doctor. I like it when he uses my first name. It makes me feel as if our relationship is becoming closer, finding a more relaxed place, entirely capable of turning into something else.

'Information?'

'We just need to know *how* you knew the locations of those human remains, seeing as no records seem to exist going back that far.'

'A lucky guess?' I am teasing, I know. I cannot help it. I am so naughty.

The good doctor sighs, closing his weary eyes for a brief moment. I sense the poor man is in much need of his morning coffee. 'David, please.'

'Why don't you ask Adam yourself instead of consistently badgering me for information I cannot give you?'

'That is *precisely* why you have been brought into the station this morning. To help us do exactly that.' The good doctor regards me for a moment, unsure how to approach the subject of my wildly differing personalities. He takes a breath, grabbing a chair opposite mine, stretching his long spine before offering me a genuine smile I am momentarily taken aback by. 'Come on, David. Surely you *want* to get better. Surely you want those men out of your head?'

'More than you will ever know, my dear fellow,' I reply stiffly, not in any way wishing to expose my unfortunate position.

'Then help me, so that I can help you.'

'Help *you* understand?' I am perplexed by such a question, confused as to how this poor man believes he can ever help me.

He nods.

I take a moment. Would the good doctor even want to understand? Would he care? *Would any of them?*

'How do I get Adam to talk to me?' he asks. I wish to leave this room, offer the good doctor a hot cup of strong coffee. Plenty of sugar. The poor man looks as if he needs it.

'You need to play nice, Doctor Flanigan,' I respond, not meaning to sound so flat. 'You need to play nice.'

'Nice?' I can see he is in no mood for my games. He has misunderstood my meaning. What a shame.

'How did you get those scratches?' The good doctor is staring at my forearm, my sleeve raised above my wrist, the bandage he carefully wrapped around my right hand still smelling of him. I tug it down, covering my potential embarrassment, further questions unrequired.

'My birds,' I reply coldly, needing to add nothing more on that subject. *Just my beloved birds.*

Twenty-Five

Newton

I left the interview room on the edge. On the edge of what, I had no idea, but whatever it was, it felt a little too close for comfort. I poured myself a coffee, drinking it in one go, most of it not even touching the sides, my taste buds unwilling to acknowledge a single drop. The police had absolutely *nothing* to go on, David's continued ability to summon dead bodies on cue, something they could *never* charge him for. Once again, he'd been pulled in for questioning, only to pull the wool over my eyes, now to be released without further action, the police left as baffled as I was.

'You okay, Newton?' I turned to see DS Alice Baker standing by my side, leaning in to grab an empty coffee cup from the countertop. Her perfume was nice. Distracting. I liked it.

I nodded when I honestly just wanted to shake my head in

frustration. I wasn't sure what it was about David that bothered me so much. I was used to patients with mental illnesses, of course. It was part of my job, nothing new, yet David made the tiny hairs on the back of my arms stand to attention, and I genuinely had no idea why.

'I don't suppose there's a spare bed going begging somewhere?' I joked, wondering if I could get away with pouring myself another coffee before falling asleep under the nearest table. I hoped she wouldn't take my innocent question as a proposal.

'You could always curl up in the corner,' Alice laughed, pointing towards an abandoned space to one side of the room, piled high with discarded folders and unwanted items—a bit like me. It fitted how I felt, my eyes ready to close on the spot. It seemed there were two things I didn't fare well without in life. Coffee, and sleep. Alice didn't know it, but I genuinely liked her. She was always the first to offer a smile I probably didn't deserve, able to ease my racing mind with a flash of a smile I found alluring—the woman easy on the eye. I had no idea what made her tick, what she liked. I didn't even know where she lived. I could ask her out, of course, but would that make me look desperate, stupid? Would she say no? I couldn't overthink it. I was too busy trying to stay awake.

Twenty-Six

Simon

It isn't raining, but if I close my eyes, I can hear a distant hum of patter against the old shutters of my parents' 1920s property. I take a slow breath, thinking of this old house—my childhood home. It isn't something I often do, but today seems to have tipped the balance of logic towards melancholy. Sitting alone in my mother's kitchen with only the sound of a rattling pipe for company feels impossible. Still, I cannot dwell on my apparent illness any more than I am willing to acknowledge a past I can no longer change. Instead, I clear away several dirty dishes, making a cup of hot cocoa to ease the pain of my racing thoughts.

The old clock in the hallway is still, so I amble into the darkened corridor to wind it. A once treasured sound of my childhood, this ageing grandfather clock now spends many hours in silence. I wind it carefully, the mechanics springing to life, its low, distinct tick filling the space once more, cushioning a void I do not entirely understand. I wipe a thick layer of dust from its once gleaming face, unsure how much grime can gather so rapidly. It has been too silent here since Mother's passing. Quieter than I could have anticipated, that's for sure. No longer do my ears ring with chatter from her daily chores, dinner she needs to prepare, her singing often allowed to fill the space with infectious enthusiasm. I unclick the basement door that rests soundlessly beneath the staircase, needing time alone with my memories. I reach out, my hand finding the light cord with ease, a familiar soft buzzing below me as the basement flickers into dim focus.

I have always loved the sound my shoes make as they tap merrily down these steps. This once treasured, albeit dust-filled environment below my mother's beloved home, a most revered place. It used to make me feel as if I was escaping reality, even for a limited time. She was unaware that I had turned this disused space into my "special place", poor woman, though none of that matters now. It became a place I entertained my guests, you see, our soft moans of pleasure able to lie unabated in secret, away from the imposing atmosphere above.

I giggle softly as I remove a cobweb that has attached itself to my hair, my recollection attuned, taking in these familiar surroundings as if I never left. I reach the bottom step with ease, grateful that nothing here has changed. Everything is as I left it, concealed — unbeknown to the rest of the world, the whole place berating a society that could never understand me. It is a shame I barely recognise my guests now, their faces turning to dust along with the steady decline of this decaying house. I take position on my once loved high-backed chair beneath a dangling light bulb, a spotlight cast upon my trembling body the only warmth provided. I barely recognise the corpses that sit in a circle around me. If it wasn't for the clothing they died in, I might not remember them at all. It is extremely upsetting.

Michael still sits where I placed him, hands in his lap, back straight, well presented should anyone visit—precisely how Mother would have liked him to be. Proper, correctly attired for such an auspicious occasion. Oh, how I remember my beautiful man. An accidental sob rebounds into the space, no fear of potential reprimand from the woman who hated any expression of emotion. Michael was my first love, you see, the first man I enjoyed spending time with—my earliest encounter into the world of homosexuality. Michael was the very first male I ever brought home to meet mother. The first man I allowed to *touch* me in places reserved only for those who deserved my special attention. I do not understand why such memories make me feel so downhearted now. Of course, Mother could never openly approve. She despised what she knew I was. We did not speak of such things. A mother and son should never discuss matters of the heart. It is not appropriate.

I glance around. A further *fifteen* men now sit before me, a requirement, a necessity, nothing more. Once my beautiful boy was dead, there was nothing more for me to do than increase the number of dead men around me. I did not expect to grow as fond of the sound and sight of death as I did, the electrifying echoes of men dying in my loving embrace, unanticipated. The feel of their cooling bodies as they lay next to mine, their fading, lustful moans—blood I can still taste long after they departed this earth. I close my eyes, recalling a time long past, glancing across the room in irritation. I rise to my feet, anger burning inside my chest for what that woman willingly put me through.

'How could you do this to me?' I spit loudly into the face of my most precious corpse. Mother does not respond. Her usual pained grin has been replaced now by a set of teeth that threaten to fall from the skull in which they are attached, eye sockets that hold no stare, unkempt strands of hair that no longer appear as thick and glossy as they once did. Beneath her favourite gloves are nothing more than fragmented, skeletal hands, resting on bony, unfeeling knees.

'You never understood me. You did not appreciate what I needed.' I place my hands over Mother's dead shoulders, nothing but brittle bones beneath my imposing fingertips. She hated me touching her, claimed I was unclean, sinful. 'You made everything bitter.' I stand upright, straightening my spine, no longer wishing to show my mother how weak I truly feel. She believed me feeble for many years, of course, my choices something she could never understand. So it is apt she found herself sharing eternity in the company of the very homosexual men she claimed to despise, dying almost as slowly as they did. The men I loved dearly once, left now to rest with the woman who loved *me* dearly once.

I kneel at the feet of my once adored creator and cry. I sob like the little boy she lovingly tucked into bed after the nightmares had abated. That same little boy who grew into a man she learned to detest. 'Why couldn't you have loved me for who I am?' I scream into her dead, blank face. 'It's your fault this happened.' I cover my ears as her hateful voice fills my head, death surrounding me now, the muffled screams of my beautiful male callers as they took their last breath on this magnificent earth, more than I can stand.

'I hate you, Mother,' I spit into her once beautiful face. 'I hate you.'

Twenty-Seven

Newton

With nothing else to do, I found myself driving across town to David's house, a veil of suspicion clouding my misguided judgment, my intention purely to speak to the guy on *his* territory—uncover whatever traumatic incident had no doubt triggered his deepening symptoms. Away from the prying eyes of the police, I felt he might open up to me. I arrived, however, to a locked building, no one inside to answer my repeated, consistent banging. *Where was he?* The only other location I could think of was Old Trent Road. The Frederick residence was a place of solace for David, although why, I had no idea. The house gave me the creeps. It baffled me how so many beautiful old buildings could be left forgotten— withering to dust, still owned by the dead, no court in the land able to change that annoying truth.

I abandoned my car on the pavement outside the house

and made my way around the back of the building, the terrible state of the front door prepared to give me nightmares for weeks. I knew, if anything, David would be in the kitchen, talking to either himself or Simon's long-suffering mother. He seemed to do that a lot. I could barely make out the shape of him moving around, the windowpanes looking as if they hadn't been cleaned for years. He was cooking, his back to me, occasionally mumbling to himself and a presumed invisible person in the room.

I fought the urge to wipe decades of dust and grime from the glass in order to gain a better vantage point, knowing it would draw attention I wasn't prepared for. It might even provoke an unfortunate side effect of pushing the ageing windows from their frames entirely. They didn't look as if they had been touched since 1936. I could understand why David had chosen Simon as one of his alters. Empty houses could well afford a man the headspace he might not otherwise achieve elsewhere. Time for reflection, private isolation. Personally, I would have found somewhere nicer than here, of course, but who was I to assume anything? Beggars couldn't be choosers.

I hesitated. I needed to speak to David but wasn't confident it would be wise to interrupt his moment of solitude. I understood more than most how crucial alone time could be. Time to gather your thoughts, reclaim a rapidly wandering sanity.

'May I help you?' David's overbearing and berating tone shifted me sharply out of my musing, the decision made for me as he emerged in a doorway which creaked and groaned in protest of having been moved, causing me to retreat, stepping back a few paces further than intended. I almost held up my hands to steady its long-suffering frame, expecting to be crushed where I stood.

'Sorry, I didn't mean to disturb you,' I muttered, feeling stupid. 'I was hoping to speak to you, if you don't mind.' I refrained from adding "in private". I didn't wish to be alone with David for a second longer than necessary.

David sighed, flicking a wrist towards the dimly lit kitchen, allowing me access I wasn't sure I wanted. Even in the brightest sunlight this place looked dark and cold. It wasn't pleasant. 'What *are* you doing here?' he asked.

'David, I—'

'Simon,' he corrected sharply, holding the palm of a disgruntled hand a few inches from my face. 'You are speaking to Simon, my dear man. If you do not mind.'

Twenty-Eight

Simon

A rustling outside the kitchen door is irritating, adding to my already bristled composure. Nobody knows I visit this house. Nobody cares what I do when alone, requiring much-needed privacy to reflect and unwind. I peek through the window to see Doctor Newton Flanigan hovering by the door, no doubt unsure what he is doing here. Oh my goodness, what is it with this man that seems to crawl beneath my skin so readily? I pull open the door before he is able to make a hasty retreat and change his mind. He appears sheepish as if he's been watching me. Is a man not entitled to some privacy? I hope he does not notice tears still lingering in my tired eyes. I look for a wedding band, finding no hint of skin rendered a lighter shade than the rest of his fingers. He isn't a homosexual. I know of such men. They take far better care of their appearance than this wretched fellow ever could.

Every inch of my body is screaming, demanding his imminent removal. I need him to leave me alone, never return. He tells me he wishes to speak with David or Adam, yet why my company is not good enough, I do not know. How very rude. I allow a sigh, flicking my wrist towards Mother's prized kitchen, allowing him entry I do not want. I step away from the door to allow him inside, oddly aroused by his scent, his laboured breath. To be honest, I do not care what troubles this fellow, I have enough of my own to contend with. I scoff, almost forgetting my manners, my thoughts still with my beloved companions below my restless feet, my mother's words still in my head.

'I was hoping to gain some valuable information—'

Valuable information? *Seriously?* 'You know, you really shouldn't probe.' I pour water into the kettle before placing it onto the stove. 'Tea?'

Flanigan shakes his head, too busy to be seen in my company for long, it seems. Is my tea not good enough for him? How typical.

'Probe?' he questions. I despise his voice. It grates against my current disposition, conflict building in my mind for how attractive I otherwise might find him.

'You will make him angry.' I am jesting, yet Flanigan does not know this.

'Who?'

'Jacob.' *Who else?*

'Is Jacob here?' Why does the man sound nervous by the concept?

I avoid acknowledging a laugh that suddenly finds its way

into my throat. 'Oh, you would know it if he was.'

'Why's that?'

I take a breath, closing my eyes, no longer wanting to share this space with a man who uses far too much soap and forgets to comb his hair. 'I forgot, I have no milk.' I turn around sharply, no longer comfortable in the man's presence. He is standing awkwardly by the open door. 'I wish you to leave.'

'I believe this house belongs to Violet Frederick.'

I shoot him a sharp look. Was that a question or a statement? 'Indeed. She is my mother.' How dare he refer to my mother so casually?

'Is?'

'Is. Was. All is relevant in time and space, don't you agree?'

'I would like to speak to either Adam or David, please.'

'Not today.' I shake my head before I accidentally say anything further.

'Oh, yes. Today.' Flanigan steps forward, smothering this space with his overbearing tone. How *dare* he question me in my own home?

I press my lips together, retaining focus, restraining my anger. Now is not the time to lose my temper.

'Why don't you take a look in the mirror, Simon?' Flanigan is very pushy. Under different circumstances, I might find it appealing.

'Now, why would I do that?'

'Humour me. Please.'

I sigh. If it gets him out of my house, I will comply. I step casually into my mother's front parlour, glancing briefly at my reflection in the mirror over the fireplace. It has peppered in places, blackened areas now overtaking the once gleaming reflective surface, most of it obscuring my view—the shine becoming almost as lost to time as I have, gone from a world we once both knew well. I motion my face from side to side. Apart from a few stray hairs requiring a barber, stubble I do not recall growing, I look like me.

'What do you see?' Flanigan is standing in the doorway. Imposing. Just like my father.

'I see a striking young man about to throw you out of his mother's house, my dear man,' I confirm with a snigger, turning my head in his direction. 'Please, do me the honour of leaving before things become, shall we say, less than polite.'

'You don't see the face of David Mallory?'

I swallow, not wishing to express the truth of the matter that I have been looking *only* at the face of David Mallory for many years. In my heart and mind, I *am* Simon Frederick. I have all my own faculties, my own memories. I know what Flanigan is trying to do, of course. He is trying to unsettle me. It is a shame my memories now encompass mostly pain and suffering, usually ending in the tragic death of those I once loved. I am, it seems, doomed to forever suffer the fate of my old life over and over, a relentless loop something I will never escape.

'Get out of my house,' I yell, accidentally taking on the guise of a madman. My tone would have mortified Mother, especially standing in her best room, thickened dust from the basement below still on my shoes.

'Not until I speak to Adam Mires,' Flanigan booms, standing his ground.

If the man is not so infuriating, I might find him alluring. Instead, I do not wish to express my displeasure or attraction, so I look away, glancing towards an ageing photograph of Mother and I in our best finery, taken one Sunday morning before Church. I cannot do this. Not today.

'Leave!' I spit, summoning the energy to face him head-on. Flanigan shakes his head, determined. I pick up the nearest thing I have to hand, only wishing to frighten the man, force him to back away. I do not intend to hit him with it, yet my hand is already raised as I find myself swinging a heavy candlestick across this man's cheek. Why do people *never* listen? If they did, they might not find themselves in trouble. Of course, I do not wish Flanigan any direct harm, he is the type of man I would enjoy spending time with, and he would make a much-improved addition to my collection. Yet, I see no other way to make him leave here. His presence today is inappropriate.

He makes a strange sound, his cheekbone exploding with the incoming weight of the heavy object, the cold metal in my hand enough to knock the man unconscious, if not to end his life. It is not my fault. I cannot be held accountable for such things now. Mother's voice screams at me from below, bitter words of anger I do not need inside my head.

'No, Mother. It could *not* be helped,' I shout into the overbearing silence of the room. Flanigan is lying on the floor, his head an open wound, blood already spilling onto the floor, forever staining the solid wood. I drop the offending weapon, furious I have been brought to this.

I wanted Flanigan to take the hint, *leave*. Yet I am now standing in a house that feels strange, as if it is someone else's home I have accidentally invaded. Being with the doctor always seems to alter my state of mind. I do not know why. He wanted me to open up to him, to talk about things I wish I had the courage to share with him. I stare at his crumpled body at my feet. It would be funny to see the look on his face if he knew *everything*.

Twenty-Nine

Jacob

I must confess I am surprised by the continued interference of this lowly gentleman, his nose forever entangled in the business of others. I am a trifle perplexed as to why Simon and David have become so resolved by the thought of his presence, a potential intimate acquaintance no doubt their ultimate aim. Yet who am I to condone such affection? We have never met, he and I, yet he lies now before me, a shrunken idiocy with little in the way of manners in which to display any resolve.

I wish to kick him awake, nothing but a stray dog at my feet, but I would forget my manners in such an unfortunate undertaking. It would be ungentlemanly of me, I know. Instead, I am prevailed upon to receive him in his own time, forced to yield my wants in respect of potential courtesy. Of course, I wish nothing more than for us to converse at length, seeing as we have not yet been properly introduced. It is most disgruntling. My eyes rest upon a man whom I suspect, no doubt (if his reserve can be answerable to the event) that he has not been well received here today. It is a shame. Yet, I cannot be held responsible for such an occurrence. I require his momentary companionship, for there is much to be discussed and little time in which to do so.

I am standing inside the unfortunate residence of Simon Frederick, or to be more precise, that of his long-suffering, overbearing mother. This building must have been a welcome retreat for the two of them at one time, a distraction from the world outside, yet I am reminded of the motion of time, forever grasping the jaws of steady decay.

A slight movement, the repositioning of a wayward limb oddly welcome to my senses, the distraction well received. The man is awakening. *Good.* I take a seat next to the fireplace careful to retain my manners, disguise my increased excitement. He sits up rubbing his head. A dark patch of blood now stains his fingertips, the floor below ruined. I refrain from offering an unrefined utterance to the effect, yet I find it all very pressing.

I am glad when he notices me, our eyes connecting for a brief moment that has the ability to delight my senses. My goodness, he is a striking fellow. I can appreciate why Simon and David have taken such affection towards him.

'What the *hell* did you do to me?' the man asks groggily, although it is a trifle impertinent of him to ask, seeing as I have no idea to what he is referring. I have, indeed, done *nothing*. I find his tone increasingly irritating.

'Why my dear man, I did nothing to see you in such a dismayed position.' It is true, of course, lest he should rile my irritation further. Then I may be forced to act upon my perplexed senses. 'From what I can gather, you are in this situation now due to your recent acquaintance with my dear friend, Simon.'

'Simon?' The man is muttering, a slurred vocalisation I cannot abide. 'Then who are *you*?'

'Forgive me.' I rise to my feet, my dubious surroundings rendering me forgetful of my status and position. 'Please allow me to introduce myself. My name is Jacob.'

I am given a lengthy glare, this not so *gentle* man appearing altogether obstinate in his mannerisms. How very rude.

'I wish to speak with David, or Adam,' he mutters, still clutching the side of his face. His tone is nervous. It is most ungracious.

It is unfortunate that this residence no longer employs staff to cater for our needs (that's if it ever did, of course), the poor fellow hovering mid-sentence, blood staining his skin and clothing, the flooring now requiring a deep scrub, afternoon tea something that would have gone down nicely, may I conclude. Yet as it is, we are resolved to remain parched, nothing to be done about such unfortunate matters in this instance.

'I do not believe David or Adam are with us currently,' I offer, motioning forward to help the poor fellow in his hour of need. I only wish to help him from the floor to a chair, remind him he is in delectable company. He flinches, moving sharply away from my approach. I raise my hands, meaning no harm in my actions. 'However, David has told me much about you,' I offer, wishing to denote a calm conversation. 'I do not judge you to be the type of person with whom he could so properly consult, and therefore I readily oppose seeing either man at this time.'

He is, if nothing else, punctual in his return, the laugh leaving his lips most unrefined. 'And David has briefly mentioned you,' he confirms, pressing a hand over his wounded head.

'How delightful.' I offer a relaxed smile, resting my hand against the edge of the fireplace, regretting my decision the instant I am greeted by a layer of thick, heavy dust. I glance at my palms before rubbing them together. No need to make a fuss. 'Pray, forgive me if I speak out of turn. I do not wish to be of any nuisance. I would ask, of course, what *exactly* David has divulged about me, but I do not wish to sound ill-advised.' I stand with my arms by my side, waiting for information I suspect will not be forthcoming. 'David and I speak often, you must understand, about *many* things. I have the understanding there is much to be learned about you, although what precisely, he did not say.'

I laugh, heartily, only wanting the poor man to feel at ease in my company. I have always prized myself upon my ability to receive others, entertain where possible—although it has been a while, I know. Such credible ability raised my status complimentary, once upon a time. However, this dubious fellow is unconvinced whether or not he should answer my query. 'Come, please, my good man, be seated.' I point to a neglected chaise longue, the thing in want of a good clean. No matter. It is out of *my* hands. I am grateful when Doctor Flanigan does as I ask, rising from the floor with a groan.

'I should go,' he motions to stand, his balance uncertain.

'I shall not hear of it,' I declare, brighter than intended. 'We have hardly become acquainted.' I have no fundamental understanding why the wretched gentleman finds my presence so perplexing. 'Your behaviour has, in every respect, been somewhat despondent.' It is true, of course, hardly worthy of attention.

'My behaviour?'

'Why, yes, of course.' Does this so-called doctor not appreciate the value of his own actions?

'David would *not* be pleased you're here.'

'Oh? And why would that be?' I resist an urge to laugh. It would be ungentlemanly of me. I cannot allow him to witness my darker side. Not yet.

'He seems afraid of you.'

'Oh, come now, on the contrary, my dear man. David and I are the closest of companions.' I regard the doctor for a moment, wondering if he appreciates how close he and I actually are? 'I am a doctor too, you know. We have much in common, you and I.'

'You're a doctor?'

It vexes me that he does not believe me. I refrain from expressing my distaste. 'Oh yes. I was once *very* well practised in my field. Until that unfortunate business put pay to my employ.' I swallow, wondering how much I can divulge without exposing my true nature. It matters little. It was a long time ago. Nothing of what happened then is important to this moment.

'Unfortunate business?'

'Why, yes. With Jack, of course. He and I shared a close bond, you see. Until...'

'Jack?'

I nod. 'Indeed. Although Jack wasn't his *actual* name. That was purely the name afforded to him by the press of our time. His true identity has never been revealed, and I made a solemn promise to my dearest friend I would take his secret to the grave with me. Which I am impressed to confirm, I did.' I am smiling now, recalling a time long past, a friendship most appealing, many lifetimes ago.

'What name?'

'Why, Jack the Ripper, of course.' I am given a dismissive glance.

'You claim to have known *Jack the Ripper?*'

His tone is disbelieving, condescending, his words slurred by a swollen cheek. I feel a distinct prickle of irritation rise against the hairs on my neck.

'You, good sir, ask too many questions. Do you not know it is rude for a gentleman to converse by means of questioning alone? I know almost *nothing* of your good self. Please, pray come, tell me more.' I wish only to ease this rapidly infectious moment.

'There is nothing about me you need to know.' He shakes his head, dismissively.

'I fancy, *Doctor Flanigan*, that obstinacy is a poor defect of character.' I sigh, this room, this conversation, growing now rather tiresome. 'Jack was always asking questions, forever pointing accusations my way.'

'I thought you said you and he were close?'

I take a breath, my mood shifting. 'Oh, indeed we were, once. But unfortunately, we were ambitious fellows, both seeking fame and fortune. Surely *you*, of all people, can understand such a concept?'

The doctor nods. I am grateful for the prevailing silence.

'Jack was a valued surgeon, as was I. But, unfortunately, our kind was not accepted.'

'Your kind?'

I smile. 'Men who prefer the company of other men.' I pause, hoping he understands. 'Jack and I were close. If you appreciate my meaning.' I close my eyes, recalling such a valued time in my life, regretting much of what happened thereafter.

The doctor laughs. It is inappropriate. He is shaking a trembling hand towards me. 'Hang on a minute. So, you're trying to tell me that Jack the Ripper was *gay?*'

I am perplexed. What is his meaning? *'Gay?* Sir, I do not believe that happiness has anything at all to do with a preference for—'

'Sorry, I mean homosexual.'

I am confused yet continue my explanation. 'We preferred the company of men, yes.' I do not wish to confirm that, for me, nothing has changed in *that* department. I have said enough.

'But Jack the Ripper killed prostitutes.'

His pointed words rile me, ensuring I straighten my spine

stiffly. 'Filthy whores, they were. Nothing more. Please, I do not wish to recall such wanton images.'

'The Ripper killed five women—'

'Four,' I cut in sharply. 'Jack killed *four* women. I, however, lay claim to four of my own. Not that any of those were documented.' It is a shame, yet nothing can be done about that now.

'No. Jack the Ripper killed Mary Ann Nichols, Annie Chapman, Elizabeth Stride, Catherine Eddowes, and Mary Jane Kelly.'

I have not heard those names spoken aloud for so very long. It is oddly perplexing to my ears, ensuring I must take a moment to gather my thoughts. 'Oh, no, sir. Mary Jane Kelly was one of *mine*.' I see the look of shock appear on the poor doctor's face, yet I am unable to fathom his thoughts.

'*You?*'

I nod. I am proud of my most famous deed, a deed that became infamous, although unfortunately not in my good name. 'It is unforgivable that Jack took the credit for her as well. I was aggrieved that it equally ended our friendship.' I do not wish to say anything further. I have said enough, and I feel discouraged by such painful recollections. 'I must speak no more. What I tell you now can give no fresh pain. You, sir, have been the most unexpected of visitors.' It is true. He has indeed lowered my mood.

'So have you,' he replies, condescendingly. His eyes set wide, his words crackling due to an unanticipated facial injury. I am glad when he rises, a swift exit seeing him head towards the front door. However, I cannot allow him to leave just yet. There is still much to discuss. Much for him to learn about *me*.

Thirty

Jacob

I do not often get to enjoy an audience with such a captive congress. Of course, David and I converse regularly in private, but I am usually forced to remain in perpetual silence, my outward existence rarely appreciated. I cannot allow the doctor to leave without understanding the truth of *who* I am.

'Doctor Flanigan? Will you not address me some more, my dear man?' I rise to my feet. My only aim is to ensure he turns to face me, yet his eyes are set wide as if he requires nothing more than to leave this house, escape my presence, claim back sanity he is unaware has left him. It is most aggrieving. I have done *nothing* to warrant such a distasteful, unappreciated response.

'I have nothing more to say to you, Jacob,' he mutters, one hand already on the door handle, the other clutching his throbbing face.

'You must understand, that we lived in a wonderful new world of industry and discovery, Jack and I. It was a vibrant time, a vibrant city. We were medical students together at the Royal London College of Science, something to prove, a purpose to fulfil, the whole of London society a fragment of the larger world in which we wished only to live and thrive.'

The doctor hesitates, stepping away from the front door, the doorframe of the parlour becoming his willing protector. I am grateful for his attention.

'I gave Jack the idea, you know.' I close my eyes, recalling our late-night discussions, the practice we eagerly required, our highly anticipated surgeon status incomplete.

'What idea?' The doctor is standing close enough to the doorway for a potential retreat if needed, yet he no longer seems desperate to leave, curiosity overtaking his attention.

'For his participants.' Those wretches became much-required subject matter on which to practice our devoted skills. Indeed, they should have *thanked* us.

'Participants?'

'Willing or otherwise.' I am being unkind. I cannot help it. *Filthy whores*, every one.

'You mean, victims?' Doctor Flanigan raises an eyebrow, momentarily forgetting his pain until the swelling reminds him, forcing him to wince.

I nod.

'Okay, if that's true, then why are *you* not famous?'

I take a breath, requiring a moment of reflection. 'I ventured far from London's depths in pursuit of my participants, assuming if I found young women who would *not* in any way be missed, I could hide my deeds from the rest of the God-fearing, law-abiding world, protect them from what they could never understand I *needed* to do. Jack, however, had a different plan. He readily welcomed the fame and notoriety that came from his documented misgivings.'

'And you?'

'Me?'

He nods. 'Yes. What did *you* want?'

I wanted *Jack*. I wanted what every good citizen requires from life. Love, companionship—an appreciation of who I was and what I felt I might one day become. I cannot, however, disclose such inner, painful emotions to the doctor. It is hardly appropriate. Instead, I smile blankly, wandering over to the window of Simon's mother's once cherished home to stare beyond to a world I no longer recognise.

'I, sir, wished to be happy.' It is not a comment I have intended to spill so readily. I am staring out of the window, unable to acknowledge this lingering truth. A change of subject is required. 'I find it disgraceful how *women* seem to find it entirely acceptable to wear nothing but their underwear these days.' I am looking onto a street filled with women in their under garments. It is unattractive, ungodly. I glance towards the doctor leaning against the doorframe, his potential escape accessible, his face still throbbing. I can see it in his expression. 'Don't you?'

He regards me, contemplating my underappreciated viewpoint. I wonder what he is thinking. He does not say anything. He is a hard man to read.

'*That* is why I had to kill Mary Jane Kelly. I needed to

show the whole of London society that I was a far more accomplished surgeon than Jack ever could be. However, it was sadly to become the end of our friendship.'

'How?' At least the doctor is participating again now, ready to relieve my one-sided conversation.

'Because I made quite a mess of the poor wretch, as I am confident you already know.' I offer Doctor Flanigan a sinister smile that is unfortunately not reciprocated. 'Jack wished to display *precise* surgeon skills, showcasing to high society he was a man to be taken seriously.'

'Really?'

'You do not believe me?'

'No.'

'Then why do you believe Jack and I chose our participants?'

'Because you hate women.'

I swallow, momentarily forgetting my place, my manners. The doctor is correct in his assumption, although not for his readily presumed reasons. I press my lips together. '*Hate* is a strong word, do you not agree?'

'No. Not really. It is fully documented what Jack the Ripper did to his victims, how he treated those poor girls.'

I allow a sigh I do not intend, wishing wholeheartedly he would refrain from using the word *victims*. 'Poor girls?' I almost lose my composure, my lunch. 'Those creatures were nothing more than common whores. Disgusting vile wretches who received precisely what they deserved.'

'And I suppose that has nothing to do with the fact that Jacob Pointer was apparently a gay—sorry, *homosexual*—man, living during a time that did not accept men like him. You hate women purely because you hate what *you* are, what you see when you look at yourself in the mirror? Am I correct?'

How dare this man presume to know my mind? He is referring to Jacob as if he and I are two separate entities, my previous actions wholly invented for the purpose of this very conversation. I do hate myself, always have, my inability to change anything about who I am ensuring the ultimate path I took. I cannot confirm this, of course, instead needing to reclaim this moment, retake my power. My inner demons that have never left me. They threaten to dislodge my composure, overthrow my sanity.

'Come, sir, will you not sit?'

'I don't need to sit down.'

Oh, but I do. I take a seat on the edge of the chaise longue, hoping for a moment of consolation, disturbed now by the way this conversation is turning.

'If you knew Jack, why won't you name him?'

The doctor is relentless. 'I promised I never would.'

'I don't believe you knew Jack the Ripper at all. That's why you can't give me his real name.' The man is walking towards me as if he *knows* me, has nothing to fear from my presence. However, it is not something he wishes to undertake lightly. It may not be suitable for the poor fellow's overriding health.

'Jack and I loved each other. It is not my fault he grew weary of the little time afforded us, wishing, as I did, to be accepted by a world that would never acknowledge us. I refute your pained words. You mock me as if you believe you know me. You do not.'

'Then tell me.'

'I killed Mary Jane Kelly to show Jack that I, too, was worthy of his attention. He went out into the city each night, away from me, killing where he could, provoking much panic within the community. Two evenings after the death of that *whore*, Jack and I fought. He was pained by my interference, expressing volatile disdain for my actions with a fist to the jaw.' I close my eyes, recalling the incident that ended my life. It is a regrettable tragedy.

'Care to elaborate?'

'It was the night I met my end, the River Thames capable of claiming many lives.' I glance towards the doctor, unimpressed that I have been forced to uncover my ultimate downfall so readily. I recall the water, cold, heavy—a thick, choking mud that dragged me to my doom. 'You do not know of my end, sir?' Was my downfall not documented?

He shakes his head. I sense he does not wish me to add to my story.

'I did not intend to fall, of course, or lose my footing, Jack's wrath most unanticipated.' I cannot tell him I never learned to swim. I never told Jack. If I had, things might have been different.

'And what about the others?'

I close my eyes. 'Others?'

'*Your* victims?'

I smile, wildly recalling an unbridled passion for wilfully slicing those whores to pieces. I cannot say such words aloud, though I found it most pleasurable. 'None were documented.

It is unfortunate. I moved their bodies. Hid them away.'

'You hid them?'

I nod. 'To a place where I could sit and watch them decay to the dust they deserved to be, in a hell I had willingly created for them.' I must appear deranged to this fellow, insane, unstable. I cannot help it. It is the way of things—disused barns, overgrown woodlands, remote lakesides, each holding secrets yet to be unearthed. It must be challenging for poor Doctor Flanigan to appreciate my art. His job, of course, is to understand the minds of the wretched, yet I assume he could *never* understand mine.

Thirty-One

Newton

I couldn't get out of that house fast enough. I'd heard some impulsive stories in my time, but this? David was a master of diversity, able to change his tone of voice with relative ease depending on who he claimed to be from moment to moment. Even the language he used was impressive, representable of whichever character he was portraying at any given time. If I closed my eyes, I might believe I'd accidentally slipped face-first into a Charles Dickens novel. *Speaking of which.* I climbed into my car to inspect my face in my rear-view mirror, my cheek feeling as if it had been caved in with a sledgehammer. *Thank you, David.*

I prodded a bruise threatening to erupt, angry blood in my hair, glad at least I still had all my teeth. Nothing seemed broken. *Thankfully.* Apart from my ego. I glanced towards the house. A hollow, shapeless form lingered in the hazy windowpane I tried not to stare at, the last few minutes surreal. Jacob Pointer was undoubtedly the troublesome character I'd built in my mind, yet I wasn't anticipating a full-on "Jack the Ripper" connection. I understood, of course, for reasons known only to himself, David had created his alters from dead killers. But *Jack the Ripper?*

I had to physically prevent myself from racing to his window when he spoke of women wearing nothing but their underwear, (wondering if I was missing something interesting) before realising he was speaking from the viewpoint of a Victorian. To any self-assured Victorian gentleman, modern summer dresses would have indeed appeared indistinguishable from undergarments worn by women of that time. I thought about the unfortunate body I'd witnessed, the way her insides had been cut out, organs carefully placed across her torso. Exactly like the Ripper's victims. I knew Paul was irritated with me for forcing him to retrieve centuries-old bones, yet I couldn't dwell on mud-covered corpses, the Ripper victims, or David Mallory as I dialled my friend's number, the incoming tone threatening to burst an eardrum and create yet more drama I didn't need.

'Any chance I can get Thomas Mallory's care home address?' I held my breath, expecting a torrent of abuse I couldn't avoid forever. No time for pleasantries today. We might be friends, but Paul had specifically told me to leave it alone. It wasn't my fault I found some.

A sigh. 'Why?'

'I want to see if he can shed some light on his son.'

'You know he's got dementia?'

'Of course.'

'*Fine.* You got a pen?' I wasn't expecting him to sound so calm, anticipating an ear bashing, his berating tone hitting me with almost as much force as David's candlestick.

'Hang on,' I muttered, scrambling for something to write with, something to write *on*, grateful to Steph and her obsession with leaving pens in my glove box. I hastily wrote David's dad's address on the back of an unopened envelope.

'You might not get much from him,' Paul concluded, sounding busy as always, his multitasking quite impressive. That didn't matter either. My aim was to meet the guy, find out whatever I could about David. I didn't reply. 'You okay, Newt?'

I couldn't tell my oldest friend that I had just encountered the potential personality of a dead Victorian who'd claimed a victim of one of the most prolific serial killers of all time. Plus, my face was still throbbing. 'Sure. Just tired. Been a long week.'

'*You've* had a long week? Shit, try digging up bones I wasn't meant to be going anywhere near.'

I sighed. *Here comes the sarcasm.* I was waiting for that, although I probably deserved it. 'Yeah, sorry. I'm just trying to get a feel for David—'

'Why are you so obsessed with him?'

'*You* asked me to take a look at him in the first place.'

'I only wanted you to assess the mind of a guy claiming to have buried a two-hundred-year-old body—'

'That's precisely what I'm trying to do,' I cut in. I still had Jacob Pointer in my head and a headache now to complete the image.

'Okay, so when should I expect the profile for a killer I *can* catch?'

I sighed, knowing I was procrastinating on the subject of David Mallory. There was much about him that made no sense. 'Meet me in Billy's after work for a drink. We need a catch up anyway.' And I definitely needed a drink.

'Okay, but Newt?'

'Yeah?'

'Be careful.'

~

I hate care homes. They promote a feeling of impending doom around every corner, invoking panic I can never rationally explain. Hospitals are no different hence I avoid those too, where possible. I stood by the main door, next to a solitary rose bush, grateful for a moment of distraction, several bees frantically collecting nectar, the fresh scent of rose petals welcoming. When a tall, narrow hipped woman appeared, she expressed the look of a stern headmistress—reddened cheeks, a small, unsympathetic mouth completing her unassuming face. *Bloody hell.* I couldn't smile even if I wanted to. I didn't need the discomfort such action would provoke. I couldn't overthink the concept that I looked as if I'd been beaten to a pulp.

After explaining who I was and showing her my identity badge, I was reluctantly allowed entry, grateful for the nod of an overworked head as she stepped to one side. A long hallway was lined with photographs of many residents both dead and alive, familiar faces of friends and family designed to jog old memories, potentially giving these residents something to cling onto life for.

'Tom?' The care assistant called to an elderly gentleman in a nearby room, slumped awkwardly in a high-backed armchair as if someone had forgotten he existed. He was staring blankly out of a misted patio door, this empty space imposing. He was absentmindedly twisting ageing fingers around a length of wool as he glanced my way, an expressionless smile spread across pale cheeks. His face was lined with creases only a full life could provide, his eyes glazed as if he had been elsewhere for some time.

'There's someone here to see you.' The woman cupped his hand in hers as Tom patted it with familiarity. When she turned to me, however, her impromptu warmness slipped. I stepped back. She didn't know me, didn't need to concern herself with pleasantries on my behalf. 'Don't tire him out,' she stated snippily before leaving the room—though not before offering my throbbing face a lingering stare. I was then left with this ageing and frail-looking gentleman who equally now sat looking at my injuries. *Brilliant.*

'Who are you?' he asked. His voice crackled, yet his eyes held a kind glint, shielding a personality slowly fading with time. I stared at him, unable to fathom the idea of growing old, the concept of being unable to think straight or tie your own shoelaces rendering me momentarily speechless. How *should* I introduce myself? Should I blurt out the recent, disturbing police discoveries or David's increasingly troublesome behaviour? Indeed, how much of his *son* would this poor man now recall? More importantly, did I wish to drag up whatever painful memories might still be lingering behind his already delicate recollection?

'Get me a cup of tea, will you lad?' he asked out of nowhere, as if he needed me to *do* something for him or *leave*. He shook his head, shaking off my presence, no different to a dog shaking off unwanted rainwater.

A tiny smile pulled at my mouth, my swelling face momentarily eased by this innocent request. Tom smiled back. This old man appeared a good soul, different to his son, it seemed. Thankfully. 'Of course,' I replied, stepping into the corridor to find help and tea that now eluded us both. It only took a few moments, but by the time I'd made my way back to the visitor lounge, Tom was standing by the fireplace staring at a wooden clock with a broken glass face.

'What time is it?' he asked, staring at the clock as if he'd never learned to tell the time.

'It's just gone three, Tom,' I replied, unsure how to broach the subject of his wayward son, the reason for my visit becoming less important the longer I was in Tom's company.

'Oh.' Tom seemed unconcerned, shifting his attention back to his chair by the window.

'Do you need any help?' I felt terrible for asking, yet I couldn't stand and helplessly watch him struggle to lower frail legs into fabric much older than he was.

'Oh no, lad, I'm good.' He turned my way as if it was the first time he had noticed me. 'Get me a cuppa, will you?'

'It's coming,' I replied. I perched myself gingerly on a

hard-backed chair next to his. 'I'm Doctor Newton Flanigan,' I confirmed, realising we'd not yet been introduced.

Tom nodded, my name of no relevance, no consequence to his day. He picked up the wool and began twisting it around in his fingers.

'It helps my arthritis,' he told me, assuming (correctly) that I was wondering. 'Old hands, you see.' Tom stretched out his fingers, clenching them against his palms several times to convey the idea that twisting wool around fingers helped keep old bones agile. *Who knew?* 'Are you here to see me?' he asked.

'I am,' I replied, taking a breath. 'I was wondering if I could speak to you about your son?'

Tom glanced skyward as if something had sparked his interest, though not for long. 'Really? That's nice.' He sighed, returning his attention to the wool.

I nodded. 'Yes, Tom. About David.'

Tom shot me a cold look, sadness still lingering. 'David?' Tom placed the wool into his lap, smoothing it out in a long, straight line. 'He was an extraordinary boy, you know,' he confirmed sullenly. It had the unfortunate side effect of making him look older than he probably was. His mind was reliving some terrible past event, guilt growing in mine for having placed it there. Tom shook his head. 'But he was an odd boy. Obsessed with the Ripper stories. You should have seen his room.' I straightened, my interest piqued, begrudgingly of course. I hoped Tom wouldn't notice. 'David would keep the door of his bedroom locked, never allowed us inside. Not even his mum.' Tom closed his eyes. 'He was a strange boy. Such a loner. Yet, so bright, so inquisitive. He had much potential.' Tom laughed, recalling an old memory he didn't feel the need to share with me. 'He was just months away from securing a degree in medical science. It was a shame about the voices.'

'Voices?'

'Most unforgiving things they were. He began having conversations with himself around the age of eight, or thereabouts.' Tom shook his head, shaking off this wavering memory as if he wasn't convinced it was correct. 'I think.'

'Conversations?'

'Oh, yes. His mother and I would often hear him in his room, chatting quietly. Sometimes the conversations were heated, as if he was arguing with someone who wasn't even there.'

'Did you ever hear what he said?'

Tom shook his head. 'Ramblings mostly, nothing that made sense to me.'

I wanted to press him but knew of his delicate state of mind. Nevertheless, I was impressed by how rational he sounded. No sign of dementia at all now.

'He was going to become a surgeon, you know.' Tom smiled with old pride. 'Until things went wrong, forcing him to drop out of medical school.'

'Oh?'

Tom shrugged, waving a free hand towards me as if he didn't want to say anything further about that.

'Did he ever mention the name, Jacob Pointer?'

Tom looked as if he'd heard the name before somewhere,

although not for a very long time. I sensed he knew it well, remembered it more clearly than he was letting on. He didn't reply.

'Did David ever mention a *friend* he referred to as Jacob, or Jack?' I was pushing it, I know. I couldn't help myself.

Tom shook his head. 'I don't know.'

'How long did David talk to himself?'

'Years. Until—'

'Until?'

'Things escalated around seven years ago.'

'What happened seven years ago?'

'His mum and sister died.' Tom was fading now, his mind drifting to a time long past.

'I'm sorry to hear that.' I *was* sorry. I didn't want to leave the poor man with those memories in his head. Visions of Rachel Gates flooded my mind, this man's daughter mutilated, her brother tipped over the edge.

'Did you know that David has a *secret*?' Tom was staring at me.

'A secret?' Where had that come from?

Tom leaned forward, glaring intently into my eyes. I was about to repeat my question when we were interrupted by a nurse carrying a tray of tea and biscuits. 'Tea,' Tom declared from nowhere, sounding more like an excited child than a man of advanced years.

'Are you boys having fun?' she asked as she placed the tray onto a nearby table.

Tom sat upright, the thought of a cup of tea lifting his mood far more than I'd managed to achieve. I didn't take it personally. He held grasping hands towards an incoming cup, his fingers waving frantically in the air like a toddler. The nurse handed him a lid-covered plastic beaker, his trembling hands unwilling to cooperate.

'Thank you,' he stated as the first warm sip touched his lips. The nurse smiled and left the room, Tom now more interested in his cup of tea than our previous discussion.

We sat in silence for a moment whilst Tom drank, the man occasionally releasing a satisfied sigh that made me smile. 'You can't beat a nice cuppa, can you, lad,' he said, lifting his plastic cup towards me several times.

I smiled, allowing Tom time to enjoy his tea before attempting to reinstate our conversation.

'You were telling me about David's secret, Tom,' I queried, my voice almost as shaky as Tom's hands. 'Tom?' No answer. 'Are you okay?' I asked, the long pause threatening to engulf the room.

'Yes,' Tom replied between bites of shortbread biscuit and sips of tea that dripped carelessly onto his shirt. He had crumbs on him. The man was muttering sullenly, absent now, staring at the wool in his hand without recognition. He stopped drinking and looked towards the clock on the mantlepiece. 'My wife and daughter passed away a few years ago. But you wouldn't remember them.'

I thought about Tom's dementia, my mother's own battle with the illness, my inability to cope with any of it until it was too late, Isaac's annoyance with my continued absence. She had rare moments of clarity mixed with complete non-observance of who her family were. It wasn't a memory I needed in *my* head right then.

'Who are *you?*' Tom asked, as if we hadn't yet been acquainted, his eyes blank, unconcerned by any words I might have to offer. 'Do you want a cup of tea?'

I rose to my feet, knowing I had all I was going to get from the man today. I didn't want to push things and promote more aggravation from Paul or the staff here. 'I appreciate your time, Tom,' I offered, stepping forward to shake the old man's hand.

'Did I give you some?' Tom queried as he took my hand in his, puzzled now by my presence. I was impressed that, for an older gentleman, he still had quite a grip. It was a shame about his mind. I nodded, turning to leave, already halfway across the room before he spoke again.

'Thank you,' he stated firmly. I turned around to see him sitting upright, his eyes once again bright and sharp, wholly aware of his surroundings, his plastic beaker dangling by his side. 'I appreciate you talking to me about David. I've lived with the unknown surrounding that boy for many years. Why do odd things happen around him? Why did he not protect his mother when he had the chance? Why did he let his sister die like *that?*' Tom swallowed hard, something in his throat almost choking him. I couldn't help it when a lump formed in my own. 'So many whys,' he added, closing his eyes tightly against an incoming tear.

'What do you mean, Tom?' I queried, needing to know more, desperate for any information I could get. How much did he know about Rachel's death? *How* was his son involved? I stepped forward but Tom simply looked at me now as if he could see straight through me. I no longer knew what to say to him, my earlier uncertainty creeping once more into my mind. 'I'm grateful you were able to talk to me,' I muttered quietly before leaving Tom to his tea and biscuits, the woollen length in his palm unravelling along with his memories. I wondered how long he would be able to recall my visit today before his mind once again filtered out any truth he had once known, painful or otherwise.

It was too late for Tom to find any real closure for his past, his lucid moments few and far between. I made my excuses and left, downtrodden. The idea that Paul would, yet again, chastise my choices and mock my terrible decision-making abilities lingered in my thoughts long after I climbed into my car and drove away. I was glad I had spoken to Thomas Mallory, yet I felt sad for him, oddly lamented that his cherished memories were slowly fading forever. Dementia is a cruel disease. I did not need *that* idea in my head either.

Thirty-Two

Newton

Billy's Bar was a favourite of Paul's and the reason I'd chosen to meet him here. I was late, as always, my thoughts permanently elsewhere.

'Where have you been?' he asked, disgruntled as usual. He was propped against a wall, phone in hand, his mind a heady mixture of stress and responsibility he struggled to juggle. I knew how he felt. 'Why couldn't we do this at the station?' His South London accent was usually thick, confidant, slightly arrogant, although not today. Today his tone did not match his outward, sometimes aggressive-appearance, his features now almost as flustered as mine.

'Sorry. Got held up.' David was still in my thoughts. Which one, I couldn't say, but I needed space in which to think it all through, a friendly ear provided by an old friend, away from the overbearing buzz of the Eastcliff police station.

I wasn't confident I wanted the hustle of such an active place in my head.

Paul was still on his mobile as we entered the tiny building, a rich aroma of beer and coffee grabbing my immediate attention. There is something about coffee that offers my brain clarity I can never find elsewhere. I wondered if beer had an equal effect on Paul. It was fairly dark inside, the warmth of this space a welcome relief from the fresh summer breeze that had developed outside, the British weather as unpredictable as ever. Rows of coloured vintage light bulbs dangled from ceilings showcasing industrial steel lined walls adorned with hanging planters of all shapes and varieties. I could see why Paul liked it here. I imagined sitting happily by a window, absentmindedly watching the bustle outside for hours with no one in the world to disturb my thoughts.

'I'll grab us a drink. You grab a table,' he instructed as he headed towards the counter and an overly enthusiastic employee who immediately greeted him with a fond embrace. Instinctively, I chose a window table and sat down, glad to take the weight off my aching legs, my cheek still throbbing, grateful for a moment of solace. The town was always alive with such activity that a person could sit for hours and not notice the same things twice. From a large, imposing window of this tiny unassuming bar, I could sit and watch locals discuss their day, enquire about local gossip, comment on local issues.

'Here you go.' Paul sat opposite me as he placed a large mug of black coffee onto the tabletop, sipping a frothy beer as if his life depended on it. He released a loud sigh, confirmation that, like me, he had the day from hell. 'Jeez, I needed this,' he exclaimed, savouring the moment as if this was the best part of his week. I knew him well, understood the way he operated, happy to share his enthusiasm for such a simple pleasure. Although he was looking directly at me, he seemed to be staring through me, as if he believed me to be as transparent as I currently felt.

'So?' Paul was gulping his beer, no time for potential taste, it seemed.

For a moment, I almost forgot why we were here. 'Yeah, sorry. It's been one of those days.'

Paul waved a free hand towards me casually as if dismissing my inability to communicate, the beer in his hand more important than anything I might have to say. 'I can relate to that, Newt,' he breathed, displaying a blank expression I couldn't read. 'Anyway, how are you doing with my profile? I was expecting you to have it already.' He glanced out of the window, omitting to confirm I was usually far more organised.

I nodded, knowing I'd cobbled together the profile during my sleepless hours in front of my laptop that very morning. Did I tell him *why* I was holding back? Would he understand? I sighed. 'Your guy will be a respected member of the community. Clever, extremely knowledgeable of human anatomy, no doubt a doctor or science expert. But he won't currently be practising his profession, probably struck off for some reason. Because of this, he will be unable to access his victims directly, so he must seek them out. He is probably a gay man. Why? Because the violence he expresses towards women isn't typical, as if he feels he should be one way, but can't conform to what society expects.' I was drinking coffee between my carefully considered declarations, waiting for Paul to make the connection that had been in my head all day. David Mallory.

'How long did it take you to come up with that?' Paul was not impressed.

I shook my head. 'I wanted to check a few things first.'

'Check what?'

I swallowed, my coffee threatening to choke me. 'David Mallory.'

'Jesus Christ, Newt.' *Here we go.* 'Will you please forget about David for a moment.'

'I went to see his dad today.' I waited for Paul's acknowledgement, my request for the care home address something I knew he wasn't impressed with, despite saying nothing to deter me from my cause. There was none. 'He told me his son was obsessed for many years—'

'Obsessed with what?'

I took a breath. 'With Jack the Ripper.'

Paul furrowed his brow, shaking his head as if I'd actually gone mad. 'And you think—'

I nodded, not waiting to hear what Paul had to say on the subject. 'I *think* it might be connected.' Paul scoffed. I ignored him. 'It makes sense. Think about it. How many cases have you seen in your career that has even come close to the one we've been forced to deal with?' I knew Paul would appreciate the truth of *that*.

'But David is a delusional idiot. He'd probably confess to any cold case out there, given a chance.'

'According to his dad, he was studying for a degree in medical science. He attended medical school but dropped out.'

'Why?'

'I don't know. Thomas Mallory has dementia, you know.' I didn't mean to sound sarcastic.

'I told you that you wouldn't get much from the guy.'

'I don't think he was lying about David, though. It was almost as if he was scared of him. There's something else, too.' I took a swig of coffee. 'He wondered why so many odd things happen around his boy and why David did not protect his mother when he had the chance.' I was chewing my bottom lip, momentarily unconcerned by the developing bruising on my cheek. 'He also wanted to know why he allowed his sister to "die like that"?' I paused. 'He said David has a secret.'

'What does *that* mean?'

I shrugged.

'Did you get any information from Thomas Mallory that we can *use*?' Paul was behaving as irritated as I felt.

'Did you identify the latest bodies?' I needed to change the subject.

Paul nodded, giving me one of his "thanks for that" looks. 'Two males. One would have been in his teens, the other between thirty and fifty.'

'John and Henry Bull,' I muttered, recalling Adam's overly detailed description.

'If you say so.' Paul had finished his beer, readily looking around for a refill.

'How long had they been there?'

'You know very well the answer to that,' Paul snapped. 'I told you to leave it. The department is stretched enough as it is.'

I pulled a face. 'Sorry about that. I just needed to know.' I couldn't allow something as trivial as police funding to determine the direction of my curious mind.

'Know what?'

'That Adam was telling the truth.'

Paul laughed, leaning back in his seat as if he'd heard a ridiculous joke. 'How can he *possibly* be telling the truth? Can you hear yourself? The bodies are *hundreds* of years old for crying out loud. David is thirty-eight.'

I sighed. 'I know. I can't explain it any more than you, but I believe he deserves a closer look.'

'Why? Because he readily confessed to the locations of long-buried bodies?'

'No. Because he fits the profile of our killer. And...' I paused.

'And what?'

'The seven-year gap. David was in Manor Hill for the last seven years. Until last month.' We both knew killers didn't just take breaks. If anything, becoming increasingly arrogant as time passed. The timeframes fitted.

Paul took a breath, the resulting air released far slower than was comfortable for either of us. He knew I was right. 'Fine. I'll look into him. But Newt, if you have this wrong—'

'Yeah, I know. It's my neck on the line.' We sat in silence for a few minutes, the tension oddly annoying. 'Do you have any new information on the mutilated women or Annie Cormac?'

'We found a trace of blood on the most recent victim. It's just a trace, but it matches DNA found on a strand of hair taken from Janet Gates. It is enough to link them. It looks like we're dealing with the same killer.'

'So it *could* be David?' All they needed was to bring him in, take a sample. I didn't like the idea I was considering he might have killed his sister. It didn't bear thinking about.

Paul gave me one of his looks. I glanced away, not needing his thoughts on that subject. 'The marks and bruising found on the latest woman's body were not fresh though, already discoloured. The lab feels they were most likely caused by an older attack, maybe from a client, or her pimp.'

'So the killer didn't beat her?' It wasn't comforting.

Paul shook his head. 'As for Annie Cormac, she was last seen on CCTV outside a club in the town centre around one o'clock of the morning she disappeared, dressed as if she was looking for attention. If you know what I mean.' I did, and I didn't like it.

'Did you find out who Tony McNally is?'

'Yeah. A low-level scumbag. He's been in and out of prison since he was fifteen on drug related charges, burglaries. You name it, the guy's probably done it.'

'Why would Annie Cormac get involved with someone like that?'

'You tell me.'

'Does he have an alibi for the nights the other victims went missing?'

'Doesn't need one.'

'Why not?'

'Because the guy has been in prison for the last three months.' Paul tilted his head to one side, as if he'd only just noticed my existence. 'By the way, what the hell happened to your face?'

Thirty-Three

David

A ringing phone jolts me out of a witless dream, and it takes a few moments before I can catch my breath. No dream has ever felt so tremendously real, yet so distant, my mind struggling to hold onto the images playing violently inside my head. The room's calming ambience slowly brings me back into focus, yet I dare not open my eyes for fear of dislodging this moment of clarity. I know, of course, I cannot lie here forever, the phone disrupting my solace with its incessant noise. I place clammy palms over my ears to ease my racing thoughts, unable to prevent the vomit threatening to erupt.

'Hello?' My unexpected strained voice jolts me further out of my slumber, back into a stark reality I am not yet ready to acknowledge.

'Davy?' A small voice cuts further into my solace. It is Frank, my neighbour. His familiar, ageing vocals filling my ears as I find myself back in my front room, spread flat across the sofa. The blinds are pulled shut, my nerves in tatters, a sickening feeling in the back of my throat I cannot dislodge. I sigh, taking a breath, glad for the momentary distraction, the untethered dream of my father still lingering.

'Uncle Frank?' I automatically smile at the familiarity of this once cherished childhood voice. Frank is not my uncle by blood, more a substitute family member forged since birth. He and his wife Clara have lived next door for years. They babysat my sister and I when our parents took a night off, read bedtime stories when my mum was busy making fruit pies, creating new recipes from the fruit produced in her Victorian garden, nothing in our house ever going to waste. Yet Frank sounds solemn now, as if there is something he needs to say, but is too afraid to open his mouth. 'Is everything okay?' I sit upright, leaning across my parents old sofa, springs groaning.

Frank swallows. 'The home has been trying to reach you, son. I'm so sorry.' He is whispering, holding back tears I am currently unaware of the reasons behind. 'But I'm afraid I have to tell you that your dad passed away an hour ago.'

For a moment, I assume he is joking. My father, of course, cannot be dead. The man is strong. *Immortal.* He will be in my life forever. 'Frank, stop it. You cannot say things like that to me over the phone. It isn't funny.' I almost laugh, rolling my eyes, knowing the old man's wicked sense of humour often borderlines distaste.

Frank remains silent. He *isn't* joking. I lower myself to the floor before I fall onto it, the incoming thud something neither of us would appreciate. 'A heart attack,' he confirms into my strained ear. 'It would have been quick. He would not have suffered.'

I'm not sure if I am meant to feel glad about such a concept. Am I supposed to feel relief that my father did not suffer during his last moments on this earth? Despite our hit and miss relationship, my father has been my only constant in life, the one person holding me in place, keeping me functioning, albeit not for a continued lack of acceptance.

'Did you hear what I said, Davy?' Old Frank's voice echoes through the phone, yet he already sounds hollow somehow.

'I heard you, Frank,' I whisper, feeling as if I've missed the entire conversation.

'Your dad was proud of you. You that know, don't you?'

I shake my head, knowing Frank cannot see my disturbed features, a lump already forming in my throat for a truth Frank has never known. *Proud?* The very word insinuates I am somehow a good person. I am not. The very declaration now renders me unable to speak. I close my eyes a mere moment, that's all, yet it is enough to allow my thoughts to travel, my mind to wander. Frank continues to speak, yet I am no longer listening, lost deep within my own head, confusion apparent.

'I will speak to you again, of course. To arrange—' Frank's voice trails off. We both know he wants to say, "to arrange the funeral."

'Of course,' I mutter in shock, not able to focus on anything.

'Your dad was a good man. He will be sorely missed.' Frank is crying. I cannot comfort him. It is a shame.

I thank my father's oldest friend for his honest, thoughtful words and hang up feeling numb, lost in a world where my emotions no longer make a shred of sense. It is as if the universe is slowly devouring me, piece by fragmented piece, threatening to leave nothing behind of my once rational personality. I'm convinced that, at one time, I must have felt *something* other than repulsion and confusion for my own existence. My father has been my one consistent throughout everything that has happened over the last few years; losing my mum; losing my sister, Rachel; my unfortunate incarceration; Dad losing his mind. Now, it seems, I am on my own. Worse still, I can no longer tell my father how much I love him. I hope somehow, somewhere, he knows.

I wonder if he is with Mum now. I want to hold onto the idea that my parents have been reunited in that other place, and that everything will be okay for them. Thoughts of my dream return once more, lingering in my head long after it has faded. Was it a sign? The end of my relationship with a father I adore, yet failed often to tell him? The end of my shallow life in a bustling town I assumed I was a willing part of? The end of my childhood, my life? Nothing will ever be the same again now. Of that, I am certain. Yet where I go from here, I simply do not know.

I wander aimlessly into the kitchen. Nothing seems natural, as if the world has slowed down without me. It is probably just my brain, I know, yet I pull open my freezer door and stare at my cherished prizes, the icy air alien to my skin. Glass jars of differing sizes adorn each shelf, a brimming collection I am proud of, carefully labelled, cautiously stored. I have been locked inside my head with The Others for so long, my collection is simply a way for me to claim something for *myself*—something that is purely for *me* and no one else. Nobody will ever understand that, of course. Sometimes even *I* do not understand.

From this angle, my freezer looks sinister, jars crammed with frozen, bloodied body parts, tattooed skin preserved for later attention, my genuine aim to create wall hangings from them at some point. I have often wondered if passing visitors will comment, a secret smile on my face as they deliberate over my creations. Would they know they are human skin? Who now will appreciate my work as I'd always hoped my father one day would? Who else can I share my feelings and thoughts on such matters? I close my eyes, recalling the very day he learned the gruesome truth of his only son, the way he looked at me, those all-seeing eyes, witness to my true existence for the first time in his. But of course, dementia took that moment from us, too. It is a travesty, I know. I wonder if he remembered that day, when alone, no one to deter his limited considerations. Is that the secret my father wished for me to atone for? It doesn't matter. Nothing will ever matter again now.

Thirty-Four

Newton

By the time we left Billy's, Paul had ignored more phone calls than was probably acceptable. He was hoping for an hour's break, no more, the working day already at an end, our brains needing sustenance, a light beer, another coffee. We were standing in the fresh air, the day's sun still lingering, several cups of coffee in my belly, two beers in Paul's, our stress temporarily sedated. Paul was on his mobile phone to the station, his abandoned officers requiring assistance, as usual — my friend trying to locate his sanity. I jabbed an index finger across my cheek, my head still throbbing from the blow it had taken at David's earlier hand. Although still swelling, I was grateful it wasn't as bad as I'd anticipated. I moved my jaw from side to side, glad it was intact, my headache temporarily eased with the comforting sensation of caffeine. I momentarily chastised myself for hiding the truth from my friend, oddly unable to explain the reason, blaming clumsiness instead. I knew what he'd say anyway. I should have seen it coming. I should *not* have been at the Old Trent Road house. I know. I get it.

Yet maybe I *should* tell Paul what happened. It might be enough to see David arrested, placed on an assault charge, get him off the street and give me an opportunity to talk with him again—the safety of a police station now appealing. I turned, ready to explain what had really happened, but Paul was already waving a half-hearted goodbye my way as he trudged along the street towards an awaiting taxi.

My own mobile rang, my wayward thinking dislodged.

'You need to lock me away, sir,' a small voice emerged. *Adam.*

'Adam?'

'Indeed, sir. Please, I beg of you. You are the only person who believes my truth.'

I sighed, probably too loudly. I couldn't help it. Even *I* was growing tired of it all now, David's incessant demands for attention something I did not need. 'They can't charge you for something you didn't do—'

'I murthered those people, sir. Five men and an unfortunate young woman who were in the wrong place at the wrong time.' He paused. I wondered for a split second if he was still there. 'He's planning his next victim.'

'Who is?'

Silence.

'Adam?'

'He is planning, plotting, sir. *Please.* You must stop him.

Prevent his wretched deeds.'

'I can't help you unless you tell me what you are talking about.' We both knew, of course. I was trying to remain neutral. Diplomatic.

'If you do not lock me away, I cannot be responsible for what he will do next.' Adam hung up, leaving me in the middle of a busy street, an angry dialling tone in my ear and several furious car horns aimed my way.

I was nervous about seeing David after what happened earlier. I couldn't explain why, yet I needed to figure this thing out. If Paul wasn't going to help, I guess it was down to me. When did life turn so sour for David Mallory that unwanted attention now formed his entire existence? Poor Tom, stuck in a care home, stuck inside a mind he could no longer trust, his memories fleeting. How could he trust his own judgment? I sighed, a gentle sea breeze tugging at my soul. How could I trust mine?

Thirty-Five

David

The consistent drumming against my front door is not something I enjoy. Neither is the sound of the good doctor calling my name loudly through the letterbox. I pull open the door, my face a collection of irritated twitching muscles I fear might accidentally express my annoyance, give away my position. It is not intentional, of course. Yet, it is giving me a headache.

'What is the problem, Doctor Flanigan?' I query sharply, stepping out of the way as the man rushes into my hallway. We have not spoken since I was taken to the police station for questioning, accused of knowing the whereabouts of forgotten bones. What he requires of me now is anyone's guess.

'Adam called me,' he states. The good doctor is slightly out of breath, as if he has been running. Does he assume I care? I am grieving. I do not require further drama adding to my already traumatised emotional mindset. I do not wish to speak to or *see* another living creature for a while. Solace is something I deem most valuable at this painful time. The smell of strong coffee ensuring this fellow now appears wired, over opinionated.

I sigh. That man can be infuriating. 'May I get you a drink, Doctor Flanigan? A cup of tea, perhaps? *Coffee?*'

'I spoke to your father today.'

My attention is caught, yet I do not wish to convey my current emotions or the fact such news is disturbing. If I discover the good doctor has had anything to do with his recent passing, I will not be held responsible for my actions.

'You did?' I turn, staring at him, wondering what I am seeing behind his troubled eyes. 'Then you must also know my father passed away this very afternoon.'

The doctor regards me for a moment. 'No. I'm sorry, I had no idea.' I believe him yet resist the urge to strangle him where he stands. His face is a twisted mixture of confusion, something in his eyes confirming he is struggling to recall the contents of his last moment with my father.

We head into the kitchen where I open the fridge to retrieve milk, glancing towards the top shelf adorned with the recently acquired tattooed skin samples I have yet to dry out and prepare for framing. The doctor does not notice, of course, busy seating himself at my mother's table, my late father still on his mind.

'I assume at some point, you will explain what *exactly* Adam wanted and why you felt it so important to speak to my dying father. You do know the poor man had advanced

Alzheimer's?'

The doctor nods. 'I did, yes. I'm so sorry for your loss.' His words sound genuine, yet I am left wondering if they haven't been uttered for the benefit of duty—sympathy he does not otherwise possess. 'Your father actually had a lot to say to me.'

'Oh?' I am pouring milk into teacups, not even bothering to ask if he takes milk in his tea. I know he prefers coffee, of course, yet I no longer care.

'Do you mind telling me what happened to your mother?'

My goodness, where on earth did *that* come from? At least buy me dinner first before you pounce so readily, my dear fellow. I hover in the looming space between my refrigerator and the countertop, not wishing to look directly at the good doctor. My father and I have not spoken of my mother for seven years.

'My mother?' I sense a wobble in my tone. It is inappropriate, yet regretful that I cannot retract my question.

'Your father said you didn't protect her. What didn't you protect her from, David? He also wanted to know why you allowed your sister to "die like that".'

'My poor mother had an unfortunate accident. Do you take sugar with your tea?' The good doctor is usually a welcome relief to my senses. Not today.

'No, thank you. What type of accident?'

Oh, dear. Why all the questions? 'I thought you came here because *Adam* called you?'

'He did yes, around thirty minutes ago. He said someone was plotting something. His next victim.'

I laugh. I cannot help it. 'Victim?' I question, feeling suddenly amused, if not slightly accused. 'Did he say *who*, exactly, is plotting this next victim?' I am perplexed.

'I think we both know.' The good doctor is pointing accusations my way he cannot verify. *Careful.* Some things are best left alone.

'Enlighten me.' I reach for a bread knife. I cannot help it. It has become an automatic defence mechanism of late. A way for me to protect myself in a world I can no longer abide.

'Jacob.'

I sigh with audible relief, placing the knife back on the board, stroking the handle. 'Jacob?'

'Adam believes he is planning to kill someone.'

'He *told* you that?'

'Not in as many words. You still haven't told me about your mother.'

I sigh, bringing two cups of tea to the table as I sit opposite the good doctor, our hands almost touching. 'What exactly do you want to know, Newton? That *Jacob* is planning a murderous deed? Or the truth of what happened to my poor mother?'

'Both.'

Such *greed.* Tut, tut, my dear man, I thought we understood each other better than that. I sigh again, unwilling to do more than sip my tea, noticing the good doctor hasn't even acknowledged his. 'Why would Adam tell you such disgraceful things about Jacob?' I query.

'He didn't. I just assumed—'

'Oh, you *assumed.* Assumption is a very dangerous quality.

I hope you know that. It has an irksome downside of getting people into trouble.'

'So why would Adam call me, sounding upset?'

I chuckle. 'Adam is *always* upset. By now, you should know this more than anyone. We tend to ignore him, The Others and I.' I glance towards the good doctor, intrigued by his appearance. 'What on earth happened to your face?'

He presses a hand across a painful-looking bruise above his cheekbone, reddened with angry blood beneath the skin. 'As if you don't know.'

I am taken aback by this rude response. 'How am I to know what has happened? Unless you tell me.'

The good doctor regards me for a moment. 'Simon wasn't thrilled to have me visit his mother's house.'

'Oh, my goodness,' I am laughing now. I cannot help it. 'Forgive me, Newton. You seem to find it relatively easy to upset The Others.' I can, of course, understand why. The man is infuriating. Alluring indeed, but infuriating, all the same. 'Jacob does not enjoy the limelight. If you met him, you would understand—'

'Oh, I met him.'

'Oh?' I look shocked. I cannot suppress it. Jacob only appears when my stress levels have elevated, surpassed normality. I glance towards the good doctor's cheek, wondering what might have happened during their encounter. I do not ask. 'Do you not believe that *Simon* might be the one plotting?'

'Is he?'

I cannot tell him. It would be unfortunate at this stage. It would ruin the plan we have carefully worked on for the last few weeks. 'Are you not the one supposed to be working that out?' I drink my tea, neither of us offering anything further to this already strained conversation.

'May I use your bathroom?' the good doctor asks suddenly, rising to his feet, his tea untouched.

'Of course. Top of the stairs. Door to your left.'

The good doctor nods, leaving me to drink in relative peace. I have a headache, an unexpected funeral to arrange, my father's personal effects to put in order. The last thing I need right now is *this* conversation. I lose track how long he is gone, peace being something I do not think I need until I find myself alone with my thoughts. When several aggravating minutes pass without his return, I head upstairs to check, reaching the top step, noticing the bathroom door is open. Curious, I glance around, my bedroom door also now ajar. My bedroom is my sanctuary. *My private space.* I never leave *that* door open. With a heavy sigh, I step into my room, to the unwanted sight of the good doctor rifling through my things, looking at my cherished collections, his nose where it is unwanted. *Oh, dear.* This will never do.

'This is not the bathroom,' I state, more forcefully than intended. No matter. He should *not* be in here.

The good doctor turns sharply, knowing he has been caught, unable to do anything about that now. 'I'm so sorry,' he mutters, motioning to leave. I step in front of the doorway, preventing his retreat. *Not so fast.*

'Find anything of interest?' We both know what he has found. I need his acknowledgement, although I hope he hasn't peeked under my bed. Such a discovery would be uncomfortable for both of us.

'I was curious,' the good doctor confirms flatly. 'Your father—'

Of course. 'I should have known my father would be involved, somehow.' He was *always* far too talkative for my liking, too impulsive. My father would have told him of my collection if his dementia allowed such a memory. My *obsession*, he called it. 'The man never understood me,' I confirm, glancing towards a lifetime's worth of Ripper memorabilia that any self-respecting collector would be proud of. 'None of them appreciated that it was, in fact, Jacob, not I, who collected these precious artefacts.' The doctor is observing newspaper articles that adorn my walls, unable to prevent his prying, wandering eyes. 'It took him over ten years to gather everything you see before you now. He was most aggrieved that he and Jack found their friendship ruined by such a terrible incident.'

'Yes, Jacob mentioned something about being friends with Jack the Ripper.'

'Oh, they were much more than friends, my dear fellow.' I pause, narrowing my eyes. 'But you didn't believe him. I can tell, by your tone.' I resist the urge to grin. I sigh, knowing I need to explain my past. Yet where would I begin? It is the very reason I spent seven long years locked away. I can hear them now, loud and clear. Jacob, Adam, and Simon—each one attempting to claim my undivided attention.

'Be quiet,' I mutter, my head filling with noise I do not need. It has been an unfortunate part of my existence for so long, a most depressing day.

'I didn't speak,' the doctor replies innocently. He is still scanning the contents of my room.

'Not now. I cannot. This is not the time.' Jacob is speaking to me, Simon too. Adam is yelling, as always, profound, bitter words leaving his mouth I wish I had the capacity to silence. Yet it is purely down to *Adam* that we are all here now—each of us destined to experience our lives on a relentless loop because of what he set in motion.

'Are you okay, David?' The good doctor is behind me, yet I am unable to respond. My thoughts are overtaking my senses. Nothing good ever happens when this occurs. I cannot always be responsible for my actions.

I lower myself onto my bed, needing a moment to calm myself. 'Forgive me. Stress sometimes has the terrible side effect of upsetting my senses. My father only passed this very day, and I haven't yet had time to process it.' Of course, it is true, yet I cannot tell the doctor the truth of my rapidly declining disposition. Not yet. 'I cannot always keep The Others away. You should not have come here.' I glance his way. The poor fellow looks perplexed. 'They *like* you.'

'Who do?'

'The Others.'

'I didn't get that impression.' The good doctor sounds nonchalant, the wound on his face beginning to look a little angry now. He touches it, remembering.

I smile, rising to my feet. 'Simon finds you attractive, in an odd way, although he is upset by the concept, you understand. It is unfortunate. The poor fellow had to deal with a lot in his life, as you can imagine.'

'Are you talking about Simon now, or yourself?'

I smile, offering an inappropriate laugh. 'My good man, we are the same person. Have you not figured it out yet? Each of us were born to different times, to different mothers, yes, yet with one thing in common.' I glance his way, needing him to appreciate the *truth*. 'Me. I am the link to them all. I am the one soul who lived through every life I can still recall, too vividly.'

'But why kill?'

He has pressed a nerve. 'I was unhappy with who I was.' I still am, yet I cannot tell him everything. I glance towards my wall coverings. 'Those prostitutes were dirty whores who got exactly what they deserved.' The doctor is glaring at me now as if he cannot absorb what I am saying. I cannot express enough that those types of women disgust me, not because of their sex, but because *I* could never conform to what society wished me to be. Why should *they* be allowed to flaunt themselves so freely, when I am unable to be myself in private?

'Are you speaking on behalf of Jacob?'

'Is there a difference?' He still does not appreciate my words.

'So why is Adam determined to repent?'

I shake my head. 'Because *his* innocent love started it all.'

I close my eyes, remembering my one true love, my first love. The *only* man I ever wanted to be with. James. I do not wish to remember him. It makes me sad. I am troubled now, more aggrieved by the idea of losing *him*, in fact, than my father. I cannot tell the good doctor that I have been searching for the reincarnated soul of James Lambert Collier throughout every lifetime I have inhabited, forced to live without him ever since. Sixteen dead at the hand of Simon Frederick, four at the hand of Jacob Pointer, more to be had if *he* had not met with such an unfortunate end, our mothers the overriding demonic presence that drove it all. Women, it seems, have been cause for much personal suffering. Adam wanted to be happy. *I still want that.*

'And what about you?' The doctor is listening calmly. It is unnerving. I understand why he makes a good psychologist.

'What about me?'

'What do *you* want?'

An idea forms in my mind, a gem, nothing more. Yet it has the added bonus of raising my mood enormously. 'Would you come with me?' I motion my free hand towards the door.

'Where are we going?'

'I have something to show you that you may find intriguing.'

Thirty-Six

Newton

I did not intend to snoop inside David's bedroom, but it was a compulsion I couldn't help. Thomas Mallory's words were still lingering in my mind, his mannerisms, that uncertain disquiet attitude. The way he stared into space as if dislodging old memories he didn't need inside his head whilst clinging desperately to the ones he did. He must have passed away while I was with Paul, the outside bustle passing us by, our minds elsewhere—my last words to him the last he might have heard from anyone. I'm confident I said nothing that would have brought about such a sudden, unexpected death, yet I couldn't be certain I wasn't *somehow* to blame. Equally, I had no idea why I'd now agreed to indulge David's fantasies. Curiosity seems to have got the better of me. Either that or I am an idiot. Either would work against me at some point, no doubt.

'Where are we going?' I asked. I was sitting in David's car, uncomfortably staring out of the window towards a passing town overrun with people I no longer knew.

'Old Trent Road,' he replied calmly, his subdued tone unnerving. There was something on his mind, yet what it was, I couldn't tell.

I wanted to ask why, but I think I knew the answer. Old Trent Road seemed to have a pull for David that no other location did. It was perhaps because Violet Frederick still owned it, her disappearance all those years ago ensuring no one ever came forward to claim it. I didn't even know if the poor man had any family besides his mother. A mother he seemed obsessed with. She probably was his life, at one point. I wondered briefly if that was why David had chosen Simon, chosen *that* house, the darkness surrouding the place providing an edge he might not have otherwise been able to claim. I glanced his way, something not sitting right with my logic. I couldn't tell what. I am usually a studious thinker. Yet, there is something odd about David that has left me questioning everything I believe I know about life, death, the way of things—none of it making much sense to me anymore.

David was eager to get inside as we pulled up in front of the ill-fated Old Trent Road property. 'Come, Doctor Flanigan,' he called as he rushed along the path away from me, key already in hand, excitement teetering on trembling lips—his shaking hands doing nothing for my state of mind. 'You don't want to miss what I have to show you.' He was too excited, something in his thoughts I'm certain wasn't there earlier. David was usually calm, calculated in his responses, at ease with himself and the world. Now, I wondered if David wasn't the one racing into that house at all.

I had no idea what I was letting myself in for, yet against my better judgment, once more, I followed my wayward feet into the darkened hallway of a house I detested. Faint laughter filled the space as I closed the front door behind me, my mind screaming at me to run for my life. An angry bloodstain still lingered on the front room floor—my blood, infused now with sludgy dust that only prolonged time can create. It hit my senses rapidly along with something else, something new. I couldn't place what, other than the fact this house needed a damned good clean. Some paint. *New owners.* The basement door was open. Okay. *That* was new.

'David?' I called, daring to poke my head into the dank space below, trying to ignore the odd smell that hit me full-on—stagnant air drifting skyward.

'Doctor Flanigan, wait a moment,' he called gleefully, the words echoing through this desolate space nothing but white noise giving me the creeps. After a brief moment, he clambered up the steps, meeting me in the hallway, out of breath, his hair now combed back neatly against his neckline, a grin on his face.

'Everything okay?' I asked, expecting to be greeted by either Simon or Jacob, wondering what on earth I was doing here.

'Come with me,' he sneered, acting like a schoolboy who wanted to show his parents something he assumed deserved attention. David led the way into the basement, the only light being a swaying light bulb overhead. The entire space smelled off, wrong, coated in a veneered layer of ancient dust that floated mockingly in the air, forcing to me place my hand over my mouth in disgust.

'What on earth is that smell?' I asked as David continued to retreat downward.

'Age, my dear fellow. Age and secrets.' I didn't like his tone or choice of words. In the darkness, it sounded odd, demonic.

Age and *what*? I remembered David senior's words. *David has a secret.* My brain was screaming again. I ignored it.

'Do you know why this house was never sold?' he asked. I wasn't listening, barely able to see my feet in front of me, my eyes not yet acclimatised to the encroaching darkness. I shook my head, concentrating more on keeping my balance than answering his ridiculous question. Another snigger. Then David flicked a second light switch, allowing the space around us to illuminate with a soft amber glow. Its dimly lit corners were filled with cobwebs and damp, old boxes left to rot where they sat, broken chairs, old paint tins, stepladders no longer fit for purpose. And then, centre-stage and beyond rational logic of anything I had ever witnessed in my entire life, sat a circle of corpses.

I blinked, not convinced I was witnessing this right. *What the hell?* I considered that maybe David had slipped something into my tea whilst I wasn't looking, though I didn't recall taking a sip, this moment rendering me incapable of rational processing. I opened my mouth to speak, but no words emerged, my narrowed eyes straining to accept my current surroundings and what now stood before us.

'What do you think?' David asked, stepping eagerly towards me, his arms spread wide as if showcasing something he was genuinely proud of.

'Oh my God. What the hell?' I stepped back, needing to get away from this madman.

'Do you like it?'

Like it? I glared at him, his darkening features even more distorted in the overriding gloom of this space. Had he finally lost his mind?

'David, what is all this?' I couldn't take it in.

'This, my friend, is Simon Frederick's collection.' He stepped towards the unfortunate corpses, propped on ageing chairs, facing one another in a circular configuration as if engaged in a group counselling session that had ended some time ago without their knowledge. There was nothing left of them now but skeletal remains, clothing hanging from rotted flesh, still seated where they were placed, much care taken to retain their original positions. David revelled in the details as he touched one tenderly on its skull, sending more dust flying into the air. I winced. I understood the stench now, at least. Decades of rotting flesh, slowly dissolving into crumbled wood and cold stone beneath our feet.

'You look surprised, Newton,' he whispered, as if he didn't wish to disturb his sleeping guests. He wasn't wrong. I hadn't expected this place to be welcoming, of course, but *this* was the last thing I imaged I'd see down here. 'Maybe you should take a seat, my dear friend.' It did not sound like a request.

'Why?' To be honest, I wasn't sure my legs would hold me

up much longer. I needed to relocate the steps. Get out of there. Fast.

'Because you will want a better view.'

I glanced at him, still confused, my eyes unable to communicate with my brain. 'A better view of what?'

He smiled, breathing deeply against the heavy dust surrounding us, taking in this environment with enthusiasm. Something struck me on the head although I didn't initially notice, too busy staring at death already around me. It was ironic, considering. 'Why, of your forthcoming death, of course.'

Thirty-Seven

Simon

After all these turbulent years, I cannot believe I finally get to do what I love best in the world. I have David to thank for this, of course. He understands more than anyone how I have been struggling of late. I have tried, many times, to add to my beloved collection but, until recently, David has been most aggrieved by the concept. Today that *will* change. We have something in common now, something that will bring us together, aside from Adam, of course, Jacob too. If we could shed him from our circle, we would have gladly done so by now. As it is, we are stuck together for eternity, our shared history ensnaring us as equals.

I am standing in the basement, surrounded by familiarity I assumed might become lost to me forever, Doctor Flanigan at my feet, awaiting his natural end, the man soon to be subjected to a uncomfortable night without warmth. I take a breath, gazing into the face of my dear, dead mother. I cannot help such things.

'You would have loved to see the man in our company today,' I say aloud to the prevailing darkness, no natural light required for me to find my way. 'He is a handsome chap, with his unruly hair and charismatic, slightly bumbling persona. You would have liked him.' I tilt my head, saddened now by how she appears. 'I am sorry *your* looks have faded over the years, your features far less appealing on the eyes than they once were. Still, aren't we all destined to follow the same path in the end?' I stroke a hand across my mother's best Sunday hat, wishing only to make her look presentable for the entertainment she is about to witness. My goodness, has it been so long since I last had any fun?

It is a rarity that I get to sit long with my gentlemen friends, although in fairness, I recognise each one less with every visit I make to this crumbling basement. It matters little, of course. What is done is done. No one can change the past. I am despondent as I stroll around this space, glad my cherished possessions are still here, undisturbed by David's current, *misplaced* guests. Yet, we are the same, David and I. Jacob, Adam too. I should be more tolerant of his needs, more understanding.

I walk slowly over to Michael and kneel at his feet, clasping my palms across his once beautiful knees. They are mere bone now, of course, nothing more, but I am immediately transported to a time when he and I were at our happiest, this godforsaken world unable to sedate our passion. Michael Yarrow was my first love in a world never able to tolerate us. I would often sit naked at his feet, my head resting across his knees, staring lovingly into his deep brown eyes, my own allowed to wander freely across his torso, to other body parts, readily waiting. Of course, the subsequent men who came afterwards were a requirement, nothing more, a way for me to dislodge the pain and suffering I had nowhere else to direct my attention, transforming *my* unease and rejection onto *them*. It was ultimately not my fault that, in the end, my death toll formed a cumbersome equation. I could never have assumed I was capable of killing so many until my mother became entangled with my suffering, changing who I am forever.

I cannot help but offer a sigh that seems now to penetrate these dense walls, reverberating like an icy wind on a winter's evening. Had Mother shown anything other than repulsion towards Michael and I, things may have been different. I might not have had to kill so many. I might not have had to kill *her*. As it is, she brought this onto herself, made me the way I ultimately became. Of course, she assumed Michael and I were friends, acquaintances, initially welcoming him into her home and her life. I am certain they even shared the occasional fond moment, a cup of tea, the possibility of acceptance warming my heart. It was temporary, I know. I should have appreciated that. Indeed, had she not found us in a compromised position, I am confident things *could* have been different for us all.

I hate my mother now almost as much as I did the very night Michael met his end at the hand of the woman who birthed me. Of course, she did not mean to hit him, and he equally did not mean to lose his footing. Yet, he tumbled down the staircase like a rag doll, naked as the day he was born, caught out in our act of passion, her only son merely wishing to be understood. Equally, if my mother had shown any kindness after that tragic event, expressed her sorrow, none of this need happen. But, instead, she stood at the top of that looming staircase, glaring at us both as if we were no better than demons sent from hell to disarm her, my arms wrapped around my dead naked lover, willing him back to a life that could never be.

If I could cry for the loss I suffered, I would. However, tears have long since dried to dust, no different to how Michael now looks, still here, waiting in the darkness for my loving embrace. Mother did not initially know I kept him in the basement, utterly as disgusted with the terrible smell that lingered in the house for several weeks as she had been towards me the night he died in my arms. In fact, her hatred formed a gem of an idea that saw me hunt and kill homosexual men for months afterwards, my only intention to hurt my mother in the way she had scorned me so badly. I was on a mission to hunt every male I could find who was willing to accompany me home. I hate what mother has done to me, how she took away the one person I truly connected with.

She took weeks to die, starving in the darkness, tied to this chair, bound and gagged, sobbing like the pathetic wretch she was. I left her alone in the dark with Michael so she could get to know the very man she detested enough to kill, get to know the subsequent men who ultimately took his place. More importantly, she finally got to know her son. I dressed her in her Sunday best, of course, gave her the best seat in the house, forced her to sit and watch as my beautiful Michael turned to a putrid mess before her eyes, her own body slowly succumbing to its own death—each one of those men beaten and tortured in her presence. She despised us purely because of who we were, and so, I made her suffer as she had made me suffer. It was the least I could do for my snivelling wretch of a mother. It is a shame she did not thank me, in the end.

Thirty-Eight

Newton

I dared not move, although, to be honest, I'm not convinced I could even if I wanted to. My hands and feet were tied firmly with rope, readily chaffing my wrists and ankles, my skin increasingly sore with each uncomfortable movement. David was rambling to himself as if the corpses in our presence were alive and well, requiring his deluded attention—mine thankfully remaining unnoticed as he ambled around me in this dimly lit environment. He wasn't aware I'd overheard his ranting, of course, his private confession something he probably expected to keep to himself. My head was throbbing, yet again, my thoughts twisting violently.

I remained as still as possible, my pounding heartbeat and trembling legs uncooperative, the unforgiving floor below me damp, my muscles as deadened as those unfortunate victims around me. My capturer was deluded it seemed, deranged. I didn't want him to acknowledge that I was now conscious, his ridiculous ramblings keeping him occupied. Neither did I wish to further provoke David's increasing wrath, yet I needed to think fast, create a plan, get the hell out of here whilst I could—preferably in one piece. He was conversing with those corpses and The Others as if it was the most natural thing in the world to him, his frantic whispers almost demonic.

Is he awake?

Why ask me?

Someone should check. We do not wish the poor fellow to pass over without giving him uncensored access to the main event.

We should let him go—

No one is asking you, Adam. Stay out of this.

I didn't dare dwell on this heated, one-sided conversation, the only thing on my mind being the so-called *main event*. It was ironic that the one person amongst them actually able to help me, currently existed inside the mind of a psychopath. It wasn't a comforting consideration. It was questionable which personality greeted me at any given moment, my time with David Mallory seemingly knowing no bounds.

Eventually, David shifted his attention towards me, lifting my head from the floor, checking my breathing. I almost held my breath in a misplaced plea for my life, though such an act might have a negative side effect of making him assume me already dead. I released an unanticipated groan as pain shot through my back.

'Oh, you're awake,' he stated, too brightly, tugging my body roughly. He grabbed my arms, lifting me into a seated position that felt no more comfortable than lying on the floor.

'David?' I struggled to catch my breath, knowing I couldn't play dead without running the risk of ending up in that unfortunate position.

'Oh, darling, I expect he's around,' a small voice filtered into my ears. 'Somewhere.'

'Simon?'

A subdued laugh, a little wink. Did this guy seriously assume I was going to play along with his game?

'You have to let me go.' I have no idea what I was thinking, making such a stupid suggestion. As if *that* was going to happen any time soon.

'Tut tut, Newton, my dear man. May I call you Newton? I feel we got off on an awkward footing the last time we met. I'd like to rectify that, if at all possible. I would like us to be friends.'

Friends? Was this guy serious? Simon strode around me, touching my legs, my arms, running his hands too keenly over my inner thigh. I flinched, not comfortable with such close proximity. 'Do you know how excited I am to have you in my mother's home?' he asked giggling, somewhat schoolboy-ish mannerisms, worryingly coming onto me with ease. 'You will comply, won't you? I do not wish to have to gag you whilst I perform my duties.'

Duties? What on earth was he talking about? 'Comply to what?' I asked, my voice gruff.

'Why, we will connect as only men can.' He giggled again, brushing a free hand across my groin.

Seriously? I reeled backwards, hoping I was overthinking

the entire thing, imagining a scenario that only existed in my head. Surely he wasn't planning on doing something stupid? I glanced towards the corpses surrounding me. What the hell had he done to *them*?

Simon pulled his hand away. 'Oh, dear. You're not going to be a willing participant, are you?' He sounded troubled by my apparent rejection.

I shook my head. 'Why don't we talk about this?' I was trying to remain calm. I was failing. Psychopaths could be volatile, it seemed. *Who knew?*

'Now now, darling Newton, there will be time enough for chit chat later. I usually like to smoke after sex. I hope you don't mind. It helps me relax.' He brushed my face with an icy palm. I pulled away, forcing him to rise to his feet abruptly. 'We are on a schedule. Time is of the essence. David will wish to take over at some point, and you *need* to be alive when that happens, believe me.'

'I beg your pardon?'

'To witness our incredible finale.' He waved wild arms into the air as if acting out a theatrical scene I wasn't yet aware of.

'Finale?'

'Patience, my dear man. David, Jacob, and I have been planning this for a long time. Of course, *you* were not meant to become our ultimate trophy. That was a mere coincidence, a fitting end. It is very exciting. I have my needs too, you know.' He laughed, more to himself than to me.

I had no idea what the man was talking about. What *ultimate trophy*? My mind wandered uncomfortably to Jack the

Ripper, those poor girls currently awaiting justice in the morgue, Annie Cormac. I couldn't stop myself when I began to struggle, attempting to free my hands, gain back control I never had in the first place.

'There there, my dear fellow. Stay calm. All will be revealed in due course. I promise.' He giggled again before leaving the basement, chatting to himself as he ascended the steps, light-footedly skipping towards a sliver of light above.

A few unbearable moments later, he returned. 'I do apologise for Simon, Newton. He cannot always control his urges?'

'David?'

David offered me a knowing nod. He did not smile.

'Untie me, please. You need help. I can help you—'

'Do not patronise me, my dear man. It does not become you.' David's tone was clipped, his temper rising.

I bit my lip. I could usually read people well, yet having four potential personalities at your disposal is oddly confusing. 'Untie me and we can talk.'

'I'm afraid I cannot do that.'

'Why not?'

'Simon Frederick killed sixteen people, you know.'

'Apparently so.' I glanced around, fully able to witness the aftermath of such a vile act.

David stared at me. 'Count them.'

'What?'

'Count the bodies. If you don't mind indulging me?'

I had no idea what the man was talking about, yet I sat upright as best I could and began counting the unfortunate corpses that sat forgotten around me. 'Nineteen,' I stated, counting twice to make sure.

'Exactly. Nineteen.'

'But you said—'

'Sixteen. Yes. That is correct. I did.'

I stared at the corpses, nothing left now but unsightly, skeletal remains.

David was smiling, grinning wildly as if he knew a secret I didn't. 'Fifteen gay men whom Simon willingly attacked, brought here alive, raped repeatedly whilst he made his mother watch, before killing brutally, ensuring they sat staring at her with eyes wide open, mouths agape, faces forever set in pure horror. If you include mother dearest.' David walked over to a corpse dressed in 1930s attire, a hat still on its dangling head, gloved hands clasped across bony knees. He leaned forward, kissing her on the cheek. *My god, how disgusting.* 'That makes sixteen.' He strolled over to a further corpse, lingering a trembling hand against its shoulder, closing his eyes at the acknowledgement of a single tear. 'This gentleman was collateral damage. Poor Michael died by accident, a terrible thing. It should never have happened.'

I narrowed my eyes. 'So, who are the other two?' I honestly did *not* want to know.

David smiled, clapping his hands together as if he was overjoyed by the thought that something so important had slotted into my mind so readily, setting everything neatly into place. 'Those, my dear fellow, are *mine*,' he concluded with a stiffened nod of his head. He stepped around the circle of supposed companions until he came to a space where two discarded corpses sat. They appeared naked, nothing but skeletal remains, tethered to chairs by chains. They had no hands. No teeth. How had I not noticed?

'Do you think I can exist with *three* killers living inside my head without them rubbing off on me?' he laughed loudly. 'Unfortunately, my other participants are sadly still out in the world somewhere, probably buried by now, two of them awaiting justice in a police mortuary. But I cannot help that.' He sighed, disheartened by such an unfavourable concept.

'What are you talking about?'

'You should know, Newton. You saw the last crime scene.' David was still smiling, still staring into space as if I should already know.

I glared into David's eyes, my thoughts unwilling to absorb his words. 'You're the Eastcliff Ripper?'

He bowed. 'At your service, my dear man.'

Of course, he was. *I had always known it.* I cursed myself for allowing Paul to suppress my nagging suspicions. 'Tell me, David. Why didn't you move the other victims?' I glanced around. And, why, if this had indeed become some strange commemorative site, did he not bring them here?

'Oh, that was unfortunate. The first girl was, of course, my first kill. I was still learning the trade.' David closed his eyes, remembering. *Learning the trade?* Seriously? 'I was highly stressed at the time. Jacob had already expressed a notion of how easy it was to kill, had told me such for many years. He assumed the poor wretch was a prostitute. The way she dressed, always prancing around, her walk, so common. You must understand Jacob wasn't used to seeing women dressed in so little. It was a mistake. I know that now. We've all made them. Rachel masqueraded as a school teacher by day, harlot by night.'

I shook my head, glaring towards a face I didn't wish to acknowledge. 'Rachel?' My question was unrequired, my brain only now just piecing together the jigsaw puzzle that had been staring me in the face this entire time.

David nodded, waiting for me to join the dots.

'Your sister?' Why did I sound so shocked?

'How was I to know that dear Rachel was on a well-deserved night out with friends. Jacob, you see, had convinced me she was soliciting herself for money. It was unfortunate, I know, yet I rectified that early mistake, of course, ensuring I focused on actual prostitutes for my participants.' David was hovering above me, threatening to make me dizzy. 'I managed to take a few trophies of Rachel's with me, thankfully. Her breasts, a hand.' He took a deep breath as if revelling in the moment, not at all concerned by the fact that he had murdered his own sister. 'That was until I was rudely interrupted by the arrival of *Adam*. The man was furious. Ran from the scene screaming I would be sorry for everything, my penance forthcoming, the deluded man claiming we would all burn in hell. When I returned later that morning to collect her, the police were already on-scene. The next girl, however, was not so lucky.' He pointed to a corpse sitting in front of me, her toothless skull nothing now but a distorted head shaped bone. 'It is a shame my mother then died unexpectedly, a few days after we lost poor Rachel.'

'You killed your mother too?' I didn't mean to sound so flippant, the question simply my wayward thinking. I wasn't expecting him to say *yes*.

'Of course I did.' David grinned, something telling me he no longer cared for polite etiquette, my thoughts on him no longer relevant. I felt sick. 'She found my sister's hand, you see, in a bag hidden at the bottom of our freezer. I was simply waiting for my opportunity.'

'Opportunity?'

'To figure out how to preserve it better.' David turned his attention to the two female skeletons in front of him, the subject of his mother no longer holding his attention.

'But why bring them here?' I asked, nodding towards bones I wished didn't exist. Did he butcher them at the scene of death? I assumed he must have. The other women were brutally slaughtered where they fell.

'To *hide* my crimes, of course, as Jacob and Simon once did. I needed to continue our journey. Simon had the entire thing perfectly planned. Seventeen corpses were still here. The unsolved disappearance of his mother. This place was and still *is* the perfect location to keep our beautiful trophies.'

'But you took their hands and teeth?'

'Only for identification purposes, silly. Prostitutes should *never* be named or be allowed any dignity. They should disappear from this earth and become nothing, because they *are* nothing.' He laughed, stroking a hand across one of the girl's skulls. It tipped violently to one side, almost coming away in his hand. 'This one didn't appreciate my craft.'

'Your *craft*?'

He nodded. 'Yes. I made her sit in front of a mirror whilst I pulled her teeth out, one by one. Her mouth was a bloodied mess. It was unfortunate.' He was laughing now, remembering.

'So where are they now?' I couldn't imagine such suffering. I didn't want to know.

David laughed. 'The teeth?'

I nodded. *What else?*

'Why, safely in my freezer at home, of course.' He spoke as if such a question was unrequired. *Obviously*, his trophies would be in a freezer. How rude of me to ask? 'If you'd only allowed me to see the photographs of the recent crime scene when I asked you, I might have been able to help clear up a few things long before now. Tut tut, Newton.'

David shook his head, shaking off a thought he didn't need. 'My latest participants were left disposed because, these days, Adderson Street seems to have become a place for dog walkers and joggers. I find it annoying, my time never my own for long.' He was staring at me, his demonic features as black as the surrounding shadows. 'I fell in love once, you know.'

I didn't care.

'There was a gentleman who worked in the local supermarket, a most attractive fellow, not unlike your good self.' David grinned. I wasn't impressed.

'Rachel had discovered I was gay, you see, prone to hearing voices, believing me quite troubled. She overhead me saying I was going to claim the shelf stacker for myself, add him to my prized collection. It was Simon speaking, not me, but Rachel confronted me about it, subsequently warning the poor sod to stay well away. We argued. Rachel punched me. She was arrested. It was very messy. Yet because Simon had ventured into that supermarket and not me, no initial connection was made that she and I bore any ties. Sadly, just three days later, poor Rachel and my mother were both dead, and Simon had stabbed that defenceless shelf stacker three times in the back.' David was so flat in his tone, so matter of fact. I wondered when the man had become such a monster.

'And what about these two?' I nodded towards the chained girls.

'I was stressed, as you can imagine, the week I'd had, most depressing. I wanted to take my time with them so I brought them here in the boot of my car. What is a man to do?' David stepped behind the two girls and placed his hands over the backs of both chairs. 'They died together at least, this one watching in horror as I killed this one.'

'May I speak to Adam?' I genuinely thought I was going to throw up.

'No. Of course not. He would help you. We can't have that. You see, there are three of us, and only one of him and you are yet to witness the best part. You need to *be* a part of our ultimate goal.' David took a slow breath, unconcerned by decade's worth of disintegrated skin now left to float around this space.

'What *ultimate* goal?' I questioned. Simon had said the same thing. I was busy struggling with painful ropes against my wrists. I couldn't help it.

David smiled. 'Allow me to show you.'

Thirty-Nine

David

I cannot control my excitement a moment longer. Still, I must remain focused on the task at hand. My good friend, Newton, is not yet fully aware of my circumstance and his undeterred fate, the idea of including this man in my beloved collection making me wonder why it took so long for me to realise.

'My dear, Newton. What if I told you there was more to this life than what we see on a day-to-day basis? More than most of us could ever dare imagine. What if I told you that death isn't the end of us? I assume you would think me mad, a complete lunatic.' I glance towards him, not needing a response. 'I would have, too, at one point. Yet, as I have since discovered, there are greater forces at work in the universe than any single human being can understand. Not until the entire story is told, at least. Only then dare we see things differently. And it changes everything. It changes your life. It most certainly changed mine.'

I am speaking to the good doctor, yet he is looking at me as if he is able to see straight through me, assuming I have lost my mind. He is waiting for the punch line, to understand some undetermined secret he wishes for me to reveal before the poor man loses *his* mind by the sound of my bizarre words. I am speaking in riddles, I know, skirting around the edge of something neither of us can comprehend. I enjoy playing games, you see, taking control where others assume there is none to be had.

'I have witnessed a far greater, expansive realm than my physical being alone could ever dream possible. And it is magnificent, Newton, of that I can promise you.' I am staring into space as if I can see beyond the confining walls that surround us now, the darkness of no consequence to the sight I behold in my mind's eye. 'You see, my friend, I have always existed and will continue to do so throughout time itself, no matter what happens to me along the way. I understand, more than most, the importance of each person who has touched my life via the passing of time.'

The good doctor has no concept of what I am talking about, yet I am able to sit calmly opposite him, my legs crossed, speaking openly, potentially for the first since I have known the man, expressing myself with ease. After all, this is what the good doctor does every day. He evaluates people, watches them, witnesses their motives and learns what makes them tick—allows them to talk.

'It is a shame, however, that because of what I have discovered, I now live every day with demons inside my head.' I am relishing the sound of my own voice. Am I now willing to apologise for Adam's previous outburst, for Simon's sharp, infected tongue? For Jacob, whose persistent presence appears more inside my own thoughts than of his? Each personality is, after all, a product of my soul, my crazed identity developed because of who I have always been throughout the very essence of time.

'And what exactly *have* you discovered?' Newton asks, once he is certain I have finished my assumed theatrics. I am impressed by how calm he is, yet he is hoping I will hurry up and get to the point. I can tell. He presumes he has no genuine need to be here. He is a busy man, I know.

'Memories, my dear Newton,' I conclude, unappreciative of his blatant interjection. 'Memories.' I smile as if I know something he isn't yet aware of. It is unnerving, yet oddly enchanting. 'Because, my dear fellow, when all's said and done, I am still here, still existing in the form I know well. For me, everything is the same as it had always been, yet, at the same time, continually changing. It is all very bizarre.' I laugh, my emotions allowed unfeigned freedom of this darkened space. 'It genuinely feels as if I have been awakened, and, in truth, it is only *this* life that subsequently becomes the fallacy. The concept is strange, I know, yet tremendously beautiful, don't you agree? It is as if I have become *everything*, no sense of fear or confusion. I am completely free.' The good doctor stares at me, a lingering look on his face I struggle to read, my god-like stance undeserving of attention.

'Free?' Why does he sound so ignorant in such matters?

'Free to express myself as I willingly see fit.' Maybe I *am* a god? Sent from the heavens to save humanity from itself.'

'In the form of Adam, Jacob, and Simon?'

I nod, grinning wildly now. I cannot help it. I have no idea why. It isn't funny, I know. Maybe I am a paranoid schizophrenic after all? Delusional, ridiculous, comically unhinged. I have certainly lived with the label long enough. I close my eyes, forgetting my place, my manners. 'Forgive me. Sometimes the voices can overtake my senses. It isn't always a pleasant experience.'

'So, you're saying it's pleasant, *sometimes*?' Now, who sounds condescending? Forgetting *his* manners. I shake my head, perturbed by the good doctor's unrewarded musing, his little joke unappreciated.

'Tut tut, Newton, you know I don't mean it like that.'

He shakes his head, uninterested.

'The most profound aspect of this entire thing is that I became acutely aware of everything that is my true authentic self at a very young age. I was able to recall, in vivid detail, every life I ever lived, every memory I ever created, every person, animal, and possession that had come into and left my life up until that very moment. I became aware of multiple levels within my otherwise subconscious state, recalling old memories with ease. You see, Newton, the idea I have lived many different lives that span centuries is now a completely normal concept in my mind. Indeed, how can any of us think differently?' I stare at the good doctor, hoping he understands my meaning, watching him as if I have all the answers. I don't. He assumes I do not know what I am talking about. 'The truth is, Newton, that my problems stem from neither

DID nor schizophrenia.'

There is something in his expression, yet what, I cannot tell. Ignorance perhaps. 'So, you're now trying to tell me that you believe you have lived before?' he asks, sounding as if he wants to laugh. I do believe his mouth might have fallen agape by the sound of my words. Be careful, Doctor Flanigan. Simon may wish to place something inside your mouth. *Forcefully.*

'Indeed. Many times,' I confirm, maintaining momentary control. I grow silent, not daring to speak further for fear of breaking this precious moment. 'To cut a long story short, by the time I was eight years old, I'd attempted suicide, twice. It was unfortunate, and I would prefer not to go into details, but I was poorly equipped in my mission because I'm still alive to tell the tale. However, something happened to me that I have never truly been able to understand, no matter how hard I try.' I take a breath, old memories still lingering. 'Do not ask me why. I have spent the last three decades of my life trying to figure it out. I have learned that sometimes we can pull memories from our past when close to death. I don't, of course, understand the concept, and I appreciate it is difficult to understand someone who wakes in the middle of the night screaming, speaking an old English dialect I did *not* learn in school.' I can no longer bring myself to look at the good doctor. He has no concept of the many traumas I have suffered. It is not something he can ever fully comprehend.

'Don't get me wrong. I was never worried or frightened by the prospect. There was never any anxiety for the fact that I have been able to recall such memories. I was moments from death, you see, the bathwater keeping me warm as my heart stopped beating.' I recall that fateful day, depression not something children are meant to experience, painful memories often drifting unhindered that, at the time, I did not understand. I stare into space, needing to be heard. 'I was in awe of this amazing new being I had unwittingly become, knowing instinctively that if I were to stay longer in this new and wondrous realm, more answers would come to me. Additional space would in some way open up, allowing me to connect with something else. Something I was yet to comprehend. In that bathtub, I was in limbo. My soul had not yet left my body, my brain still clinging to life. I had no idea if what I was feeling was the afterlife, or wayward thoughts playing tricks on me. But I knew I was dead, instinctively. I could not have been watching my own body if I wasn't already dead. And, despite being eight years old, I was oddly okay with that conclusion.'

The good doctor is watching me from the floor, his hands tied behind his back, his legs bound and tethered. It is refreshing expressing, for the first time since my mother's death, who and what I truly am.

'But I digress. You wish me to reveal *everything* to you.' I step gingerly into the corner of the basement, excitement reignited, opening a hidden wooden panel along the far wall. It is not visible unless you know it is there and I have waited for so long to share my abilities with someone else. Another doctor who might appreciate my work. Yes, of course, he is a psychologist, not a medical doctor, but we share a title, all the same.

The girl struggles as I pull her listless body from behind the wall, her flaying legs dragging across the dusty floor. Like the good doctor, she is also bound, gagged too, drugged to ensure continued compliance, both guests ready for their ultimate sacrifice. I glance towards the good doctor whose eyes are wide open in obvious shock. I smile.

'You *really* do not want to miss a thing, Newton,' I breathe, my loins beginning to tingle with eager anticipation I am not expecting. I will shortly slice this wretch open, displaying surgeon skills I have been unable to express in front of anyone else for many years. Not since my time with Jack. Back when everyone called me Jacob. I wish only to show the good doctor my careful hand now, how skilfully I can remove body parts with ease. Once this whore is dead, Simon can then take over, have his way with the good doctor before ending *his* life, adding two more prized possessions to our ultimate trophy room. I stand tall, thoughts I cannot dissipate allowed freedom of this space, my body quivering with anticipation. It is intoxicating.

'Hey!' the good doctor is yelling, trying to unravel himself from Simon's restraints. I laugh, knowing Simon is far more practised in the art of rope tying than this man appreciates. He has had a lot of practice. It doesn't matter. I do not expect he is capable of freeing himself any time soon. None of these other wretches ever did. I glare at the wriggling thing in my grip, her terrified focus returning, a mere slip of a girl, little more than a teenager. She has already ruined her life with drugs and sex. Now I intend to show her that Jacob and I do not care for such wretched sights. She has no one to blame for this but herself.

'Let her go.' The good doctor's words are distracting, prickling my irritation. Maybe he requires a gag too, before Simon *forces* him to gag. I smile, allowing a chuckle at my private musing.

'Now, now, Newton, that is not part of the plan.' Simon loves to hear the groans of his beloved men as he thrusts himself inside them. Indeed, as we are one and the same, I, too, will enjoy the pleasure of the good doctor's company. I almost urinate with excitement, accidentally of course. This has the potential to become the best day of my life so far. I do not wish for my guests to miss a moment of it. It is regretful there are no smiles on these monotonous faces to potentially dispel this moment—no acknowledgement from insipid voices that do not yet know me, or what I can do. No matter. It will be over soon. I am almost irritated that it is growing late, the day already at an end. Taking a piece of wood, I hit Newton across the head, ensuring his silence is maintained in my absence. I will return. We will resume our game very soon.

Forty

Adam

I am abjectly aware everything ultimately occurring within the last two hundred years began with *myself*—my cowardly crimes procuring this lunacy, entrusting us all to a lifetime of hell. It matters little how remorseful I am. My soul is already damaged therefore I will be damned for eternity. There is nothing to be done. My fate is sealed. It is however, disturbing to know The Others are never far from mind. Indeed, I am growing increasingly tired of their controlling ways, the way they hold me forever accountable for the way of things, our pained duration and shared suffering, something I can never now change.

We are but a single soul, of course. I know this. I am not an imbecile. We stem from the same entity, savagely ripped asunder by the death toll I readily brought forth in my youth. Yet, I am damned if I know how to prevail over such a travesty that has continued this web of suffering throughout time itself—damned, it seems, no matter what I do.

It is fortunate that I have been given an unexpected moment of conscious thinking this morning, my unhinged conscience allowing the time I require to potentially free both captives. Such an act might, therefore, provide *them* enough time to see me precisely where I belong, locked away, out of sight. I am fully aware that only then will the citizens of Eastcliff sleep safely in their beds once more, including poor Doctor Newton Flanigan himself.

Of course, I have very little time upon which to act, grateful that David is easily distracted, exhausted by a restless sleep he has found no comfort in. This house is never a place he can settle. It has allowed me to surface, take over where his failing mind has ceased to exist. This morning, his father's funeral arrangements have provided the perfect moment for me to step in, overtake his senses—take back control of this uncomfortable situation. After all, the poor man deserves a break from his distorted logic. He has had a lot to deal with of late. He must leave this house for an hour or two, other, more pressing matters to attend to.

Poor Doctor Flanigan has been knocked unconscious, a night spent against unforgiving stone something I feel most aggrieved by. I must act swiftly. I am horrified by my noxious surroundings as I race forward, unable to acknowledge the painful truth of his fate as I grab limp arms and legs. A young woman is lying on her side, some feet away, her face swollen with painful bruises, most of her clothing taken, features distressed. She glances my way, fear lingering in her deep-set eyes, including an even deeper hatred for me she has nowhere to place—nowhere to disguise the pain she feels I have willingly brought upon her. I grapple with heavy ropes, loosening each one enough so the doctor can easily break free when he awakens, yet nothing that will allow David to notice. I tap pale cheeks rapidly, needing him to rise from his slumber in order to help *me* help *them*.

I motion towards the girl but she is already attempting to scream beneath her firmly gagged mouth, desperate words emerging as muffled grunts, her body pressed violently towards an unwelcoming wall the poor thing believes far more appealing than I. I mean her no harm, of course, but I exist inside the very body causing this poor wretch much suffering, this mind prepared to end her life without remorse. She cannot understand anything beyond this sickening notion that genuinely ales me.

I peel the gag from her mouth, allowing much-needed air I'm certain she feels she might never experience again. I cannot express heartfelt words to her. I would not know where to begin. This is, after all, entirely *my fault*. I step away. Her breath remains shallow yet thankfully free now from the muffled silence she has been forced to endure. She may scream if she deems it safe to do so. I want to smile, offer my honest affection, but she will not understand, of course, so instead I step across the floor, removing myself from the trembling side of this young thing so she may feel safer than she might otherwise assume.

'Please, Doctor Flanigan, sir. You must awaken.' I am focusing on the doctor, shaking him with enough aggression to reinforce my shameful behaviour to the shivering thing behind me. He, too, has bruising on his head, blood in his hair, his limbs uncooperative, hanging loose, no chance of a swift recovery merely because I procure it so. I close my eyes, already feeling David's unwanted return. With little time afforded to me, I race from the basement, those jagged stone stairs able to ravage me too, my feet uncooperative, the soft light above painful after enduring the looming darkness below.

Of course, David would have taken the doctor's mobile phone, ensuring the man devoid of help. I search the parlour, the kitchen, eventually locating the loathsome object inside David's jacket pocket, still hanging where he left it in the hallway. I grab it, ensuring I position the garment as I found it. It would not do for David to notice the thing is missing before I finish my quest. If I am swift enough, he may not learn of what I have done until both captives are free. I race into the basement once more, the poor young female scrambling now on her belly towards the open basement doorway. She freezes when she sees me, expecting the worst.

We linger for a moment, locked into each other's eyes, neither confident of the other's intention. She cannot know I mean her no harm, of course, yet she is right to be frightened. I do not notice the chain around her ankle. I swear that if I did, I would have unlocked the padlock, ensuring her ultimate safety, an easy retreat to be had. As it is, I am focused only on placing the doctor's mobile phone inside the pocket of his breaches, ensuring the girl can see what I have done here today. He is beginning to stir. Thank goodness. I turn my attention once again to this female who has now reached the stairwell. Will she believe I only wish to help?

'Please, miss. I wish you no harm,' I promise, knowing it is not myself of whom she must be afraid. She flinches as I kneel by her side, loosening ropes already slicing into her delicate wrists, threatening to scar her young arms, leaving a lasting reminder of this ordeal. 'When *he* returns, you must fight.' I am desperate for her to understand my words, my logic, appreciate a truth from which I can never escape. I rise to my feet, no longer feeling myself. *He is returning.* They are no longer safe. I race up the steps, into the hallway, much-needed air almost eluding me in my haste. If I am able to get as far away from this place as I can, it might give them the time they need to claim back their much-deserved freedom.

Forty-One

David

Rarely do I stay overnight at the Frederick residence, Simon's perpetual needs hardly important. Yet I sat in that kitchen for hours until sunlight trickled through the ageing curtains, unable to find any rest at all. Now, lack of sleep has irritated me, aggrieved that I have been forced to leave my work behind for now, along with my two guests. I shouldn't have hit Newton across the head again last night but exhaustion tends to tip my mood, the unfortunate requirement of my father's funeral needing to be dealt with. I must leave Old Trent Road, for now, leave the good doctor and that whore alone in the darkness together, free to get to know each other in my absence.

It feels like only yesterday since we buried my mum. To be now burying my father in the same grave so soon is utterly inconceivable. It is a shame things were never the same after she died. My fault, I know. My selfish delusions saw me existing in a bubble where, in my unashamed bewilderment, I assumed she would be around forever. Then she was gone. Her chair was empty, and somewhere along the way, something profound inside me changed too. I wish I had my mum to talk to now. She would have helped make sense of my untethered brain. She always understood everything. She was good like that. I couldn't dwell on our last moments together, the sheer fact she did *not* understand Rachel's frozen hand, something that will live with me forever.

Frank has been kind enough to explain my father already had his funeral wishes in place, handing me a letter he kept in his possession for this very occasion. He wanted a simple affair, nothing lavish. Thomas was a simple man. Upon his passing, he did not want flowers. Flowers were for girls, or so he claimed. A simple coffin. No brass fittings, nothing over the top—nothing that would cost too much or place any financial difficulty onto me. It was ironic his nursing care costs had already achieved that end. It doesn't matter. Not that my parents had much, their home being the most expensive part of my inheritance, already firmly in my possession.

It is unfortunate I must leave my precious work unattended for now, but today is the funeral, a simple day made possible due to those previously planned arrangements I wasn't even aware existed. When I arrive, old Frank is already standing outside my house, hat in hand, dressed in black, head held low as a long black car snakes along the street towards us, my father's simple coffin laid carefully in the back. I do not want to do this. Not today. There is too much still to be done elsewhere, so much I cannot leave unattended for long.

Frank nods solemnly when I greet him, my face flush with nerves and private suffering I cannot express, his own untold emotions in check, his composure required for my benefit only. I appreciate Frank's compassion in such matters. It helps, if only a little. 'Are you ready?' he offers flatly, holding out a trembling hand I automatically take in my own.

I shake my head. 'No.' I am not ready to say goodbye to my father any more than I was prepared to say goodbye to my childhood, my mother, my sister, my past. Still, this has to be done. I know that.

We climb into the back of a mourner's car, a passing stranger offering a solemn look I can do without. It isn't right that it is just Frank and I now forming the mourning party. My father deserved better. The car slowly makes its way out of the road, down the hill, away from familiarity, no words spoken that would make any difference to our lowered mood. It is almost a relief when we arrive to a church filled with faces, a sea of black against an ocean of blue beyond, many people spilling into the lane from the oceanside church grounds, heads down, some crying, others offering condolences. A seagull flies overhead. Frank smiles, believing he knows what I am thinking. *Oh, the irony.*

I keep my head bowed low throughout the ceremony, no words to share with this group for a father I am still unsure I knew at all. How does that make me look? An absentee son who visited the care home on the odd occasion, who rarely called, rarely cared, who doesn't even now wish to speak on his behalf? Frank holds my hand throughout, unapologetically, the small boy he once knew steadfast in his memory, nothing more required of this painful moment. His shoulders shudder occasionally as he holds back private emotions, my needs today more important than his. By the time we venture into the churchyard beyond, I am exhausted, wishing I'd worn sunglasses to hide my shamed face. It is a wonder the place hasn't already devoured me whole. I am, after all, a sinner.

I am greeted by many faces, offered sympathy from mouths I find no comfort in, looking and feeling as lost as Annie Cormac did during her first night in my care. The vicar seems a kind man, his appearance as solemn as these moments have taught him to be as he kisses my cheeks, holding my trembling hands in his with words of condolences and sympathy. He lays my father to rest above the body of my mother, both parents together now as we stand around a small plot, each privately muttering our solemn goodbyes.

My parents' grave appears nothing more than a recently dug plot, earth that will continue to sink beneath soft ground, requiring continued levelling by the local council. The headstone has already been removed in order for eternal details to be added, so a simple wooden cross temporarily bears a lasting tribute to my long-suffering parents.

Ellen and Thomas Mallory, reunited in heaven.
Loving parents
Dearest Friends

Beyond the Veil

Forever cherished

I stare at a single wreath of flowers laid by Frank, despite my father's insistent instructions to the contrary, weeds already making a break for freedom around the freshly dug soil. I smile, picking up an empty crisp packet that has found its way onto the grave, stuffing it into my jacket pocket for later removal. I dig my hand deep into its lining as a moment of panic hits my gut. *Where the hell is Flanigan's mobile phone?*

I do not mean to falter, but I need time alone, so I make my excuses and leave, hovering anxiously next to a bench and a rotting tree stump that feels hot against my legs. I am frantic, digging around empty pockets that mock me in the prevailing sunlight. I feel sick as I stare towards a piece of faded metal adorning the back of a once cherished bench, its wooden facade rotting along with the memories of the person it is dedicated to. "For Anna. Never forgotten. Henry." I am amazed how love really can be eternal for some people. For the lucky few, it seems, my mind wandering freely now to James. Jack. Michael.

'I'm so sorry I wasn't a better son to you,' I find myself offering the silence of the afternoon, a low chatter behind me denoting the voices of my father's friends and acquaintances, each experiencing a personal recollection of a man lost to the ravages of dementia. I wipe away a stray tear before it dares to fall. It would make me look weak. *I am not.* It is uncomfortable, talking to myself, although it is something I do daily, I know, and I am compelled to say the words aloud now anyway. If my parents can, in any way, hear me, I want them to know how I feel.

'I loved you both so much. I hope you know that. I'm so sorry I never showed it when it mattered.' I lift my head, wanting the universe to hear me. 'Please forgive me.' A light breeze lifts my words as if I haven't spoken at all, making me forget such irrelevant thinking as I slip silently out of the cemetery, back to Old Trent Road and a much anticipated, pressing matter at hand. I wonder if I have lost that vital piece of potential evidence on-route here today, Newton Flanigan's mobile phone potentially lying in the back of some random funeral car, my terrible deeds all but prepared to seal my fate, once and for all.

Forty-Two

Newton

I have no idea how long I was out cold. By the time I opened my eyes, my head was pounding, the gloom around me overshadowed by an overwhelming stench. For a brief moment, I had no idea where I was, no recollection of the last few hours, what time is what, how long I'd been here— David's last movements lost to my increasingly failing memory. I took a moment, my attempts to shift back into focus not forthcoming, blood inside my mouth. Had the man hit me *again*? I was about to chastise my inability to see unwanted attacks coming, when I remembered the young girl. Her frightened, shallow breath lingered some feet away, although, in the darkness, I wasn't confident I hadn't invented her too.

'Annie?' I called into the dark, hoping I'd imagined her face, wanting desperately for the *real* Annie Cormac to be sleeping off a hangover on someone else's sofa, unaware of David Mallory's putrid existence or current extensive search for her whereabouts.

'How do you know my name?' a small voice emerged. I closed my eyes grateful, at least, she was still alive.

'Are you okay?' I coughed. My throat was so dry I felt as if I had been strangled, David metaphorically choking me to near-death where I lay. To be honest, I wasn't convinced he hadn't already tried it.

Annie was lying on the floor, barefoot, dressed in nothing but her underwear that did nothing to hold off the incoming cold. I struggled to confirm anything of her frightened eyes in this dimly lit space, searching desperately for a glimmer of *something* that would tell me she was dealing with this better than I was. A single light bulb overhead flickered and buzzed sinisterly, providing something to focus on other than corpses that appeared diabolical in this light. I had no idea how long they or Annie had been here, forced to endure each other's less than appreciative company. I narrowed my eyes. From this vantage point, poor Annie looked petrified. Christ knows what she'd already been subjected to.

She was staring blindly towards the basement steps, a sliver of natural light emanating from above. The door was open. *Why* was the door open? Indeed, *how* was the door open? I struggled to adjust my position to gain a better vantage point, ropes that had once tightly tethered my wrists far less painful than they were previously. Were they coming loose? I pulled my hands free with ease, exasperated that the ropes came away swiftly. Sitting up, I caught my breath, my moment of relief evident. *Yes!* I almost yelled out with joy before I noticed a chain around the poor girl's ankle.

'Did he hurt you?' I asked. I needed her to confirm she was all right, still in one piece. My sanity depended on it. No reply. 'My name is Newton. Newton Flanigan. I'm a clinical psychologist with the Eastcliff police. I promise I *will* get you out of here.' I offered my young companion reassuring words I needed more than she did, as I set about freeing my tethered ankles. Her eyes were set wide, fearful, cowering in the corner, staring into space, nothing more than a terrified child uncertain of a world she couldn't possibly understand. I struggled to imagine her ever becoming involved with either drugs or sex work.

'Are you okay, Annie?' I repeated. Her silence was unbearable as I clambered to my feet, shocked by how heavy and painful they felt. Annie nodded, yet was unwilling to offer any confirmation that would express a comforting reassurance *any* of this was okay. I needed clarity over a situation I didn't expect to be placed in. What an idiot. Why did I honestly believe David only wanted to *talk*? I shook my throbbing head, my top lip now joining in swollen protest. I spat a clump of blood across the dusty stone floor, my jaw aching, my scrambled mind all over the place. Mine certainly wasn't the first blood spilt here, of course, but it had better damned well be the last.

Annie took a breath as I shuffled around in the gloom, stretching my legs, checking my injuries. 'How do you know me?' she whimpered. She had been gagged, I remember clearly, yet she was now able to speak to me with ease. I assumed, somehow, she must have pulled it free.

I sighed, attempting a reassurance I wasn't convinced I pulled off. 'We've been trying to find you.' I did not tell her, of course, the police were expecting to recover a body. I assumed if David hadn't been so blasé, they might very well have done by now.

Poor Annie was staring wildly at the bodies surrounding us, unable to remove her attention from the grotesque image they provided. I wanted to tell her to look away, not to dwell. 'Where *are* we?' she asked.

'It's a long story,' I muttered, scrambling across the room, lifting her from the floor, tugging ropes that equally came away freely, freeing her arms, the poor girl so weak she could barely move. I tugged the chain, only to find the thing firmly attached to the wall.

'He untied them,' Annie stated, noticing a cold look of confusion on my face. She was crying now, trembling, no better than a small child lost in the wilderness.

'Who?'

'*Him,*' she whispered. Her eyes were darting around, terrified David would return at any moment to finish what he'd started. I almost turned in expectant trepidation, glad I refrained, knowing it was Annie's fear speaking and not David Mallory *actually* standing behind us. I didn't need to make her feel worse than she already did, and I certainly didn't need that image in my head.

It didn't take long for me to realise that Adam must have been granted temporary access to David's mind, *thankfully*—a much-needed moment of clarity now something that, after spending the last few days trying to figure the guy out, I was extremely grateful for. I wondered where he was, listening overhead for any sign of unwanted movement. I tugged the chain, its weight disproportionate to the tiny frame of Annie. Why would Adam leave the poor girl chained like this, unless, of course, he hadn't noticed? I needed something, anything, to break her free, the crumbling wall damp enough to potentially aid my impossible mission. That's if I could find something heavy enough to do the job. I glanced around, searching for anything that might free her. A crowbar. A hammer. A piece of wood. I paused. The basement door *was* open. Dared I go out there? Would I find a key to these shackles, or David?

This entire place had sat unused and unappreciated for decades, these unfortunate bodies confirmation of a sad truth no one would ever want to acknowledge. I needed to focus on getting Annie free. Nothing else mattered. I tugged at her blood-soaked ankle. It looked sore. She winced. I apologised. I frantically scanned the basement for anything I could use to pry open her restraints.

'It's okay,' I said, lifting Annie into a seated position, disgruntled that she wasn't any more comfortable for my efforts. It wasn't okay. We didn't have much time. She was crying again.

I was out of breath by now, iron chains not something I expected to tackle today, my attempts to locate something to break it with, thwarted by a throbbing headache. Annie was trembling, her body barely clothed, her limbs shaking with fear and cold. There was fresh blood in her hair and eyes. It was obvious that David had hurt her. I removed my jacket, draping it around her shoulders that she hugged to her body as if I had just saved her life. I couldn't understand why David had brought her here alive, thoughts of those other girls meeting their terrible end where they fell, something I struggled to accept. I was grateful, although I couldn't tell Annie, obviously. I dared not glance towards those chained bones, David's past actions already seeing him murder two young girls in this space.

'What happened?' I asked, hoping to shed light onto how the poor girl came to be here.

'I don't know,' Annie breathed, my jacket unable to sedate the chatter of her teeth. 'It happened so fast.'

I appreciated how David could potentially remain unnoticed in the dark, yet I couldn't bring myself to ask where poor Annie was when she met him, why she was readily available to the attention of such a monster. I wanted to ask about Tony McNally, a future she'd all but destroyed, but I stayed silent. She was alive. Everything else could be dealt with in due course. What I needed now was to leave her, go and find help. I rose to my feet, hoping for salvation, anything to cure this impossible situation. Annie pulled my arm. I shrugged her off.

'It's okay,' I muttered. It wasn't.

It was a shame that in the prevailing darkness I lost all sense of direction, this basement hell-bent on removing any possible clarity I assumed I had, my injured head too muddled for rational, basic function. I headed towards what I thought was the staircase, yet unintentionally went the wrong way, the very panel concealing the girl ensuring I entered an entirely different part of the basement by mistake. Annie's terrified protests rendered my efforts useless as I rounded a corner, straight into a corpse dangling from an ageing rope, its jaw hanging agape, readily groaning now against its equally ageing weight. Annie screamed. I wanted to do the same.

'Oh, Christ,' I breathed, more to myself than anything. I blinked, hoping to retrace my steps, relocate my sanity. I was seconds from freedom, seconds from salvation when Annie let out another terrified yell. I turned around to see David standing at my back.

'You found him then?' he muttered, his teeth clenched, his face angry. Before I could register what was happening he grabbed me around the throat, forcing Annie to subsequently scurry back towards the far wall, still screaming, this day slowly tipping us both over an edge we could never have known existed.

Forty-Three

David

It is unfortunate that, by the time I return to the house, I can already hear movement from below; urgent whispering I cannot *abide*. I have been gone just over two hours, no longer. I assumed the blow the good doctor took to his temple last night would be enough to ensure he slept soundly throughout my unheeded absence. However, it is irritating to know he is awake, threatening now to ruin my day further. I scan the property for his mobile phone, certain I will have placed it somewhere safe, praying it didn't fall out of my pocket during my absence. I am convinced I put it in my jacket pocket. No matter. I will search again later. I creep into the basement, having already removed my shoes, needing to retain stealth in this moment. I know these steps well, more than able to step into the gloom below me in silence. I have done this many times before, you see.

The good doctor is *free*. How annoying. I resist the urge to sigh. He might overhear my approach, and that will *never* do. He is standing near my special guest as if he actually believes he can save her. Oh, dear, Newton. A low creaking is reverberating gently against a joist somewhere in the background, the darkest corner of this space revealing its secrets—the very sound a hangman's noose makes once a body has met its defenceless end, strong in my ears.

'You found him then?' I ask. I do not mean to sound complacent. I am still grieving. I am standing at the foot of the stairs now, my fists clenched, teeth on edge, the hairs on the back of my neck standing to attention. The girl screams, forcing the good doctor to turn, facing me head-on as if my presence here is unexpected. How *did* he remove his ropes? Simon would have ensured they were tied tightly. I might have been impressed with the man's abilities had things been different. However, I cannot dwell on such a concept now as I lunge forward, grabbing him by the throat before he has time to react.

I am surprised by the good doctor's strength, the feel of his hands around mine, pulling himself free of my unwanted grip—our momentary grapple exciting. It only makes me *want* him more, if I'm honest. Makes Simon *need* him in his prized collection. I am more than ready to inflict pain yet, so it seems, so is the good doctor. The young wretch is crying. It is disturbing. I wish for her silence, almost forgetting my place as I automatically turn my attention to the snivelling thing in the corner, ready to lay her to rest, once and for all. My error is swift, misplaced, enough for Newton to punch me, tipping me off-balance, off my feet. I land with a thud, temporarily calmed.

'Who is *that*?' The good doctor is out of breath, staring towards a face I have not seen for many years. He is standing over me now, fists clenched, breath heavy. I do not want to be reminded.

'That, my dear Newton, is Simon Frederick.' I close my eyes, not wishing to recall that fateful day. I rise to my knees, willing myself with every ounce of strength I can muster to look at the remains still hanging where he'd met his untimely death. *Where I'd met my end.* At least the good doctor will now understand the truth behind the mystery of the missing Frederick family.

'He killed himself?'

Does he seriously need to ask? 'No. Of course not. *Adam* did it.' I laugh. It is not appropriate, yet Adam is nothing more than a thorn in my side I cannot dislodge. I remember vividly how he hung himself in that corner, old pain in *my* heart I can never appease. 'He was only trying to end it, you see, end *us*. He couldn't have known we would come back, time and time again. It is just the way of things. The way it has *always* been.'

'Is that why you kept the bodies down here all these years? For Simon?' Newton is staring at the hanging body now. A body I inhabited once.

'You're a clever boy, aren't you, my dear Newton?' I cannot help the arrogant tone that echoes through the darkness. 'But I'm afraid it is why I can never allow you to leave this place.' Annie lets out yet another scream, forcing the good doctor to pull her close.

'Let Annie go. She's done nothing to you.' Newton is staring at me with pleading eyes, a subdued tone, a subjective longing in his mannerism I do *not* like.

'*She's a whore!*' I spit, causing everyone to jump, myself included. Today has been most unforgiving. I take a breath. 'You *both* deserve what's coming to you.' There is no time left for niceties, nothing more to be said. I lunge towards the good doctor, my thoughts on ending this thing I've willingly begun, my emotions wandering to places I can no longer tolerate. Seeing my approach, and without hesitation, Newton grabs a nearby body, tossing the ageing bones towards me as if the thing is made of paper mâché. Dust, bones, and ragged clothing spill into the darkened void. I cannot help the grunt that leaves my throat, anger bursting from me the instant he dared touch my most *prized* possession. I stagger backwards. The good doctor lunges forward. He pounds his fist into my face, sending me sprawling to the stone flooring below. I hit my head, my temple exploding, the good doctor believing he has knocked me out.

Yelling. Heavy footsteps. I want to scream. He does not know I locked the door behind me when I entered the basement. More yelling, muttered grunts of 'shit' and 'bloody hell' originating from the good doctor's *filthy* mouth as the door handle refuses to turn. Tut, tut, Newton. Such foul language is hardly appropriate in front of a young lady, no matter of her own failing status.

I lie on the floor, the wind gone from my lungs. If he wants to escape, he will have to come close, search my pockets for the keys in my possession, the key to the chain around that whore's ankle mocking us both. Footsteps again, accompanied by low grunts as Newton gingerly steps towards my presumed unconscious body. I am spread out on the floor, assumedly out cold, blood in my hair and the scattered bones of the man I once loved lying around me. He cautiously leans across my chest, his breath so close to my cheek it is almost overwhelming. I sense something hard in his trouser pocket as he searches for something in mine—wishful thinking, I know, yet it provides a moment of hope. He is tugging the keys from my pocket, so close, his breath laboured, his only aim to free the girl and race to freedom. I cannot allow that to happen. I grab his leg, this moment oddly exhilarating.

'Going somewhere?' I grin, sitting up, my grip firm around his calf. I need to prevent this potential escape, nothing of this godforsaken day going as planned. The sudden intrusion causes an automatic reaction, forcing Newton to kick out wildly wishing, of course, to regain his freedom, liberation not yet afforded. I clamber to my feet, anger building, a disgusting taste of fresh blood in my mouth. 'Just look at what you have done to Michael!' I scream, the man nothing now but devastated carnage at my feet. I grab Newton's arms, slamming him against the nearest wall, the young girl still screaming, her shackled ankle preventing much assistance. Newton grunts, slides to the floor, enough time provided to see me race up the stairs. I push past the screeching wretch. I do not mean to make her fall, the chain around her ankle mocking the fact she is going *nowhere*. She falls silent. I cannot dwell. I unlock the door, slamming it behind me, my appearance matching that of a deranged madman. I cannot overthink the concept. It is hardly appropriate.

~

I am pacing the kitchen, glad Simon has been spared the travesty of witnessing Michael's devastated corpse for himself. I dare not think about the bones currently lying scattered across the basement floor beneath me. His life's work. *Our* life's work. My beautiful, innocent *Michael*. I am devastated. The good doctor cannot know what he has done. Of all the men in that basement, the one I loved most in the world is now torn to pieces, the necklace I gave him for his birthday lying broken on the floor. I want to scream, race into the garden and dig a hole, bury them both alive so they may choke their last breaths amid soil and earthworms. I want to scoop Michael up, bring him into this kitchen where he can be safe from further harm. I dread what Simon will think of this.

I need to calm down. I can fix this. I can make this better. I run cold water over my freshly cut cheek, the good doctor's fist having an unexpected, impressive impact. The only thing I want is to head straight back into the basement, slice open that *bitch* where she sits, her guts spilling into the darkness, absolutely nothing the good doctor can do about *that*. I then want to beat *him* until he no longer resembles a human being. It is, after all, precisely what he deserves. I thought we were friends. I thought he *understood*.

Movement from below again, whispered voices that echo

through the floorboards, mocking me, taunting my existence. Are they plotting? Do they expect to somehow overthrow me at the top of the staircase? I resist an urge to smile. Never have I been forced to face such demanding participants. They are usually so compliant.

I sit at the kitchen table, a tremble in my hands I cannot sedate. I merely wish for a moment of solace, a moment to gather my thoughts, consider my next move. I almost do not register the distant sound of police sirens, the outside world holding no sway over me now. I hold my breath, knowing they won't come here, yet my nerves are shattered, all the same, this day threatening to devour me whole. The good doctor has a way of doing that to me. And to think, I was beginning to have private, lustful thoughts about the man. Ideas I have not allowed myself the pleasure of experiencing for a long time.

I am lost in my thinking when the sirens grow closer. I rise to my feet, flashes of blue already streaking across Violet's once beautiful hallway floor. No. *How is this possible?* I instinctively check my pocket, remembering the misplaced mobile phone. I rise to my feet, knowing what has happened, a sinister grimace creeping readily across my reddened face. Curse you to hell, Adam Mires. Curse you for *everything*.

Forty-Four

Newton

I hadn't known him long, but I'd never seen David so angry.
The man was usually difficult to rattle, his persona
unrelenting, often annoying. Now, as I tried to compose
myself, bruised and battered in both body and mind, I wasn't
certain *what* to think of him.

'Are you okay?' I asked the looming darkness, out of
breath, hoping I wasn't out of time, needing to know that
Annie wasn't seriously hurt. She had fallen badly, twisting her
ankle, her chain still tethering her to the wall. I hoped she was
still breathing.

'Yes,' she sobbed quietly. 'I'm okay. Are you?' It was nice
of her to ask.

'I will be when I get you out of here.' I tried to joke, I
couldn't help it. I was shaken, terrified for the both of us,
embarrassed I'd failed to overpower David, this space slowly

devouring me where I sat.

'He put something in your pocket,' Annie whispered. I could barely make out the shape of her trembling body lying at the foot of the basement steps, the bones that lay at my feet adding to my unforeseen discomposure—both visions disturbing. The noose was still creaking.

'Who?' What on earth was she talking about? And, more importantly, *when* had I missed this important event?

'*He* did. Earlier. When he loosened the ropes.' I thought of Adam, automatically reaching into my pockets, fumbling around like a madman, knowing, of course, that poor Annie would assume this just another one of David's games. When my hand pressed against something hard, solid, I couldn't believe my luck. My mobile phone. I scrambled to my feet, pressing the "on" button, my impatience obvious as I hurriedly willed my ageing phone to spring to life, the basement lighting up around us with an unexpected glow. I didn't have much power, didn't have much time, but it would do the job as long as I could get a signal. Frantically, I called Paul, hoping he wouldn't ignore me, every purr of the dialling tone too much for my ears, every second we were forced to wait, too long. I was pacing, stepping around death and decay, willing my phone to keep a steady signal, a lifeline to the outside world balanced now in my unsteady grasp.

'Newt, where the hell are you? I've been trying to get hold of you since last night.' Paul had no idea how grateful I was to hear his voice. He could yell at me later. I'd be glad to listen.

'Shush,' I breathed rapidly, practically spitting into the mouthpiece, frantic desperation obvious. I needed my friend to shut up, my battery already flashing red. 'David has locked us in the basement of Old Trent Road. Send help. *Now!*' I sounded crazy, unhinged, glancing around a space full of corpses. 'And plenty of body bags.'

'What the hell are you talking about?' Paul didn't sound impressed. 'Who the hell is *us?*'

I glanced at Annie. 'Annie Cormac.'

'Are you fucking *kidding* me?' I thought that might get his attention. I resisted the urge to smile. Now was not the time for jokes.

'As if,' I muttered, hoping David couldn't overhear, needing Paul to appreciate the urgency.

'She okay?'

'For now.' I was simply thankful she was alive. If I hadn't agreed to indulge in David's earlier fantasy, I dreaded to think of the alternative. I wouldn't be here, and Annie might not be breathing. 'Just hurry the hell up.' My phone decided to take that precise moment to die, the low beep that shot into my ear almost making me scream into the incoming darkness as my mobile fell silent. Annie was crying again.

'It's okay. Don't worry. The police are on the way,' I reassured her. I had no idea which of us I was trying to convince. I could only *hope.* David was stomping around overhead, slamming doors, throwing chairs, seemingly dragging tables across the floor, cursing loudly. We didn't have much time, a frantic few minutes passing before I vaguely made out a siren in the distance—the comforting buzz of Eastcliff feeling a million miles away. I held my breath, not expecting salvation so rapidly, no matter how quick to respond Paul and his team might have been. After all, he wasn't superman.

Forty-Five

David

I did not expect my day to turn out like this. I have to think fast, no time now to contemplate my next move. I grab the largest knife I can find in the kitchen drawer and head towards the basement—my only thought being to protect the work that has taken so long to collate. If the good doctor is plotting from behind that closed door, he will shortly feel the full force of my untethered wrath. After all, he is only just beginning to appreciate who and *what* I am.

I turn the key, no time to concern myself with anything other than taking hostages (should the situation call for it), bide myself time I am fully aware I do *not* have. The darkness is overwhelming, as is an unexpected stench of sweat and urine that hits the back of my nostrils as I step into the dark. The knife in my grip is prepared to cause irreparable damage should I find myself in want of swift appeasement, my eyes adjusting to these dimly lit surroundings as if I, too, belong here with those whose lives I callously took. I dare not look at the floor. I do not wish to see Michael like *that*.

'Have you not figured it out yet, Newton?' I call into the darkness. A tiny shuffle, my eyes adjusting to a vision of them both pressed against the far wall, huddled together as if their very lives depend on protecting each other. How ironic. How *pathetic*. I wonder if they have heard the sirens. I smile. It is unappreciated. No matter.

'Figured *what* out?' Newton is asking, yet I get the distinct impression he does not require an answer.

'That I am *all* the people in my head, my dear friend. I have been known by many names over the years, of course. Adam Mires. Jacob Pointer. Simon Frederick.' I pause. 'David Mallory. You see, Newton, we do not stop being who we are just because we are born into a different body. Most people do not appreciate this. They do not remember the lives they have lived before. *But I do.* I remember them all.' I am laughing now as I make my way across the basement floor, knife in my hand, grin on my face.

'You're nothing but a twisted murderer.' Oh, dear. The good doctor is being impolite. Newton, you are making this far too easy for me.

I continue, unheeded, unaffected by chastising words my dear friend cannot know has the power to scourge me forever—such cheap remarks simply adding to my declining state of mind. 'As Adam, I tried to repent for crimes I did not intend to commit, failed in my mission and suffered the consequences. As Simon, my mother controlled my every

351

waking movement until eventually, I snapped, the killer I already was allowed to break free once more. As Jacob, I befriended the *wrong* man, fell in love with someone I shouldn't have allowed into my life. Yet, Jack taught me more than anyone ever could.' I sigh, taking a much-needed moment of reflection. 'I have been looking for him, you know.'

'Who? *Jack the Ripper?*' Goodness me. I can see the good doctor honestly now believes my mind is broken. It is amusing how he is able to retain his sense of humour, considering. I laugh, rolling my eyes, tilting my head towards a ceiling no longer able to contain my secrets.

'The *one*, Doctor Flanigan. I've been looking for *the one*.' Does he not yet understand? 'James. Jack. Michael.' I glance down, the poor man now lying in pieces at my feet. Newton follows my line of vision towards the bones of my beloved, unwilling to linger long, knowing, of course, what he's done. I smile, though it is not a happy memory that now floods my mind, a distinct thumping on the ageing front door above, threatening to break this moment along with the equally aged woodwork beyond. This old place cannot stand such unwanted intrusion, its walls damaged by time and pain. Not unlike me.

'All I *ever* wanted was to be openly gay. To be *loved*. Is that so wrong? Do you know how that *feels?*' I am staring into the face of the one man I assumed might understand, yet he shows no expression at all. I was wrong in my assumptions. Never mind.

'You live in the twenty-first century, David. Being gay is

not a crime.' The good doctor is mocking me, shaking his head as if he cannot understand my insecurities. He may be right, but it baffles me how he still does not fully understand. I shake my head.

'But I can never forget the things I was callously forced to endure.' I take a breath, taking a moment I do not have. I glance towards the narrow shaft of light overhead, peppered now with flashing blue, angry shouts from strangers in authority threatening to invade my private space. 'Adam did not appreciate being gay. Homosexual men were hung, their *sins* seeing them at the end of a hangman's noose.' I sigh, those visions still strong. 'Simon merely wished for the approval of his mother. Yet, myself aside, they all lived through a time where gay men were *despised*, seen as filthy — punished for their apparent *crime*. I saw many men like Jack back then. Many a good man to be had. Doctors, men of state, men in control. They were married, of course, hiding dark secrets none could share with the world.' I take a moment to consider the whores we once hoped to rid this world of, each one far more sinful, filthy, and ungodly than I *ever* could be.

The good doctor does not respond, focused instead on the disruption above, my time running out. Should I kill them both now and be done with this monstrous moment, once and for all?

'I have been searching for my beloved for many years. I know he's out there somewhere in the world waiting for me.' I lick my lips, hoping the presumptions formed in my head are not unfounded. 'At one point, I honestly thought it might be you, Newton.' Why I am able to say such a thing aloud, I do not know. Maybe the darkness is helping.

'*Me?*'

Why does the doctor sound offended by such a concept? 'Of course, you.'

'But I'm not gay.'

'You're not married, and you never speak of female friends. You have no photographs in your home of any past girlfriends. No wife.'

'That's none of your business—'

'I have been trying to make sense of my life for so long. Why is such a concept difficult for anyone to understand?' I tap a trembling hand against my temple, the knife lingering, its metal edge glinting in the gloom. 'I despise them all, living in my head, because there is no way for me to *ever* escape.' I press my hands over my ears, but I cannot drown them out. 'You're lucky. You get to forget your past, move on—live a completely new existence from a brand-new perspective, your mind unable to recall old pain. But we can only ever be who we have *always* been.'

I am furious now, gripping the knife too tightly. It is digging into my skin, drawing blood. I will never get another chance like this. With no more time afforded me and the front door above already forced inward, I move forward swiftly, plunging the knife deep into Newton's stomach before he can react, warm blood oozing over my closed fist. It is troubling that I almost urinate with unanticipated excitement, yet if I can't have him, no one shall. 'Don't you see, my dear Newton? *This* is what I live for.'

The good doctor stares deeply into my steel eyes, nothing

of what he sees there inviting. He glances at his wound, fresh, unexpected, my hand still holding the knife. I know this is the end for me, the end of what I know, yet I cannot leave this world without the possibility that maybe, somehow, I can take my dear friend Newton with me. Perhaps we can return together, resume a new chapter with fresh enthusiasm, new memories to be made. Newton might not even remember what I did. *What I had to do.*

'You could have changed. Done better,' he croaks, slipping to the floor, the infuriating man forever the *psychologist*. This is why I like him so much.

'My dear fellow, how can you not yet see my truth? It is *love* that made me what I am. Love made me do what I did. Love. Anger. Pain. Everything I can never change about myself, or The Others.'

'You *brutalised* those girls.' He slides onto his back, blood loss already too much for the poor man. I kneel by his side, cradling his head. That silly girl screaming manically behind me, uncertain what to do, trembling violently, still tethered to a wall. It doesn't matter.

'Have you *never* felt such pain and suffering that nothing and no one has the power to appease you?' I smile. The good doctor's eyes are dimming now. He doesn't need to reply. We both know the answer. Indeed he has. We have both suffered. It is a comforting thought as my dear friend slowly succumbs to my demands, because finally, he might now understand.

Forty-Six

Adam

I am sitting inside a jail cell, wishing for the capacity of mind to express happiness of the concept. It is, after all, the one thing I have searched for, the *only* thing I required. Yet, I find myself saddened by what has happened, my elevated mood ebbing away with unpleasant thoughts of poor Doctor Flanigan and a young girl whom I have seemingly caused much suffering. The constables have kindly issued me with paper, a pen. My only requirement now is to write to the doctor, express my sincerest apologies for what has happened, hoping I may somehow find peace. It is most regrettable, I know. Most unlikely it will ever happen.

My Dearest, Doctor Flanigan,

I take this valuable opportunity to express my deepest regret for how things have ended for us. I am grateful to find myself finally where I belong, behind unyielding walls that will now become my justified penance. I tried in the past to end things for us all, yet my fruitless efforts created more suffering, my time on this earth destined to set my existence on repeat, the same mistakes made unrelenting, failing to right old wrongs, heal painful wounds.

This all began with me, of course, yet never did I assume things would escalate the way they ultimately did. You see, I have always been envious of those around me, innocent individuals able to live their lives with no regard for forgotten histories, no memory of time gone by. I have been forced to relive my suffering. I may never understand why. Penance perhaps—God's calculated way of ensuring my deserved punishment. Or, maybe this is hell. I have no honest way of knowing.

The one thing I do know, however, is that the terrible deeds we carry out on earth are bound by some unseen law to set in motion a twisted loop of torment that continues until we correct our mistakes, right our wrongs, atone for our sins. In my case, I secured the wrath of The Others, my will slowly silenced by their desire to be heard. I am thankful David committed crimes finally linking back to him. Your good self is witness to that end, as is the young girl who did not deserve to be drawn into this travesty. I am confident I will spend the rest of my natural life in jail. It is, after all, what I deserve.

I have no one to blame but myself, I know. I alone am responsible for the way of things, my actions. I am the reason Jacob was uncertain of his existence, my crimes ensuring Simon's need to prove himself to his mother, the world. David ultimately became a victim of us all, his mind unravelling with the magnitude of a past no one should be forced to address.

I could take my life. I have done it before. I could do it again. Yet would such an act secure me the release I desperately seek, or see me living some future life with another name, painfully rediscovering everything I am? For now, I cannot take that risk. I wish only to spend whatever time I have left in this life, growing as strong as I am able, so that one day, in some potential distant future, I may find the strength to take back control that has been so cruelly removed from me for so long. I can be better. I may, one day, be able to do better.

Perhaps we will meet in another life, you and I. Hopefully, under far better circumstances.

Until then, I wish you a fond farewell, my dear, Doctor Flanigan.

Your good friend,
Adam Mires.

Forty-Seven

Newton

When I opened my eyes, I was strangely disconnected from myself, the events of the last few hours preventing any appreciation of reality. I blinked, barely able to comprehend several shapes some feet away, whispered voices I struggled to pinpoint. I was lying on my back, cheap sheets pressed against my half-naked torso, a needle in my arm, aching all over. For a moment, I struggled to understand what had happened.

The hospital loomed into perspective, yet it was as if I was watching from a distance. Paul was pacing the corridor, wearing out his shoes, exhausting his need for answers. Hours could have passed and I would not have known. His face was ashen grey, a hint of terror lurking behind his usual bright eyes, threatening to spill hidden feelings that might expose his true nature to all. He was a proud man who rarely expressed affection, especially towards me, his emotions kept private, our friendship therefore maintained—his working life separate from everything else he knew. And yet there he stood, beaten, weathered, afraid of losing a friend before his time.

'It's going to be all right,' a soft voice muttered, gentle hands pressing against a body that hardly felt like mine at all. 'Try to relax.' The nurse continued to straighten sheets already too tight across my ribs, an overwhelming stench of disinfectant in the air. I wasn't expecting to wake up in a hospital bed, safe. A disconnection to the last few hours had prevented any honest appreciation of what it was like to exist anywhere other than prevailing darkness, not, in fact, expecting to wake up at *all*. I turned to my side, grateful for Paul's approaching features, unshaven, empty coffee cup in hand. When he saw I was awake, he smiled, shook his head, sighed.

'Where's—'

'Locked away. Where he belongs. I'm sorry I didn't believe you. I had no idea David was connected to any of this.' Paul looked tired.

I lifted my hand, waving off unnecessary apologies, the moment for gloating long gone. My insides felt as if they had been sliced out. *Oh, the irony.* The only thing I needed was confirmation I was alive.

'And Annie?'

'Safe. At home with her family. Where she belongs.'

I closed my eyes. Dead bodies littered the insides of my eyelids. Something like that wouldn't be easy to dislodge. 'Is he talking?'

'Suddenly "no comment" seems to have become his phrase. Luckily we have his DNA, and there will be plenty of evidence to wade through. We already found his stash.'

'Stash?'

'Bags of teeth. Tattooed skin. Body parts. His freezer was full. They found the clothing and personal items of five women in vacuum-sealed bags under his bed. From these, we hope to make formal identifications.'

I tried to sit up, shocked by my friend's words. I'd consumed tea a few feet away from that fridge, inches from evidence I couldn't have known he had in his possession. I'd been in his bedroom, sticking my nose where it didn't belong. No wonder I became a target.

'David killed his sister.'

'Christ. I guess I shouldn't be surprised.' Paul swallowed, his face a mixture of confusion and frustration. He scratched his head. 'Four victims to identify then, assuming Rachel's belongings are among the stuff we found. To be honest, we weren't even looking at David.' Paul didn't appear impressed to admit this truth. He saw the look on my face. 'Yeah, I know. You can say it if you like—'

'I wouldn't dream of it.'

'I assumed David was just another nut job who would have confessed to killing *Jack the Ripper's* victims if we placed the idea inside his head.'

I failed to smother a smile.

'What?'

'Nothing.' The irony of that statement would be lost on

my friend anyway. 'Simon Frederick's body was at the house, as was his mother's.' I didn't need the reminder. I still couldn't believe it.

Paul sighed. 'Any more you want to tick of my identification list?'

'I wish.'

'Are you okay?' Paul lowered himself onto a chair, his tone serious now.

I nodded.

'There will be an investigation but it will be a painstaking job to identify most of the bodies found. We'll need to check missing person cases from the 1930s, see if we can put names to the faces, so to speak.' I knew what he meant. No face in that house was *remotely* recognisable now. 'We may be able to bring closure to families of some of the victims, but I doubt *all* will be identified.' He sighed. 'We can't charge David for those deaths, of course. That all happened long before he was even born. Luckily he won't be getting away with the recent murders, kidnapping, attempted murder.' Paul glanced at my bandaged gut. I nodded again, grateful. 'We will take a statement from you when you're feeling up to it. What I don't understand though, is why he didn't kill Annie Cormac and leave her as he did The Others?'

'Arrogance. David was beginning to feel untouchable.' I swallowed. 'Apparently he wanted an *ultimate* trophy.'

'He actually said that?'

I nodded.

'What ultimate—'

'*Me.*' The thought stuck in my throat. 'Two for the price of one. Two personalities satisfied, three if you count Jacob.' I was talking more to myself than Paul. The details didn't matter. Paul only needed facts.

'The police found photographs at the Old Trent Road property of several men after they had been murdered. Some images showed Simon lying naked with the corpses. Others showed him inserting things inside them with large objects.' Paul glanced at me, uncomfortable visions he didn't need in his head probably matching the ones that had now popped into mine. I think I might have gripped my buttocks together in automatic protest. There was literally no circumstance that supported the idea of me *ever* looking at those photographs. We fell into an awkward silence. 'Bit of a sick bastard, really,' Paul concluded.

He was right. He was. Yet I couldn't help disagreeing with his blanket statement anyway. Yes, David may have been an exceptionally troubled soul, but everything that happened had occurred because of painful emotions and memories all four men were forced to live with. I couldn't tell Paul my thoughts on this. We had very different views on these matters.

When Paul handed me a letter from Adam, I didn't know what to expect, how to react, or what to do with it. What could he possibly say to me that he hadn't already confirmed in painful graphic detail? 'Read it later,' Paul concluded, 'or throw it away.' I wasn't sure I could do either.

Oddly, I had Adam Mires to thank for the fact I was here now at all, alive, able to tell the tale. How did *that* make him a bad person? He was a lost soul in a world that didn't and couldn't understand who he was, everything happening to him afterwards, out of his knowing control. It was left to my unfounded assumption that, ultimately, our choices send us along the paths we take, and so we must therefore take responsibility for what happens along the way. *We* control our own destiny. No matter what life throws our way.

The Case of David Mallory

<u>Dissociative Identity Disorder</u> Versus <u>Reincarnation</u>

Who is David Mallory? He is not a man I assumed I would remember, yet he has inspired me to record findings I equally did not expect to discover. Is he a sufferer of DID, a paranoid schizophrenic, or a deranged killer? Dissecting the man might prove a challenge, no way of uncovering the reality behind a hidden façade many will dismiss as ludicrous. We each have a story to tell, living through personal, self-gratifying experiences. It is a sad and painful truth that, in the end, our lives equate to little more than nostalgia we will eventually lose to the passing of time, recalling old events incorrectly as our memories fade. David displays vivid paranoia, yet does that make him schizophrenic? Equally, do differing personalities prove dissociative identity disorder? How did any of this turn him into a serial killer?

What if human beings *are* genuinely able to recall much

older lives that existed before the ones we know now? If a human mind *is* able to retrieve such memories, would we appreciate what we find lurking there? Would it tip the rational balance of a sane mind? What's more, what if who we are today has already been shaped by a predetermined history, a long distant past no longer consciously remembered? What if this life is *not* all there is? Would such a question be so difficult to answer? No one has ever proved otherwise.

The Ancient Egyptians believed in reincarnation. It, therefore, stands to reason that a soul would, under that assumption, become reborn as the *same* soul but inside a *different* body. A person would maintain the same personality, the same way of thinking, the very ideals that shaped their developing identity remaining intact. It would only be the time in which they exist *now* that changes, genetics, of course, personal circumstance—ever-evolving periods in time, the year of their birth. If those Ancient Egyptians are to be believed, it might be entirely possible to be reintroduced to this world with the same needs, feelings, wants, and desires as experienced in a past life. And, if such a conclusion is to be reached, it means that death really isn't the end of us at all.

We have all, I assume, at some point in our lives, heard nonsensical tales of ghosts, reincarnation, soul mates, higher spiritual entities, to name a few. Stories we contradict, their potential existence too outlandish for rational, sane consideration. We smile, roll our eyes, nothing more than fictitious ramblings of would-be madmen, our lives too busy for such intractable connotations. Yet, because we know little more than the existence we have created for *ourselves*, we have nothing, it seems, to compare anything else to. Everything we know about life becomes the only contrivance that matters. We have readily convinced ourselves this is it. *This is all there is.*

> *When you're dead, you're dead. That's it. You're gone.*
> *Goodbye. Adieu. Farewell. Anon.*

So I am left now with a genuine question I cannot readily answer.

Is this life all there is?

David Mallory readily claimed identities of four separate men, (himself included, of course). A classic characteristic of DID. Yet nothing of those four identities give reason to assume any dissociative disorder at *all*. They were *real* people, three of which experienced tragic deaths, and yes, although an assumption can be made that David wanted notoriety for his existence, I cannot ignore the fact he did not create a set of characters from his inability to deal with reality alone, instead claiming those of *actual* dead people.

I, therefore, cannot help but conclude that there is more to this than meets the eye. Adam Mires, Jacob Pointer, and Simon Frederick were not figments of David's over-elaborate imagination, and this is not typical of DID. Sufferers of this condition usually "invent" each personality (subconsciously, admittedly) to suit their personal, often tragic inner beliefs.

David harbours characters of dead men. I am baffled how he has been able to do this—switching from personality to personality, knowing things only those dead men could have known, including the locations of bones long buried.

Take Adam Mires, for instance. He appeared to be a frightened young man, wanting redemption for murders he claimed to have committed over two hundred years ago, attempting to take back control he never had in the first place. Simon Frederick killed for fun, his mother a major contributing factor to his ultimate downfall. Jacob Pointer made a startling claim to Jack the Ripper's last victim, Mary Jane Kelly. A copycat killer, yes, but he wanted the credit. As for David Mallory, he was calm, disconnected from the world around him.

David's personalities cannot be mere inventions but extensions of himself, manifestations of different people born to different times, all sharing the same soul and experiences. I do not understand how he has been able to vividly recall these old lives in such a way that they can manifest readily. Dissociative Identity Disorder is rare, of course, yet of those studied, most personalities are *invented*, not from an over imagination, but necessity. Most sufferers exaggerate specific areas of their personality in order to better cope with emotions. Most are troubled individuals, unable to express anger, pain, insecurities, and so bring forth alternate characters that allow them the freedom to express themselves the only way they know how. By hiding behind the personalities of different people, sufferers of DID seem able to better cope with life in general.

The Jekyll and Hyde phenomenon springs to mind. Good and evil, light and dark, yin and yang. Two sides to the same face, each holding power to display kindness or wrath, depending upon any given mood, the people we meet, our emotions. Yet, for the most part, we are capable of keeping these feelings and mood swings in check, displaying a low-level change in personality that is deemed *normal*. I could conclude that David researched his personalities in order to convince himself he wasn't responsible for his crimes. That he chose his character arcs to hoodwink those around him into believing he *was* innocent in everything he felt was otherwise out of his control.

Each of David's personalities was a killer in their own right. Men who lived poorly, died young. Yet, there was no initial evidence to support this truth apart from a confession made by chance, Adam Mires wanting penance, David himself unwilling to corroborate this fact. It was indeed Adam who exposed them all, in the end, Adam who saved my life, saved Annie Cormac's. If David chose those men specifically to promote fake grandeur, why did he not openly confess to *all* those old murders committed when he was given the opportunity to do so? It would have confirmed a secret desire to be caught, claiming ownership of long-forgotten murders to direct suspicion onto himself he was otherwise unable to admit. As it is, he has remained as aloof and unwilling to cooperate as the day I met him.

I remain perplexed how he knew the locations of bodies buried over two hundred years ago, no media coverage in existence to support such knowledge. If David was pretending to be Adam Mires, how did he know where to direct the police to those old bones?

Jacob Pointer died in 1888, his body fished from the River Thames after it was found floating face down. I could find little more about him other than David's confirmation that the man had developed a hatred for women of ill repute, his crimes borne from a need to feel better about *himself.* David claimed to be friends with Jack the Ripper and that Jack himself was a gay man. There is, of course, no tangible evidence to support such a concept, so I am unable to comment on that, and it does not matter in this instance. However, David was indeed obsessed with the Ripper stories; therefore, it is easy to deduce he made up a connection to Jack in order to make himself appear more important than he actually is. His vile crimes certainly fit this obsession.

I remain shocked, however, by the tone of voice readily used by both Adam and Jacob, language no longer in popular circulation tripping easily from David's tongue. DID sufferers do *not* go to such lengths to create elaborate character tropes. If reincarnation is to be believed, and, if Adam Mires was indeed the earliest memory that David had inside his head, it is tangible he would have felt repentant for his actions. From an early age, we are taught right from wrong, even those who experience a turbulent upbringing and troubled mental health. We each have a conscience, so can therefore express a reality based on what we know is *right.*

Adam Mires' earliest *apparent* crime was falling in love. He was a gay man living in a time that did not understand him, his desires viewed as ungodly, a disgrace upon a community that did not know better. Ultimately, his suffering would have made it plausible to kill the one person he loved more than anything, the one he couldn't be with, couldn't live without. Each murder thereafter was unplanned, a way for him to survive another day he felt he didn't deserve.

Simon Frederick only ever wanted his mother's approval, trying and failing to conform to her relentless demands. In the end, I assume it became too much for him. He was gay. He was in love. His mother did not approve. Therefore, killing fifteen homosexual men would have felt a release he was otherwise devoid of experiencing.

We cannot exist, of course, anywhere else but inside our own heads. As a result, we fail to notice the bigger picture. We fail to see our entire lives stretching out in front of us, a quandary of uncertainty, repetitive routine, frustration, telling ourselves that tomorrow, eventually, we will find our happy place in a world we understand very little about.

As I write this, I am reminded of how quickly time changes around us. Seasons relentlessly come and go, people come and go in and out of our lives, and when all is said and done, the only thing left are memories of what once was and what will soon be no more. You never think about death until, without noticing, death is upon you, pressing against your very soul. It creeps up, unnoticed, silent, like a cool breeze that chills you. I am no different. I often fail to recall a time in my existence when I truly felt at peace. How many of us think about our mortality until faced directly by it? Death is seemingly the biggest fear we have. And then there is the biggest question of all?

What is the meaning of life?

What if the meaning of life itself is to *learn* from each moment we live, taking our pre-shaped personalities and subconscious teachings with us into the *next* life? Such a revelation would confirm the existence of soul mates, ghosts, spirits. We spend so long wondering about the universe, the point of existence. Would it be so terrible if we had this all wrong? Are we holding onto our current lives for all the wrong reasons? After all, none of us know any differently, do we?

Do I feel sorry for David Mallory? No. Do I believe in reincarnation? I really cannot say. I only know what I have learned during my time with him, the things he has taught me about life, about death, about everything in between, the man ultimately taken to the brink of sanity. Everything else, as they say, is pure speculation.

N Flanigan

Acknowledgements

A few years ago I trained in psychology and life coaching. It opened my mind to how the human mind works and allowed me to become appreciative of those few we barely get to understand. I have read dozens of books on the subject, my fascination growing ever more curious. *The Flanigan Files* series came from the idea of wanting to understand the human condition. Our brains are far more fragile than most can ever comprehend. Each novel tackling a different mental health viewpoint, each character suffering pain that is projected onto others. The hope for this series is for readers to hopefully gain a better insight into the minds of those among us whom we would never willingly spend time with.

My thanks goes to SRL Publishing, for their excitement and enthusiasm for what *The Flanigan Files* can achieve. To my husband, as always, whose valuable insight into this plotline has been so very vital. To my course tutors and authors of all those incredible books I have read about psychology and the human mind. Keep up the great work. Without you all, this series wouldn't have been possible.

SRL Publishing don't just publish books, we also do our best in keeping this world sustainable. In the UK alone, over 77 million books are destroyed each year, unsold and unread, due to overproduction and bigger profit margins.

Our business model is inherently sustainable by only printing what we sell. While this means our cost price is much higher, it means we have minimum waste and zero returns. We made a public promise in 2020 to never overprint our books just for the sake of profit.

We give back to our planet by calculating the number of trees used for our products so we can then replace them. We also calculate our carbon emissions and support projects which reduce CO_2. These same projects also support the United Nations Sustainable Development Goals.

The way we operate means we knowingly waive our profit margins for the sake of the environment. Every book sold via the SRL website plants at least one tree.

To find out more, please visit
<u>www.srlpublishing.co.uk/responsibility</u>

Milton Keynes UK
Ingram Content Group UK Ltd.
UKHW040242130923
428520UK00003B/1